Avenging

the

Edward A. Horton

A Novel

by

Tommy Carbone

Books from Tommy Carbone

The Lobster Lake Bandits

Mystery at Moosehead

The Elephant Mountain Gang

Mystery at Maine's Moosehead Lake

I am Penobscot – A Novel

Growing up Greenpoint – A Memoir

Woods and Lakes of Maine - Annotated Edition

Hubbard's Guide to Moosehead Lake and Northern Maine

Annotated Edition

Exploring the Maine Woods

The Hardy Family Expedition to the Machias Lakes

David Stone Libbey – He was Penobscot

The Penobscot Man – Life and Death on a Maine River

Katahdin, Pamola, & Whiskey Jack – Stories & Legends from
The Maine Woods

Avenging

the

Edward A. Horton

Vessel:	Edward A. Horton
Tonnage:	66.46 Tons
Master:	E. M. Hodsdon
Ship Numbers:	8623
Built:	Essex, Mass., 1870
Owner or Fitters' Names:	Harvey Knowlton

Illustration from Frank Leslie's Illustrated Newspaper, Nov. 18, 1871.
Caption: The American Schooner "E. A. Horton," Recently Cut Out From The Canadian Port Of Guysboro' By Massachusetts Fishermen.
(Flag added by the author.)

Avenging the *Edward A. Horton*
A Novel

An historical fiction novel about the 1871 capture of the schooner *Edward A. Horton* by the Canadian government for alleged poaching inside the three-mile limit off the Nova Scotia coast.

Cover photo and design by the author. All interior photos are from the authors collection, sketched by the author, or with permission as noted. Additional illustrations from public domain works are as listed in the photo and illustrations credits appendix.

This is a work of creative historical fiction. Certain events, names and places are based on published accounts; while other events, dialogue, characters and places are non-factual, coincidental, and intended for the purposes of a novel. The appendices include further details on the reports from the 1871 historical event.

ISBN: 978-1-954048-37-9
2024-06-28-5.5.8.5-ISPBK

1. Gloucester – 2. Schooners – 3. Fishing – 4. Nova Scotia – 5. 19ᵗʰ Century History – 6. American History – 7. Maine – 8. New England

www.tommycarbone.com

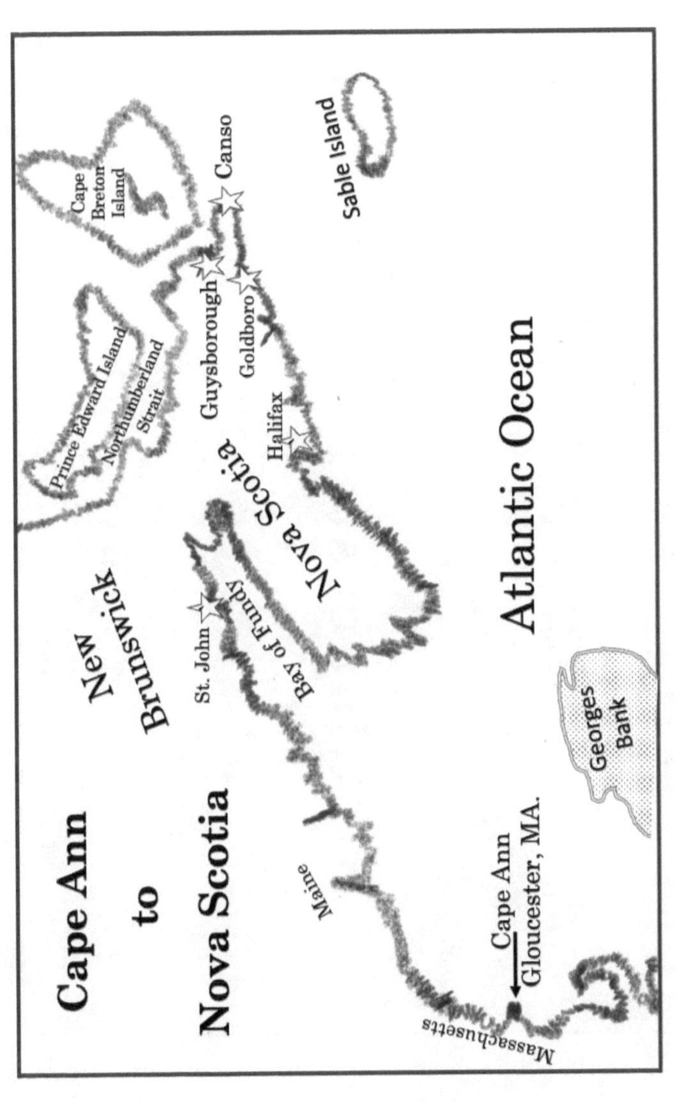
Cape Ann
to
Nova Scotia
New
Brunswick
Maine
Massachusetts
Cape Ann
Gloucester, MA.
Georges
Bank
Atlantic Ocean
St. John
Bay of Fundy
Nova Scotia
Halifax
Goldboro
Guysborough
Canso
Sable Island
Prince Edward Island
Northumberland
Strait
Cape
Breton
Island

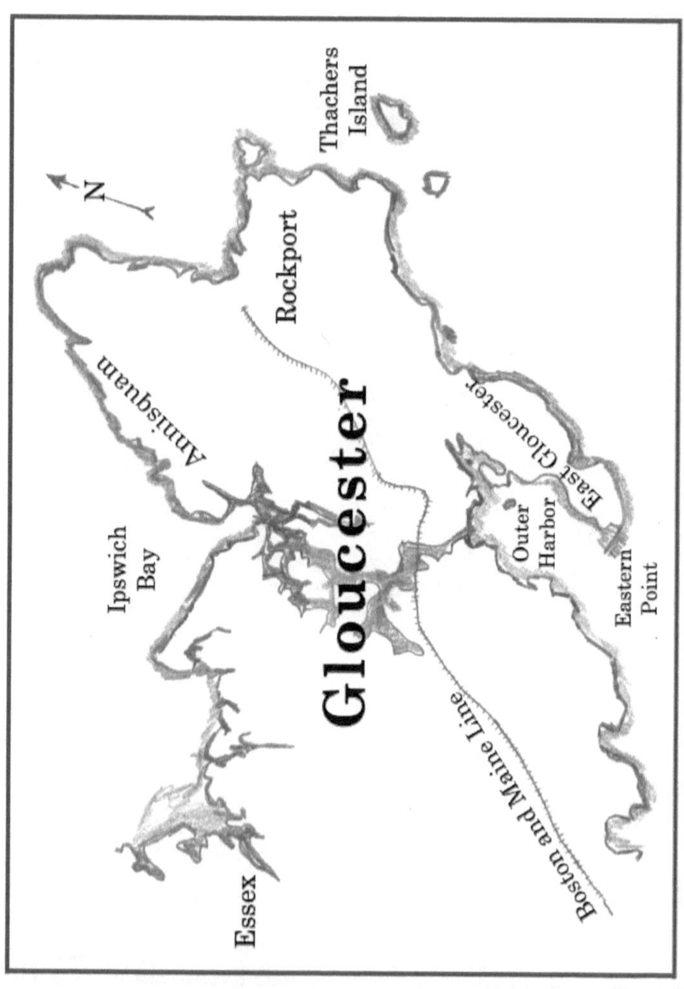
Thachers Island
Rockport
N
Annisquam
Gloucester
Ipswich Bay
East Gloucester
Outer Harbor
Eastern Point
Essex
Boston and Maine Line

Select Sea-Faring Terms

Aft – towards the on board rear of the ship.

Aloft – to be atop the mast.

Amidships – middle of the vessel.

Beckets – ropes used to lower and hoist dories from the deck.

Blocks – pulleys.

Bowsprit – the spar extending beyond the bow of the ship.

Broker – to return home with no share from a fishing trip.

Catchee – a boy on board the vessel who helped as deck hand for odd jobs. He 'caught' the painter for returning dories.

Comber – a large curling, sea wave.

Drogue – a bucket or canvas type bag, attached on a rope to the boat for use as a sea anchor.

Duck – the term for heavy sail cloth, from a Dutch word. Much of the early flax and hemp sail material originally was sourced from Holland and thus the adoption of the term.

Fathom – depth of water measurement. One fathom is equivalent to six feet (1.8m).

Fish pen – a wooden pen on the deck where fish were thrown before processing for storage in the hold below.

Fisherman – the term not only for one who fishes, but also used as a term for the vessel.

Fore – the front of the ship, towards the bow.

Forecastle – the crew's living quarters, below deck, at the fore of the ship; also spelled as fo'c's'le or forec's'le.

Foreyard – the horizontal beam, known as a spar, to which the foresail is secured.

Galley – the schooner's kitchen. For a ship such as the Horton, this would have been part of the forecastle.

Halyards – various ropes used to raise (or lower) the sails, each with specific names, i.e. peak halyard, throat halyard, etc.

Hawsers – thick ropes for mooring, towing, or securing a ship.

Heave to – to adjust the sails and rudder to hold position.

Jonah – fishermen's term for bad luck.

Leeward – the side of the ship away from the wind; sailors say it as, 'looard.'

Log-line – An early instrument for measuring the ship's speed. Also known as log-reel, or log-ship. A piece of wood (the log) was attached to a spool of rope with knots at measured distances. The log was constructed with a weight to remain by water-friction as the ship sailed away from it. Using an hourglass, the sailor could determine the speed at which the knots played out.

Painter – ropes attached to the bow or stern of a dory or boat.

Port – looking forward to the bow, this is the left side of the ship.

Raft – a term for a large school of surface fish.

Red jacks – above-the-knee boots worn by fishermen.

Seine boat – a rowed boat, up to forty feet long. Used in companion with the two-man, shorter dory when seining fish.

Seine net – a net used from the seine boat to a dory (usually) to close around a school of fish.

Sou'wester – fisherman's oilskin hat with a wide brim and long in the back to protect the neck from the weather.

Starboard – looking forward to the bow, this is the right side of the ship.

Thole pins – a wooden pin fixed in the gunwale between which the oar is placed when rowing.

Windlass – a winch affixed with ropes or chains to lower and raise an anchor or other heavy objects.

Windward – the side of the vessel bearing the wind.

This is the song of the seaman,

Bending low at the haul;

This is the song of the fisher,

Tending his miles of trawl;

This is the song of the reefer,

Changing suits in a squall.

This is the story of the _Horton_,

A Glo'ster schooner, avenging the rights of all.

A Patriot Wronged

"I purchased a glass of stiff Glo'ster grog
for a salty son of the sea,
And he confidentially leaned on the bar
And spun this yarn for me."

**October 10, 1870
Herrick Tavern
Gloucester, Massachusetts**

A meeting of
Captains J. William Gott and Harvey Knowlton, Jr.

"It was unavoidable I tell ye!"

His two fists caused a wave of ale to jump from his mug, roll across the tilted pine-log table and onto his bait-stained wool pants. The seaman shook as he made his statement, not out of cowardice, but from disbelief and anger.

"We were outnumbered two men to one. And we, unarmed, except our harpoons and gigs. I tell ye, Captain, we were no match once they showed their Union Jack colors with drawn bayonets."

He drained what remained of his ale in one swallow. "The scoundrels violated every rule of the sea! Coming up alongside under false pretense. Disguised as a fisherman and even flying the stars and stripes! The crewman watching from up in the nest, saw no concern for alarm on their deck—until it was too late. It wasn't any fault of his and I told him so."

His hairy hand lifted the dented tin mug and he banged it on the table three times. "Then they stripped her naked and kept her in the harbor under watch!"

The bar wench, on her continuous rounds, replaced his empty with a full mug. A silver, ready in my hand, I dropped it in her apron pocket. I gave her a nod to leave a second mug next to my still nearly full first. My eyes fixated on the raised plate design on the stein—a two-masted schooner, bare booms, idle at berth— it was like having sharp cod-salt rubbed into my open wounds.

I pressed the lid of the mug open with my thumb. "Did you get a good look at any of them?" I asked.

The captain in my employ raised his head to me. His black eyes, nearly hidden behind his bushy brows and puffy beard that had creeped up his cheeks during six months at sea, bored into me. "You bet I did, Captain Knowlton. If I was as good with a brush as with a tuna-spike, I could paint you a portrait of the arrogant leader!" His eyes narrowed at the thought of the scoundrel.

"What was the name of their ship?"

"Arrg! Can you believe it? She was the *Sweepstakes*. They be no better than pirates after bounty if you ask me."

"And the captain's name?"

"I'll never forget it until the day I die. Reminded me of those traitorous Bostoners who had no spine. Tory it was." The emphasis he placed on the name caused his dried saliva to blow from his upper lip. "Jonathan Tory." This full name he stated with a drawn-out growl.

"Were you able to take off my grandfather's instruments?" It was a question I had to ask the captain; for the navigational instruments were of sentimental value to me.

Captain Gott shook his head. The crusty seaman brushed at his brillowy, black beard; his tone softened. "I sure miss the *Lily Rose*. Him takin' her from me, I mean from you Captain, it just isn't right."

I lifted my mug. The warm ale complimented the bitter story Captain Gott told of how it came about he lost command of the *Lily Rose Snow*. She was a new schooner to the Gloucester fleet of the firm *McKenzie, Knowlton, & Horton*. As a major stockowner in the company bearing my family's name, I was determined to acquire my rightful property once again. The Dominion government had over-stepped its claims on too many United States fishing vessels. It was time to take a stand, even if President Grant couldn't be bothered to protect our vessels, our livelihood, and our American rights on the high seas.

Before going home to Rocky Neck, I wired an update to my partner. Edward Horton was, on that day, in D.C. lobbying the United States Fishing Commissioners on behalf of our firm's affairs, and for all the Gloucester vessel owners. He was on an errand, for which purpose to most every owner was common sense, and shouldn't have needed explaining. And that being our rights to earn a living from that which the seas provide and to be unmolested while doing so.

10-October-1870
Edward A. Horton
Willard Hotel, Washington, D. C.

Captain Horton,

Captain J. William Gott returned from Canso by rail with crew. I've assigned him to captain the Phantom to Long Island Sound. Best to keep him away from the Dominion waters for a time. Doing the same with my brother Joseph will not be as easily managed.

Better you than me to be speaking with the Massachusetts Congressional delegation on this matter. I certainly do not have the patience for their excuses in protecting the scandalous President who seems more interested in gold prices than protection of the Union's citizens and property. If you should see Mr. President smoking his cigar in the hotel lobby, be cautious – he may consider you a 'lobbyist' in requesting he perform his duty to protect the property of the citizens of the United States.

Sincerely,
Harvey Knowlton, Jr.

The Chase

One Year Later

"Our captain's name, all know, was Knowlton;
Our first mate's last the same,
Our schooner she hailed from Gloucestertown,
And the *Horton* was her name,
Brave boys!
And the *Horton* was her name."

Thursday – September 7, 1871 – 9 p.m.
Off Cape Jock, Nova Scotia

Captain Joseph Knowlton stood alongside his first mate at the chart table. He removed from his pocket the telegram and placed it in the drawer of ship's correspondence. The message from his older brother Harvey, received at the last port, was of the usual tone—remain cautious and stand your rightful ground.

A lantern secured to the quarter's ceiling rocked to the sway of the waves. The younger man examined the chart. He traced an arc across the Northumberland Strait to Point Prim Light with his divider.

"Humph," grunted the captain. "You're troubling yourself for naught. We're well outside any imaginary three-mile line. Even if Dominion measurements are double or triple scale to suit their whims."

Without looking up, the mate measured another line from the tip of Cape John to the tip of Point Prim.

"Humph." Captain Knowlton walked close to the chart. "Seventeen miles by your mark." He waited for a reply. "Well?"

"Aye, Captain. Seventeen miles."

"You go up and get a sight on Prim Light." Captain Knowlton handed his first mate a spy glass. "The steersman will have her seven miles nor'west on the horizon at this hour."

Without a word, Mate Oliver started for the ladder.

"And because, my young nephew, you've questioned my navigation, you can have the watch until four bells."

Oliver Knowlton paused on the top step. He'd only been checking the charts out of interest in learning, he hadn't meant anything by it towards his uncles' bearings. Now, having to remain awake until the men turned out of their berths meant he'd be getting no rest before the difficult work seining began. He held his tongue.

The captain, seeing the mate pause, added to his orders with a shout through the open cabin door. "Mate, outfit the two dories and seine for vittles and water while you're on watch."

Up on deck, Oliver didn't bother to look through the glass. The Knowlton skippers had been fishing these Canadian waters for four generations. He trusted Captain Joseph Knowlton knew his ship's exact position in the strait between Prince Edward Island and the Nova Scotia mainland, and the captain knew it as well as the mate at the wheel holding the course. Oliver stood by the rail gazing out over the dark, endless water. Infrequent breaks in the clouds displayed shimmers of moonlight riding the crest of waves across the channel. He struck a match to his pipe bowl.

It wasn't the captain's navigation that was worrying Oliver's mind. No, it was the tactics of the American fishermen's enemy.

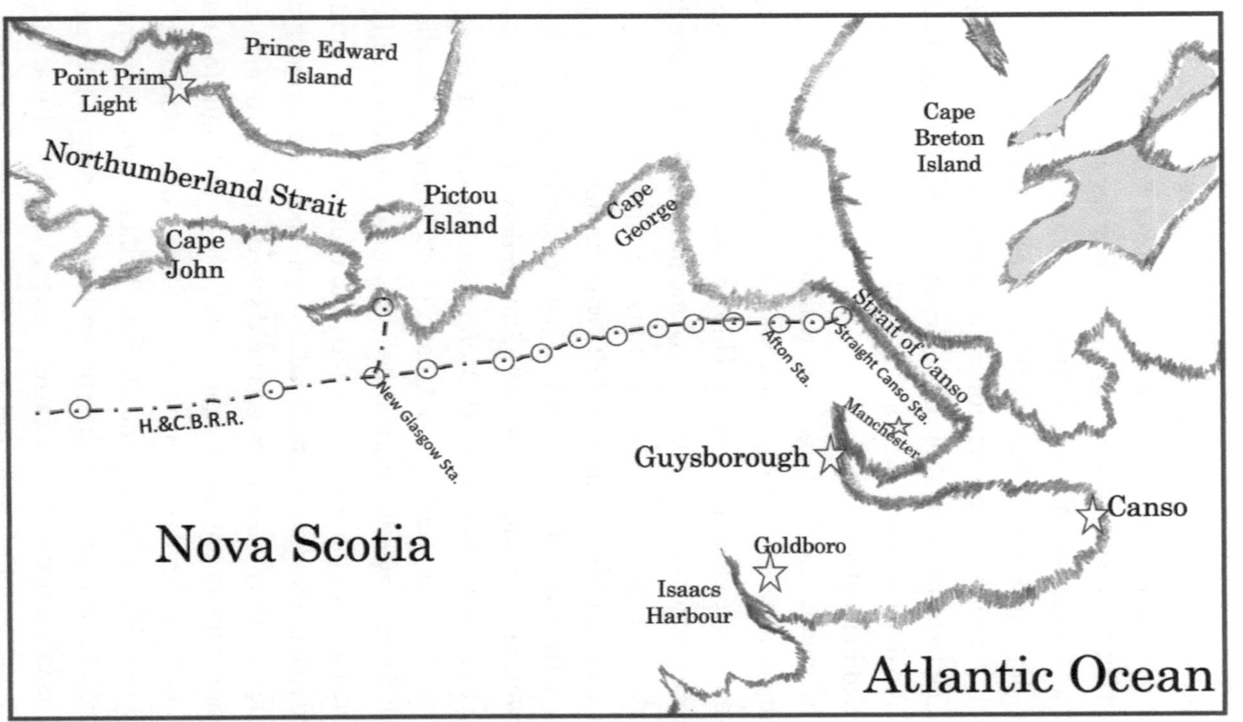
Point Prim Light
Prince Edward Island
Northumberland Strait
Cape John
Pictou Island
Cape George
Cape Breton Island
Strait of Canso
Straight Canso Sta.
Afton Sta.
Manchester
New Glasgow Sta.
H.&C.B.R.R.
Guysborough
Goldboro
Isaacs Harbour
Canso
Nova Scotia
Atlantic Ocean

With the situation beyond his control, he went about his work obeying orders to ensure all was ready in the dories. The dorymen were his responsibility and his single concern that night. He stocked the bow's tiny dory locker with filled water jugs, cheeses, and hardtack. The dories, like the seine, required food and water for a day's fishing, and more importantly for three days survival in the event she was separated from the vessel. When the food was stored, he inspected the bailer, bell, horn, lantern, handline, thole pins, stern plug, and the painters. A frayed painter was removed and a newly-repaired line of hemp was tied in its place.

The mate went about his work without distraction. He knew the importance of his task, for it was three years ago that two dorymen were caught in a fog and blown away from a Knowlton company schooner. One was crew member and close family friend, Frank Sweeney. Frank and his dorymate rowed for five days until beaching on the coast of Newfoundland, surviving on what little water they had in a jug, catching rain in their sou'westers, and eating raw fish. Simple dory supply kits had since become a standard on all *McKenzie, Knowlton, & Horton* vessels; other Gloucester vessels hadn't yet taken up the practice.

Oliver inspected the gear while trying to wash out the earlier interaction with his uncle, or rather, the captain; but the words rolled round-and-round in his head. Joseph Knowlton, as captain, was never wrong—not as long as he'd sailed with him; or anyone had sailed under any Knowlton master. He pulled tight to knot the bow tarpaulin down. His thoughts turned to the stories he'd heard from his uncles and grandfathers. In their years, fishermen never had to consider outfitting the dories for fishing on the seas; they hadn't a need to. The earlier generations fished mackerel with hook and line from the deck of the vessel. The surface feeding mackerel were lured alongside with chum dropped overboard. Fishing was done with lines rigged with jigs—a bulb of lead fashioned with hooks all around it. A line fisherman would handle seven or eight lines from the deck. Once dories came into use, then the men fished on the open sea, untethered, sometimes three miles from their vessel in those years—eight or more dories were set with two-man crews spread out across the vast ocean with no other power to get back than their arms and oars. Ah, it seemed the newer method using a single larger seine boat, and a single dory to close the net, was safer and more productive than all those dories left to drift over the waves, invisible in the often-present fog of the banks.

Yet, fishing from the deck was dangerous, too. His grandfather and crew of eighteen were lost in the George's gale of 1851, along with seven other vessels of the Gloucester fleet. Men died from being swept overboard or when the vessels plunged into the sea, split into pieces under the force of the gale.

"Ho there, mate."

Oliver turned to see his crewmate, Duncan. "Ho."

"You got the early watch I see," said Duncan, as he passed.

"And the late as well," returned Oliver.

He watched Duncan step to the deck box, where he began to grind bait into chum, barrels of which they'd throw overboard to attract the schools of mackerel.

Oliver leaned against the rail under the fore staysail. His pipe smoke mixed with the smell of the herring Duncan was cleaving into chunks. The beacon from Prim Light flashed. Sure enough, as the captain knew from even his position below deck, the light was nor'west. The beacon, at the horizon indicated to Oliver the *Horton* was drifting beyond twice the three miles from the northern shore. For Oliver, the youngest of the crew, six miles from land wasn't enough margin to be complacent. There was always a good chance to be boarded by the Dominion cuttermen.

He felt were the Canadian revenue cutter captains were merely government-sponsored pirates. With angst he searched the sea for ship's lanterns, worrying which might not be friendly to their occupation.

For four, long, dark hours Oliver watched the sea surface for signs of mackerel and the horizon for other vessels. At the bottom of each hour he updated the log with the relative location of the vessels in the strait. On a significant deviation, he reported at once to the steersman on duty to ensure all eyes stayed alert. The two fishermen passed a few moments together guessing the names of the neighboring vessels, none of which were within three miles of the *Horton*. The ships were too far off in the gray of the night to determine if they were American or Canadian, never mind a particular vessel they might know. Their diversion was mostly for conversation during the lonely, night hours on deck.

Diligently, Oliver made the rounds of his watch. He ensured two men were manning the pumps and neither was asleep. He checked the *Horton's* red and green beacons to ensure they were shining with plenty of oil to burn.

In the galley, when he turned in for a mug up, he made short conversation with the crew members who were too anxious to sleep—all were waiting on the mackerel. Mates Duncan and Cornelius sat on lockers near the cook's stove. Oliver mediated

their argument on the finer points of handling a seine net. All rummaged the food locker for grub the cook had set for the night crew. One fisherman sat on the floor with his legs braced against the mast, a lantern swinging in its gimbal over his head. In his right hand he held one of the captain's books, in his left a mug of coffee with a touch o' rum. It was a known fact, from Boston to Portland, that the Knowlton skippers always shipped with a fair library aboard their vessels. The volumes of stories were available to any crew member wishing to crack the spine. There were always a few fishermen who sought the schooners in order to read the latest books, stories they'd share with their children when home.

Oliver bent his head to read the title on the spine of the book his mate was holding. He'd read all the books of the Horton shelves at least once. "You planning on trading down to a birch-bark canoe, Anson?"

"Nay. Seems this Walden-woodsman and his Indian guide carried their boat through Maine more than they paddled it."

Back on deck, through the hours of the night, various crew came and went performing their duties without being told. Oliver lent a hand to keep himself awake.

The seine net was checked. Barrels were lashed to the rails. All loose items were stored away below. With the wind coming up, all was made ready to drive the *Horton* to beat the other vessels to the catch—no matter if they were Canadian or American ships. It'd be each vessel for themselves once the mackerel surfaced and a chase was underway.

At half past three, Oliver heard the cook's call. "**Ho-ho.** Mug up all you Gloucester hardies. **Ho-ho.** Roll out, mug up or miss out."

Relieved of his watch by a fisherman who had slept soundly for six hours, Oliver proceeded to the skipper's quarters. He set the captain's mug squarely in the tables hold.

"All prepared, mate?" Captain Joseph Knowlton, his right upper cheek still covered in shaving soap, looked at Oliver in the clouded mirror over the washbowl.

"Aye, Captain. The lead dory is prepared, as is a second, along with the seine boat. The men are turned out in their oilskins."

"Very well."

Oliver watched as Joseph drew the blade along his cheek. He found the captain's morning ritual odd. With a full facial beard the captain was known to keep his cheeks freshly-shaven, and particularly so when they were to be off chasing a school of mackerel.

"You'll be aloft, mate." The skipper wiped the remaining soap from his face.

"Not in the dory, Captain?" asked Oliver, taking in his own face in the mirror. He pulled at the blond hair of his four-month beard thinking he could use a shave himself.

Tossing the towel aside, Knowlton faced his nephew. "You'd rather be on the water, mate?"

"Captain, you've always put me in the dory. I figured…"

"It's high time you had a larger stake in bringing this vessel to Glo'ster with a full hold." With that, the captain headed for the companionway. Oliver followed. He watched the captain climb down over the rail into the seine boat with the men.

Oliver gave the orders to raise full sail. When he reached the top of the mast, the first hint of dawn was lightening the horizon in the east. He turned his head northwest to keep his eyes accustomed to the dark. The fate of the men's take would be on him. He squinted; searching for the phosphorescent signs of mackerel trails across the surface of the water.

Chants rose from the men of the seine boats already being towed by their vessels. The singing drifted across the strait, mixing with the off-tune squawks of the gulls who'd arrived in anticipation of a chase. From north, south, and west muffled echoes of shanties rose from the fishermen all readying to drive for the fish. Aft of the *Horton*, the seine and dory in tow on painters, his own crewmates sang:

> *"A Yankee sloop came down the strait,*
> *Hah, hah, rolling John!*
> *What do you think that sloop had in her?*
> *Hah, hah, rolling John!*
> *Mackerel to the deck,*
> *all hooked within three-mile a shore.*
> *Hah, hah, rolling John!"*

Oliver grimaced. He thought the men ought not sing such a song when a cutter could be lurking in the dark close enough to hear.

"Be ready, men!" The captain's command was literal, as well, Oliver knew, an order to change their tune. They obeyed but would sing until the seine boat painter was cast off the *Horton's* stern. For then it'd be all work; their sweat mingling with sea spray, until the last fish was hauled over the rail and sent below.

> *"Singing, Row, Row, Row, bullies, Row,*
> *Oh, the Gloucester girls they've got us in tow.*
> *Singing Row, Row, Row, bullies, Row,*
> *Oh, the Gloucester girls they've got us in tow."*

In watching the red and green vessel beacons scattered over Northumberland, Oliver noticed a near vessel trimming sails. He yelled down to the steersman. "Nor by nor'west!"

Captain Knowlton stood in the seine boat, adjusted his sou'wester to hold in the breeze and wondered if Oliver was going to be brash enough to crowd the other vessel. He made no comment.

Oliver directed the steersmen. "One point east'ard. And mind that green light looard?"

"One Point East. Yes. Green light looard," yelled the man at the wheel.

Within five minutes, Oliver commanded they tack back west toward Prim Light.

He called to the deck hands. "Slack the foretops'l halyards." The topsail slapped in the wind.

The cook poked his head out from the galley. "Oliver, I've got the dinner cookin'. The way you're driving the *Horton* the cho'der will be more in my pockets than in the pot!"

"Sorry, mate. We'll be holding this course." Oliver watched the sea. "And, cook, you'd better close down the stove and get in your oilskins."

"Aye-Aye, sir." The cook hustled down to his locker.

In the seine boat, the skipper commanded the crew. "All right, boys, be ready."

"Ready? It seems mate Oliver is driving us in circles," stated Anson. The seine fishermen readying their oars laughed.

"Nay." The captain yelled, pointing to his mate in the crow's nest. "That there's the first college man in the Knowlton family. I figure he's calculating on something only he can see."

Duncan and Cornelius in the dory were laughing and singing. "Mark it in your book, Duncan, this will be a day we have the Jonah," chided Cornelius to his dory mate.

"Aye. I ought to charge the captain for my loss of a day's fish. Why he'd give his position in the mast to that boy is irresponsible. Oliver couldn't find a mackerel in a fish house."

Their banter went on and on. They were simply along for the ride behind the schooner until a school of fish might be spotted. Cornelius opened the wooden locker to see what food might be aboard. He broke off a piece of the cook's molasses cake to share with Duncan.

The phosphorescent green streaking over the water wasn't visible to the crew of twelve in the seine boat. Nor could the two-man crew of the dory see it. The extra hands on deck would have been hard pressed to know where to look. Only Oliver, high in the mast, began to smile. The school had turned and evaded the pursuing north-bound vessel. By the movement of the ships to the north and west they had taken notice of the same. The streak of green was headed down the strait—right toward the *Horton*.

"Cast the painter!" Oliver yelled. "Drag that net no'thward, men!" He pointed.

Without delay or further humor the crew heaved the net. The seine men rowed. They sang.

"Row, Row, Row, bullies, Row."

In the dory, Duncan and Cornelius sang the loudest to make up for their loneliness compared to the twelve men in the seine. The pair were two of the crew who were most fond of the shanties. Together they sang a harmony that added a depth to the chant. With each line of the song they fed their end of the net and let the current pull them away from the seine boat. The cork-buoys on the top rope bobbed on the waves. In their excitement and jolly singing, they'd only then noticed their predicament. This caused a lapse of judgement and Connie let the end of the net go as he bent low into the boat to check under the seats.

Captain Knowlton was too busy at first to notice that the dory had drifted away in the wrong direction. When he saw the net sagging, he stood and gazed into the darkness. The swells hid the dory at first. He tried to hear what seemed like an argument between his two dorymen; their arms flailing at one another.

"What's the trouble?" Knowlton called out. "Row in here and help!"

"Can't, Captain." The dory was carried farther away on the wind and waves.

"Why the blazes not!" The captain yelled through cupped hands.

"We would, but wouldn't you know, Oliver left us without oars fastened on the sides, Captain."

Just then Oliver rang his bell and yelled from the mast. "School is under a half mile. She's a raft and coming strong, Captain."

Captain Knowlton stared at his two helpless fishermen who were drifting away on the rises of the sea. He checked where Oliver was pointing. He assessed the swells, the tide, and the distance to the shore, against his obligation to fill the hold and pay his men and the owners. The crests and troughs weren't anything unusual for a dory to handle. Besides, with the fish approaching there was no time to row for the dory. It was the men or the fish.

"Don't worry, Captain. Oliver left us plenty of food if not the oars. Swing back after you haul the school. Now go drive'er, boys. Drive 'er!"

"Keep your lanterns lit until the sky is light. Throw a drogue out if you've got one." Captain Knowlton only left those two men to the mercy of the sea for he knew they were able seamen and it was a calm sea—calm enough for Gloucesterman anyway.

Cornelius had already tied the largest bucket they had to a painter and heaved it over. If it slowed their drifting at all, he hadn't noticed.

It was only then that Oliver noticed the dory not in position. His attention left the splashes of the speeding school. The fish were headed directly towards the chum and the waiting seine net. They were as good as being sold back at Gloucester. He commanded the deck hands to drop the spare dory over the rail and to help with the net. Then he left the fishing to the crew and kept his eyes focused on the two men who would need saving.

"Pull that line tight, men!" Captain Knowlton yelled to the hands in the spare dory. "Don't let it slack or they'll go right over us."

Whether it was their confusion from all the boats in the strait, the rising sun, or dumb luck, but that school swam themselves directly into the *Horton's* seine net. There was no need of a chase, with the men having a mile of hard rowing, to get in range of the fish. All the fishermen in that seine boat that day would swear it was the easiest catch they ever made. And one of the fullest nets they'd ever circled around a school.

From his position high on the mast, Oliver could tell the school was going to be a heavy haul. He took a final bearing on the drifting dory, and when the *Horton* eased alongside the seine boat, he slid down the rigging. Along with the steersman, the cook, and the extra hands they secured the weighted net between the *Horton* and the boat.

Then the men went to work heaving those fish up over the rail. The dip net, on rope of the strongest Cebu hemp, was lowered into the deeply stretched seine.

The captain called out, **"Heave-ho."**

On deck the crew tugged with a chant.

"Pull, pull, pull, bullies, pull.

Oh, how the Gloucester girls are waiting at home!"

Over and over the dip net went.

Repeated again and again went their chant.

The fish were placed on the ice that was put aboard at Canso three days prior. Four small thirty-pound halibut were pulled from the net and placed in a barrel off to the side, in order the cook could smoke them for the crew.

There was no time for noon dinner. Even the cook hadn't a moment to leave the deck. Not until the fish were packed, the net was straightened in the seine boat, and the dory was hauled over the rail, did the captain shout his order.

"Set sail for Cape Jock."

Together at the wheel, the captain and Oliver consulted the tide, the wind, and the last known drift path of the lost dory. She'd been out of their sight for hours.

"They'll be southeast for certain." The captain knew so by dead reckoning. Oliver wouldn't dare question it.

Down below, the crew had removed their oilskins and were having a mug while warming themselves by the stove in the forecastle.

"You don't suppose Cornelius and Duncan weren't smashed on the shag rocks of Cape Jock in the combers, do you?" asked Anson, his pipe hanging from the corner of his lip.

"More likely, Connie blasted up those rocks into a pebble beach with his swearing alone. In order to make a soft landing," said another.

While the men made light of their missing crew, all were worried about the two men. Although the seas weren't stormy that day, they knew the tide through the strait brought rollers to make a ride in a dory unnerving, especially without the means to steer into the rises.

"Most likely they've been picked up and are having a rum in a tavern by now," said the cook.

Nods of agreement came from the exhausted men, who all knew the Northumberland Strait was full of sail and steam vessels in the chase for the season-ending mackerel run.

"We ought to find them easy enough. As long as the captain doesn't take us into the Amet Island Shoals to retrieve those two," said a fisherman who was consulting a chart of the strait. "It'd be mighty embarrassing to run aground here."

"Nay, mate. Never he'd do that. He'd send us out in the seine before taking the *Horton* in there!" replied Anson.

As it turned out, the dory holding Cornelius and Duncan had drifted right over the shoals and it was at that moment about to enter the Eastern Passage on the incoming tide.

From the mast, Oliver had spotted them. The *Horton,* with the captain at the wheel, was routing around the shoals to head them off.

Captain Knowlton called out, "Drive her, men. We'll reach them before they go into the breakers on Cape Jock." The crew jumped at the halyards each hand knowing what to do before the commands were heard. The schooner skimmed over the water.

With the spyglass held to his eye, Oliver also noticed another ship flying the American flag was east in the passage; about four miles out. The ship was running slow, without her topsail lifted.

Within the half hour, the *Horton* was within rowing distance of the dory. "Here you go, mate Knowlton." Oliver turned to see the captain holding two pair of oars. "Take another man and row these out to Duncan and Cornelius."

Dropping the dory over the side, Oliver and Anson delivered the oars. Aside from having to continuously bail the dory from the sea washing over, the two men didn't come out of it too bad. They were no more wet than usual. And of the cheese and bread they joked they'd made a relaxing cruise of the afternoon. This was only after they'd given Oliver a seaman's round of swears, but then the joking began.

"You could have left us a jug of rum, Oliver," shouted Duncan while rowing back to the ship.

"Aye. Or a young maiden to make us our lunch at least," added Cornelius.

No matter if it was Oliver's fault, or the men's for not checking for oars before casting their painter, it didn't matter for the jeering. Had Oliver not been a relative of the captain, the tongue lashing would have been far worse. He let them have their fun given it all turned out okay in the end. With all the chiding while watching the dories approach, none of the crew noticed how close the other American vessel had gotten to the *Horton*'s port side.

"Ahoy, there!" The call from a speaking-trumpet came from the captain of the other vessel flying the stars and stripes. **"Permission to call,"** came the request.

Captain Knowlton responded with typical seaman courtesy and invited the captain aboard. The first noticed oddity was that the captain of the other vessel was rowed over to be lashed to the

Horton's iron rungs by a twelve-man seine boat crew and not in a dory.

Maybe it was the crew's lingering laughter at the expense of Oliver, or the high of the *Horton's* largest mackerel catch of the season; whatever the reason, Captain Knowlton (and the entire *Horton* crew) received a most unwelcomed surprise once all thirteen unknown seamen were on the deck of their schooner. Such a Cape Jock welcoming committee *might* have been anticipated, had Captain Joseph Knowlton not been in such good humor from the successful mackerel haul. His mood turned as sour as herring pickling-juice once his recognition of the injustice being committed was realized.

Harbor Blues

"What looms upon our starboard bow,
what hangs upon the breeze?
It's time the good ship hauled her course
about the old Saltees.
And by her wondrous spread of sail,
her long and tapering spars,
We found our morning visitor was an English man-of-war."

Friday – September 8, 1871
McKenzie, Knowlton, & Horton, Co., Wharf Office
Rocky Neck
Gloucester, Massachusetts

Harvey Knowlton Jr. stood at the paned window beside his rolltop desk on the second floor of the *McKenzie, Knowlton, & Horton* wharf building. Outside the morning clamor of fishermen, deckhands, and laborers made up the familiar stirrings of a harbor at dawn. Rigging was clanking. Hammers were pounding. Ropes with tackle were being dragged across the docks. Oars were rhythmically slashing the water as men rowed to their schooners to pump the bilge. The sky was a deep blue, except on the horizon where the sun was glowing orange. The harbor was calm and the water a deep sea-green.

Knowlton went through his morning routine to make an account of the company vessels. The east coast map on the wall, from Delaware Bay to Newfoundland, was marked with tiny colored flags on tacks, each representing a schooner. The *McKenzie-Knowlton-Horton* fleet were scattered from Long Island Sound to Canso. The *Emma S. Osier*, the *Proctor Brothers*, and the *Lizzie and Namari* were off Georges Bank. The *Phantom* was fishing in Block Island Sound with the *Mary Burnham*. Smaller boats of the fleet were clustered a few miles off shore where they were lobstering and hand-lining. Several others, he estimated, were ten miles off Cape Ann, including the *Alice Wonson*, a vessel being kept close to home—at least for the foreseeable future—given its recent troubles with the Canadian neighbors to the north.

The exact whereabouts of the *Edward A. Horton* was his largest unknown. Not that it mattered, his entire map system was merely approximate for vessel locations. Between the infrequent wires from each ship's master when they made port for ice or supplies, the flags were mere representations for Harvey's peace of mind.

Harvey worried about the *Horton* most of all. The sixty-six ton, two-mast schooner, was the firm's newest. He knew his brother Joseph would be chasing the mackerel to the last possible day of the season; a day dictated by the weather, the sea, and of the fish, and not the calendar. Joseph would have driven the *Horton* somewhere northwest of Canso, Nova Scotia by now. Of that, Harvey was certain. Beyond that, Joseph said little in his wires about his location. The younger brother was always concerned about revealing his whereabouts, and rightly so, as the Canadians kept better accounts of American vessels off their coast than Harvey could possibly track back in Gloucester.

Last he had heard from Joseph was nine days ago, when the *Horton* was in Canso being outfitted for four more weeks of fishing. Joseph had wired his brother Harvey about his progress and plans, or at least the plan as best as Joseph knew it, and that was to follow the fish. Since April, the *Horton* had chased schools of mackerel from Georges Bank, across the Scotian Shelf, to the Grand Banks, and now west towards the mainland.

The weather had been favorable sailing up to the banks. To remain out for another month, Joseph wrote he sold their initial catch at Canso. He'd made a modest profit for the men and the company, but it would have been a disappointment to him, and the owners, to return to Gloucester without trying for a larger share. Joseph informed his brother that he was confident the crew would fill the hold and then head for home with a substantial harvest of fresh mackerel packed on ice.

Harvey pulled out the *Horton's* pin. He had no inclination from Joseph whether he planned to sail around Cape Breton or through the Strait of Canso. Harvey figured Joseph would sail the same as he would, and that would be the direct route, same as the fish, no matter what attention the *Horton* drew in going through the narrow passage toward Prince Edward Island.

With either route, Harvey had plenty to worry about. In theory, the seas were always neutral territory; but that old adage only applied so long as civilized governments ruled and reasonable captains were manning the helms of navy and cutter vessels.

He held up Joseph's wire and read the last line again, '*I was told from a Gloucester friend while in Canso, Lily Rose has traveled to England.*' Harvey knew just what Joseph's words meant, even if thinly disguised to the unknowing. To Harvey, this act signified the Dominion government, in conspiracy with England, had no intentions of honoring neutral territory, or applying fair justice, or even to return the Knowlton's ship. The last official correspondence Harvey had from the Canadian courts was the *Lily Rose Snow* was safely under guard at a Canso mooring awaiting final judgement. To this date, the *McKenzie-*

Knowlton-Horton firm had grudgingly paid the imposed fine and spent hundreds of dollars on court fees. With the latest move from the thieving Red Coats, he resolved he might never see his ship again. He pulled the *Lily Rose Snow* pin from Canso Harbor and dropped it in the English Channel.

"Mornin', men!"

Harvey could tell by the responding voices Edward had stopped alongside *Defiance Too* to give his daily words of encouragement to the workers. This company vessel was commissioned by the partners with a design to outrun any Canadian cutter under sail or even steam given the advantage of wind. She was two weeks from being moved *from the ways* and into the harbor for fitting out. The men could be heard from the deck of the vessel giving Edward the morning report of their progress. He, in turn, praised them for their diligence and asked questions. This was his way of reminding them of the order of operations for the day without bossing.

The wooden, rickety stairs creaked until Edward reached the first landing outside the office. There he rested without entering. Harvey went back to the inventory of the vessels and schedules. The creaking continued. In keeping with his morning ritual, Edward continued up a level to the sail loft.

His thunderous voice bellowed a *"Good Morning!"* which came as a muffled reverberation through the gaps of the plank-walled building. Edward had taken personal pride in another of their schooner builds, for which the sails were being sewn in the rooms on the third floor. Of all the phases of construction, he enjoyed seeing the white sheets of duck-cloth strewn across the loft most of all, possibly because of his own start in a sail-loft as a boy. The structure of the one-hundred-and-twenty-ton schooner, the largest of their fleet, for which the sails were being sewn was now being assembled in Essex. It was to be christened for Harvey's uncle, Nehemiah "Nemo" Knowlton III, but even Edward hadn't yet learned what his partner was planning for the specific name of the vessel.

The rising sun diffracted through the scratched window overlooking the harbor. Dust particles floated through the air with each step of someone in the front attic. The sounds of rigging being dragged toward the forward winch indicated Frank Sweeney, a loyal chap since starting as a cabin boy for Knowlton's father, had begun his day to the directions Harvey had left for him in a note.

The thick oak door to the office opened with a groan from the hinges. Edward's corpulent frame filled the opening as he took a breath.

"Mornin'!" Edward began to take his coat off, but pulled it back on. "Harvey, my friend, if you don't die of worry, you'll freeze to death up here." Edward pushed a stick of scrap lumber into the stove.

"Good morning, Edward." Harvey looked over to his partner. "Sorry about that. I got busy with the mapping."

Edward always arrived on time each morning, if owners had a clock to report to. Harvey always arrived an hour early and only on the coldest of days took time to start the stove. To him the office, even on the coldest mornings without a fire going, always felt warmer than a schooner's quarters cooled by the ocean breezes.

Edward stared at the map taking notice of the relocated pins from where they were yesterday. "You worry yourself too much there. We've got able men as masters. They report when they can or come around the point just the same." His gaze lingered on the flag of the *Lily Rose* being moved across the Atlantic; he let the recent wound alone, so as not to trigger Harvey's anger so early in the morning.

Harvey rose and went to the stove. He knew that last statement of Edward's was not always the case. Some men never returned to Gloucester.

Edward had left the stove door ajar. The fire was ablaze and smoke was bellowing back into the loft. The heating of the iron airtight warmed the wall behind the stove. The hundred-year-old paneling was awakened from the reflected heat and the smell of dried wood filled the room. Harvey added another stick of wood, latched the door, and adjusted the damper to half closed.

"Maybe so, Edward. And you know as well as you've known me, it's what I am apt to be doing every morning if I'm not on a fisherman myself." He poured Edward a mug of coffee from the pot on the oil burner. "I figure you've already been up to see the widow Tarr at the tavern for your first and second mug ups." He sat the mug down with a smirk.

Edward's lips tightened. He let the remark about the widow Betty Tarr go floating by, as he felt it was reciprocity for his own earlier remark about Harvey's love of tracking the fleet. Together the two had their interests in the business, and in that, they were good partners.

Edward raised his mug. "Aye. This is strong coffee. But I'll stand by that Betty Tarr makes the best cup of coffee on the point." Edward shook sugar into the cup. "It's on account of the beans she imports and grinds herself."

"Aye. And seeing her husband was lost with his ship not more than four-hundred days ago, you've been drinking a mighty fine amount of her fresh brew every morning—and at supper." Harvey walked back to his chair.

"She's a fine woman. No sense in her being alone at thirty-five." Edward rolled open the top of his desk, placed down his mug and hung up his coat on the hook by the window. He stood looking down on the activity on the wharf and in the harbor. Boats were arriving with their barrels of lobster. Men were readying bait for the schooners. Decks were being scrubbed. Sails were being mended. He enjoyed the scene of work and all the people he'd get to talk to about it. "The day looks to be shaping up."

Harvey pulled himself away from his papers and gazed out the window. "Any news from Robert?"

"Wire from two days ago. He and his wife are enjoying their time with relatives."

Their third partner, Robert McKenzie had sailed to Ireland for a visit and business trip. He was the money manager of the firm and was always looking to save a dollar here and there.

"And of men?" asked Harvey.

Shuffling the papers on his desk, Edward stated, "He's recruited a half dozen to return with him. They'll be sailing to Galway Harbor by this week I suspect."

"He'll need to multiple that number by ten." Harvey's fingers pulled the pin representing McKenzie's vessel and placed it at Galway. The partner was attempting to lure men to Gloucester. The town had lost more men to the sea in the last decade than the recent war, and the firm was badly in need of labor.

The door to the office swung open. "Good morning, Captains. Mail call."

"Morning, Mate Sweeney," the two skippers said in unison.

Frank Sweeney strode to the table between his two bosses and sorted the mail into four piles. He tapped them. "Captain Horton's, Captain Knowlton's, General Company and the daily papers." Captain McKenzie's mail he added to Edward's stack.

Horton and Knowlton swung their chairs to the table and flipped through the envelopes. Sweeney filled a mug from the pot on the stove. "Gents, you'll want to see the fishing report in the daily."

The owners both reached for the paper. Edward yielded to Harvey; knowing he'd read aloud.

Knowlton skimmed the fishing pages, understanding Sweeney wouldn't have made a remark unless there was something of note. When he reached it, he knew it and read: "*Schooner Samuel Adams*, Master Nathaniel Friend, returned from a five-month voyage netting $14,465 clear all expenses. The high liner's share being $625, cook's $550, crew $328 per fishermen."

"Seems that might be a high line record," Sweeney stated, not one to miss a record concerning anything vessel or fishing related. He went on with their own good news. "The rigging for *Defiance Too* will be ready by the end of the week, sirs."

"Very good, Frank. Let us know if anything turns up that might set us back." Harvey made a note of the *Samuel Adams'* profit in his logbook.

Sweeney was hanging around longer than usual considering his affinity towards saying as little as possible. He finally spoke what was on his mind. "Captain Horton, how's about you let the fire die out before noon dinner today. Yesterday, I had the fore and aft attic winch doors swinging open with all that heat rising through the floorboards."

"Aye, Frank. There'll be plenty of cold days coming up on us to have a fire. Guess I was anticipating such with the nip yesterday before she warmed up." Horton flipped open his ledger. "Have we received a quote for the ship knees order as of yet, Harvey?"

"Not yet. Expecting a letter from David Libbey and James White. They ought to be done with fashioning the raw timber and have the knees laid up by end of this month per their last correspondence."

"Have you figured the rail fees?" Edward asked as he made a notation in the ledger book.

"I thought maybe I'd take a crew on the *Phantom* and sail up to Bangor to go inspect them. And if as promised, I could retrieve them right home on our own ship, saving the rail fees." Harvey didn't look up from his mail, but anticipated his partner's response.

Edward went to figuring. He opened the railway freight price book. In a moment he swiveled on his chair to Harvey. "Paying our men, and using our vessel, with the freight charge from Libbey's barn in Newport to Bangor," Edward tapped his pencil, "not to mention my losing you here for two weeks, would cost us twenty-five to thirty percent more than freight on the rails right here to Gloucester."

Harvey knew Edward would consider the dollar amount, particularly with McKenzie away, he having to keep Harvey in check. "True. I don't doubt your figuring."

He stood and crossed the office to a corner where they kept a supply of conversational building materials, items mostly dropped off by sellers, or as Harvey had taken to calling them, *lobbyists*, on account they would barge in uninvited. There were coils of hemp rope, of which Harvey would only use Cebu manila on his vessels. Iron rings of various sizes hung on the wall with inscriptions of the manufacturer's name burned into the pine planks to which they were attached. Sail fabrics from Europe, the far east, and west from the mills in Lowell were strung from the ceiling. They had wood samples of oak, ash, mahogany, teak, pine, and juniper—all species of wood that a vessel might use from keel to crow's nest. Shelves held samples of instruments, cooking supplies, and pumping mechanisms. Over eighty years of accumulated items took up half of the second floor for the partners and draftsmen and designers and even the ship's cooks to look over and contemplate when outfitting a vessel. Harvey knew the quality of each item. Edward knew the price.

"Now, Harvey, I know where you're going with this. You've given me the warehouse walk-around three dozen times over the years." Edward met his partner by the door to the back stairs that led to the basement storage and salvage area—where a room was full of ship knees, some taller than the men and weighing more than a horse. He had no interest in huffing himself down two flights of dingy stairs to the damp, stone-wall basement, only to have to climb back up again, after a tour of the moldy, grain-cracked knees leaning against the stone wall of the foundation. The knees and other timber had been stored there following instances when the most frugal partner of the *McKenzie-Knowlton-Horton Company* had made poor supplier choices. Robert McKenzie always tended to make decisions on price over quality. But, with him across the ocean, Harvey took the advantage to ensure they'd have an option for acquiring the best quality knees at a fair price for their future vessels.

"Edward, you know how I feel about the quality of materials for a boat. Our buying from Libbey would be to ensure our interest and the interest of the other company stockholders." He rummaged his draw and pulled out a letter. "Libbey stated he had secured quality hackmatack from the Adirondacks. That timber won't wait long before another buyer gets them if we don't."

"It seems we could get wood from Essex," countered Edward.

"True. Yet, David Libbey and James White come highly recommended," countered Harvey. "And besides that, this White fellow was the one who not only found, but fashioned by his own broad-axe, the famous keel for Simonton and Holyoke's ship built in South Portland." Harvey saw he had Edward's attention.

"That's the one felled off the side of Mount Kearsarge, up Fryeburg way. Wasn't it?" asked Sweeney.

"That'd be the one." Harvey nodded. "White got it for one dollar on the stump. Largest keel timber felled in New England in a hundred years."

Rubbing his head thinking it out, Sweeney remarked, "It was a rock maple at 28 inches, and 46 feet long! True all the length of it. To it they joined two end timbers, for a 76-foot keel overall." He walked close to his bosses, his finger raised, they knew not to interrupt when he was quoting a record. "I saw the completed ship afloat in Boston Harbor. Horrible what design they put that keel in. A freighter! Anyway, there isn't another hard-wood tree along the east coast the likes of it. Any builder wanting that length again would have to send for Oregon Douglas Fir."

Edward patted Harvey on the shoulder and walked back to his desk. He'd known he'd been beaten on reputations of men in the industry, the likes of Libbey and White two of the best. Besides, he recalled the Knowlton family had a nephew who'd served with David Libbey in the war. It was likely Harvey felt a patriotic duty to buy from the Mainer, and he wasn't about to deny him that pleasure.

As intended, Harvey knew Edward loved to speak of his connections from Portland, Maine to the Oregon woods for timber. Having knees from Libbey and White would provide a good story for him at the tavern.

The partners compromised. Harvey could get the knees from Libbey, but Edward didn't agree to the expensive trip for Harvey to freight them on the *Phantom*. A train ride in order to have a look was all he could agree with, so long as Harvey wasn't gone too long.

"Okay, Edward, we'll have the Libbey and White knees shipped directly here by rail after I make an inspection."

Sweeney set down his mug and headed for the attic. His focus was to be on the *Defiance Too*; he'd let the owners argue about knees.

Later that afternoon, darkness in the harbor made the vessels with their naked masts look like a forest of bare trees. The sail loft above was quiet, the workers had been gone for hours. The wharves were deserted.

Knowlton and Sweeney left the warehouse and walked together up the hill toward the house. At the post office, Knowlton stopped. "I think I'll check for any mail, Frank." He took a step toward the narrow double doors.

Sweeney, continuing on, stated, "Stop down for a pint after your supper, Captain Knowlton."

On opening the door, the post master, Allen Humphries, blurted out, "Captain, I was about to run this telegram up to your house once I closed for the evening."

He handed Harvey a slip of paper.

In the dimness of the tiny office, Harvey squinted at the paper. "Keep this quiet for the time, Allen."

"Right, Captain. Will do." Post Master Humphries locked the doors. He then watched Harvey turn back toward the harbor and enter the kitchen entrance of Tarr Tavern.

Advice of Friends

> "Farewell to friends, farewell to foes,
> Farewell to dear relations.
> We're bound across the ocean blue—
> Bound for the Province nation."

At his usual table in the room at the back of the kitchen, Harvey found his partner. There, between checking on the kitchen staff and attending the guests in the tavern front dining room, Widow Betty Tarr would often sit in conversation with Edward. Given an opportunity while the hostess was taking orders and out of listening range, Harvey informed Edward on the contents of Joseph's wire. Then, he informed his partner of his plan to get the *Horton* back to Gloucester.

Edward listened while eating his pot pie. When Harvey concluded his whispering, he wiped his chin with a napkin. "That's what you've devised on your sixty-second walk from the post office up here to the tavern?" asked Edward. "I think we'd better inform the United States Fishing Commissioners. They will send notice to Halifax demanding return of the Horton, and we can pursue the legal route." Edward lifted his glass of ale to his lips.

This casual attitude should have been what Harvey was expecting, but the telegram had stirred his own feelings and he anticipated his partner would feel the same. A response of wait-and-see from Edward was his typical stance, to let government do their job. Harvey wasn't in any mood for it.

"I'll be going down to talk with Sweeney. I'll be there when you're through with your supper." Instead of going home to his own supper, Harvey went directly to the Knowlton boat house, above which Frank Sweeney had his room.

Before the door was even closed, Harvey shoved the telegram into Frank's hand.

To Captain Harvey Knowlton
Gloucester, Massachusetts

Edward A. Horton seized.
At Guysborough.
More to follow.
         Joseph Knowlton, Master

The captain sipped the ale Frank had poured. "Frank, you've been part of the Knowlton family of fishermen since you were a young boy. How old were you?"

"Aye. The year I was born, my father was sailing for your grandfather. I was orphaned from the storm that swept my dad off the deck—that was in twenty-four. Your grandfather Nehemiah Knowlton Jr., let me and my sweet, beloved mother, Lord rest her soul, live here in the boathouse right off."

"And over the years you gave my grandfather, and later my uncle, more than an honest day's work."

"I'd like to think so, sir." Frank's eyebrows tightened; he wondered where the captain was going with his statements.

"Nothing necessary to think on. I know it—even when you were simply a boy untangling nets on our wharf. And by the time my uncle was in charge of the fleet you'd gone from being a cook and fisherman to our top master rigger for the firm."

"I've always enjoyed block, tackle, and rope, sir." Sweeney thought on it. "And of my time as cook for your uncle."

Neither Harvey, or Frank, wanted to mention the sinking of the *Patience to-Knight*, which was more the cause Frank had retired his oilskins and was now the chief rigger for the company. The day that vessel had gone to her grave, Nehemiah Knowlton III, Harvey's uncle, was the master of the vessel and he'd gone down with his ship.

"Ah. It's more than that. You've always had a sense for what a vessel would need before her deck was nailed on. You're a valued man in the rigging."

"Maybe so. Again credit to your grandfather for the schooling he saw I had with the books, and then your uncle putting me on the ships."

Harvey was silent for a time. "You see, Frank, I don't think I've ever asked anything of you beyond your duty. You've known your job, you've done it well, and I've depended on you as my uncle had."

"I trust I can be depended on, Captain." Sweeney raised his mug in a toast.

Knowlton raised his in return. "Yes, you can." He nodded and thought about what he wanted to ask. "On this business of the *Horton*, I'd value your opinion on the matter."

Sweeney sighed. "Aye. I may not be a stockholder in the company. Yet, as you employ me sir, I have to say, the actions of the Dominion government shan't go unpunished. You and I know—and I mean no disrespect to Captain Horton—that lobbying to Congress isn't likely going to get your schooners back. Especially considering the actions of the Grant administration to date."

"Lack of action, more likely," injected Knowlton.

"One ship fined was bad enough. But three now!"

"It seems to be they've confiscated enough ships to require we hold another tea party. This country wasn't founded on diplomacy. I doubt we'll win with that approach now." He held out his mug for a refill. "Frank, what do you think my grandfather or uncle would have done?"

It didn't take but a second for Frank to respond. "Either of them would have sailed to fetch her home, by any means necessary." Frank saw the sparkle in Harvey's eyes, but before the owner could agree, there was a shout from the lawn behind the boathouse.

"Ahoy!"

By the time Edward reached the door, both Harvey and Frank could hear him coming, from the squeak of the steps to his heavy breathing. He looked in the un-curtained windows on his way across the front deck. He burst into the room.

"Harvey, I've a thought." The dinner napkin was still tucked in behind Edward's shirt collar, barely hidden by his dark-blue captain's jacket. "You ought to head north to meet with Libbey and White about those knees sooner than later. I suspect you'll be gone as long as it takes. I'll mind the shop and make sure everyone knows I'll have no way to contact you for the time." He inhaled to catch his breath.

Sweeney and Harvey sat with their mouths open, about to say something. Each knew what Captain Horton was implying. They were not to question Edward's sudden acceptance of Harvey's quickly devised plans.

Harvey rose from the rocker. The two partners bid Frank a "Goodnight" and walked up to the main house.

"Why the change of heart over use of diplomacy, Edward?"

"Turns out, after you left the tavern, Collector Babson sought me out."

"Ah, I take it our harbor customs officer has heard the news?" Harvey didn't have to ask the question. The seizure of the *Horton* was probably well circulated in the official news of the day.

"That he did."

"And, was he fired up to assist us in Washington with more talk? This now the third ship of ours seized?" Harvey lifted the latch of the picket gate to his walkway.

Edward shook his head. "He wanted me to caution my more *emotional partner* with prudence."

"Did he now! That's what he said? Your more *emotional* partner?" Harvey grabbed hold of Edward by the shoulder; his laughter erupting on the thought of the label.

Ellen, waiting on Harvey for supper, opened the back door to see the two partners standing between the open gate.

"When will you be sailing?" Edward asked, not having noticed Ellen.

"Not sailing. I'll still go by rail. That way my arrival in Guysborough will be less noticeable."

"When then?"

"I'll wire Libbey in the morning for an appointment at his first convenience."

"What? You're really going to waste time with a stop in Maine? I was implying that'd be a good excuse for your absence, that's all."

"Not a waste at all, Edward. Such a trip will not raise any suspicion of my travel north, and a few hours spent inspecting that timber will ease my mind." He shook Edward's hand in parting. When he turned, he noticed his wife at the door.

After dipping his hands in the washbasin, he sat while she served his haddock chowder with a freshly baked biscuit.

"What is this about a rail trip to Maine, Harvey?" asked Ellen.

"Ah, this smells wonderful." He took a spoonful. "And tastes as good."

He looked out over the masts in the harbor as he waited for her to be seated. "I have some news of the *Horton*. It's a situation which requires my intervention, my dear." He broke off a piece of a biscuit. "I'll be away for an undetermined amount of time. It'll be important my whereabouts remain unknown. Should anyone inquire, refer them to Edward."

Tory Celebrations

> A pirate of the seas with trickster ways,
> Johnny patrolled the Province bays.
> American ships—his favorite prey,
> And it was the *Horton* he seized this very day.

Friday – September 8, 1871
Customs Wharf
Guysborough, Nova Scotia

"Are we going to stand by and watch them steal our catch and remove our sails, Captain?" Oliver raised his arms, waving them towards the *Horton*.

From the wharf, standing alongside his crew, Captain Knowlton ground his teeth at witnessing what was occurring on his vessel. For Joseph, the most disturbing sight was watching the Canadian cutter captain, who was at that moment on the deck of the *Horton*, standing feet apart with his left hand on his hip and his right grasping the uppermost spoke of the helm. The pompous captain, in his red jacket with white fringe, was smugly nodding as his men tied the Canadian Flag to the *Horton's* mast.

"Well?" asked Oliver.

"Keep your calm. You're a Knowlton." Joseph made his statement through his closed lips, while not taking his eyes from the cutter captain. He stood tall, forced to endure Captain Jonathan Tory, of the *Sweepstakes*, ordering his crew to pull all the sails and guard the *Horton*. Like red ants, the cutter men hoisted the furled sails onto their shoulders and marched across the road into a warehouse.

Captain Tory then ordered the American flag to be flown at half-mast with the Union of Stars down. He stood on the bow and yelled loud enough for all the spectators to hear.

"This ought to discourage the blatant violation of the fishing treaty and Canadian rules." Then, calling out, he enticed the Nova Scotian fishermen to unload the *Horton's* catch in order to hold an auction. This, he claimed was goodwill. "In order to avoid spoilage," he remarked, "and to allow our own Guysborough fishermen what is rightly theirs."

"I'd say, that is going to be one record of a catch you stole from us."

The statement, coming from behind Joseph, caused him to remove his gaze from the smirking Captain Tory and turn around. All the fishermen who had gathered on the wharf parted to leave a sole man standing in a half circle of men. The speaker stood a head above all the other Canadians to his left and right. His black knit cap was stretched over his cannon-ball head, leaving only the lobes of his ears exposed. His lips were barely visible behind his upturned moustache when he said, "That's right—you thieving Yankees! You stole our catch."

Oliver's right hand reached for the fisherman. He had just about grasped his neck, when Captain Knowlton yanked his hand back. He glared at his nephew. "Not the time or place."

Joseph stepped towards the scowling Canadian fisherman who had his fist clenched by his side. "What's that about stealing *your* catch?"

"You heard what I said. We were in the strait about to close on that school and you crowded right in behind us."

"That's a lie." Oliver made a leap past his uncle.

With his right arm across the young mate's chest, Joseph grabbed Oliver's arm with his left.

"The way I saw it, you weren't nimble enough to chase the mackerel, or smart enough to anticipate their diving." Knowlton moved in front of Oliver and closer to the Canadian.

"Are these Yankees causing you trouble, Captain?" In the heat of the discussion, Knowlton and Oliver did not take notice that Captain Tory had disembarked and was standing beside them.

"No, Captain Tory. We was only having a row about those mackerel they stole from us."

"Why you lying bluenose!" Oliver made a third move towards the fisherman. Knowlton grabbed him back again.

"Captain Knowlton, you might want to keep better control of your crew, or in addition to the impoundment of your vessel, loss of catch, and heavy fine, you'll see him locked in the damp cell within the dark hold of the cutter *Sweepstakes*." Tory removed his white glove and pointed at Oliver. "What might your name and rank be?"

Recognizing maritime law for what it was, and not wanting Oliver to get himself into deep water, Joseph answered, "He'd be first mate Knowlton, of the Schooner *Edward A. Horton*, Gloucester, Massachusetts."

Captain Tory's eyes narrowed and he focused on Joseph. "Two Knowltons then. Related?"

"Mate Knowlton is of the Knowlton family, yes," continued Joseph, not giving Oliver a chance to possibly further offend the captain, get himself in a mess, or give away his relation or even his first name; the less Tory knew the better.

"Well, Captain Knowlton, I seem to recall," Tory stole a glance at the *Horton* to check on progress, "about a year ago, *you* were the first mate when I impounded another Gloucester schooner. *That* one I caught near to Canso for violating our fisheries law."

A growl came from Oliver's throat, as he held back the words he wanted to use. He checked himself as his uncle stepped closer to the Canadian captain.

The taunting was severely testing Joseph's patience. "Oh, I recall your Canadian strong-arm tactics well enough, then as now. The day we sail away on both the *Lily Rose Snow* and our *Edward A. Horton*, I trust you'll be here to give us a send-off."

A loud voice erupted from behind a large group of Canadian fishermen who had gathered to hear the Dominion and Yankee captains talking. **"The only way, Yankee, you'll see your *Lily Rose* ship again is if you were to row the Atlantic to Gloucestershire and walk to Bristol—'cause your ship is long gone. Isn't that right, Captain Tory?"**

A gale of laughter rolled through the crowd.

Tory's glare searched the men. The voice was distinctive enough for him to know who made the remark. He only had to locate the always-worn, blue and gray plaid tam o' shanter on the head of the man. There weren't too many people who were in the know on the location of the *Lily Rose Snow* and he was determined to find out how this person knew. He spotted the hat with the head turning away, the man's gray-blond locks of hair curling from under the wool.

"Skipper Tom MacDonald, I'll be wanting to speak with you later." Tory pointed at the man he'd searched out.

The fisherman briefly faced Tory with steely gray eyes. Joseph took in the face that was shadowed by the tilted hat. The sailor's black mustache covered his lips, and his white beard, streaked with black hairs, grew from his upper cheeks to hang over the collar of his wool shirt of the same colors. The Canadian fishermen whispered together. MacDonald disappeared within their circle.

"Now, those of you who want that fish at a good price, get to work." Tory returned his attention to the Knowltons.

"Captain Tory, is what that man, who you named as MacDonald, telling the truth about the *Lily Rose Snow* being sailed?" asked Joseph. He already knew of the ship's sailing from his contacts in Canso, but he played along to put the Canadian captain on the spot. Before the captain could respond, he added, "If that is so, seems you've violated the decisions of the courts."

"Ah, no need to worry yourself, Captain Knowlton. It's all legally binding per the court of England. Your concern now needs to be how to pay the fines on the *Horton*."

Oliver stepped forward. "Pay the fine? You've stolen thousands of dollars of fish." His voice rose in an excited pitch. "That's more than enough to cover any false accusation. I declare we weren't inside any three-mile-limit. That's a fact."

"Mate! Hold your tongue." Joseph was getting irritated with Oliver's outbursts, even if he was making a factual point.

"Captain Tory, please excuse the first mate. However, I stand by that we were not within the three-mile-limit and will testify to such." Knowlton's head looked left and right. "As will the other vessel captains who were fishing in the strait." Knowlton scanned the crowd to see if there were any Gloucester or at least American skippers in the crowd to back him up. He didn't see any stepping forward.

"Oh, Captain Knowlton, I never said the *Horton* vessel itself caught fish within the restricted boundary."

Joseph was amazed at the captain's statement. "Then why, sir, have you impounded my schooner?"

"I am surprised, a seaman as experienced as you do not know the reason. However, seeing as you have little control over your first mate, I can't expect you could handle the crew of your common fishermen."

"Explain yourself, sir!" Joseph took a step closer to the cutter captain. Oliver, and the full offended crew, did the same.

"Those two," Tory pointed at two men of the *Horton* crew standing behind Joseph, "they were fishing from the dory. I watched them myself through the spyglass. You hoisted those men, the dory, and the fish they caught into the Horton. In doing so, you forfeited all rights, property, and fish taken from

Canadian protected waters until such time fines are paid and a court decision is issued.”

Joseph and Oliver turned to their two crewmates.

“It was only to pass the time, Captain.” Duncan raised his hands in an open gesture.

“We only kept two flounder, intending to make a gift to the cook. It didn’t seem to us we were close enough to shore to be within the limit.” Cornelius shook his head.

The Canadian fishermen in the crowd, who had not dispersed, roared with laughter at hearing the reason the Yankees had lost a ship and a full hold of mackerel. In response, the American fishermen booed and hissed at the tactics of the cutter captain.

Captain Tory, seemed distracted and was ignoring the commotion for the moment. Joseph and Oliver both followed the captain’s gaze. He gave a nearly imperceptible wave to a young woman wearing a long blue dress and holding a matching umbrella over her head.

The taunts from the Canadians continued toward the crew of the *Horton* for their loss. Joseph returned his attention to his arguing crew members.

“I told you not to cast a line!” shouted Duncan over the jeers of the onlookers. Oblivious to their surroundings, Cornelius and Duncan continued their bickering and placed blame to one another.

“I see you’ll have to clear this up with your men, Captain Knowlton. And you’ll excuse me as I have something to attend to.” He took a step toward Joseph. “And as you’re aware from your firm’s prior infractions the court proceedings on these matters can take many months. You and your crew will do well to find your way from Guysborough.” Not wanting it to seem a threat, he added, “We’ve not rooms enough in this small town for so many men.”

Surrounded by a guard of his sailors, Tory made his way across the street to the woman waiting near the brick office building. A sign indicated it was the offices of the Dominion Customs Service and Coast Guard. The second floor was the Tory residence, courtesy of the government. Captain Tory's office was a half-round extension on the building with windows from floor to roof overlooking the harbor.

Knowlton turned to his two dorymen who were still deciding on whose idea it was to fish. "Duncan! Cornelius! That'll be all. We'll address this at another time."

"It appears your first mate is otherwise occupied," whispered the troublemaking fisherman in the tam o' shanter who'd made his way to the side of Captain Knowlton.

Joseph looked at MacDonald and then searched for his nephew. Oliver had stepped part way into the street away from the crowd. His eyes were locked on the young maiden who had beckoned to Captain Tory. He watched as the two entered the building and he kept his gaze on the door, even as the arguing was going on behind him.

"By the look of it, Captain," Cornelius stated while pointing at Oliver, "our mate there has eyes for the enemy." Cornelius had only made the remark in jest, but the statement drew further unneeded attention. The captain held his response; his expression was enough to advise Cornelius, and all the *Horton* men, they'd better be keeping their thoughts to themselves, or he might just abandon them there in Guysborough.

Across the street, on the second floor of the building, the woman stood at the window. From below, his face hidden under his sou'wester, Oliver blended in as just another fisherman in his jack boots, black jersey, wool pants, and unshaven face. He could tell her gaze held no interest in the activity of the fish auction taking place on the deck of the *Horton*, and, rather, she looked far across the harbor. Tory stood by her side, his hands motioning some explanation.

The Canadian fisherman with the oversized head, who had started all the trouble by accusing the *Horton* men of cutting off his vessel for the mackerel, set to provoking Captain Knowlton. "I heard you two are from a close family of fishermen." He motioned at Oliver who was still a statue; gazing upwards at the building across the street. Standing close by Joseph's side, he said, "Your mate ought not to stare down the likes of Captain Tory as he is." The fisherman, not observing Oliver's true focus, and getting no bite, added, "And the *Horton,* if I'm not mistaken, it's owned by your brother's firm – eh?" He started away down the wharf.

"What was your name, sir?" asked Joseph, wanting to know more of how this captain knew so much.

On finally setting his hook, the fisherman spun around. "Ah, I be Captain Stewart Tory. A name you'd be wise to remember. And you ought to commit my vessel to memory as well." His finger pointed to a two-masted schooner with white and red trim. "So as you don't crowd me again. She's the *Province Princess.*"

Not taking the bait to look at the vessel, Joseph instead followed the stench he was getting a whiff of. "Tory? Related to Captain Jonathan Tory I suppose?" Joseph had begun to understand the gurry that was fermenting in the barrels of the town.

"Aye." His teeth showed through his grin. "He's my elder brother." The captain motioned toward the *Horton.* "You'll excuse me. I've got some mackerel to purchase—on the cheap."

Knowlton watched as the brother of the Canadian cutter captain placed his bids for the mackerel he didn't catch. He bought nearly the entire hold, other than what he gallantly allowed the women of the town to buy for their evening meals.

Bait fish couldn't have been bought for the low price he paid for those prized fish. No other locals would dare outbid his offer. When the bidding closed, he directed his crew to load the barrels onto the *Princess*.

"He'll be sailing to Canso to sell those barrels for a handsome profit," stated the Irish fisherman in the tam o' shanter. Since Joseph didn't acknowledge his statement, MacDonald added, "It's not the first time this has happened with the two Tory brothers in close waters. Should it make ye feel any better." He touched his cap with his finger and disappeared up the street.

Not wanting to give Captain Tory any satisfaction, Captain Knowlton stood motionless on the wharf and kept his stare on his ship. His crew sat on barrels, crates, and lobster pots waiting on direction for what to do next.

By noon, Captain Knowlton and his crew had watched the *Horton* be stripped of sails, all navigational instruments, and ropes. And with practiced execution all the fish had been sold off. The American crew were only permitted to board the ship to gather their personal belongings and to collect their ditty bags. The cook was outraged that he was forced to leave his knives and jars of spices. He was further insulted that the Canadian officer, left in charge by Captain Tory, would allow no China or silverware from the captain's quarters to be taken on shore.

On account of his learning from the loss of the *Lily Rose Snow*, Knowlton demanded the officer sign an inventoried list of the *Horton's* stores. This included every patent log and line, all mallets and wrenches, every rigging pulley and foot of halyard. Each barrel, tarpaulin, gaff, pail, axe, auger, and every sail needle.

Oliver made a special project of listing every volume in the *Horton's* library. While only a few dozen books, he took a long time at listing each title in large handwriting. When he requested additional paper, his Canadian escort left him alone long enough so that he was able to roll two of his favorite books within his jacket.

The entire process took the better part of the afternoon. This delayed Captain Knowlton from wiring an update to Gloucester until late in the day, as he would not leave supervising the counting of inventory to no other of his crew, for fear Tory would kick his assigned agent off the vessel.

Finally, Joseph Knowlton demanded the United States Flag be turned over to him, and that request was taken to Captain Tory. It was denied and the flag remained flying upside down and below the Canadian flag. This insult incensed Joseph, Oliver, and all the *Horton* crew, as well as the other American fishermen who'd arrived in the harbor. Words were had between the guards on the vessel's deck and the American men on the wharf.

In order to avoid fights or violence with the locals, Captain Knowlton arranged for his men to travel out of Guysborough before nightfall. Five decided to go to Canso for a chance of meeting a Gloucester captain. It was their intent to hire on as extra hands. As it was already late in the season, they didn't want to lose even a week of work. Duncan and Cornelius, who'd been shamed for their fishing from the dory, considered it in their best interest to get home to Gloucester at once. They began querying the crews of American vessels with the hopes of finding one going towards Cape Ann. The remaining four decided getting home was also their best chance to hire out for the remainder of the season, so they hitched to that plan.

A Rockport captain, who'd sailed into Guysborough to purchase extra salt and fresh provisions, was sailing the *Paul Revere* home on the late-evening high tide. He offered to take the men, saying, "It will be my patriotic duty." Captain Knowlton elected to travel home on the *Revere* as well, in order to attend to affairs with his brother Harvey in person. Although the crew were welcomed aboard, they were reminded they'd have to contribute to the chores and there were only three spare bunks to share in turns between them.

There was a single holdout who decided not to sail home. His plans were discussed over a meal in the captain's quarters of the *Paul Revere*.

"Are you certain, Oliver?" Captain Knowlton sliced into his pork chop, the first fresh meat he'd eaten in weeks.

"I'm certain. You tell the men I'll be going home by rail."

Enjoying his meal and wine, compliments of the *Revere's* captain for the indignities they'd endured, he instructed Joseph on what to tell Harvey. "You can explain since I've never traveled through inland Nova Scotia and Maine, I'll be spending my earnings from this trip in order to see what's there."

"Ah. There's nothing but pine trees and bears." Joseph was thinking about his young nephew's safety; not on account of bears, but the Province lawmen, for it was he and Harvey that promised to look after their nephew when their sister died; although, by now he realized, Oliver was old enough to take care of himself.

Joseph took a swig of rum and tried another approach. "You know, Oliver, Harvey and Edward will have all the crew outfitted for another vessel before they get home. You'll be wanting to earn on a vessel, I'd bet."

"I'm sure the company can do without me for a trip or two. Since college I've known nothing but the life of deck and berth. I need a change. Walking on solid ground that isn't rising and falling would be welcome."

The uncle admitted to himself that further talking would have no effect on the young man's plans, whether speaking as captain or relative. He wished him well, handed over the pay owed to him, shook his hand, and trying to hold his head high, started forward to the forecastle of the *Revere* to play cards with the men. They'd need to be kept occupied. The captain of the *Revere* handed Joseph a bottle of rum to take forward. "This will ensure they keep close to you below deck," he said.

Before leaving the ship, the good captain, J. Paul Jones of the *Revere,* assisted with one final detail. In the darkness, he and Oliver hoisted a dory over the harbor side of the ship. He rowed the fellow American to a wharf at the end of town. The townspeople lingering about the wharf gave no concern to a dory rowing in the shadows of the harbor. It wasn't until the *Revere* raised sails an hour later, that the men of Guysborough took notice of the departing Americans. Shouts, jeers, and laughs came from the still-celebrating Canadians who'd gathered to see the Yankees off—unknown to them one man short.

She Holds the Key

Down by the sea, near Guysboro town,
There lived a young maiden; subject of the crown.
She spent her days pining for a life of grandeur,
But lived her life reading about knights of yore.

Saturday – September 8, 1871

With the rise of the sun, Oliver was a new man. Nobody in Guysborough was aware a sole fisherman from the *Horton* crew had been left behind. In the captain's quarters of the *Revere,* he'd shaved his beard, had his hair cut short, and dressed in a dark blue suit he'd bought from the captain. The leather shoes took some getting used to in place of his jack boots, so he walked the few streets of the town, breaking them in while getting his bearings. His excursion didn't take long, the town having but two roads parallel to the harbor and four streets leading away.

On the outside porch of the boarding house where he'd rented a room, he watched the early morning bustle of the sleepy town of Guysborough. Two small boats returned with their morning's catch and sold the barrels to the dealer at the fish house. A seine was turned over for a scraping by two permanently hunched fishermen. Shops began to open their doors.

Oliver was deciding on where to take his breakfast, when the decision was made for him. He stepped off the porch to the shade of a nearby tree.

The young woman from the afternoon before was walking ahead of Captain Tory, who was alongside a woman much closer to his age. They were headed his way. Oliver's heart jumped. He assessed their direction was for Guysborough's only formal dining establishment, the *Tory Arms Hotel* (owned by another brother to the captain). In timing his steps, he arrived to hold the door open while gazing directly into the young woman's eyes. She thanked him and paused slightly longer than required for passing through a doorway.

"Thank you, young man," stated Captain Tory, as he escorted his wife inside through the still open door.

"You are welcome, Captain." Oliver tried to hide his disdain for the man, and more so, for the collection of medals and ribbons displayed on the captain's full-dress uniform. He could not get the image of the same man wearing the stained oilskins of a fisherman when he boarded the *Horton* under false pretenses from his mind. Yet, Oliver was relieved he had easily gone unrecognized in his gentlemanly attire and calm, deep voice.

To the right of the lobby there were two dining rooms. The three Torys were escorted to a table where another high-ranking Canadian seaman was waiting. No other patrons were seated in that room. Requesting to have the morning light to read his newspaper, Oliver was led to a window table just through the arch of the adjoining room. A steaming pot of coffee was left for him; the rich smell, without the lingering odor of fish and sweaty crewmates, made him glad of his decision to not sail on the over-crowded *Revere*. A warm scone broke easily in two, the center crumbling to the dried currants within. They were a welcome change from stale hardtack and gritty, flaky biscuits made by the cook in a crude cabin oven. The words of the conversation around the corner drew his attention away from his contemplating the lightness of the cake-like biscuit in his mouth.

"I hear you are to be promoted!"

"Oh father, isn't that wonderful!"

"How do you know of this?" Oliver heard Tory ask the officer.

Pretending to read his newspaper, Oliver heard the officer tell the captain how their superiors had been impressed with Tory's continued ability to capture American schooners—several of which had already been pressed into service for the Royal Navy. The officer explained that before he'd left Halifax, he'd learned Tory was to become the Province of Nova Scotia's Chief Customs Officer, the honor to be awarded at an upcoming ceremony.

"I should hope not!" was Tory's response.

To which, Oliver heard the wife make her one and only comment the entire morning. "But Jonathan, that would mean you'd be more on land than on sea."

Captain Tory wanted to hear nothing of the sort.

"I am a vessel captain. How can I capture vessels violating the three-mile limit, or other rules, if I am in an office in Halifax?"

Oliver shifted his chair so that he could lean back and see through the arch. He held the paper up to conceal most of his face, but he had a side view of the mother and daughter.

"Halifax! Oh, Father, that would mean we could live in a real town. Wouldn't that be splendid, Mother? I could go to the university there. Imagine the library!"

Mrs. Tory nodded to her daughter. Oliver interpreted the smile of the mother as her also being delighted with the idea of a city life. However, she did not add her opinion out loud.

"The waters between Canso and Cape Breton Island hold the best possible chance for capturing vessels violating the laws. I'll remind you, my dear, of the prize money you get to employ following each impounded schooner. That would no longer be, if I was bound to paperwork."

Before the breakfast was concluded, Tory advised the officer that he expected the men to leave the *Horton* provisioned as it was seized. His plan was to actually add to the ships' stores in order for the vessel to be sailed to England. He laughed when he relayed to his officer about the assurances he'd received from the Royal Navy commander. "They assure me that legal action from the Yankee owners would be fruitless."

On hearing this, Oliver could not even eat his eggs. He decided to avoid sending a wire on this development to his uncle Harvey, on the possibility of the message being intercepted. His only option was to write a letter, even if it could take weeks to arrive in Gloucester. It might possibly even arrive *after* the *Horton* was sailed away.

The morning's best overheard news was that Captain Tory was to sail to Canso that very morning in order to make an inspection of the cutter operations at that harbor. Oliver lingered once the Torys had left. At the table, he read his paper. Through the window, he watched Tory and the officer board a two-mast vessel that put out to the bay. The wife waved at the ship, then parted from the daughter; each going their own way. Thirty minutes later, Oliver just happened to be available in order to open the door to a clothing shop just as Miss Tory was exiting.

"Thank you, sir." Miss Tory paused on the threshold. She at once recognized the sharply-dressed man. She had earlier noticed his smart suit and clean appearance, two characteristics not often seen in the Guysborough fishing community, even from the ranking officers of the customs service. "Oh, it's you, from this morning at the hotel. Do you happen to be Guysborough's official doorman?"

"At your service, Miss." Oliver was pleased she had a sense of humor about her. "And no. No official town title for me, but I am in your service as long as I am about the place." He took her hand to assist her down the stone steps. "My name is Oliver Knight," he told her, taking his grandmother's maiden name.

"Pleased to meet you. I am Alice Tory."

"Well, Miss Tory, I will keep a watch out for you, and any doors you may require opened here in town. I will do my best to assist." He bowed.

Not having many gentlemen to speak with, unless it was one of her father's crew who were always asking her to dine, she found this new arrival enchanting. "How long might you be staying here in our *quaint* town, Mr. Knight? I assume on some errand?" She started to walk down the main street that ran parallel to the river.

This interest provided Oliver with an excuse to keep the conversation going and he walked along beside her. "I wish I could be definitive with an answer. My business is quite open ended."

"And what business is that?" Alice turned the corner and began to make her way up a side road.

It was then that Oliver realized he had not planned any business to remain in Guysborough, other than to keep an eye on the *Horton*; a truth he had not even disclosed to his Uncle Joseph. And maybe there was one other reason he desired to remain in the town—and that was held in the eyes that were then watching his own. Neither reason was sufficient to answer the girl's question. But he was quick on his newly-found shore feet with a business venture.

"I represent a shipping interest with plans to possibly establish a warehouse. My task is to evaluate the potential opportunities and vessel access to the harbors." His face brightened on hearing his words. The business sounded legitimate and Guysborough was a developing harbor community. "However, as this business is sensitive for securing locations at the best price, I might not have been wise in giving out this information."

Alice Tory stopped her slow walk. "Mr. Knight, are you implying I have a mind to gossip?"

"Oh, not at all, Miss Tory. I only mention it because…" Her sparkling eyes and large smile revealed her intended sarcasm.

"No need to worry, sir. Such affairs hold no interest to me. This hamlet of a town barely holds any interests at all." She began to walk again, and as she did, she looked his way. "At least until today."

Going along beside her, Oliver was quiet for several steps. He hadn't been paying attention to where they were headed, and wondered if she considered that he was following her at this point. "I didn't mean to imply, but you might understand that certain business men might take advantage of such information to raise property prices."

Alice made no comment. The road had begun to ascend a small hill. They were now walking along a tree-lined carriage road.

"Each morning I take this walk after my breakfast."

"I didn't mean to intrude," he said.

Her finger went to her lips to indicate silence. Alice peered beyond the low bushes into a clearing. "Oh. Look. A small flock of Horned Larks," she whispered.

Oliver pushed aside a branch. "Imagine. They really have horns."

"Don't be silly, those are…" Alice tilted her head at seeing his smile. "Follow me, we're almost there."

"Where?"

"You'll see." She went on ahead.

"How did you know those birds were there?" he asked.

"Did you not hear them?"

He tried to remember. "I guess not. I must have been thinking too loud."

At the top of the small hill, which could not have been more than a hundred feet above sea level, there was a view of the bay and small coves. On watching Oliver draw the coastline in his notepad, Alice described what was visible from their vantage point.

"Guysborough Harbor." Alice motioned with her hand to their left. "And to our right," she turned, "that is Mill Cove with, of course, Chedabucto Bay leading to Queensport and Canso eastward."

"Interesting. I didn't realize there would be an opportunity to have this view around here. The land seemed so flat from the harbor."

"This is the only elevation nearby to Guysborough. You can see why I enjoy the walk here." She leaned against a lone tree. "Not that I have any interest whatsoever in your business, but you can see the coast from here to Canso Harbor is open to the sea. Any of those miles of shore would make a terrible location for your venture of a wharf."

She said this without looking at him. His eyes locked on her profile. He wondered what her thoughts would be for something of interest to her, given her mind for such details.

They turned, and side-by-side walked back towards the small town, stopping at times to observe the waxwings, chickadees, and a pine siskin. At her prompting, Oliver tried to learn their calls and songs to distinguish bird from bird.

Alice gave him up for hopeless. "You might do well to stick to your shipping business," she playfully stated.

Oliver stopped before they reached the road that ran along the waterfront. "Is there a library in the town?"

"In Guysborough? A library!" She laughed. "Don't I wish. Why do you ask?"

"I was hoping to review local maps. The ones I brought don't seem to be useful."

"You'd have to go to Canso for maps. I'd love to go myself, to visit the library there." Her eyes focused on his for an invite. "Besides that, not that I have any interest, but the maritime office there has a cabinet stuffed with maps. Old and new. Charts of all of Nova Scotia and the outlying islands."

"Sounds exactly like what I need."

She watched his suntanned face brighten even more. "Too bad you can't get in." Alice continued down the lane. With barely a turn of her head, she added, "Not without the daughter of a cutter captain anyway." She walked on.

"Why's that?" he called, taking three long strides to catch her.

The girl stopped so abruptly he nearly ran into her. "For *she* knows where to find the key to the mysterious map room on the second floor."

Miner Days

"Don't fret your life with needless strife,
Yet let this teaching stick;
You'll find, old man, in the world's big can
It sometimes pays to kick."

Wednesday – September 20, 1871
Barn of Mr. David Stone Libbey — Lumberman
Newport, Maine

"These are fine looking pieces of timber." Harvey Knowlton ran his hand across a knee of hackmatack that was standing against the barn wall. He turned to the two Mainers. "I thank you, Mr. Libbey and Mr. White, for accommodating my request to review the lumber order."

"You are welcome, Mr. Knowlton," responded David Libbey.

"You don't see any issue in shipping the full order to Gloucester by month's end, do you?" asked Knowlton.

"No issue at all. James, the boys, and I will complete the shaping this week per the drawings." David pulled the barn door across the threshold. "I must mention I was surprised to receive your telegraph advising of the need to inspect the lumber."

"It is important I tell you both, this was my own idea. My partner, Mr. Horton, had accepted the quality of your work from reputation alone. From what I've seen here today, he was correct."

"That is wonderful to hear. However, I was not implying you traveled here to check up on us prior to shipment," responded David.

His brother-in-law James added, "No. The surprise was your traveling here while dealing with the seizure of your fishing vessels by the Provinces." He stopped out of hearing range of the buckboard that was waiting on Mr. Knowlton. Both James and David were no stranger to the ill-feelings between the Yankees and the Nova Scotians, most of whom supported the Confederates during the war. There was also the century-long competition of logging and river-driving; each claiming to be the better men in the woods and on the rivers.

Knowlton acknowledged the comment with a nod. He knew the latest vessel theft by the Province government had been news all along the east coast. "Well, gentlemen, this business with the Dominion authorities has been a financial burden, not to mention time consuming for our business." He continued to the wagon. The men followed him across the dooryard to the dirt-path of a road. "Though, I will admit, this traveling through Maine has given me a long-needed reprieve from the hourly responsibilities back in Glo'ster."

"Are you sure we can't put you up here for the night?" asked David. "We've plenty of room."

"No, thank you for the offer, but I must be on my way. I promised my partner, I would try to make an additional visit while up this far north to a supplier in Brewer."

Before getting into the hired coach, Knowlton addressed James. "Mr. White, you are the renowned Maine woodsman who scouted and felled the *Simonton-Holyoke* great keel from Mt. Kearsarge, isn't that so?"

"I am." James nodded at the recognition from the well-known fishing captain and vessel owner.

"If you should ever find a tree of that size again, know that I am good for the price on it." He thought on it, and then added, "No. We are good for ten percent over any fair offer you might receive from others who hear of it."

James shook his head. "Captain Knowlton, I doubt there will ever be another hardwood tree of that size found anywhere in New Hampshire, Maine, or all the way up to Canso in the Provinces."

Knowlton's eyes visibly opened wider at the mention of Canso.

David added, "I went to those woods the following year, walked eight miles from the Fryeburg train, to see the stump myself." He made an indication of its size with his arms. "Having lumbered all throughout Maine, the Adirondacks, and the lower Provinces, it was a trunk I'd only seen once in my life."

"I suppose you are correct, Mr. Libbey. Although, it can't hurt to be on the lookout." He shook their hands, climbed onto the wagon seat, and gave a wave as the driver pulled away.

That afternoon, Knowlton had no intentions of departing from his train for a stay in Brewer. In need of sleep, his eyes closed, and he continued on the line north to the border. In his drifting in and out of rest, he thought about the *Horton* and the continued injustices the Dominion government had subjected on his business and his fishermen.

At the final Maine line station in Vanceboro, Harvey wired Edward that he'd inspected the ship knees at the barn of the lumberman, David Libbey. The telegram offered no further news, explanation, or plans. There was no need. Edward already knew of Harvey's next destination.

After his transfer to the Canadian rail, Harvey crossed the St. John River at Carleton, New Brunswick by ferry, and spent the night at St. John on the Bay of Fundy. Exhausted from his travelling, he sat in a red-upholstered chair by the window of his room. The ships in the bay, slowly rising and falling on the dark sea, made his eyes heavy. By eight that evening he was slumped low in the chair, snoring to the rhythm of the distant fog horn. The bed he paid for was unslept in. In his dreams, he was at anchor in a Canadian harbor.

He was a fisherman.

His uncle was the captain.

A Dream of Four Years Earlier
September 1, 1867
Captain's Quarters of the *Patience to-Knight*
Canso Harbor, Nova Scotia

"Captain, why are we not chasing the mackerel up the Northumberland Strait."

"Mate Knowlton, it's certain I don't need to remind you of the three Glo'ster ships, in the last six months alone, that have been seized in the Strait?"

"And a hundred other vessels have filled their holds for Boston markets, doing what they came here to do."

The captain leaned back in his chair, about to respond, when the cook called.

"Ahoy, Captain. Dinner." Cook Sweeney carried in a basket of ramekins. The China plates clinked as he set the table for the two Knowltons.

In the presence of Sweeney, more than a cook or a fisherman to the Knowlton family, the young Knowlton assumed a privilege of familiarness.

"May I speak freely, Captain?"

The elder Knowlton removed his pipe from his mouth. The younger took this as a sign of approval for his request. Harvey Knowlton, Jr., circled around the captain's table and sat in a chair.

"Uncle Nemo," began Harvey, "if you're going to be cautious and have us not chase the fish, then…"

"I'll stop you right there, mate." The captain raised his hand as his nephew was about to speak again.

Cook Sweeney's eyes slowly opened wide. Astonished at the exchange, he had stopped setting the dinnerware. For a mate to address a master as anything but captain, was as unusual as a week without fog on the banks. Even more shocking was Harvey using his Uncle Nehemiah's nickname, one he hadn't heard stated since the nephew was a boy. "I'll be going. Your dinner is…" Before Sweeney could explain the fare he'd prepared, the captain spoke up.

"You'll remain here, Cook Sweeney. As a sailor near all your life, I'll be expecting you to confirm what I am about to remind the mate here with regards to a ship's command."

The cook's eyes moved to his left to take in the junior Knowlton's shocked expression.

The captain addressed his nephew, but all the while speaking towards a wall displaying navigation implements. "These instruments, some were my father's, and his father's before that."

The nephew, knowing this, sighed loudly with exaggerated emphasis. Harvey was well aware that his Uncle Nehemiah Knowlton III was proud of the sailing antiques, as was he, but he had little patience for a sailing lecture at the moment.

With a scowl at hearing the breath, the captain turned still eyeing a meticulously polished brass compass in his hand. He then untied a sextant that was secured to the quarter's wall above a thick, smooth board that served as a writing desk. "My grandfather, your great-grandfather, taught me to sail with some of these very same instruments. A few of them, like the ring dial and astrolabe were out of use for a century even by that time." He motioned to the antique pieces of brass, wood, and bone. The uncle ran his hand over an ebony and brass quadrant with carved ivory scales, then a cross-staff that was two-hundred years old, and finally a sextant with an arm plated in gold.

Sweeney nodded as he watched the captain's regard for the instruments. He swallowed hard with pride, because besides his paid duties, he'd made it his responsibility to polish the instruments with attention deserving the memories of those who once held the brass and wood to the skies over the Atlantic Ocean.

"This spy glass, it's over four feet long. It was used by our navy during the revolution, a gift from the Dutch. Your grandfather, my father, purchased it for his first vessel."

"Captain, what does this have to do with fishermen going fishing?"

Sweeney shook his head. He poured the captain his spot of rum and began arranging the ramekins of braised beef, carrots, and bread pudding.

"Thank you, Cook Sweeney. You've performed another ship's miracle aboard this fisherman."

It was a deserving compliment, considering the food was often basic, but all the more special considering their location and means of preparation. Any dinner beyond a fish stew or "salted horse" (and sometimes it was just that), was always highly regarded by the crew. The cook acknowledged the captain's praise without interrupting the speech he was giving his nephew.

"Mate, these instruments show the tradition of sailing navigation. A captain must always know his course. He is responsible for his ship." He paused to taste the beef. "Seasoned wonderfully, as usual." His head nodded to Cook Sweeney.

The captain moved the ramekin of beef towards his mate. The nephew waved it off.

Sweeney sighed.

Captain Nehemiah Knowlton III continued his lesson. "And more importantly, a captain is responsible for his men. In return, the men are expected to obey orders. For as long as men have gone to sea, and when I sailed with my father, and he with his father, the rules of hierarchy on the ship were obeyed. Always. No exceptions. Whether between a common deck hand—or a relative."

"Pardon me, Captain. I will not forget your position again. Or mine. It was a nice speech, yet, I argue we ought to go fishing."

Captain Knowlton shoved a spoonful of carrots into his mouth. He took his time chewing, lest he lose what patience he had left. "You may have learned half of the lesson. The other half being forgotten, is the captain gives the orders aboard a fisherman on when and where to fish."

Harvey, as much as he wanted to be a proper seaman, a Knowlton of the finest kind, he was a youth full of impatience to be a high liner with a desire to return to Gloucester and be noticed. His uncle was trying all the patience he had in reserve at the moment. He rose. "Then, Captain, until you are to order us to fish, I have to wonder why I am aboard if not to chase the mackerel. When I captained a vessel …"

The mate was interrupted. "You don't need me to remind you that the last vessel of which you were master, was lost on Georges."

Harvey's face tightened. It was always the same—his uncle bringing up the schooner that was blown over shoal water in a gale whenever he wanted to make a point. All the men were saved, but that was of little account. The vessel had been financed by his Uncle Nehemiah Knowlton III, and Harvey's father, Harvey Knowlton, Sr. But as these things tend to go, in a lapse of judgement Knowlton junior had splurged for a night of fun in Boston with the insurance money he was to deliver to the agent. He'd intended to make good before the vessel sailed. His luck in earning to pay the debt was worse than the luck he'd had gambling. Time had run out, and the ship was put to sea, unknowingly uninsured by the owners, to never return. It was a loss of near four-thousand dollars, not to mention a season of fishing. Harvey Knowlton, Jr., was thus working to repay his father and uncle on the loss—he'd become a mere mate under the watchful eye of Captain Nehemiah "Uncle Nemo" Knowlton.

The uncle, as captain, was at the end of his log-line of patience. He desired to finish his meal in peace. "Mate Knowlton, you'll return to your duties. Make ready to set sail with the tide at first light."

The nephew could not help but smile, assured he had convinced his uncle to go up the strait in search of fish. He stood with renewed energy.

Captain Knowlton, noticing the changed disposition in his nephew, sought to take the wind from his mate's sails. "Inform the men we will be going out to sea. To the banks."

"The banks! There will be no mackerel out there this time of the season."

"Dismissed!"

Sweeney took the opportunity to disappear up the companionway after the junior Knowlton. Throughout his years sailing he'd born witness to arguments between fishermen, but not one between his captain and first mate; and never an argument between two who were so closely related. He sat on a barrel in the galley, wondering how it might all turn out.

Captain Nehemiah Knowlton III did not finish his meal. He stood in front of the painted portraits of his father and grandfather on his cabin's wall. *"I apologize, Captains, if ever as your mate I tested either of you in the manner my nephew has tested me this day,"* he thought to himself

When the captain summoned his first mate at four a.m., he was informed by the deck watch that Mate Knowlton could not be located aboard the *Patience*. A more detailed search showed the shore skiff was missing, along with Harvey's ditty bag. The captain consulted his father's pocket watch and then his tide table. Now, he was being tested beyond his ability to remain patient.

Captain Knowlton knew if he waited over the rising tide for his first mate to possibly return after a drunken row in Canso, he would be seen as weak amongst his men, and that could never do. He was a Gloucester captain of a ship with responsibilities to fish. Without guilt, he resolved to let his nephew row his own way in the world.

He arrived back to his cabin as Sweeney was setting the morning coffee, eggs and biscuits on the table.

"Good morning, Captain. Mug up." A usual hearty greeting from the captain was not returned. Sweeney poured the coffee, yet unaware of the deserter nephew.

"Cook Sweeney, what is this?"

The cook paused in his juicing of an orange to see the captain holding a folded paper with the captain's wax seal applied.

"It was folded in this napkin." The captain's stare accused Sweeney of its being there.

"I had not noticed it, Captain." Sweeney watched as the captain sliced open the note. The clanking of rigging filtered down the companionway.

After reading the note, Captain Knowlton slipped it between the pages of his journal. "Cook Sweeney, would you please on your way forward inform the second mate to report to me."

Without a minute delay, the *Patience* sailed east on the tide with a newly appointed first mate; and he was not a Knowlton.

Later That Same Month
September 25, 1867
Goldboro Settlement Miner's Hotel
Guysborough County, Nova Scotia

"You'll be sure to stay a mile away from any miner working a piece of the river. They tend to be territorial over their pools. Four pine boxes had to be ordered this year already." The man stopped and held a lantern to better see the expression on his new guest's face. There was none. "I mention it because you appear to be new in these parts."

Harvey Knowlton, Jr., said nothing; his face displayed no surprise. There was no need to disclose his prior mining history. He followed the owner of the hotel down a narrow hallway of unpainted knotty pine boards, the knots staring like eyes in all directions.

"You'll be sure to buy your own bedding. Tonight you'll have to do with what you have. The store's closed and I'm off to have my supper after I show you your room, Mr.?" He held the lantern up again, to better remember the face. "What did you say your name was?"

"Handron. Zadok Handron."

The owner continued speaking as he walked on ahead. Snores filtered through the thin walls. "You'll be sure, Mr. Handron, to keep quiet hours here after four in the afternoon." The owner, reminded of his rule, lowered his voice. "The miners are up early and they get sore if woken before time. I'm less inclined to board to troublemakers."

He stopped outside an opened door to a room. A painted number seven was hastily marked on the rough-hewn door.

"You'll be sure to purchase your mining outfit from the mercantile up the road. It's my brother who owns it. You'll be sure to tell him you've taken a room here at Isaacs'—that's my name. You'll notice there are no locks on the outside of these doors. You'll leave nothing in the room when you leave each day that you'd want to say was yours. You'll pay for your next night each morning before you leave. You don't come back, that's your problem, not mine. A candle is on the table to the right." He spun and his shadow disappeared into the darkness.

Striking a match, Harvey inspected the room. On the table with the candle was a wooden water bucket. He lifted the candle and touched the match to the wick. The glow reflected across the water in the bucket showing it was covered in a filmy-white substance. There was a plank bed with no mattress or pillow. A curtain-less window was blocked on the outside with close-growing bushes. A bed pan in the corner was reeking of a lingering odor. He tossed it out the window—pan included. The same was done with the water bucket. Turning back towards the hall, he latched the door, untied his blanket from his sack, and rolled his coat into a pillow. Over a forecastle bunk, the room had two advantages. He was alone, and there was no smell of fish. It was easy to fall asleep on the hard board, although, he slept with his knife at his side.

Harvey, under his assumed name of Zadok Handron, kept mostly to himself, a trait common to the pick-axe men and panners. What was uncommon to Knowlton, was his well-off financial situation. To the inside of his coat pocket, he'd sewn a roll of bills from his season's fishing earnings, an amount of over four-hundred dollars. Although his Uncle Nemo had allowed no privilege in being familiar while aboard the ship, he did not hide from him the combination to the ship's safe. Harvey Knowlton Jr. hoped his uncle was regretting that lapse in captain judgement.

Through the 1867 months of October and November, Knowlton remained in Nova Scotia mining in the Goldboro area. He'd mined once before, albeit out west, and had skills enough to surpass the others in locating what gold there was in the Canadian Province. His hard work was rewarded with claims enough for him to leave the miners hotel. He took a room in a local home with an old bachelor farmer who welcomed the rent money. In utmost secrecy, he made consistent deposits in a Halifax bank, including nuggets he secured in a safe deposit box.

Over the winter months, Knowlton kept his anonymity and traveled to Brewer, Maine. There, he found work with the *McGilvery & Stetson Shipyard.* His skills and knowledge of ship building, even without him trying, were recognized beyond someone as a day-laborer and he was promptly promoted. While he appreciated the higher pay, he struggled to keep his expertise around vessels hidden behind his miner's beard and newly acquired mannerisms of a Province panner of gold. It was during these months when he first became acquainted with the lumber supplied from Maine's forests, and in particular, with the tamarack for ship knees supplied from one of Maine's most respected lumbermen, David Libbey.

On the first Saturday afternoon in January of 1868, the temperature was ten below zero. The wind was running up the Penobscot River, penetrating his wool coat. When work ended for the day, he was walking along Wilson Street to his rooming house. The bitter cold sent him into a business he passed every day on his way to and from the shipyard. From the Brewer fur trader, Manly Hardy, he purchased a fur-lined coat and trapper hat—two items he felt were necessary for working along the river at the boatyard. With Mr. Hardy, he discussed game in the Maine woods as Manly's wife, Emmaline, measured him for the coat. While she did, Knowlton sung a sea shanty to the Hardy's three-year old baby girl.

> "O, Fannie, I'll sing you a song, so listen to me,
> Heave away, away, blow the man down.
> It's about what you'll find, should you go to sea,
> Oh give us some time to blow the man down."

April 1868

The winter months had passed by quickly with Harvey working long hours as a carpenter. With his new appreciation for shipbuilding, he spent his evenings at the desk in his room by the light and warmth of an oil lamp sketching designs for vessels. On the drawing of a sleek schooner's bow he penciled the name, *Defiance*. Harvey carefully folded the schematic into a leather case—wondering if he'd ever have the fortune to build such a vessel.

Soon it was spring. The streets were clogged with the throngs of river drivers preparing to head north. Harvey feared that if he continued working in Brewer, he might be recognized by east coast fishermen who would stop in the harbor for supplies. He entertained thoughts of taking to the woods and rivers with the woodsmen. After considering the meager pay of lumbering, he returned to Goldboro, and the solitary quiet work of mining. In the third week of April, he mined two large nuggets. His experience told him they would be worth several thousand dollars.

Quietly, he left Goldboro to deposit his gold in the box at the Halifax bank. With his new found wealth, he took a room at the city's grandest hotel, had a bath, and bought new clothes. In the lobby tavern, he relaxed in a chair next to the fireplace. From a glass, and not a tin mug, he enjoyed sipping a warm spiced-rum. Piled near the kindling box was a stack of newspapers. A headline from a two-month-old issue grabbed his attention.

Halifax Daily Times
Captain Knowlton of Gloucester Drowned at Sea
February 10, 1868

The schooner *Patience to-Knight* was found hull up, west of Canso Bank. The *Patience*, from Gloucester, was located only after two survivors told of their misfortune. The ship's cook and an another, survived five days adrift in a dory. The cook was determined not to die until he was found. Said he, *"The captain, Nehemiah Knowlton III, his dying wish was that his grandfather's instruments be returned to Rocky Neck. And that, I promised to do before my death."* The cook and mate did not know what became of the rest of the crew. Some were seen getting into dories. A search only turned up the vessel, which was sunk as a derelict to not endanger the ships passing the area. The cook stated the captain went down with the ship as he made one last throw to the dory of a cross-staff. The cook caught it. Within moments, the *Patience* flipped on her side and the captain was hit with the boom. The cook and mate said they planned to return to Gloucester by train as both were too shook up to travel by sea for the time being.

The once sailor's hands trembled as he held the paper to the flames. The next morning, Harvey Knowlton, Jr., withdrew his money and all but three of his smaller nuggets from the Halifax vault and booked passage to Boston on a steamer.

The return of Knowlton did not go unnoticed. For when he disembarked, he was not the unknown miner Zadok Handron any longer. Fishermen of the Gloucester fleet, in port selling their fish, were accustomed to watching passengers arriving. He was immediately welcomed home from those who recognized him. Amidst questions on where he'd been, he received condolences on the loss of his uncle. The men told him of the whereabouts of his brother Joseph's vessel and news of the Gloucester fleet. None of this he asked for, they simply walked with him as he went to find a rooming house. Word of his arrival reached Gloucester that very week. The gossip included news about the city life he was spending lavishly on.

The Monday following, he was at breakfast in his hotel. A hand pushed down the pages of the *Boston Times* he was reading. Opposite, he found a face he recognized smiling down on him. Without hesitation, the clean-shaven Knowlton rose and shook hands with the man of rotund figure. "Why, Captain Horton, what brings you to Boston?"

"I might ask the same of you, Mr. Knowlton. Your being here, and not in Glo'ster." Edward A. Horton took a seat at the table. "It's good to see you, Harvey. I might not have recognized you without your seaman's beard." He touched his own trimmed facial hair. "It was required the owner point you out on my query."

Harvey ran his hand over his cheek. "Hmm, yes. I found that here in Boston away from the harbor, a rosy-cheeked fellow gets better service than one with a bushy, fisherman's beard."

Horton laughed. His own cheeks red from his normal cheerful disposition.

Soon the conversation turned to family. Edward Horton was surprised to hear that Harvey had only recently learned of the sinking of the *Patience* in recent days. "I apologize, Harvey. I was one to think you were ignoring the news. Or worse, were dead.”

“I have to admit, these past months I have not been much of a news reader. Novels have had a better effect on my disposition than the snide remarks of the journalists.”

“Ah, I see.” Edward approached the subject of his errand. “Your mother has asked if I might convince you to come home.”

“And my father?”

“You know he is the silent type.”

Neither Edward or Harvey needed to say more about the senior Harvey Knowlton. His known wish was for his sons to get jobs on land; as he had done. It wasn’t that he’d blame his brother Nehemiah for taking the boys to sea, or his son for the death of his brother, but everyone knew how Knowlton Sr., felt about the risks of going to sea.

In his heart, Harvey knew his father wouldn’t say much about the sinking of the *Patience,* or his absence; it was well understood that the fishing life was a dangerous one and nothing further needed saying. They’d had it all out before.

He looked away from Edward. “I was planning on going home, once I could figure what to say.” Harvey lifted his coffee cup, but without drinking placed it back on the saucer. “I’ve been absent for so long. My not knowing of what occurred. To have not been on the vessel.” He turned back to Edward. “How things were left between myself and the captain. I don’t know how to explain it.” Harvey didn’t tell Edward about the guilt he was feeling, and how he wondered if he’d been on the *Patience*, if the outcome would have been different for his uncle, or at least he’d have also been drowned and spared the pain.

“Nothing is expected. No one blames you for what happened to the *Patience* and crew. Sweeney says that had the gale not surprised them, they surely would have outrun the cutter.”

Edward saw the surprise on Harvey's face. "Yes. That's something the Province papers have not included on their pages in their reporting. Sweeney says the *Patience* was at least seven miles from shore where they were fishing."

On the train north to Gloucester, Horton told Knowlton of how some of the individual fleet owners were combining into companies in order to gain economy of scale and deal with risks; risks he claimed not only from the sea, but to deal with losses imposed by hostile neighbors. Knowlton knew exactly what Horton meant.

By the time they reached Gloucester station, Harvey knew what he intended to do with the small fortune he made mining. His parents were to be cared for until their deaths, regardless of what would become of him and his brother Joseph—on land or sea. Following that expenditure calculation he made Edward Horton a proposition that was accepted without reserve.

By the end of April 1868, the business charter for the combined *McKenzie-Knowlton-Horton Company* was filed in Boston. Harvey's first order of business was to commission a new ship to replace the *Patience*. Work on the *Lily Rose Snow*— on account of his mother's favorite flowers and her love of snow—began in the shipyard next to the Knowlton home on the fifth day of May. She was launched *from her ways,* one year later, on Mother's Day 1869.

Frank Sweeney, the cook, who had lost his taste of cooking at sea with the loss of Nehemiah Knowlton III, applied his skills at finish-carpentry to the captain's quarters on all the firm's vessels, in addition to his directing the rigging. It was discussed within the Knowlton family on what should become of the rescued instruments. There was only one rightful decision. The instruments Sweeney had saved from the *Patience*, he fitted to a custom-made wall unit in the captain's quarters of the *Lily Rose*. There they could help direct the captain, if not by direct use, then through memory.

Harvey Knowlton Jr. sailed the *Lily Rose Snow* as captain for a year before Edward Horton convinced him he was needed more in the firm's daily management from the offices in Gloucester. Captain J. William Gott, a terribly-able Gloucester captain was then given the helm. In the summer of 1870 skipper Gott had sailed the *Lily Rose* towards Canso—chasing the mackerel— until he returned to tell Harvey of what had occurred to the vessel.

Thursday - September 21, 1871
King's Square Inn, on the Bay of Fundy
St. John, New Brunswick.

Harvey stirred from his dream. For a moment, he thought he was back in the tavern with Captain Gott, but it was only on account of the rum he'd spilled over his shirt. A vision of Gott's description of the Canadian cutter captain was the last thing he saw before opening his eyes to the sun rising over the Nova Scotia mainland. He rose from the chair. It was time for him to make that captain's acquaintance—face to face.

A Miner Again

Wednesday – September 27, 1871
Destination: Guysborough, Nova Scotia

On this morning there was no one wanting to sit next to Harvey Knowlton as he rode the train as far as he would go by rail, and that was to Afton Station in Nova Scotia. The roughly dressed passenger collected his baggage and hired a wagon to take him the twenty miles southeast to Manchester.

"Appears you plan to do some panning." The driver sat holding the reins, watching Knowlton load his belongings. He'd transported many miners outfitted with shovels, pick-axes, and sifters piled in the buckboard. But this was the first miner he'd seen wearing a fur trapper hat. "You also a trapper?"

The question, unbeknownst to the driver, provided Harvey with the confidence in his disguise. Since leaving St. John, he'd spent the last six days on a side trip to Goldboro. There, in familiar places of his past mining, he supplied himself with the second-hand gear he was now loading, along with a wardrobe of used clothes, all but the hat and his coat; those he'd had stored away in his attic for the past four years.

In Goldboro, where Harvey had purchased the mining tools, Isaacs, the owner of the mercantile, gladly sold him—for a second time—picks, shovels, and pans. After the man left the store, he'd laughed with his wife. They'd recognized him as Zadok Handron, who'd been a customer four years prior, although neither made any mention of their recognition to Harvey himself.

"That drifter surely never panned enough gold to pay for the first outfit I sold him," stated the husband.

"Guess he'd figure on trying again," said the wife. She added, "And we'll be the ones making the money. We ought to try and sell him a new hat this time around!"

While there, Harvey left some intended impressions with those he spoke to in the depressed mining town. When he walked away carrying his gear, all those in the town assumed he was going into the woods of Goldboro to stake a claim. They were wrong.

"No trapping. Just mining." Harvey kept his answer short; he didn't intend to say much to the wagon driver. The teamster, however, wasn't only driving the horse team, he was driving for a conversation.

"Seems everyone has this idea all over Nova Scotia these days. Tried mining myself for a time." The driver gave the reins a shake to move the team down the road. "Didn't make enough to buy a dinner. Now I'm driving a team and making a good living." When there was no response from his passenger, he set to watching the ruts.

At a roadside tavern the horses were watered and fed. Inside, the two men ate in silence. Expecting no further conversation from his passenger, the driver retrieved the daily paper. His snickering and laughing caused Knowlton to raise his head from over his bowl of French onion soup.

"I have to admit, this business of the government seizing American vessels is the best laughter since Denman Thompson passed through poking fun at the hayseeds." The driver poked at the paper. He'd taken his passenger for a Province man, or at least not someone from America. "This newsman has a way of telling the story of two vessels taken from the same owners. Poor Yankees, they never seen what hit 'em. Or rather, what sailed under their bows."

Dropping his hard end-crust of bread in the bowl with a splash, Knowlton scowled at the driver and grabbed the paper. "Let me see that."

The carriage driver, offended, was about to resist, but eyeing Knowlton's size, he shrugged the man off as just a rude miner. He'd dealt with plenty of them.

Canso Weekly

Two Septembers in a row. That's right, our daring Captain Tory has seized a second vessel from the same Gloucester fishing firm whose vessel the *Lily Rose Snow* was confiscated and the crew convicted last year at Cape Auguet, south of Cape Breton Island. As is typical, the Americans were violating the three-mile fishing rule. In his latest victory for Province fishermen, on September 8 of this year, Captain Tory and his crew led the *Edward A. Horton* into Guysborough Harbor. That morning the schooner was seen within the three-mile limit. Two of their dory men were hand-lining over the Amet Island Shoals, close to the Eastern Passage. There, Captain Tory saw the dory men haul in fish. The *Horton* was seized immediately by the brave crew of the Canadian cutter *Sweepstakes*. Rumor is the earlier seized ship from the same outlaw firm is now at service for his Majesty from an undisclosed port in England. The second ship will likely join the first before year end. The Gloucester fishermen ought to learn their lesson and keep to Yankee waters.

Knowlton's face reddened. The writer of this piece was no different from his obnoxious journalist kin. Harvey's firm had paid all legal fees even though it was contested that the seizure of the *Lily Rose* was illegal and with no merit of a fishing violation. The ship, by court order, was to have remained in Canso until legal proceedings were completed—what was considered a final formality. Once again, there were violations of legal rulings.

With restraint, Knowlton made it to his destination of South Manchester without unloading his opinion on the driver, or giving away his identity as not being from the Provinces. Shouldering his pack, pickaxe, and other gear, he held his compass. With the driver watching, he walked east into the woods. A mile later, assured he was alone, he struck for McCaul Point. His line of direction was based on the compass, a crudely drawn map, and his knowledge from his limited experience with the shores of Chedabucto Bay from his fishing days. The entire bay side was deserted of habitation, making the hills ideal for a lone miner camp. The woods afforded a bounty of dried firewood. Fresh water was available in the hilltop ponds. Most valuable of all, the site was within rowing distance of Guysborough and a dory sail to Canso. He struck camp in a hollow offering concealment. As he really had no intent on mining, each location along the point was as good as the next. And if someone should happen along, they'd only find the tent and gear of a miner—an occurrence that would draw no suspicion.

Two hours later, his camp setup completed, he was in Guysborough Harbor. The clammer, who shuttled him across the channel, even was helpful in telling him where he could inquire to purchase a dory. By this time, it was evening and he was stuck in town for the night. He took a room, had a bath, and ate dinner at the tavern—where he was eyed suspiciously by the fishermen. He ignored their looks, paid his bill, and intended to have good night's rest. For an hour he stared at the ceiling, not able to sleep. He put his boots back on and went down to the wharf.

The *Edward A. Horton* was the largest boat in the harbor, other than the revenue cutter. Harvey took a seat on a barrel on the opposite wharf from his schooner and smoked his pipe. He watched a man carry a lantern to the captain's quarters aft. To get a better look, he climbed a ladder to the roof of a fish house. In keeping in the shadows of the chimneys, he focused his spyglass on his ship. He continued to watch the *Horton*. No other watchmen or guards were seen on the boat or along the wharf.

With only the night sky above, he thought it through. An infrequent bell from a ship at anchor broke the silence. He concluded that Captain Tory was figuring that no American sailor could free the *Horton* from the shallow, narrow channel of Guysborough Harbor, at least not under the cover of darkness. Harvey knew the harbor was unforgiving to those not familiar with the channel. The river had a reputation for grounding vessels in the shallows of mud, sand, and stone. Most captains of larger vessels only sailed from the harbor during daylight hours when there was a high tide. Such requirements would make it impossible for Harvey to sneak away with the *Horton* as the townspeople went about their business.

At midnight the church bells rang. With no further activity on the ship, Knowlton assumed the sailor had gone to bed. He was wrong. The man, carrying his lantern, appeared on the deck and over the rail he went. Up a side street, swinging the lantern and whistling a low tune, he walked. Knowlton followed at a distance to see the man enter a home. This development was the best he'd had in weeks. If it proved routine, it meant the *Horton* was left unguarded during the nights. That the Canadians had calculated an American crew could not sail the *Horton* out of the harbor at night, allowed Knowlton the best night sleep he'd had since leaving his own bed in Gloucester.

Thursday – September 28, 1871

In the morning, Harvey, as Zadok Handron, purchased a dory boat, a small sail, salt pork, and a supply of bread, cheese, and honey. The rest of the day he spent making himself known as a miner looking to make it big. The storekeepers, and residents alike, whom he spoke with gave him little interest. Guysborough county was full up with drifters intending to make it rich— although, as they all told him with a sneer and a laugh, none had.

Handron was confident, not discouraged, by the statements from everyone he encountered who made it seem he'd be just another failed miner. He made it known, to anyone who asked and those that didn't, that he'd be mining the rocks from McCaul Point to Clam Harbor River. With his alibi in place, he rowed over to his camp on the point, and as far as he knew, not close to any potential mining deposits.

At midnight, adrift in his dory and concealed under the shadows of moored vessels, he watched the guard again leave the *Horton* and go home. Then, under the cover of darkness, while all of Guysborough slept, he sounded the depth of the harbor channel. This was a difficult task for a single man. He had to hold the dory in relative stable position on the tide, drop the line, and update his depth chart. Across from one shore to the other, he took his bearings and mapped the floor of the channel. After three cold hours, he had only obtained three parallel passes.

With the harbor fishermen readying for their day, as evidenced by windows in the shore houses showing light, he made one more run, this time to the *Horton*. It didn't take him long, even in the dark, to discover the sails and most of the rigging were not on the vessel. This was to be expected; Captain Tory certainly intended for it to be all the harder for any crew to make away with the vessel. What was unexpected was the state of the provisions and ships' stores. All was as Joseph had told him. It appeared not one fresh water jug, crate of hardtack, or other food had been removed. This was unusual for a ship that was intended to be stationary for some weeks. Shielding the light of a lantern with his hand, he investigated the captain's quarters.

Several books from the ship's library were stacked on the desk. A bottle of rum was to one side; no doubt from the captain's cabinet. Knowlton's jaw tightened on seeing the lock pried open. A book was on the table at the captain's chair; the page marked with a feather. A mug was positioned nearby.

Having to spend a night on the cold, hard ground was not relished at all, especially when there was a ship full of empty bunks, but he hurried over the rail back to his dory. Thankfully, his reconnaissance of the *Horton* profited him with a jug of rum. A few long swigs and he slept under the canvas tent until noon.

Friday – September 29, 1871

Through early afternoon, Knowlton passed his hours in the town. He ate at a restaurant, made small talk of his morning's supposed mining, and took inventory of the waterfront warehouses. In particular, the largest two-story building facing the wharf was frequented by Canadian cutter men. Between their two ships and the warehouse building they made a steady parade shuttling supplies. A quick walk behind the building showed three doors and several boarded windows.

In the shade of the fish-house, he sat on a barrel, and lighted his pipe. He smoked while considering where in the warehouse he'd find the *Horton* sails.

"How's the mining, Mister Zadok Handron?"

Knowlton looked up to see a man of piercing eyes, dressed in new wool pants, wearing a tilted tam o' shanter hat over his yellowing-gray hair that curled out from under it.

Before Harvey could answer, the man continued, "If you strike gold, I'll have to follow your lead. Fishing these days isn't keeping me barely in boots."

"Looks like you're doing okay. Considering." Knowlton motioned with his pipe at the man's shining boots.

"Ah, I've got to keep up appearances." The man sat on a neighboring barrel. "As I know your name from your boasting around this small town of ours, mine is MacDonald. Tom MacDonald." He waited for some recognition to show on Knowlton's face. When none came, he continued, "Maybe you've heard of me. Accused smuggler and scoundrel of the Cape Breton waters. According to your own enemy, Captain Tory, anyway."

This last statement provided the facial expression MacDonald was anticipating, if not for his own name, than for that of Tory's. MacDonald went on. "Oh, you might be a miner. But seeing you were skulking about the *Horton* last evening, I figured you for someone else. Maybe Edward A. Horton himself?" MacDonald eyed Knowlton with a sideways glance. "Or more likely, from what I've heard about the *Horton* from Gloucester men over in Canso, you're more likely his partner. You seem to resemble the young captain who stood on the wharf there," he pointed, "when Captain Tory made a mockery of the American crew and vessel." He turned back to Handron. "Yes, I was there," he said to the surprised look.

Coming into view at the end of the alley was a seaman of considerable rank, evidenced by his attire adorned in golden ropes and the epaulets on his shoulders. He was taking such long strides, the young woman attempting to keep up alongside him was at a near run. Part of their conversation carried down the alley.

"But father, it's only a trip to Canso. In order to go to the library."

Out of the corner of his eye, Harvey noticed MacDonald had slunk back into the shadows of a doorway. The officer had stopped to face the pleading woman.

Harvey recalled the vivid description of the Canadian from Captain Will Gott, near a year ago.

"Tory is a rotund man, but only in the belly, it sticks out as if he were carrying child. The figure is all the more strange on account of his imposing height. I, sir, and you as well, are tall men, being over six feet. But this Tory, he was a half foot over me. On account of his height, he wears a sword of extreme length in his scabbard. His hair is white, at least I think it is white, unless he is carrying on the old England tradition of wearing a powdered wig under his hat, even outside of political chambers. He looks ridiculous in his tight-fitting, red uniform. His eyes, they are too small for his head. Over them are the bushiest eyebrows that start too far from the peak of his narrow nose and extend nearly to his temple." Gott paused. "And most out of place was a gorget worn around his neck at the collar. Oh, not the gold or some metal fabrication from before the Revolution. This was a fake replica, made of a silver-colored linen, embroidered with a navy battle scene. Most out of place."

It was as if Captain Will had painted a picture, and the likeness had come to life before Harvey there in the alley. His listening to the figure speaking, reminded him of a tone and volume of a captain addressing men on deck, and not a voice necessary towards a pretty, young lady.

Tory put his hand on his daughter's shoulder. "Alice, I heard from my men you were seen in Canso just the other day. With some unknown man. I'll not have my daughter cavorting around behind my back with some stranger." He kept on his way. She followed him into the warehouse.

"How a pompous man like that could have spawned such a pleasant and level-headed young woman, I'll never know. I suppose the sins of the father should not be passed to the children," stated MacDonald as he sat back down next to Knowlton. He extended his hand. "Seeing the resemblance, might I have the pleasure of meeting the brother of Captain Joseph Knowlton?"

Knowlton didn't know what to say. This MacDonald could blow his plan faster than a gale coming up on Georges Bank in winter. He offered his hand; he was not sure yet what MacDonald was angling for.

"Don't worry. I won't be saying anything to Tory. Not just yet anyway. I'm thinking, as fishing hasn't been so good lately, and I'm pinned down at the moment from my side business, maybe you and I could come to an agreement."

With apprehension, Knowlton nodded. He considered he didn't have much of a choice at the moment. This smuggler-fisherman obviously was more observant of the goings-on of the harbor than all the Canadian officers put together.

MacDonald, sensing Knowlton's surprise, offered some explanation of the proposal. "I can see you're wondering how

I've come to figure out your secret. This I shall reveal, but not here. First, we need to not be seen with one another. The last thing we'd want to do is smudge the reputation of miner Zadok Handron around these parts, by being seen with the smuggler Tom MacDonald."

MacDonald gave Harvey directions to call at his home later in the evening—specifically after dark. "I'll be waiting in the back barn, it's my workshop and rigging storage. Not the one nearer the house—that's for the animals. Use the door that faces the woods. It'll be open. We'd not want to cause any suspicion with my daughter at the house. You'll be wanting to come alone. I'll tell you then how I knows all about ye." MacDonald peered down the alley toward the street. He decided against that exit, and instead lifted a loose fence board between the buildings. Before stepping through, he whispered, "I've heard many stories of you Captain Harvey Knowlton. We'll make a good pair." With a wink, a nod, and finger to his tam o' shanter, he ducked through the passageway, pulling the board closed behind him.

Billy Boy

Friday – September 29, 1871 – Evening
MacDonald's Cove
Guysborough, Nova Scotia

Harvey spent the remainder of his afternoon in an unsettled state. The fact that one person in Guysborough knew his true identity could prove fatal. Worried about being discovered, he sat in his dory under the wharf and waited for nightfall before beginning his walk out of town.

At eight that evening, he arrived at the home of Tom MacDonald. For a fisherman who claimed to be *light on the hooks*, Harvey was surprised to see a two-story brick home, sporting four chimneys, and having covered porches on two sides. Behind the sheer curtains the rooms were brightly lit. A man's voice was singing a recognizable tune to someone playing the piano. Harvey concealed himself behind an oak tree and peered in the window. One young woman was playing the piano, and a man, with his back to the window, was singing to another girl seated on a long, curvy couch. A fire of four-foot logs was burning in the immense hearth.

When the man thrust his hand in the air to hit a note, Harvey saw the face of the girl on the couch. She was the girl he had seen earlier in the afternoon—Captain Tory's daughter! Harvey thought, *'What kind of trick was MacDonald playing?'*

The words of the song were muffled but recognizable through the closed window panes.

"Won't you tell me Alice darling,
that you love none else but me?
For I love you Alice darling,
you are all the oceans to me.
Oh, tell me Alice that you love me,
Put your soft hand in mine,
Take my heart sweet Alice,
Tell me that you'll be mine!"

The tune Harvey knew. It was from Willy Shakespeare Hays, with *Mollie Darling* replaced by *Alice*. The man's voice had a certain quality that puzzled him as much as seeing the cutter captain's daughter at the home of a smuggler.

Startled from a tap on his shoulder, he spun with his fists at the ready. MacDonald ducked and put a finger to his lips. He beckoned with his head towards the barn. Harvey followed the quiet-as-a-bobcat smuggler in a zigzag through the trees.

Pulling the door closed, MacDonald scolded the captain. "I told you, Captain Knowlton, to meet me here at the barn. You might blow a hole in the ship's deck before we've even started the battle."

Not intimidated, Harvey demanded an explanation. "Why is Tory's daughter in your home? Is this some sort of trap?"

"Not in the least, Captain Knowlton. As I said, we must not invoke the sins of the parents on the children. Miss Alice is friends with my daughter, the one at the piano. I had no idea she'd be visiting this evening." MacDonald diverted to a boast. "I brought that piano home for my daughter from an English ship that was to deliver it to Prince Edward Island. I lightened their load considerably that day." He adjusted the light of a lantern lower, which was made dimmer on account of the smoke-stained glass chimney.

"Who was the man singing?" asked Knowlton.

For the first time, Harvey noticed MacDonald hesitate; he looked at the ground. "That there, I do not know. He arrived with Miss Tory tonight. I've only seen him twice before—when he's been walking around the town. Seems he's been here for a few weeks."

The captain scanned the barn. He was still unsure if MacDonald, who'd claimed to know all the business of the town, was telling the truth. His composure regained, Knowlton pointed a finger at MacDonald. "How did you know who I was?"

MacDonald removed his plaid cap and placed it on the bench beside him. "Ah. You see," he said, while ruffing up his flattened hair, "my profession often takes me to the harbor at night. There, minding my business, I saw a man out in a dory last evening. At first, I thought he was fishing. It's not uncommon for Yankee miners to fish in the dark. They have to. Tory would just as well fine an American miner and confiscate a dory same as he would a schooner."

From inside a bale of hay, MacDonald removed a brown jug. He was about to put the bottle to his lips when he remembered his manners. From on the workbench, behind a pile of stacked, rusty horseshoes, he produced two tin cups. Holding the lantern at an angle, he tilted and squinted at the insides of them. He blew out the dust. "You see, I was aboard the *Horton* last night when you came over the rail." He swished the cups in a bucket of water that was hanging on a hook near the door. "I'm ashamed to admit it to you, seeing the ship belongs to ye and your family. But I was scouting to see what I might procure. I'll come clean with you on that."

Knowlton was not at all surprised. He puffed on his pipe and kept his thoughts about MacDonald stealing from him to himself.

"Then, the watchman left for the evening, as he always does. Tory won't account that you'd try to sail out in the night. He figures with the sails stored in his warehouse, the ship is secure. By the way, he has rooms of confiscated sails, he always claims they've been lost—even if the legal proceedings award the sails to the owners again. Then he sells them for profit through a broker." He handed Knowlton a mug filled to the brim. "Most usually, right back to the vessel's owner."

"Thank you." Knowlton said, taking the mug. "I'd toast you, however, I'll reserve that for when I hear what you have in mind, should I agree to it." Harvey tasted the rum. "Ah, very smooth. You've good taste in Barbados water. To that I'll toast."

"Aye." MacDonald raised his cup, his eyes narrowed and his lips tightened, as he held back a grin. "Then I'll toast you and all the Yankees. Anything we can do to foil Tory's plans, I'm with you." He sat back down on the bench. "So, last evening, I sees this fisherman, as I thought you were, come aboard the *Horton*. I was behind the forec's'le companionway—thought for sure you'd spotted me—but then, I recognized you as the miner who'd been talking it up about town. I'd heard all about you— bragging about where you'd be panning and digging, and what you'd be doin." MacDonald drained his cup and refilled it. "The talk seemed a bit much for a miner. Those I've come across usually tend to be the quiet type about their business."

He topped off Knowlton's mug. "Then I watched you go aft and below. I'll admit too, I was going to tackle ye and drop ye overboard." He cocked his head. "When a miner figures to get in on my trade *procuring*, then, I'd have to do, what I'd have to do." With the raised cup hiding his lips, he gave a nod, and stated, "You'd have to understand, wouldn't ye?"

"I would not. Especially, since that there is my ship." Knowlton cupped the bowl of his pipe in his hand. "But go on."

"Aye. When you didn't take nothing, but this bottle of rum," MacDonald patted the jug and winked, "you got me to thinking. I took you for a common thief at first."

Knowlton stared at the jug.

"I see I need to explain. When you only stole, I mean took your own rum, I was pretty raw about it, as it was surely going to be my own. It seemed pretty odd to me though as you went aboard only for a drink." The wick burning bright, he turned down the lantern to allow only enough light for the two to see each other's faces; the rest of the barn was in shadows.

"Being a night watchman myself of sorts in the harbor, I let you go so as I could keep an eye on what you'd do next." MacDonald leaned in closer. "When you headed across the harbor, I pushed off in my own dory. You had me baffled. At least at first." A horse in the paddock whinnied. MacDonald went to the barn door and looked out through the crack.

"I followed after you over to the point. When you fell asleep at your camp, I recovered the rum." MacDonald grimaced. "It's an embarrassment. I admit." He took a drink. "It 'tis good rum, Captain, if there's anything to that. Anyway, I was there and the flames from your fire were still enough for me to get a look at your face."

"What else did you take from me?" Knowlton stood and began to feel his pockets. Catching the watchful eye of MacDonald, he sat back down. Through the lining in his coat, he felt for the vials where he'd stored his gold nuggets. For the moment he'd have to be satisfied the smuggler didn't empty them; he couldn't risk showing the only hand he had left.

"Shh! Keep your voice down. Nothing. Once I knew….or had a pretty good feeling 'bout who you were, I knew I couldn't take nothing from ye. On the ground next to you in your tent, I saw the chart of soundings you'd been working on. Then I knew what you were doing in the dory. And that's when it came to me as to who you were. No miner had reason to sound a channel. Neither will no miner brag about who he is, and what he's doing where. Never no miner I heard about anyway."

Knowlton nodded. "So, what's your proposal? Going to blackmail me? Hold me for ransom on my plan to recover my own ship?"

"Nah. Nothing like that. I intend to help ye."

Laughter was heard outside. MacDonald jumped up and stumbled to the door. Knowlton followed.

The three young folks were making their way to a carriage that had appeared on the road.

"That'd be Tory's official carriage. Come to take Alice home."

"Thank you, Miss MacDonald for accompanying my singing on the piano." Said the young man.

At recognizing the voice, Knowlton started to push his way past MacDonald. A firm grasp held him back.

"Please, come again. You have a wonderful voice, Mr. Knight. My father only has me play 'Billy Boy' for him to sing."

MacDonald snickered. "She's right. I love that tune."

The man's voice faded away as the carriage drove down the lane. Miss Tory could be heard laughing.

> *"Where have you been all the day,*
> *Billy Boy, Billy Boy?*
> *Where have you been all the day,*
> *Me, my dear?*
> *I've been out with Alice Tory,*
> *And she's stolen my heart away—*
>> *stole my heart away."*

"Ah. So, I take it you know the young lad then, Captain?" MacDonald asked, once they'd stepped back away from the barn door again.

"Yes. I do."

The smuggler was putting one and two together in his head. "Would he have been a sailor on the *Horton*?"

Knowlton's head was spinning. First MacDonald. Then Tory's daughter here. And now Oliver, mixing in with Tory's daughter.

"Would he have happened to be the first mate to your brother Joseph?" MacDonald pressed for an answer.

Knowlton nodded.

"I didn't know it until just now. When I heard his voice and seen you make a move towards him. He was there that day in the harbor, with your brother and the crew. Had a bit of impatience in him, the lad did. And on that day, he had a fisherman's look about him. Beard, oilskins, and red jacks. You see he's made quite a different impression." MacDonald indicated they step back to the bench. He tilted his empty mug. "We've time for a mug up."

He uncorked the bottle and poured. "He showed his temper for sure that day. I thought he might take a swing at Captain Tory. Good thing I see now he didn't. Must be working some plan of his own I say, with the captain's daughter being a pawn."

"No! Oliver is more of a man than that." Although, Knowlton wasn't exactly sure what Oliver was up to. "I'll have to be going. As you've seen my chart, I've more soundings to make."

"Have a seat, Captain. It's early. The night watchman is still in the captain's quarters reading from your books. He used to be the town librarian, until the library burned down. Besides, half the town is still awake. You've three hours before you can row your boat without anyone taking notice."

Over the next two hours, and after a good amount of rum being drunk, mostly by MacDonald, who'd taken out another jug, Knowlton listened to his proposal. It was MacDonald's opinion that the Yankee skipper needed three things from him. The first, was a captain who knew the harbor. MacDonald stated he could sail the *Horton* safely through to the bay. The second, was his knowing where the sails and rigging were located so they could quickly and quietly be recovered and fitted to the ship. Third, MacDonald calculated the number of men needed for a skeleton crew, plus Knowlton and himself, to rig and set sail the ship. In addition, that same crew would be in need of a place to lodge while waiting to sail. And no better hideout, explained the smuggler, was there than the barn they were currently sitting in. In MacDonald's near drunkenness, he set his price at one thousand dollars.

Knowlton acknowledged the first challenge of sailing the channel. He wasn't all too confident in his soundings and having a sailor familiar with the harbor could be invaluable, although he'd hate to be beholden to another. He decided, for the time, to accept MacDonald's offer, so as not to offend him, until such time a better plan could be made. Getting to the sails without detection was of course a critical matter. With a few questions, it was determined that MacDonald knew the warehouse and how to access it through a backdoor.

Knowlton didn't need any advice on the number of crew he'd need to sail his schooner and was adamant he'd be the one to furnish the men. When MacDonald continued to doubt how an American could get a secret crew there in Guysborough, Knowlton wagged a fist in front of the smuggler's face.

As for the payment, Harvey told MacDonald in no uncertain terms would he pay more than five hundred dollars for assistance, plus cost of food and lodging for the men. Without much of a fight, likely helped by the rum, MacDonald agreed to the payment and terms.

By midnight, MacDonald had fallen asleep on a bench in the barn; the empty jug held tightly in his hand. Walking the lane to town between the ruts of carriage wheels, Harvey thought about the new developments he hadn't figured on. Certainly MacDonald knowing of his identity could be trouble. Under the star-lit sky, he rowed his dory to camp on the point. By the time he reached his tent, Knowlton was resolved to not abandon his own plan, only to be dependent on a smuggling, questionable Canadian, who was prone to getting drunk, and had his own grudge against Captain Tory.

He lit his lantern and sat on his bedroll. From the leather tube on his belt, he removed and unrolled the harbor map he had drawn with his initial depth measurements. To it, he added the location of Captain MacDonald's home and barn. To himself, he admitted the hideout would be hidden far enough from town, and close enough for the crew to easily get to the ship.

The housing for the crew decided, he set his mind to Oliver. What to do about his nephew required some thinking. When Harvey and Joseph's sister had become ill, they'd promised her the boy would be cared for, should anything happen to her. After her passing, Oliver lived with Harvey and Ellen for a time. But, as soon as he was of age, he moved out, rented a room near Gloucester's fishing wharves, and worked his way through college. The independent Knowlton streak ran deep within him.

Harvey packed the bowl of his pipe to consider his approach with his nephew. Realizing he was pettifogging he went about his more important matters requiring the darkness and concealment of the harbor fog.

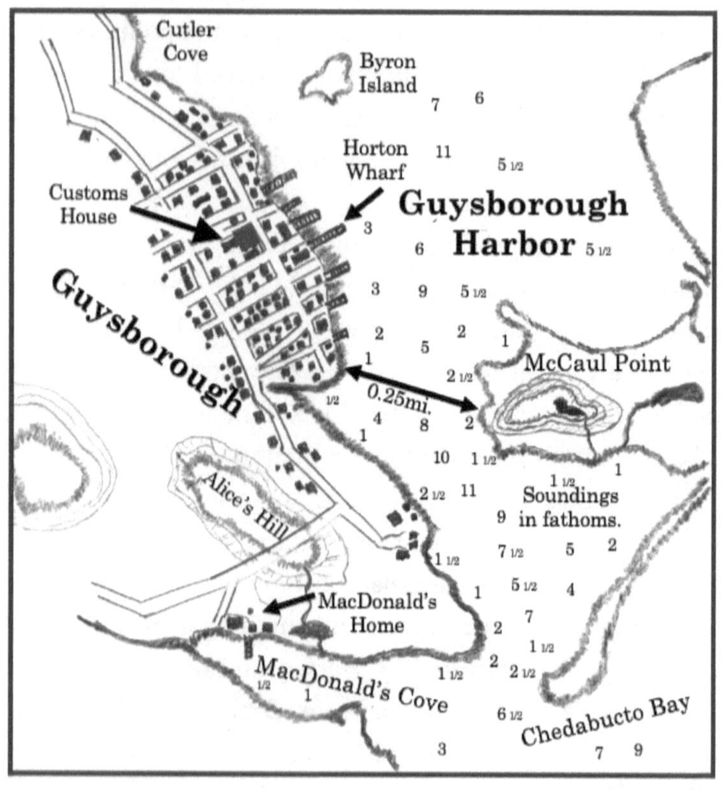

Cutler Cove
Byron Island
7   6
Horton Wharf   11   5 1/2
Customs House
Guysborough Harbor 5 1/2
3
6
3   9   5 1/2
2   2   1
5
McCaul Point
1
2 1/2
1/2   0.25mi.   2
4   8   2
1
10   1 1/2   1
Guysborough
2 1/2   11
1 1/2
Soundings
9   in fathoms.
7 1/2   5   2
Alice's Hill
5 1/2   4
1
7
MacDonald's Home
2
1 1/2
2
MacDonald's Cove
1 1/2   2 1/2
1/2   1
6 1/2   Chedabucto Bay
3   7   9

Choosing Sides

"Dory here, an' the Horton there,
Far from you at Glo'ster;
O'er the waves, I wish letters to home
To pledge I haven't lost her."

Saturday – September 30, 1871
Guysborough Harbor

After sneaking aboard to verify the watchman on the *Horton* kept his midnight departure time, and seeing no other official Canadian vessels were guarded with a night crew aboard, Knowlton struggled again to sound the channel alone. By three in the morning his arms no longer able to keep the oars from banging, he rowed back to his meager camp and collapsed on his bedroll.

Nearly after sunrise the squawks of Black-legged Kittiwakes woke him from a deep sleep. He pushed aside the flap of his tent to see a wall of fog over the bay. Mist droplets fell from the tips of the evergreens. The foghorn from the nearby light groaned in a low tone. He thought, *'Only a seaman could sleep through hours of the horn to be awoken by chirping birds.'*

With no chance of being able to go back to sleep, he boiled the last of his salted-beef and prepared a pot of fisherman coffee. Between sips, he spat the grinds at the gulls that kept approaching to steal his breakfast.

Under the cover of the still lingering fog, he took to his dory. With landmarks more visible on the Guysborough side, even through the mist, he remeasured a few of his most questionable chart markings in the turn of the channel beyond sight of the town. Dropping the weight over, and over, he thought it was going to be a Gloucester miracle to navigate around the head of land, during the black of night, in water that dropped from ten to two fathoms in several rods. There was no feasible plan he could come up with, other than to sail the harbor in the night, so he resolved to keep at his measurements. He kept at it until the sun began to burn away the mist. With a tug on the painter, he pulled his dory up through the mud of the landing below the fish house.

All eyes were on him as he crossed the hotel lobby. "I'll be needing a room and a bath," he said to the counter clerk.

The owner of the hotel came from his office. He eyed the disheveled miner. "That'll be two dollars. In advance." He indicated the trail of river mud behind Harvey. "And another half dollar on account of the mess. A full dollar should you decide to walk up the stairs in those boots!"

Taking the hint, Harvey removed his mud-caked boots without taking another step. A lady sitting in a chair let out an astonished gasp. He tipped his fur hat at her, walked across the room in his holey, stocking-feet, set the boots on the outer porch, and then mounted the stairs to his assigned room.

In the mirror, Harvey eyed his face. It had been three weeks since he'd learned of the *Horton* being seized, and he hadn't trimmed his facial hair in that time. The silver fox-hair of the hat flaps blended into his own. With scissors he did the best he could with his bushy eyebrows and the strands extending from his nose and ears. The beard he left as it was; for a miner would certainly spend no time on such grooming.

With a clean set of clothes on, he set about on his errand. In the tavern, at a window table, he consulted the fisherman's report in the paper. He placed a pickled duck egg in his mouth and washed it down with warm cider. Mostly, his eyes he kept on the sidewalk that led along the wharf. On account that MacDonald had said he'd observed the young man walking in the town, he watched and waited.

By the time he'd finished four mugs of cider and as many eggs, Knowlton had tabulated the midnight tide for the next two weeks. Now that he knew when he might get the *Horton* through the shallows, all he needed was a crew, the sails, the right wind, and no trouble from the armed Canadian cutter crew. His arms across his chest, he stared at the tide chart and shook his head. The weight of what he required for his plan to work, left a knot in his stomach. He wondered if his coming north to steal his ship was a fool's folly.

The sun streaked down the harbor and reflected off the blackened wood of the *Horton*. Taking in the lines of his ship, even without her sails furled on the jibs, was all he needed to resolve to take her home. His thoughts were on his options when he almost missed the object of his spying pass along the opposite side of the street. Waving at the barkeep, he placed coins on the table and hurried to the road.

When the person stopped to lean up against a wharf post, Knowlton hid himself behind a stack of bait barrels readying to be loaded to a vessel. He watched as the man adjusted his black top hat, seemingly taking in the *Horton*. The tide was coming in and a Canadian revenue cutter was making ready to sail, surely to go poaching in their sanctioned ways. Neither Knowlton, or the man he was watching, made a move. Both watched the vessel *Crowned Glory* navigate through the channel. With her sails raised, she set on her course through the bend of the river. Sailors at the bow blasted a horn and rang a bell at the fishermen, who in their smaller vessels did not give way until the last moment. The sailors yelled profanities related to 'slimy bait' at the men in their dories. The fishermen responded with hand gestures of no great respect.

The man leaning on the post was distracted in watching the ship. Knowlton approached unnoticed and stood directly behind him. "Do not turn around, Oliver." His nephew, startled, almost turned. "Don't look! Wait five minutes. Then, meet me in the alley between the warehouses up the next street."

It was a risk. Knowlton was unsure of why his nephew hadn't gone home to Gloucester. His change of appearance from fisherman to gentleman was a puzzle, particularly in Guysborough. The fact that he was at the home of smuggler MacDonald, and, of all things, accompanying Captain Tory's daughter was most alarming. Knowlton wasn't sure where Oliver stood at the moment. He was counting on him being a Gloucesterman, and more than that, a Knowlton.

"Uncle Harvey, why such a disguise?" Oliver looked over his uncle who stood in a dark alcove behind a pile of molded timbers.

"I might ask the same of you." He indicated the suit and high hat. "And since I outrank you, if not on a vessel right now, at least in family hierarchy, you'll explain first."

His nephew nodded. "It's not easy to say, Uncle. All of it happened so fast."

"Seems you've moved in quicker than a George's January gale on the captain's daughter."

The nephew was caught off jib-kilter. He was not expecting his uncle had known as much. "Aye-Aye, sir. That part happened as a matter of the heart. I assure you, it's nothing to do with sympathizing with the enemy, as you must surely be of mind." Oliver watched for approval in his uncle's eyes. He noticed only a bit of egg yolk stuck in the brillowy, beard hairs, but no indication could be seen in any movement of his uncle's lips.

"You might do better to explain yourself."

Looking around the alley, Oliver didn't make any attempt to speak.

"Well?" asked his uncle.

"Sorry, sir. I was wondering about your changed appearance. Zadok Handron? He is you uncle, the eccentric miner everyone about town has been poking good fun at?"

"That I'd be." Knowlton checked over his shoulder to ensure there was no one about. "Word is you've not only changed your clothes, but are now an Oliver Knight."

"That's right. I couldn't well be a Knowlton for the business at hand." His hands opened towards his uncle.

"So, you took your grandmother's maiden name." Harvey squinted. "And what business is it that you're now in? Singing your version of *Billy Boy* for all the town to hear?"

The young man's cheeks turned red.

"Yes, I heard it. From MacDonald's barn last night."

A board creaked. The two Knowlton's turned.

Tom MacDonald stepped through the passageway he'd disappeared through yesterday. "You two might be good with disguises, but your caterwauling will give you away if you don't keep your voices down. I might hear ye a half a league away—if my head wasn't pounding as it 'tis." He pulled off his tam o' shanter and rubbed his forehead. "Mighty kick in that *Horton* rum, Skipper. Now, you two know where I'll be. You split up and make your way there without making yourselves noticed. I'd be surprised if you can do that, considering the two of ye stick out worse than a bowsprit lantern in a fog in this fish town." He turned back the way he came through the fence board. "We've things to settle out. The sooner the better."

That afternoon, in MacDonald's barn, Oliver explained his doings in figuring to watch the *Horton* so as to provide information to his uncles in Gloucester. The matter of Alice Tory was seen as a complication, but Oliver assured his uncle he would in no way cause his feelings to endanger the plan to recapture the schooner.

MacDonald, for his part, gave scant details about his idea for the anticipated night to sail the vessel. He was particularly secretive about his scheme to disable the Canadian cutter crew who slept in the barracks connected to the warehouse. The three lamented over how they might rig the sails and move the massive *Horton* out of the shallow, narrow harbor without being detected by sight or sound.

When MacDonald went to the house to bring back some dinner for the three of them, Knowlton confided in his nephew about his concerns. Standing by the barn door to keep watch for the smuggler's return, he whispered, "Oliver, I'm not sure what MacDonald has in mind. Or if he can be trusted. I advise we must act in a way we can be assured of success on our own."

The nephew agreed. He stepped forward. From his inner pocket he unrolled a map displaying the Dominion's seal.

Captain Knowlton slapped his nephew on the back and could not hold back a laugh. "But how?"

"Miss Tory has a fondness for books. Let's just say, the Canso maritime office, where they house a good collection of literature for officers and their families, may eventually find they are missing this copy."

On seeing the map of Guysborough Harbor, full out to Chedabucto Bay with sounding depths and a marked channel, the older Knowlton was more confident than he'd been in a week. It was an older version to be sure, and not a navigational chart, however, it would be useful to compare to his own depth measurements. Oliver tucked the map back inside his coat.

Over a dinner of Captain Macdonald's Scottish porridge with eggs on biscuits, the Knowlton's listened to the smuggling skipper's gripes about Captain Tory. MacDonald's vessel the *Irish Lady* had more than once been boarded by the cutter captain. What MacDonald saw as his rightful property, as he was in possession of it following his illegal transportation of the same, duty free, had been confiscated time and again by Tory, all in the name of the crown.

It was apparent to Captain Knowlton that MacDonald had no likeness for Tory, or authority in general. Under these circumstances and revelations, Harvey and Oliver listened to what MacDonald knew about the Canadian warehouse, in what room the *Horton* sails would likely be found, and the lackadaisical attitudes even Tory's own Canadian crewmen had for what they felt was an unfair treatment of fishermen.

By the time the uncle and his nephew left the barn, it was late in the evening. On the outskirts of town, far from the ears of MacDonald, the two made their plans for the following day. Oliver returned to his boarding house. Harvey went to sea.

Sunday – October 1, 1871
Just After Midnight

The water was calm as Knowlton made his way across the harbor to his camp at McCaul Point. As he did not plan on taking more depth measurements of the bay that night, he made what preparations were necessary in the dory for supplies, and set off across Chedabucto Bay. The wind was light, and he raised his sail. With the moon overhead, the shore to starboard, and the boat skimming over the waves, he found himself humming. As his craft lighted across the bay he sang a sailing tune he'd sung hundreds of times—but this night some of the words he changed to fit his mood.

"Dixey Bull was a pirate bold,
He swept our coast in search of gold.
Two hundred years have passed away
Since he cast anchor in Bristol Bay."

When he sailed into the passage between Durells Island and the mainland, he furled his sail and took up the oars. In a low voice, he continued his song.

"Pirates, your flag and anchor pull,
For Horton killed your Dixey Bull.
That's how Horton won the day.
And killed his man in Bristol Bay."

He'd made the twenty miles in four hours and some odd minutes. During his sail, he'd recalled twenty-seven verses of the old New England tune. Unpacking his dory in a rocky inlet of the island, he finished with this verse:

"Where each one had his fortune made
And we all got safe on shore.
We'll ask one another to dine together
And not plough the sea anymore."

He boiled a chunk of salt pork he'd had soaking in fresh water during his sail. Dipping a piece of hardtack into his tea, he watched the sun rise over the Canso Islands. Hidden under a stand of thick evergreen trees he spread his blanket, covered his face with his hat, and slept.

Sundays were often a day of rest for the fishermen when at port. Captain Knowlton, still disguised as a miner, was hopeful he'd find several vessels he might know at anchor. He rowed over to Canso harbor around the noon hour to find a meal. As expected, the taverns were overflowing with Province and American fishermen. Over his dinner of herring with onions and a glass of wine, Knowlton made his observations of the various men in the dark, low-ceilinged room. Fishermen, in their shore clothes, were eating, drinking, playing cards, and telling stories of the sea.

He signaled the barkeep for more wine. His eyes were scanning the room when he locked on a surly looking fellow, who was sitting alone, watching him. The man rose from his table, gripping a tall ceramic mug in his hairy hand, and strode across the soggy floor boards.

"You don't look like a fisherman from here," growled the man standing over Knowlton. "What brings you in?"

The captain indicated his plate and cup. "Having a meal. May I offer you something?"

The men at the table next to Knowlton's laughed in a roar. The man held up his hand to them. "This is my tavern. You don't buy me anything." His eyes narrowed on Knowlton. "You look to be one of those miners that come in here and skip out on the bill. Have I seen you before?"

Knowlton had been in the tavern before. Many years ago. He didn't recognize the owner, nor did he think the owner would recall he was in fact a fisherman. He kept his voice hushed in order to disguise any New England accent or recognition from an American fisherman. "I don't see how. This is my first time here. Name's Zadok Handron. My mining has been down Goldboro way." Knowlton reached into his pocket and produced a handful of coins. "No need to worry. I pay my way."

The owner reached down and took what Knowlton owed. "Very well. Now that we understand one another." He nodded to the barkeep and then strode back to his raised table.

The keep refilled Knowlton's wine. The captain went to pay the barman but was interrupted.

"That is on me." An American fisherman passed a coin to the keep and sat down next to Knowlton.

"Grateful to ye." Knowlton raised the glass.

"Ah, it's to satisfy my curiosity, if you would. Any luck with the mining?"

Knowlton looked over at the familiar face. He struggled to hold back a smile and a jubilant hello. Across from him sat a Rockport fisherman, who'd started out on a Knowlton family vessel a decade earlier.

"Oh, I've had a little," he said, with a Province accent as best he could. Being in friendly company, Knowlton retrieved a tiny gold nugget from his pouch. He kept his hand over it. "Now, don't go making any loud proclamations in here." He revealed the gold.

"Hah. I could put a word in for you to my captain and you'd make more preparing trawl lines in a week for what you've got there."

"That old sea hag, of the *Sea Witch*? It'd be a better bet to get a fair deal from a Canadian cutter captain, than Skipper Warren Osler paying a fair day's wages." Knowlton struggled to keep his amusement hidden.

The fisherman was not amused. A scowl crossed his face. His fists balled up.

Knowlton could no longer contain his smile and had to act quick to avoid another visit from the owner. "Keep your cool, Gillis," he whispered.

Peter Gillis sat back in his chair; astonished at being named by the grubby-looking miner.

"How do you know my name?" He stared long at Knowlton. "And that of the honorable and fair Captain Osler of Glo'ster?" His voice faded off at a hint of recognition in the face before him. "Captain Knowlton? Why? What is this?" He waved at the outfit the captain was wearing; his hands working in a frenzy. It had been near a decade since he'd seen Harvey Knowlton and he wasn't sure what to think.

The tavern owner had again taken an interest in the miner who seemed to be causing a disturbance with his regular clients. He again appeared beside the table. "I'll remind you two about the policy of no brawling in my establishment." His hand held a club secured to a leather strap on his belt.

"No worries, sir, this here is a fr—"

Knowlton coughed to interrupt Gillis.

Catching himself, Gillis continued, "a friend of an old acquaintance of mine. I just discovered it. Quite a surprise to know someone in common is all. All the way here in Canso."

The tavern owner grunted and went back to keep order from his high stool.

A group of fishermen at a table across the room had been watching their friend Gillis and the miner. He gave a side-nod of his head towards the door. Turning his attention back to Knowlton he said, "If I've figured it right over the past two minutes, getting by my surprise, you'll be here after the *Edward A. Hor*…." Gillis stopped himself.

"You were always a smart one, Gillis. Now I don't believe I know any other of the crew sailing with you directly." He watched as Gillis's mates were making their way outside. "You'll understand then that I'd appreciate you keep your guessing to yourself at the moment. It ought to be known though, I could use a man of your ability with rigging and halyards."

Gillis nodded. "We ought to speak outside, Captain. I'm trying to figure how I might help you. A Glo'sterman in need is not to be left aground."

Under a wharf near where Knowlton had stashed the dory, the two men held council. They knew they had to keep the plan to as few men as feasible and that would be the least number to sail the *Horton* home—if it could be done. Gillis recognized the danger. A Canadian cutter captain was as sure to give chase as to fire his cannons at a vessel being stolen. The men chosen would have to be of New England stock; those not afraid to fight for American freedoms and to be jailed if it should come to that, or even die for the cause. Gillis volunteered to be the first for the mission.

Given the importance of a strong crew, and of knowing his shipmates, Gillis suggested Knowlton meet his old friend, Captain Osler, to decide how many men the captain might spare besides Gillis. Together they knew an advantage could be gained if a crew for the *Horton* could be assembled from a single schooner.

Captain Osler required no convincing. Within the hour, Gillis rowed with him from the *Sea Witch* to Durells Island where Knowlton was waiting at his camp. In short order Osler gave his recommendation on men from his crew who could be trusted, and had shown outrage over the Canadian treatment of American vessels. He assured his friend only the six would know of the errand.

For his sacrifice, Knowlton offered Captain Osler a nugget of gold, more than enough to cover the borrowing of his men and any catch they would have made for his ships' hold. Osler, seeing it as his patriotic duty to help Knowlton, only accepted the payment after Knowlton reminded him of his duty to the *Sea Witch's* remaining crew. They'd be short six men, a situation that would surely impact their take to market, and thus their own pockets. Knowlton stressed the gold would help the captain make up the loss to the fishermen, who'd certainly have to work harder to come out even on shares.

The *Sea Witch* sailed from Canso Harbor on the late-night tide. Captain Osler told his fishermen the missing crew had been left to recover in Canso from a food illness, and they were to return home by rail. It was a poor excuse, considering plenty of illness came aboard and the men worked all the same. A double daily ration of rum was given and he offered a significant retainer sum to all his men. His crew worked all the harder for the next five weeks at sea. Not only did they receive their bonus, but they returned to Gloucester with their fullest hold of the year—luck was with them indeed.

The Mysterious Key

> "Love comes to all soon or late,
>   And maketh gay or sad;
> For every bird will find its mate,
>   And every lass a lad."

Sunday – October 1, 1871
Guysborough, Nova Scotia

"This was the best Sunday I've had in many months, Oliver. Thank you for arranging such a wonderful picnic." Alice folded the blanket that had been on the ground. "I enjoyed our conversation this afternoon." She held up the present he had given her. "And thank you for this book."

"You are most welcome." Oliver looked at the cloth binding. Stealing onto the *Horton* during the middle of the night was agreed to with his uncle in order to determine what, if any, instruments had been left aboard. The taking of a gift for Alice was his own idea, a way to thank her for access to the map room and a bit to cover his guilt of taking one of the maps while she was busy exploring the bookshelves.

A group of chickadees lighted from tree to tree. Oliver couldn't help but notice they wore masks of black around their eyes.

Alice watched them as they skirted from branch to branch, calling to one another. "Did you know, Oliver, a group of chickadees is called a banditry?"

He told her he did not.

She turned the book over in her hands. "I've read Miss Alcott's *Little Women*, but this one, *The Mysterious Key*, I have not. I am so looking forward to reading it." She sighed.

"What is it, Alice?"

"Oh, Oliver, I so appreciate this gift. The only chance I have for new books is if father permits me to sail to Canso with him when he goes, or if he allows use of the carriage." She looked out over the bay. "The last time he promised to take me, he was too busy with his latest prize—*that schooner* tied up at the wharf." Her head motioned towards town.

He hid his recognition of the *Horton* from her and kept to the topic of the book. "Then I am all the more happy you like it," he said, while recalling the first time his eyes had seen her.

In what was remaining of the daylight, she opened and read the first few lines out loud. Her voice shook slightly from the chill in the air.

Holding up her wrap, he held it so she could slip into it. "I'll be away tomorrow for the day, Alice. On business." He took her hand in his. They walked down the same hill they'd ascended on the day of their initial stroll, and several times since.

"Where will you be going?"

"I've a colleague to meet at the Afton Station. He has some news on available properties we might consider."

"I suppose that works out well. Mr. MacDonald has asked his daughter Bonnie to travel to Queensport, to bring her aunt some items he has purchased for her home. She has asked if I could travel with her and the hired man. Bonnie's mother has been staying with the aunt, who is not feeling herself since her husband passed, for several weeks now."

Oliver nodded; he knew of the reasons for the trip beyond the apparent. Tom MacDonald needed to clear space in his work barn for their purposes. He was gifting his sister-in-law a few tables and chairs, to make room for the guests he'd be hosting. His generosity with his smuggled items also afforded the knowledge that his daughter and Alice Tory would be out of Guysborough for the next two days.

"Bonnie and I will be spending the night. May I thus anticipate seeing you on Tuesday evening for supper?" she asked.

"You can count on it." He walked her to her residence and left her with a bow at the steps.

Oliver caught the watchful eye of Captain Tory from behind the second story window of his study. He tipped his hat and went on to his boarding house.

Captain Tory turned to his officer. "Stevens, it'll be your assignment to find all you can about that gentleman. He's been taking too close an interest in my daughter for someone whom I don't know."

"Yes, sir." Officer Stevens did not move from the comfort of his chair. He was deep in thought on what to do himself about the stranger who was courting Guysborough's fairest maiden.

Tory stared down on him. "You will begin at this moment."

The officer, remembering his place and the impatience of his superior, stammered and stumbled out of the office. His first instinct was to interview the owner of the home where Oliver was boarding.

Monday – October 2, 1871
MacDonald's Workshop Barn

Inside the barn door, Oliver waited on MacDonald for directions on where to set the supplies from the wagon. He watched as the captain dragged two crates into a side room and bolted both with padlocks. Besides many more crates of various sizes, now stacked to make aisles, the barn was crowded with furniture, lumber, ropes, rigging of all sizes, and sails.

MacDonald handed Oliver a hammer and nails. "Take that torn sail fabric and cover those windows over." He pointed. "There's a ladder there."

Ten feet off the ground there was a strip of windows that ran along the top of one wall below the loft. With the wooden-rail ladder propped against the wall, Oliver did as he was told; although he considered it a bit much given their height and that the ground floor windows were already covered over.

Most of the sunlight that was filtering into the barn was thus extinguished when Oliver pounded in the final nail. Only two porthole windows, one on each end of the loft, provided cones of light into the space.

In his rearranging of his goods, MacDonald rambled on about the items in the barn. "You ought to know, Oliver, I've only had to take up smuggling to make a living on account of Captain Tory. He's made fishing from my vessels miserable with his inspections and tariffs." He took the box of brown-paper wrapped hardtack from Oliver to set it on the barn workbench. "I've done my best to keep my wife and daughter comfortable. They don't have any suspicion that their comforts are not provided by mackerel any longer." He eyed Oliver. "The silks, lace, fabrics, and other wares in these crates," his arm swept the room, "I trade with Newfoundland and the outlying islands. Seeing the government is set against me with their rogue officers, I don't see any need to send them their due in taxes."

"No explanations necessary, Captain. Your revenue cutter captains don't seem to be loved by Province men any more than Americans." Oliver unloaded three jugs of water from the wagon. "Captain, I must also apologize."

"For what now?" MacDonald pointed for Oliver to place the jugs on a shelf.

"You must realize, I am in no right way with your daughter, *or* Alice Tory, under my premise of being Oliver Knight."

"Aye. Your secret is safe with me. It is a necessary lie at the moment." The skipper lifted a jug of rum off a shelf. He poured two mugs half full. "Your identity will be safe until you happen to disappear on the same tide as the captured schooner."

"See, that there's the problem. I've been worried in how I'm to reconcile with Alice on my name and who I really am." He swallowed the rum in one drink. "And why I've had to do what's been done. Might I ask you to pass along an explanation? A temporary one, at least until I can get word to explain to Alice." Oliver arranged several blankets over crates which were to serve as bunks.

His mug refilled, MacDonald pondered for a minute. "It wouldn't be the first time a *pirate* took a prisoner along. The stories of Dixey Bull and John Phillips are as fresh in the minds here as herring circling in a weir." MacDonald winked. "I might find a corked bottle with a message in your hand written to Miss Tory. I think it could wash up in my cove a few days after the *Horton* has sailed." He tore a blank page from the back of an old book. "Here. Write a note. Explain you'd come along the wharf that night at just the wrong time."

"Do you think that'll make it worse on Miss Tory? I wouldn't want her thinking I was killed or thrown overboard by the scheming crew." The young man took the paper and sat on a stool.

"Nay. The days of real pirates along this coast are past and even the British have given up impressment of Americans. It'd be believable that you'd been taken as a cabin boy though." MacDonald laughed as his story expanded in his mind. "I'll even have my Bonnie deliver the bottle to Alice."

Oliver contemplated the yarn. He wrote several lines, knowing the *Horton* would be far from Guysborough by the time Alice was to read his note. Twice on the page he wrote he'd contact her as soon as he could. He slipped the page into the empty rum bottle that MacDonald tucked away in a crate. "You don't suppose Mrs. MacDonald or Bonnie will come across our preparations here in the barn, do you, sir?"

"Nay. Not a chance. My wife will remain at her sister's house for a visit. Bonnie will tend to the chickens out back, and her pony in the side shed, but never does she venture into my workshop." MacDonald made an assessment of the barn. "Besides, it doesn't look more out of the ordinary, well, other than the bedrolls."

"Look here." Hidden in the floor boards, he showed Oliver a trap door to a root cellar. "The men will need to be ready at all times to hide down there. Not only from Bonnie, but should any neighbor come calling for me. Or…" He adjusted his toorie-less tam o' shanter that was sitting crooked on his crown.

"Or?" prodded Oliver.

A deep bear-grunt came from MacDonald. "Sometimes that Captain Tory likes to overstep and send his men to inspect for rum where it's none of his concern."

"That would be very unfortunate."

                    Tommy Carbone

"Aye. I'll place some red herrings around town so he and his men are kept otherwise occupied searching for my treasure in other past hiding spots of mine." He kicked some straw over the boards. "But be sure they are ready to hide all the same."

Through the Woods

Over the sea and through the woods,
to MacDonald's barn we go.

Tuesday – October 3, 1871

In the hours before dawn, four of the recruited gallant crew, led by Captain Harvey Knowlton, made their way on foot from Canso to Guysborough. They were Daniel Richards, John Penney, Charles Webber, and Isaac Dyer. Over the water, Peter Gillis and Malcom McCloud set sail in Knowlton's dory; taking with them the men's ditty bags and necessary gear.

The march covered a distance of over twenty miles. The men were slow in their travel since they had to keep to the cover of the woods. It was particularly worrisome after sunrise. Each time a wagon would pass along the road, they remained motionless behind trees in order to avoid detection.

At Queensport, as the men were hiking within the tree line parallel to the road, they came upon a settlement of houses. Outside a cottage, they spotted two young women standing on a porch. Each was dressed in ankle-length, light blue dresses adorned with ribbon accents—one of red, the other of blue. Their heads were covered in wide-brimmed hats, with matching ribbons. A man was near the barn preparing their wagon.

"Now, isn't she a beauty?" whispered Daniel Richards.

"Yes. Aren't they both!" John Penney removed his hat and wiped his sweaty forehead.

Knowlton peered around a tree. The five fishermen stood silent; except for their breathing, which from their hard march could be heard even over the chirping birds. Two older women appeared through the doorway. The men, pinned down from moving, listened to the conversation.

"Bonnie, please tell your father I appreciate the furnishings he sent."

"Yes, Auntie, I will. Thank you for having us and making these beautiful matching dresses." Bonnie MacDonald kissed her aunt's cheek. She turned to the other woman. "Will you be home soon, mother?"

"Maybe in a fortnight or so." The mother hugged her daughter.

Knowlton watched as Alice Tory took the hand of Bonnie's aunt. "I had a wonderful time singing with you last evening. Thank you so much for the stay."

The mother and aunt waved as the horses pulled the carriage down the dusty road.

Knowlton signaled for the men to march on. Once their column was away from the homes, behind him he could hear the whispers of the men. For more than ten minutes they did not cease in talking about the two maidens.

"If they'll be in Guysborough, I may have to become a Province man," said Richards.

"I'll be a step ahead of you," added Penney.

Captain Knowlton stopped and waited until they were close around him. "Men, I'll remind you all, we must remain quiet while we are in this region. Besides that, the one girl in the party is the daughter of the cutter captain that seized my vessel. The other is the daughter of the smuggler MacDonald I've told you about."

"The one whose barn it is we are to bunk in?" asked Richards.

"One and the same." Knowlton took a drink from his water-pouch.

"Seems an unlikely match of friends. A cutter captain's daughter and the other the daughter of the one who's to help us. Why are they together?" questioned Richards.

"I will explain when we get to the barn." Knowlton wiped his forehead with the wool hat he'd chosen in place of his well-known trapper hat.

Penney's smile broadened. "Aye. So, we'll be closer to the fishing grounds than we all anticipated after all."

Knowlton stepped towards him. "Mr. Penney, that will be enough of that," he stated. Then looking from him, to each man in turn, he added, "All of you, I need to count on you that this will not become a distraction. We are only to stay under the hospitality of MacDonald for a few days while final preparations are made. It is imperative that none of you are observed while there. This includes by anyone of the fairer sex!"

"Ah, Captain, not to worry. The observations will only be one way." Richards slapped Penney on his shoulder.

In order to allow for the women to put several miles between them and the men, Knowlton called for an early dinner stop. With the provisions of fruit, bread, and cheese—all gifts from the stores of the *Sea Witch,* they rested and ate. Richards and Penney continued to speak of Miss MacDonald and Miss Tory, though neither of them knew which girl was which. When pressed to contribute his knowledge, Knowlton refused and reminded them of their mission. This business of women impacting his plans had grown beyond the complications of his nephew and Miss Tory. Now he also had to worry not only about Oliver's affections, but maybe feelings from his newly acquired crew, all of whom likely hadn't embraced a woman for three months or longer. He knew the sooner he could have them aboard the *Horton* the better.

In his mind, as he walked along, he took stock that the older married men, Webber and Dyer, shouldn't give him any lover's troubles. Gillis and McCloud, also married, had been to the war as officers and were disciplined in all duties they took, at least that is what Captain Osler said of them. As for, Penney and Richards, both in their twenties, he'd have to be all the more watchful.

Two hours past sunset, the men arrived at MacDonald's barn. All were hungry and tired. Before being able to rest, Knowlton accompanied MacDonald to the nearby cove to locate and lead the two mates, who'd sailed across the bay, up to the barn. Going down the hill to the shore, MacDonald was advised by Knowlton that the two ladies had been seen earlier in the day. Understanding the point, with more than one implication, MacDonald assured the captain he'd keep his daughter away from any lusty eyes.

Earlier in the day, Oliver had thought about entertainment for the men. Being accustomed to the boredom of a ship waiting on fish, he outfitted the barn with a dozen books—all from the *Horton*, four packs of playing cards, and a stack of old newspapers to keep the men occupied. This seemed to work for the more aged of the group who welcomed the time to relax. However, Oliver noticed Penney and Richards were more interested in discussions on the sights they had seen on the road from Canso.

Near midnight, Gillis accompanied Knowlton to the wharf to continue reconnaissance of the *Horton*. As expected, the Canadian watchman left the ship as the bells rang twelve times.

"Every night? The same hour?" asked Gillis.

"So far, yes. Seems he's aboard for reading my books, more than as a watch." Knowlton looked around. "Those windows there," he pointed, "whoever lives in that home remains awake until near half past the hour."

Gillis followed the captain's finger as it moved to the left. "And there, that's Captain Tory's residence."

"Mighty close to the wharf, I'd say." The fisherman squinted towards the dark windows of the brick home. "And the sails?" Gillis ran his gaze over the naked jibs of the *Horton*.

"There." Knowlton's finger indicated the warehouse.

"That's a long haul to make with the sails and rigging even with eight men." Gillis rubbed his neck.

"And to be quiet at it as well." The captain watched the homes until the last light was extinguished. He and Gillis then pushed off in the dory. Knowlton was glad for the extra hands, for two men sounding the channel depth made for much easier work. Gillis rowed and Knowlton dropped the lead. By three in the morning they'd doubled over what Knowlton had begun and had tripled beyond that. The chart Oliver had provided was verified and updated with their additional measurements. The two arrived back to the barn at half past four. The others were snoring loud enough to raise the roof.

Top O' the Mornin'

A sailor's dreams desire the mermaid
her sweet voice floats through the fog.
The song he hears, by ears betrayed
on the rocks is found his ship's epilogue.

Wednesday – October 4, 1871 – Morning
MacDonald's Barnyard

Sunlight filtered through the spaces between the planks of the barn walls. The men drew their blankets over their heads. The dawn songs of the birds went unnoticed by the slumbering men. No cardinal, robin, or song sparrow could wake them from their sleep. Seamen weren't accustomed to long hikes, and the miles they walked the day before called on different muscles than those required to haul trawls. But then came a song of a different tune. Eyes opened. They rolled over on top of their wooden crate-bunks to hear better.

"Where have you been all the day,
Billy Boy, Billy Boy?
Where have you been all the day,
While I wait here?"

"Is that a mermaid's voice I hear?" asked Richards throwing off his wool blanket.

"I heard her first." Penney pushed his way to the barn door.

The two peered through the opening to see Bonnie MacDonald coming from the chicken house. She wore a flowered housedress; her curly blond hair was tied back with a green ribbon. She stood looking over the fields, an egg basket in her hand.

"My, do you think she'd make me an omelet if I was to knock at the door?" Richards flattened his hair with his hand.

"Where did you learn about wooing women?" Penney watched Bonnie take the stairs to the back of the house. She was still singing her song. On the porch, she sang as the robins pecked at the ground.

"Can she cook a bit o'steak, Billy Boy, Billy Boy?
She can cook a bit o'steak, aye, an' make a griddle cake.
Can she bake a cherry pie, Billy Boy, Billy Boy?
She can bake a cherry pie, quick's a cat can wink its eye,
Bonnie dear, Bonnie dear."

The young woman laughed at the sky.

MacDonald appeared at the door. **"Bonnie, you get in here."**

Her singing and laughter stopped. He grabbed the egg basket from her. Penney noticed the surprise in her wide eyes.

"What is it, father?" she asked, as he hurried her over the threshold by his arm.

The door slammed shut.

"That's the nicest mug up call to breakfast I've had in a good long while." Richards ripped off the end of a loaf of bread.

"And that there loaf is better than hardtack," exclaimed Charles Webber. "Now you two keep it quiet. There's coffee on the oil burner."

McCloud poured a bit of rum into each man's mug. He'd been appointed the keeper of libations by the captain with strict rations to be followed each day; Knowlton wanted no trouble from men who had too much to drink.

By the time the clock rounded nine, the men had passed over the newspapers, they had tired of playing cards, and each expressed their wish to be wet in sea spray from hauling mackerel over the side of their vessel. In their boredom, they looked for things to do. The barn had plenty of MacDonald's fishing gear, his own and more acquired from derelict vessels, so the men took to finding blocks to repair, hooks to sharpen, ropes to untangle, and other busy work to occupy their time.

But, six expert fishermen, with hours of time to kill, worked through the stores of supplies in a few hours. They poked around and discovered there was more in the workshop barn than MacDonald's tackle. They inspected the trap door that led to the root cellar, the place they were to hide should anyone be seen approaching the barn. It was a damp, board-lined hole with barely room for six men to stand shoulder-to-shoulder.

"I hope we have no need to use this hole," stated Richards.

"If this is what a coffin is, I pray to die at sea," said Webber. The men scrambled for position to climb the ladder, none of them wanted to be the last man up.

Behind bales of hay, Penney discovered trunks of fancy clothes, dishes, and silverware. Several more trunks were stacked and bound with locks, which he easily picked in his nosiness. When he was called by Richards, he shut the trunk he was rummaging in and walked around to see his mate kicking loose straw aside.

"There be a trap door here. I found it under these boxes." Richards pounded his boot on the thick wood. "She's hollow under there."

"And by the look of that lock and thick planking, MacDonald wants to keep it a secret."

Town of Guysborough

Oliver Knowlton was keeping to his routine of a walk from his boarding house on his way to the tavern for lunch, when a man in uniform caught him by the arm.

"Mr. Knight, Captain Tory requests your presence to dine with him aboard the cutter *Sweepstakes* this morning."

Oliver was about to protest the manhandling, when he noticed two other uniformed sailors behind him.

"I am Officer Stevens. I've been sent by the captain. Since you have been occupying much of his daughter's time, he knows you will not refuse this request."

At that moment, Harvey Knowlton was rowing his dory across the harbor, he himself keeping up appearances as a miner. From fifty yards away, he watched as the Canadian seamen held their boat next to the moored cutter and Oliver ascended the rope ladder hanging over the deck.

To say Captain Knowlton was suddenly the most anxious he'd been since arriving in Guysborough would be accurate. Many questions ran through his mind. *Were they discovered? Was his nephew under arrest? Why was he being escorted to the cutter?*

With measured patience he looped the painter through a rusty, iron ring on the wharf. As he'd done for most of his days in Guysborough, he went to purchase his bread, smoked fish, and cheese. While the owner wrapped the purchases, the locals who sat on the bench by the woodstove smoking and gossiping, chided Zadok for chasing a fool's errand. They mocked him, *a gold miner*, for his tatterdemalion attire. He let them have their say without any rebuttal.

Through the alleys between the warehouses he made several passes. No one was around. Cautiously, he climbed the ladder on the rear of the fish house. The smell of wood burning and fish smoking circled around him. He sat with his back against the chimney and removed his spyglass from his coat pocket. The hands on the deck of the cutter were at work tending the gear and rigging. He wondered for a time if the ship was going to be made ready to get under sail—with Oliver aboard. Two officers stood at the head of the companionway aft to the captain's quarters. There was nothing he could do but wait. He cut off a chunk of the fish and raised the knife to his mouth.

Auld Offenses Be Not Forgotten

"He that deceives me once, 'tis a fault in him;
but if twice, then 'tis my fault."

MacDonald's Barn

"How long do we need to remain in this hovel like horses?" Richards dumped his cold tea on the ground.

"It's only been a day. Enjoy your time to rest." McCloud, who'd become the designated cook, seeing as the others couldn't fry an egg without setting the place full of smoke, stirred the chowder that was warming. "If we were back on the *Sea Witch* you'd be cutting bait and smell like a herring."

"Better a herring than smelling that manure baking in the sun out back." Richards shuffled the deck of cards. "Penney, give me another chance to win back my money." He dealt.

His shipmate took a seat on a barrel. "Gillis, what do ye think the captain has in mind for a plan?" Penney picked up his cards.

"Whatever it is, will you be behind him?" asked Gillis.

There was silence. Penney contemplated; maybe his cards, maybe the question.

"You don't have to ask me," stated Richards. "I'll fight to the death. If I don't die here, the sea'll probably take me one of these days. At least this way, I get a headstone back home."

"Never you ought to speak of dying at sea. It's bad luck." McCloud dished out the chowder into wooden bowls.

"That's an old fish tale." Richards spread out his cards. "That'll beat, ya." He eyed Penney.

"You youngsters don't respect the sea," said Isaac Dyer. "Even during the war, Gloucester lost near more than twice the men at sea than on the battlefields of the south."

Richards and Penney had both heard the stories of wrecks—what fishermen hadn't. But they felt it could never happen to them. Stuck in the barn, with no place to go out of earshot, they had no choice but to listen.

"In sixty-two, that was the worst. The Georges terrible gale of February the twenty-fourth. You were there, weren't you, Webber?" Dyer slurped down a spoonful of chowder.

Webber groaned. "It was a horrible scene. It was said, of a man on the *Dreadnaught*, that he'd cursed the gale that blew in. He'd climbed the mast and his mates could not convince him to come down. His shouts could be heard by the near schooners. Men yelled back at him to close his mouth."

Webber tapped his wooden spoon on the bowl. Thinking, or maybe he wasn't, he moved the potato chunks around the top of the thick chowder—there was an order to it—a memory of the ships on the sea that day. "There were over seventy fishermen at anchor. We were all too close; spread out within only a few miles—all in a circle. Not one vessel would have had time to heave anchor in the minutes that gale blew in."

He picked up a hard-boiled egg from the table bowl. "Boats were dragged against each other and crushed like eggs." He squeezed the egg in pieces over his chowder. "Nearly every ship was all stove up. Cables, ropes, anchors, booms, masts, dories, barrels, sails—were strewn over the bank amongst the bodies of the drowned."

Dyer, the oldest in the crew, heaved a sigh. "I knew men on the *Dreadnaught, Annie Laurie,* and *Ocean Flower* who never came home that trip. Thirteen vessels and *all* their crew were lost. Two other schooners were left abandoned and their crews taken home." He shook a spoon at Richards; fish chunks plopped back to the bowl. "In that one gale, one hundred and twenty men never returned to port. The account in the paper called on collections for seventy widows and their one-hundred-and-forty, now fatherless, children."

"And even before February of that year, another twenty-two men and four schooners had already been lost to the sea." Webber ladled another spoon of chowder for himself.

Richards and Penney had held their card game; no longer in the mood for entertainment.

"I for one will take my odds with Captain Knowlton against those red coats instead of a winter gale on the bank," Gillis said, as he continued his wrapping of hardtack in brown paper. Each man would carry six days of bread and water rations aboard the *Horton* when the time to sail was called. That alone wouldn't be enough should they have to put out far to sea in a chase, but it was a contingency, and gave Gillis something to do.

"Maybe so, but I'd like to see my wife and daughter again, if that's all the same to you, Gillis. I've been to the war. I've been caught in a killer gale. Seems it don't make sense to be shot dead stealing a schooner." Webber ran a hunk of bread around his empty bowl.

Gillis stopped his work. He wondered who else in the crew might feel the same and could cause a problem in what they'd signed up to do for the captain.

"Webber, we're here to take back that schooner. Are you with us or not?" shot Richards.

"Won't make but a dent for all the vessels these Canadians have stolen from American fishermen these years. But I'll be glad to teach them a lesson." He shoved the bread in his mouth.

Gillis and McCloud shared a glance.

"You know, men, it isn't only Captain Knowlton we're avenging. This could just as well be any ship you'll sail on." McCloud stood under the overhang of the haymow loft. Sunlight filtered through the upper rafter boards; particles of dust sparkling on the drifting air floated around his head.

"What are you blabbering about?" asked Webber.

Reaching in his coat pocket, McCloud retrieved a folded paper. "This here is a list of all the vessels I know about that have been captured by this stealing, thieving, pirate government of Canada. It all started with the treaty of eighteen-hundred-and-eighteen and the three-mile law."

"Goes back farther than that," injected Gillis. "Initially, nations asserted rights as far as a stone could be thrown from the highest cliff out into the sea." He stood up. "When that wasn't far enough to restrict fishermen, they went to using an arrow. Then a musket ball, followed by a cannon shot, and now, with a gunner's projectile, if he can reach three-miles, or not, that's their mark!" A hunk of hardtack left Gillis's hand and bounced off the back wall. "What'll come next? Where does it end? How far from shore must we be?"

McCloud waved his paper. "Men, I'll read you the names of the American schooners that have been accosted in the last year alone. All I have here comes from the *Cape Ann Advertiser*. If you know of other vessels that I've missed, speak up, I'd like to add the names to my list." He took a seat and wet a pencil on his tongue. Gillis anticipated what his mate, a former army sergeant, was about to do in order to rally the seamen.

Guysborough Harbor

High above, the sun beat down. Even gulls wouldn't sit on the hot roof. Knowlton hadn't moved from his position behind the fish house chimney. He kept watch from high above the harbor; his eyes fixed on the deck of the *Sweepstakes*. Nearly two hours passed before he was relieved to see Oliver climbing over the rail into the dory. The Canadian revenue men rowed his nephew to the wharf.

Knowlton shifted to make his way down the rooftop ladder. He was surprised by a voice on the opposite side of a far chimney. "Give him time to make away."

"MacDonald? How'd you find me up here?"

"I told ye, I am the master and the eyes of this harbor, no matter what Tory might think of himself." He scuttled around, staying low. "Besides, I saw you come up here hours ago. When you didn't come down, I figured you'd seen something interesting to keep ye-self occupied. Either that, or you'd fallen asleep." MacDonald placed his spyglass in his coat. "What do you suppose they wanted with your nephew?"

"Your guess is as good as mine."

"You don't suppose he'd be playing both sides, now do ye?"

Knowlton stood up straight. "Don't you be saying that about a Knowlton." Then the captain realized he was speaking with a smuggler and traitor to his own government; what else might MacDonald be thinking.

"I'm only making an observation, 'tis all. Take cover." He reminded Knowlton he was standing. "Appears he's heading out of town. Likely to the barn." The smuggler pointed to the country road leading towards his home.

"And it appears he doesn't see he's being followed!" Knowlton slid down the ladder; MacDonald followed.

"You stay out of sight. I'll distract that officer. My team is behind the store."

The cutter officer turned at hearing the wagon coming up behind him and slowing down.

"Ahoy there, Officer Stevens." MacDonald pulled alongside. "Taking a stroll in the country?"

"Rightly so." Stevens kept at his walk.

"Might you need a ride?" The team steadied alongside the walker.

"Be off with you, MacDonald."

Up ahead, MacDonald noticed Oliver had heard the voices. He'd come back over a rise in the road and was headed toward the wagon.

"Nice day for a walk, men." Oliver kept right on past the officer and MacDonald on his way back towards town.

Being of indolent disposition, and his object of surveillance only headed back to town, Stevens turned cordial to MacDonald. "I suppose, if you don't mind, MacDonald, could you shuttle me back to the barracks?"

"Well, now, I wasn't going that way, but seeing as you're a man in need, jump on."

Halting the team as he came to Oliver, he asked the young man, "Need a ride?" MacDonald winked.

"No, sir. The sea air will do me good." He watched the wagon drive over the hill to deposit the spy back in town. Once the road was clear, Oliver turned back around to make his way to the barn.

MacDonald dropped the officer at the barracks. After his turn around, he picked up Harvey on the outskirts of town. The two captains overtook Oliver before the hill down to the MacDonald barn. With the sun throwing shadows across the road, and the crows squawking from a nearby tree, Oliver climbed aboard the wagon. He explained why Tory invited him on the *Sweepstakes*.

"It began with an interrogation of sorts. Captain Tory indicated he wanted to better know the man who was courting his daughter."

"Were you able to keep the trail cold?" asked MacDonald, too impatient to wait for Oliver's details.

The young man nodded. "Oh sure. He was impressed with my college credentials and knowledge of business. However,…"

"What? Why would you tell him all of that?" demanded Knowlton.

"Not to worry, uncle. There'd be no way Tory would surmise I was a fisherman with what I told them about my business."

"Tory's investigating you. That's certain." MacDonald removed his cap to find a match tucked within the brim.

"We'd better act fast. Tonight. Before he finds out your reason for being in Guysborough is a sham," stated Knowlton.

"Nay. You can't sail the *Horton* this evening. By the time the tide comes up high enough it'll be five in the morning. At that hour the harbor will be full of the fishermen getting ready to put out to sea." MacDonald, his pipe in one hand, shook the reins with the other to move the team along home.

"Then, we'll have to be away from here before Tory gets to contacting anyone for information on your made-up real estate venture," stated Harvey.

"I figure we have a few more days. Tomorrow evening, Tory is hosting a celebration for his men. I've been invited."

"A celebration? For what?" demanded MacDonald, who was more miffed he hadn't heard about it first.

"The captain is to be honored on Saturday in Halifax. Since he cannot take his entire crew to be with him there, he is hosting a dinner for them at his home."

"And you? Why has he invited you?" asked the uncle.

"As luck is with us, Miss Alice Tory requested my presence."

"You'd better watch yourself, mate." MacDonald leaned forward on the buckboard seat around Knowlton to face Oliver. "That skellum Tory likely only agreed with his daughter's request in order to serve his purposes. And besides, I happen to know that officer who was following you has had eyes for Alice Tory. He might not take a liking to you being there."

Oliver squinted.

"MacDonald makes a good point, Oliver. You must be cautious."

"I certainly will do so," Oliver said, looking at his uncle. He then added, "Likely, my attending will give us an opportunity to know just how many men Tory will leave here in port when he sails."

Captain Knowlton agreed with Oliver's observation. For the remainder of the ride, MacDonald briefed Oliver on what he knew about the officers of Tory's crew. He advised the young Knowlton which men he should avoid during the social evening, on account of their investigative prowess.

When they arrived at the rear door of the barn, Knowlton jumped from the wagon. It sounded as if someone were giving a speech. By the groans and hisses, whatever was being said was not popular with the audience.

Reading of Grievances

The King, he taxed our tea
for paper he charged a fee.
We fought for liberty and for fairness
against England and your Highness.
Oh, Canada should remember—our American victory story
And school your captains—especially the one by name of Tory!

**Wednesday – October 4, 1871 – Afternoon
MacDonald's Barn**

By this time in his oration, McCloud was standing on a soap box. Ropes, chains, and axes hanging on the barn wall were his stage backdrop. His back was to the door when the captain entered.

"And that weren't half my list so far! Last year alone, in the Bay of St. Lawrence, the Canadian pirates, that's what those revenue cutter captains are, they got up a large fleet of vessels to pursue violators using their own measure of three nauticals. There's more here of those injustices." He waved the paper in the air as he made a circle around the table.

McCloud paused when he saw Captain Knowlton, MacDonald, and Oliver watching him from the corner. "Good day, Captain. I was just giving the boys the history on the offenses committed against our American fishing fleet."

Knowlton scooped a tin cup of water from a barrel. "Seeing as I could hear you as we drove up, you might want to consider keeping your voice down a bit. You'll recall we're in hiding."

"No worries until 'bout seven." MacDonald latched the door. "Bonnie will be down at the church until then for choir practice. After that hour, you all must be quiet and lights out." MacDonald eyed the bales of hay in the dark, far corner, behind which he was recalling he'd stored a jug of rum. He caught Knowlton following the direction of his stare. Knowlton handed MacDonald a mug of water. He whispered, "Let's not add to their bellicoseness."

McCloud continued. "As I was saying, a year ago this time," he turned to Knowlton, "mind you, Captain, I've already covered the earlier decade." With a finger he indicated his progress on his paper. Knowlton acknowledged with a nod.

He went on. "June of this year, they took the *Wompatuck,* a schooner out of Plymouth. The crew was found guilty of fishing within the three-mile limit, jailed for three days, fined, and the craft was condemned to be burned to the water line. She was not. As I speak, she's shuttling British goods in the West Indies."

Sober grumbles erupted.

"Says my list, also in June of last, the *J. H. Nickerson* of Salem was seized. The full catch and all the stores aboard were auctioned. The men, they were left stranded with no money in Ingonish Harbor on Cape Breton. They were given no shelter. The people of the island made a mockery of our brothers. Near starving, one stole a sail-dory and made to Canso. There he was forced to beg for food. Finally, he convinced a Massachusetts captain to rescue the men, on terms they'd pay their passage home. Many of them are still paying that debt."

The growls from Richards, Penney, Webber, and Dyer could have allowed them to pass for pirates themselves.

"You sure they can't have a taste of rum?" asked MacDonald quietly to Knowlton. "Stories such as these go better with the spirit." MacDonald ran his tongue over his upper lip.

Knowlton shook his head. "Only with their meals has been the agreement until we're under sail. I can't risk the problem that too much drink, combined with little to do, can cause."

A thump broke McCloud's speech. Against the rough-hewn pine log being used as a table across empty bait barrels, which smelled as such, Richards had slammed the heavy knot of rope he was working into a balled weapon. "It isn't right for this government to seize the private property of citizens of America!" Richards swung the rope again. **THUMP!**

"Aye aye," called the others.

"But there's more. And worse—from this August past even!" McCloud patted the shoulder of Gillis who took to the call.

"Yes," Gillis rose on the cue. "My brother, some of you know him. He was on the *Clara R. Chapman*, last August. As they'd done, and we've done too, they landed at Charlottetown on Prince Edward Island to transfer the mackerel home via transshipment. Well, the cutters held them off. Would not let them land. Would not let them leave. The fish spoiled and the men went without pay for their troubles!"

"Argh!" went the ensemble.

MacDonald elbowed Knowlton. "Seems they are rousing your troops to fight a good fight. My kind of men."

McCloud read on with flare as he saw his audience engaged and enraged. "In the paper, you all know him, a better supporter of the fishermen there is not, George Proctor wrote this in the *Advertiser* that I've copied here on my paper, *'The annoyances which the officers of the Dominion cutters heap upon our unarmed fishermen, and the flimsy pretexts under cloak of which they seize the vessels, is a disgrace to any nation making any pretensions to civilization. And the apathy with which our United States government witnesses these dastardly insults to loyal subjects, is equally disgraceful on the part of those in authority.'* And very right he is! Is he not?"

"Here! Here!" Fists pounded on the pine. **Thump**—sounded the knot of rope on the log table.

Gillis exchanged a nod with McCloud to have him continue the rousing.

"Now, my mates, I'll inform you, in September of the year of seventy, the schooner *Lettie*, was seized at Gaspe. Within a few days the schooner *Lizzie M. Tarr* was taken by the cruiser *La Canadienne* near the Seven Islands. She was condemned and sold at auction to the original owner! If that doesn't chowder you up. He bid her in at $2,807, near half her original cost to him."

"Tyranny!"

"But the indignities go on. The Canadians made the captain of the *Lizzie M. Tarr* make a speech against the United States. He was placed on a chair to read a statement in which, can you believe, he had to thank the Quebec people for the *kindness* they had manifested *towards him* and attributed all his *losses and trouble* to the action of the United States government." McCloud paused for effect. **"That ought to fry your pork to a crisp!"** he bellowed.

"I know the captain of the *Tarr*," stated Webber. "He only would have said such words if he was under duress."

"How'd they get away with it?" demanded Richards.

"Ah, you don't know this government. They are still Brits at heart. Think everything is theirs. And if it's not, they tax it." MacDonald looked at his water with distaste. "Be grateful you don't have to live here."

"There can't be any more in that one year, could there be, McCloud?" asked Gillis, knowing there was indeed.

"I wish I was at the end of the list. The *Alice H. Wonson* was seized for fishing within the limit and towed to Pictou." McCloud paused and looked at Knowlton. "She was your vessel, was she not, Captain Knowlton?"

"Aye, McCloud. The *Alice Wonson* was a new ship last year to the *McKenzie, Knowlton, & Horton* firm. Sixty-four tons, similar in build to the *Horton*. Our sister ship—you might say."

"How do they get away with such crimes!" The mug in Richards's hand slammed the plank bench.

"Now, Webber, do you see what we must do? Why we are here?" questioned Gillis. "We are not only helping Captain Knowlton, but all the skippers and owners in Glo'ster, Rockport, Essex, Boston, and along the entire east coast."

"Here! Here!" bellowed all, including Webber.

"But fellows, my list is not nearly done." McCloud held the paper under the lantern light. "In September of eighteen seventy, the schooner *Charles H. Price* of Salem, sailed to Halifax in order to obtain ice for the trip to the banks. You've all done it when out on a vessel."

"Aye. Of course we have."

"Surely, you have Penney. And some day, if it isn't put a stop to, you may pay the same fee as the men on the *Price*. The captain was delayed by the revenue cutters and customs office. He wasn't permitted into the inner harbor. And his exit out was blocked by two cutters, their guns were kept fixed on him. After three weeks he was given word he was not allowed to buy ice in Halifax, or any port in the Provinces. He had to sail home. The season was lost."

"You mean to say, McCloud, the crew and the owners got nothing that entire season?" asked Richards with a frown on his face.

"That you have it. They were brokers—all of them."

"What happened to the fishermen's creed?" asked Webber.

"It only applies if your vessel is Canadian or British up in these waters. And even in my case they've boarded me more times than I can recall. That pirate Tory is the worst." MacDonald made a motion of bending his elbow to Knowlton.

Knowlton responded to the gesture. "You can see the plan of Gillis and McCloud here. Rum wouldn't mix." He moved closer to the center of the barn. "Doctor, is there any of your strong tea brewed?" He'd used the respected title of *doctor* for the cook out of tradition for one who not only could doctor a good stew, but might also be called while on ship to bind a tourniquet on a leg or arm.

"Sure is, Captain. There on the hook."

Grasping the kettle over the stove, Knowlton poured himself a mug and handed one to MacDonald. "Will do for you to drink this instead."

"Isn't the same effect." MacDonald swallowed with a grimace.

"Gentlemen, I must go on." With a raised hand, McCloud called for attention. "There are many more injustices to report. In the same month of September the schooner *I. J. Marshall*, was captured as was the schooner *Foam*. Then the schooner *Clara F. Friend* was seized for alleged infraction of the fishing laws."

Captain Knowlton stood and motioned for McCloud to pause. "Like we're planning, the *Marshall* while lying at anchor was recaptured by her owner, Captain Charles Friend. He endeavored to escape with his craft and crew. The Canadians chased him down and he was retaken while passing through the Strait of Canso. The vessel was condemned and sold at Charlottetown."

The men booed and hissed.

Knowlton held up his hand. "Captain Friend was not as lucky as us. His ship was held in a deep, wide harbor. She was easily seen by several cutters as soon as they unfurled sails. It is my belief that Captain Tory chose Guysborough to hold the *Horton* not because this is his home residence, but because he sees the channel here too challenging for American sailors to try such a scheme again."

"We'll prove him as mad as King George the Third!" cried Richards.

"We have not yet begun to fight," added Penney.

"Here! Here!" rang out the chorus.

"Heave to! My paper has more still." McCloud turned it over. "In October the schooners *Gettysburg, A. I. Franklin, Granada,* and *Romp* also were stolen from American owners. And, in November the theft continued. The schooner *White Fawn* was taken by the cutter *Water Lily*. The *Fawn* was simply procuring bait at Head Harbor, near Campobello. Who here hasn't done similar on a fisherman?"

He waited for no answer but went directly on. "Locals testified that a boy of thirteen, the catchee he was, dropped a line over the rail to catch his lunch or possibly was simply amusing himself while the captain was arranging for the bait. The schooner was held until February of this year. The owners lost the winter season, most of the stores on board were left to spoil, and the ship was ransacked, supposedly by locals, but the owners avowed it was Canadian cutter men dressed as fishermen. The crew had to pay their own way home, worse for hiring on than when they'd started. It had been better for them had they stayed in Glo'ster to pave the streets with cobblestone."

Parched from his oration, McCloud dipped his mug into the bucket. Such a speech, Captain Harvey Knowlton could not have anticipated to rouse the crew to his cause.

Gillis stood and continued for McCloud. "Five of these vessels, the *Wonson,* which we've spoken of was owned by

Captain Knowlton, and the *Tarr, Franklin, Friend,* and *White Fawn*—all of these are ships I know were owned by Glo'ster men. Surely more than these were fined, seized, burned, or kidnapped. In doing so, they've taken money from our own friends."

A fisherman among fishers, Gillis continued, "Our livelihood has been impacted by these Canadian illegal actions, even if you, or a mate you've known, had not been on one of those vessels." His right hand shot high over his head. "Our American government has done nothing to avenge the wrongs. The Royal Navy, and their Canadian counterparts, cruise the waters in large numbers with a devious purpose—that being the taking of our American vessels, stealing our fish, imposing high fines, causing our men to miss a season of work, and in the same, taking food and clothing from the women and children back in Glo'ster, Rockport, and Essex!"

Sensing the thoughts in the room and wishing to stir the men once again, MacDonald added, "And not to forget Captain Knowlton's own, the *Lily Rose Snow* being captured and sailed to England in order to conceal her!" His intent was validated by the groans and hisses from the men once again.

Oliver stood. "Mates McCloud and Gillis, you have done a remarkable job recalling the injustices from the Canadian government against the Glo'ster and east coast fleet from last year." He circled the room. "I'll remind you all that the harassment has not ceased even in this year of seventy-one. I do not have a printed list as McCloud, but I can remember clearly a good number of vessels already taken. In January the schooner *Enterprise,* of Eastport was seized. Then in July, the schooner *Samuel Gilbert,* of Glo'ster was taken for the same alleged infraction. Also in July the schooner *Lizzie A. Tarr* was chased away from Grand Jardin, Newfoundland where the captain was planning on buying bait. He was restricted from landing in *any* Canadian port. A total loss of the season. Remember, she was the vessel captured the year prior! Her captain had thought he'd made friends with the Canadians after making that embarrassing speech. How wrong was he!"

Around the table, Oliver walked, stopping behind each man. "You see, if they did not take the vessel outright, they made it impossible for the men to fish. In August, the schooner *Franklin Schenck* of Rockport was boarded and taken to a Canadian port. That brings us to September, and our very own *Edward A. Horton* seized early last month. Being on that ship when they boarded, I can tell you of the indignities we were forced to endure. We stood to watch our catch auctioned as the locals sneered, jeered, and laughed at us."

The young Knowlton stood under the lantern; the light cone spread out all around him on the dirt floor. "You all know by this time, the accusation was on account of two *Horton* dorymen who'd gone adrift. You men might know them, the most fun-loving mates to have aboard a ship, Connie Cogswell and Duncan Robinson."

"Aye. Good fishers and mates for sure," stated Dyer.

"Yes, they are. Maybe they weren't thinking clearly after being adrift. Most assuredly they were bored. You'd have been too, floating along without oars for hours." Oliver didn't mention his part in the men's predicament; his uncle made no comment either. "When they went over what they reckoned was Middle Passage, and Duncan had sight of Amet Spit Island, he reckoned they were still outside the three-mile limit."

"Too close for me to drop a line," stated Webber.

"Nay," disagreed MacDonald. "The shoals are exactly six miles from where I was raised. You'll find MacDonald's Cove three miles due east of Cape John. My grandfather's house still stands with a view of the Spit. From the point of the cape, to the island it's two and a half nautical. If those men in the dory were at the drop on the north'en side, they'd have been outside the three-mile line. Close, sure. But over it."

Captain Knowlton was examining a chart of the strait hanging on the wall. He stuck the tip of his divider into Amet Island. "They were too close either way. Yet, I don't blame them. They couldn't have known the distance, but they shouldn't have chanced it. Tory was likely counting on them losing their heads. He may even claim Amet Island as part of the shoreline. The sneak may even claim measure to Malagash Point in his papers."

"Blimey." MacDonald threw his tam o' shanter on the table. "You're right, Captain. He's a regular old pirate that Tory," stated the smuggler who was at that moment unlatching a trunk hasp with a key from his pocket.

"Still don't make it right, seizing a ship. A close call such as that," added Gillis. "For only a couple of fish."

"It's unfair and uncalled for," growled Richards.

"I thought I'd kept this." MacDonald held up an issue of the *Halifax Chronicle*.

"Isn't that you?" asked Oliver.

MacDonald's picture was on the front page.

"Aye, don't mind that. Another of Tory's antics. That was the time he had me framed up. But this here is just what I wanted to call your attention to. Under the side headline, *The Canadians Are Coming*, it reads:

'Just think of it you Yankees! The Canadian fishermen now backed with Canadian gun vessels. Seven new schooners of the best type and one powerful steamship. Read this and tremble ye Gloucester fishermen. No longer will we depend on the British gunboats which you ignored. Our own vessels will stop your games of treaty violation and contempt for the law!'"

He passed the paper for the men to see for themselves.

Across the barn the dim lantern-light shone through the hanging spider webs onto the bearded faces of the men. The recalling of the list of ships seized, and hints of many forgotten, had their tempers up. After hearing MacDonald read from the paper, their Yankee blood was boiling. Richards and Penney called to raise the sails and take the *Horton* home right then at that hour. The men were grumbling in agreement when a musical voice was heard outside.

"Father? Are you in the workshop?"

All eyes opened wide on hearing the call from up near the house.

MacDonald raised his arms and waved them up and down. "Shh! Bonnie's home already! Lower your lanterns and no more loud talk tonight, men," he said in a whisper. He quickly moved to the barn door, opening it just enough to step through, and pulled it closed behind him. They heard him call to his daughter. *"Yes, Bonnie. On my way up to the house now."*

There was no doubt, the recollection of the vessel names, many of which the men knew, had effected their resolve. The whispers of contempt for what the Canadians had done to Gloucester crews continued under the low light of one lantern. Too awake to sleep, they ate smoked sausages and cold mashed potatoes. McCloud poured out a portion of rum to each man to wash down both the food and the bitter feelings of the evening.

"Canadian cutter men be damned!" Richards yelled, albeit in a whisper.

The clock rounded midnight before Knowlton convinced the men to turn in for some sleep. However, he and McCloud remained at the table for another hour adding additional vessels to the list of recent injustices.

Bonnie-girl and Billy-boy

> A tale as old as time,
> such deception for love
> has yet been declared a crime.

Thursday – October 5, 1871 – Morning

John Penney slept for only three hours, on account he was still on his ship's watch schedule of short sleeps, but more so, he had a plan for the early bird to catch the worm. Besides, the yard rooster had been *'cocoricóing,'* as his Portuguese fishermen friends called it, for thirty minutes in anticipation of the sunrise.

The sky was beginning to lighten as Penney made his way from his bunk to the woods behind the barn. The crows in the field rose in alarm; their 'caw-caw-caw' was enough to wake the dead. Two squirrels circled up a tree, yelling at one another, their tiny claws crunched up the bark with a rattle sound. Hidden behind a clump of trees, he changed into clothes he'd found in an unlocked chest in the barn. At the stream he washed and trimmed away the curly ends of his brown beard. Using the reflection of the clear water, he admired the tattered tam o' shanter propped on his head, the match of MacDonald's *except* it being a plaid of dull red and still having its bobble. He cocked it at an angle and set off towards the road.

As he walked through the shadowy woods, he anticipated that up at the MacDonald house, Bonnie's morning had begun as he observed yesterday, and as Tom MacDonald had explained to the men was her routine. MacDonald warned them on the importance of silence first thing in the morning. He had told them, *'Bonnie will collect the eggs for my breakfast, and you'll surely hear my song from the kitchen on her return. I want to hear nothing about the song, or my tune, from any of ye. My daughter and I have shared our morning singing since she was little. You can take it as a signal that she's back in the house, for I surely can be heard by anyone within an Irish mile an' a Scottish bittock.'*

Penney paused in his steps. Even down the lane, he could hear MacDonald's singing:

"Where have you been all morning, Bonnie my girl,
Bonnie my girl, Bonnie my girl?
Where have you been all the morning,
While I wait here?"

To which, he heard the daughter's response. It was much fainter, but twice as sweet sounding:

"I've been to the market, Father dear, Father dear.
To collect the eggs for your breakfast, Father dear, Father dear."

Penney waited on the edge of the woods along the road. His spying the morning before afforded him the knowledge that after breakfast Bonnie's chores included delivering eggs to neighbors along the road. He'd taken note of her route as she walked down the lane while he remained hidden behind the trees. He had listened to her humming as she went about her way from which he hatched his plan.

On this bright morning, the sun to his advantage, he saw her outlined in the soft light. She was dressed in a blue day-dress with the lace of a white hat tied under her chin; her soft, yellow hair flowing to her shoulders shined in the sun. The egg basket was swinging to the same rhythm as her head. He wondered what song she was singing to herself. With his limited ship's-catalogue of musical lyrics, he took his second advantage of the morning to sing a song she knew.

Deliberately, he scuffed the gravel under his shoe. Bonnie lifted her head to see him walking along the road towards her. He timed his stride to arrive at the rock, the one he'd earlier surveyed for his plot, along the edge of the road. Sitting, he bent over to tie the shoe he'd left untied. While she was still thirty paces away, he hummed. When she was within ten, he was still on one knee, trying to lace his shoe. He sang lowly.

> *"Where have you been all the day,*
> *Beautiful girl, beautiful girl?"*

His head lifted when she was within a few steps of him. Rising to his feet, his head nodded a good morning, and he finished his verse.

> "Where have you been all the day,
> While I wait here?"

There was nothing she could do to stop herself; her reply was ingrained from years of singing a response to the tune since she was a toddler.

> "I've been to the market,
> Billy Boy, Billy Boy.
> To collect the eggs for your breakfast,
> Billy Boy, Billy Boy."

She laughed and held up the basket.

He smiled.

"Good morning, miss," he said.

"Good morning to you, sir. Are you lost?" she asked, her head slightly slanted.

"No!" He was off balance at the question. "Why?"

"You're certainly not from this road. I'd know you if you were."

"Ah. No, you're right. I'm not. I've only recently arrived here in town. My name is, uh, Billy. Billy McMullen."

She eyed him. "Nice to meet you, Billy. An appropriate name to go with your tune." His eyes never moved from looking into her own. "My name is Bonnie MacDonald."

He stepped closer. With a wave of his hand in front of him, he gave her a half bow. "Pleased to meet you, Miss Bonnie."

"Seems you've a bit of trouble." She pointed to the broken lace he held in his hand. "Try this." She took a red ribbon that was tied to her egg basket and handed it to him.

While he worked at replacing the broken lace, she took in his attire of black pants and a high collared white shirt unbuttoned at the neck, and worn under a waist-length coat of faded black with thin white stripes. There was something familiar in the clothes, and particularly the cap he wore. However, his reddish-brown beard reminded her more of a sea-going man, of which she'd seen many around her father's ships—men having been away from the barber's scissors for too long—than one sporting such an outfit. Her gaze focused on his blue-green eyes which reminded her of the sea.

"Seems to work." He wiggled his foot, and looking up caught her quickly avert her eyes and he noticed her cheeks turned red.

"I'm just heading back to town now and this lace should hold. Looks like you're going that way. May I walk with you?"

As she had no reason to say no, she accepted his company.

Her lightheartedness burned bright on that blue-sky morning under the bare trees. She stated, "Bonnie-girl and Billy-boy. Now I bet we could make up a few good stanzas to fit those names."

And so they did. Together they sang as they walked. She could not remember the mile to town ever passing by faster than on that morning.

Before they reached the cluster of homes on the outermost street of the town, he excused himself down a side lane. Stepping away backwards from him, she whispered in song:

> *"It was nice to meet you,*
> *Billy boy, Billy boy.*
> *Goodbye, goodbye,*
> *I hope to see you again, Billy boy."*

Victory Declared

"When in safety or in doubt,
Always keep a safe lookout;
Strive to keep a level head,
Mind your lights and mind your lead."

Thursday – October 5, 1871 – 3 p.m.
Guysborough Harbor

Behind the chimney on the fish house roof, Knowlton and MacDonald watched the street below to observe the comings and goings of delivery men arriving at Tory's residence. That afternoon there was more activity than there'd been in all the days Knowlton had been in Guysborough combined. Deliveries of meats, cases of what was surely wine, casks of ale, and flower arrangements made a steady stream through the front doors of the brick Customs House. The homes and flagpoles throughout the town had been decorated with both the Royal Union Flag of the British Empire and the newer Red Ensign of Canada. Knowlton's eyes squinted through the sun's glare over the water at the *Horton*. On the mast of his ship was the one American flag visible in all the town. She was waving in the breeze, still hung upside down below the Union Jack.

That afternoon, even the watchman did not make his way over the rail of the *Horton*. There was no need for a watch. Tory was confident there'd be no Yankee dumb enough to steal a ship from the harbor with all his men, plus those from Canso, at his residence one street up from the wharf.

Near to five o'clock, couples made their way from horse-drawn carriages up the brick steps that had been carpeted in British-red. The distinguished merchants of the town wore black jackets with long tails and tall top hats. Women arrived in gowns adorned with corsages decorated with ribbons. The crewmen of the Canadian cutters sported their red and white dress uniforms. After they saw Oliver enter the residence, the two captains sat back against the chimney and smoked their pipes.

Alice greeted Oliver and made a formal introduction to her mother. A violinist played as the guests mingled in the outer room. Oliver discreetly made mental notes of the number of officers and their ranks. The local businessmen pressed him for information on his wharf venture, word of which had leaked out. Each of them hoped to benefit from the construction in some way. He was relieved when the maid finally rang a tiny bell with the call to dinner. The seating arrangements surprised Oliver as he was escorted by Alice to the captain's table set at the head of the long dining room. To his right was Alice and on his left Miss Bonnie MacDonald. On the other side of Miss Tory, Officer Stevens held the place of honor next to Captain Tory.

Dinner was followed by a celebratory speech in which the captain thanked his men for their trusty service. He told them all of his upcoming travel to the ceremony in Halifax. When he stated he'd be accepting the accolades on behalf of all of them, applause broke out. Oliver doubted the captain would feel the same if he was required to share the prize money the government provided for each captured vessel.

Upon concluding his victory speech, the captain clapped his hands. Music began in the other room. The guests made their way to the side parlor, which extended into the round rotunda overlooking the harbor. All sofas and tables had been moved along the walls. A violinist stood between the front windows on a raised platform. Captain and Mrs. Tory began the waltz. A minute later, a few officers with their wives joined them. Alice was under protocol to accept the offer to dance from Officer Stevens. A second officer invited Bonnie to the floor. The ship owners and business men were next to honor the captain with joining in the dance.

From under the doorway arch, Oliver noticed nearly all of the unmarried young men were without a date; an indication to him of the sparse female population in Guysborough. To Oliver's dismay, on account of her relation to the captain and this unbalanced ratio, this resulted in Alice Tory being the center of attention for the dances. Although, Miss Tory did her best to deflect the men towards Bonnie MacDonald, and her other few female invited guests, there was one officer whom Alice could not persuade to any other dance partner. There wasn't nearly a waltz, or jig, for which Stevens didn't cut in on Oliver and Alice. Only for three dances in a row did Stevens not appear in the hall. For all other dances, politely, so as not to cause a scene and to show himself as the better man, Oliver allowed Stevens to monopolize Alice's time. Even as he fumed over Alice being swept away, he kept his face turned away as much as possible from the officers and Captain Tory. It was imperative he not reveal his feelings, or they might recollect his face from the day they first met on the deck of the *Horton*. So far, none of the Canadian cutter men suspected the college-educated businessman as being one of the unkept fishermen they'd seen in oilskins with a bearded face, hidden under the shadow of a dirty sou'wester. Oliver intended to keep it that way.

When the violinist packed his instrument in his case and most of the guests had departed, Tory escorted his most trusted officers to his second-floor office. Alice and Bonnie were busy chatting about the evening, giving Oliver a chance to steal away. From the outside of the office door, he pressed his ear to the crack between the double oak doors to hear the conversation within. His focus was totally on listening to the plans Tory was explaining to his men. From the sounds of it, they were also engaged in celebratory toasts.

Ten minutes had passed when the sound of a door creaked open. Startled, he spun around. Officer Stevens stood under the light of the gas lamp near a rear stairwell glaring at him.

"Are you looking for someone, Mr. Knight?" The officer, who was in full dress, including his sheathed sword, approached Oliver.

"Oh, no, sir. I was intending to give my thanks to Captain Tory for his hospitality before I left for the evening."

"The captain, as you likely can tell, is in a private conference. I will give him your regards." He motioned toward the center stairs. "Goodnight."

Oliver went his way without saying another word. He was halfway down the steps when the officer called. "And Mr. *Knight*" (the emphasis on the last name he said with a questioning tone), "you'll do well to understand Miss Tory is spoken for."

At this, Oliver turned and stared upwards once again. He was about to give the officer a fisherman's speech of etiquette, when Alice called from the hallway below. "Oliver, Oliver! There you are. Would you please accompany me to escort Bonnie home?"

Oliver, his back to Alice, smiled at Officer Stevens. He bowed and turned. "Why of course, Alice. It would be my pleasure."

From above on the roof, Knowlton and MacDonald saw Oliver exit the home with the two young ladies. The three stood on the veranda waving goodnight to lingering guests.

MacDonald said, "They'll be driving Bonnie home." A few moments later, Captain Tory's carriage arrived from the stable. The three boarded and they could be heard singing until the driver turned up the tree-lined street that led over the hill to the cove.

"It's too bad Alice is the daughter of that Tory." MacDonald lit his pipe and leaned back against the base of the chimney. "She's a nice girl. I hate to interfere with Bonnie and her choice of friends. There aren't many girls her age left here in town. When the men go off fishing and don't come back, thus, leaving widows behind, they are more likely to move with their children to Halifax."

"You and Tory seem to have a long-running feud," stated Harvey.

"I not only disdain the man for the job he has, but more for the attitude which inflates his ego." MacDonald removed a silver flask from his coat. He held it to Knowlton. The captain took a drink.

"Ye see, that gomerel Captain Tory doesn't deserve a royal command." MacDonald took a long tilt of the flask. He used his sleeve to wipe his lip and dry his whiskers. "His family and mine have been settled here for four generations. It was unknown to me that for years his daughter and my Bonnie had become school friends. If I hadn't been away so often fishing, I'd never have allowed it. Mrs. MacDonald didn't see any harm in it. *They're just girls,'* she'd said." He took another drink and passed the flask.

"I let it be. Tory, not liking my character any, didn't do the same. He was also at sea a good deal and was determined that Bonnie, the daughter of a fisherman, would not influence his precious daughter. Well, children don't understand these matters. I can't blame them. As he couldn't get Alice and Bonnie to part company, he figured he'd drive me from Guysborough by ruining me financially."

Captain Harvey Knowlton was beginning to understand MacDonald's disdain for Tory. His eyes narrowed as he focused on MacDonald's face. Even through the darkness, the man's anger was apparent.

MacDonald pointed. "Look there." A group of cuttermen were making their way around the deck of the *Horton*.

"That'd be Tory's men giving a tour of the prize to the Canso unit," said MacDonald. He continued to inform Harvey of the feud. "To get at me, he made false charges, he fined me for selling fish to foreign ports, he impounded my fishing vessels. Anything to get a rise out of me."

"I thought the harassment was only towards American fishermen?" asked Knowlton.

"Nay. They can find all sorts of violations to charge someone with. That's why I had to take to smuggling. I wasn't going to give him the satisfaction of forcing a MacDonald from the Provinces." He drank.

A smirk and a laugh erupted from him. "Turns out, I began making more than a naval officer. I replaced my confiscated fishing ships. Tory was incensed at not only how I obtained my new situation, but that I had any money at all. Oh, I kept on fishing, even let him fine a ship now and then to be out of my way, especially when I knew of a loaded cargo vessel heading to

Halifax. I've been able to keep my ears into what was happening and when."

"I've been meaning to ask you about that. How did you know the *Lily Rose Snow* was sailed to England."

"I'll let you know, on account you appear to me the kind to keep a secret." MacDonald lifted his flask. Knowlton declined. With a shrug of his shoulder, MacDonald took a double drink. "You see, that Tory, he has a brother, a fisherman, Captain Stewart Tory. He'd be more of a snitch than a fisherman. I'm told he supplements the take he makes from his catch with kickbacks for information he supplies Tory." He eyed Knowlton to check if he was being believed. "Two can play at such a game. My brother-in-law works in the wire office. His salary is meager. So, you can understand, I help him out where I can."

"I suspect you mean he receives a good bonus when he lets on about some important piece of business that comes over the wire?" Knowlton knocked his pipe against the chimney to empty the bowl.

"He may, in return for my financial assistance, provide me with news he may hear from time to time. You see, it's personal with the Torys. And, here, or in Ireland, the MacDonalds aren't ones for being pushed around."

MacDonald stood to head down the ladder behind the building. "As you can see, Miss Alice Tory holds no animosity toward my Bonnie. I suspect Alice isn't much aware of the plight of fishermen due to the unfair charges against them by the revenue servicemen. Her own father included. Such business is not of interest to a young woman—I am fairly certain of that."

Knowlton said nothing, but he suspected Bonnie was as unfamiliar with her own father's doings, as Alice of her father. He followed MacDonald down the ladder. Before the two went their separate ways, he asked MacDonald to ensure the men were adhering to quiet hours at the barn, and he, instead, went to watch the harbor.

Under the wharf, miner Zadok Handron sat unnoticed in his dory. He observed the Tory carriage returning down the main street of town. In front of the Customs House, Oliver offered his hand to assist Alice from the carriage. The two stood facing one another under the glow of the gaslights on the sidewalk; the miner watched as they talked. He could only hear muffled rumblings of their conversation and Alice's laughs, so he silently left the dory and made his way closer to listen. In the darkness on the wharf side of the street, in his dark coat, trapper hat, and his beard, he was nearly invisible as a shadow could be.

Along the street, the town's lamplighter was extinguishing the gaslights; a dark street behind him and shadows still ahead, he walked with his pole and ladder. When he approached near to the front of the residence, he stopped, giving the two young people their space.

Realizing he was waiting on the two of them to depart before he continued, Alice spoke. "You may turn out that light, sir. I am going in now."

"Very well, Miss Tory." He extended his hooked pole to turn off the gas. They listened as he walked on, amusing himself with a verse:

> "My work is nearly done, the moon is out tonight.
> And so I go along, to turn down the lights."

"Did you enjoy yourself, Oliver, at my father's party?" The gaslight mounted to the side of the house door illuminated her face with a shimmer of soft amber.

"Spending time with you, my dear Alice, is all the enjoyment I require."

"Hmm. Is that so?"

"Why do you say it like that?" he asked.

She half turned away. "By the way you let Officer Stevens have every dance he asked for, I would have thought otherwise."

Taking her arm, he turned her back to face him. "What would you have me do?"

Her quiet laugh made him take a step away.

She reached for his hand. "Oh, don't be like that. This Officer Stevens, I have no feelings for him. You should be aware of that."

"This is good news to me. But still, I could not refuse an officer of your father's, at a party at his home, to dance with you."

A streak of light ran across the cobblestone of the road. Oliver looked up to see the curtain on the second floor parted. He then saw Alice's expression had turned sad.

"What is it?" he asked.

"How much longer will you be in Guysborough?"

This was a question he was not prepared to answer. The situation with Alice was increasing in complexity for him every day.

"Let's not worry about that tonight." He took her hand and raised it. "You see that star?"

"Why sure. It's the north star."

"In the mythology of the Nordic sailors, they thought Polaris was a jewel on the end of a long spike, set through the universe. Through that spike, all the sky revolved." He noticed how the stars made her eyes twinkle.

Shattering the quiet of the night, the hinges of the front door squealed. "Alice?"

"Yes, mother?"

"Your father says it is time to come in."

"One moment please." The space of the door narrowed, but remained opened.

"You are my jewel, Alice." He kissed her. "Goodnight, my dear."

She disappeared through the door that then latched shut with a clang. He walked to the wharf. Finding his uncle's dory tied to the piling, he found a crate, took a seat, and lighted his pipe. There wasn't a light to be seen behind any window in the town—except Alice's. Every streetlamp was out. A cat was walking the rim of a bait barrel. The iron rings of the floating wharf creaked with each lap of a wave.

Unbeknownst to Oliver, a figure stepped from behind the wide-round piling at the low tide mark. Stepping over the hard sand, he snuck up on the young man. Oliver tried to stand at the tap of his shoulder, but the hand held him down.

"You ought to take up a better position in order to watch your back, Oliver," whispered Knowlton.

"Ah, Uncle. I didn't figure for there to be anyone else awake at such an hour, but maybe yourself."

"Give me a few minute head start, and then meet me behind the fish house." Harvey walked away into the darkness.

The crate Oliver was sitting on flipped over when he stood up. It rolled down the rock embankment and landed in the water with a splash. Oliver looked around for movement to see if the sound had alerted anyone. Once he was satisfied he hadn't been heard, he went to meet his uncle.

Mutiny and Murder

"Oh—I am not a man-'o-war, or privateer," said he.
"But I be merely an honest pirate, sailing the southern sea."

ABOARD the Canadian cutter, Officer Stevens had been sleeping. He had taken to his bunk in order to make early morning preparations for their sail to Halifax. A loud splash, in the usually quiet harbor, roused him from his dreams of Alice. He came up from the aft quarters and peered over the rail.

The night air was brisk. He blew on his hands. Now wide awake, he took out his pipe and packed the bowl. Across at the Tory residence, the lights in Alice's second floor rooms were still burning behind the curtains. The smoke from his pipe rose around his head. His thoughts drifted to how he could win Alice's heart. The image of her from earlier in the evening brought a smile to his face. It disappeared on his realization that he first must eliminate the stranger—Oliver Knight—from the contest.

Behind the fish house, Oliver relayed to his uncle what he'd heard from outside Tory's office. "Captain Tory sails for Halifax tomorrow. He has no plans to move the *Horton* out of Guysborough until he sails it to England. In fact, the provisions have been left aboard, and even added to, so Tory must be planning to sail before the winter. He feels the depth of the harbor is too unknown for American captains to make away with the ship. His men confirmed to him there will be no chance of stealing the ship in the short-term. They are further confident because they have removed the sails and rigging."

Harvey reached in his pocket for his pipe. Hearing the plans of Tory sailing in the morning for Halifax was good news to the captain. He knew he had to retake the *Horton* before she was further outfitted for the Atlantic crossing. Knowing this made him even more determined.

Oliver assessed the clothes his uncle was wearing. Fitted to his belt was a small-handled mining pick-axe. His wool pants were muddy to the knees. The beard on his face was unkept, covered his lips, and climbed up his cheeks to the temples. The fur hat on his head added to his animal appearance. In all his years, and particularly those of his youth and family holidays, he'd never seen his uncle, a Knowlton, a Gloucester ship captain and owner of multiple vessels, looking so rough and disheveled.

"Uncle, how did you ever choose to take up this disguise as a miner?"

The captain looked around the side of the building. The streets and the harbor were deserted. Based on his nights of surveillance, he knew it would be three hours before the town fishermen would appear to ready their vessels for the workday. With a freshly packed T.D. bowl, he resolved to finally tell his nephew his history.

"When I was but nineteen years of age, in the year eighteen-forty-nine, I sailed on the vessel *Boston* for the west coast. In San Francisco the master and owner, Zadok Handron, sold his ship. With the funds, he paid us to claim our grub stake and to purchase our mining outfit. Together, led by our former ship master, we incorporated the *Patriot Mining Company*.

"Us fishermen, turned diggers and panners, were excited to be working on land. However, our excitement was short-lived. Brokers were making more money buying ships and selling mining tools than any of us miners were finding in gold dust. Master Handron made many of the crew additional loans. Soon his own funds from the sale of the ship had given out. With no money to head back east, and no possibility of paying back their loans, several of the Glo'stermen found themselves indentured to captains sailing to Asia." He paused. "I've never heard from those men again."

Smoke rose in a circle from his exhale. "What I picked out in mining dust was enough to pay what I owed, treat my friends to a grand meal, and for one final rousing night at a saloon. After that night, I didn't have enough to book passage back east—an unfortunate mistake. In my realizing I'd never strike it rich, and knowing my father was right again, I hired on as a common hand to sail back to Boston. At ninety-five days into the voyage, two men had died of scurvy and we buried them at sea off South America."

Oliver sat motionless on a pile of scrap wood. He'd known his uncle had gone west for a time in his youth, but he never knew, or imagined he'd gone for the gold rush.

"While in the Strait of Magellan, our ship was boarded and we were held at Camerón. I was forced to sail with a pirate on the *Ranger Jack* under Captain Juan Fernando de Lecato."

"You were held on a pirate ship!" Oliver's mouth hung open to hear such a tale.

Knowlton gave a low laugh. "Of course, that was not his real name, he demanded we call him that, in full, each time we addressed him. He was more of a Spanish merchant vessel captain gone bad, than a *Juan Fernando de Lecato*.

"Whenever he confiscated a ship, the first items we were commanded to find were suits and cloth. Aboard the *Ranger Jack* he kept a tailor busy making his meticulous clothes and accoutrements of scarves, hats, gloves and boot covers. Dixey Bull had nothing on Juan's flamboyant attire."

"How did you escape?"

"Righteous mutiny." Knowlton blew a breath of air. He could see the whites of Oliver's eyes growing larger.

"It had to be done. There were ten of us fishermen held beyond our will. The pirate had fifteen men of his own. All of them loyal. It took a good deal of planning to stash weapons, to time the watches, and be at the ready. It was spring in the West Indies when the time came. I'd been a captive for nine months. We heaved the pirate captain overboard in heavy seas. The six pirates on deck were fought, and, likewise, three others went to the sharks. Roused at the noise, the others came up from below and fired on us with muskets. Two of our men were shot. They died that day. We rushed the gunners, as was the plan of self-sacrifice, in order they could not reload. The hand-to-hand combat was bloody and lasted all the afternoon. When the last pirates surrendered, we dropped the flag, and sailed to Boston.

"On entering Boston Harbor, I tossed my journal of my three-year adventure over the rail with the wish I'd forget my darkest nightmare. The pirates were hung. Their bodies left on display in the Common, as was done in those days, until the crows picked apart their faces. I returned to Gloucester and fishing."

Oliver's eyes were wide with interest. How he'd never been told this family story before was shocking to him. "I'd only heard of you taking leave of Uncle Nemo's vessel to try mining. I had no idea of your west coast adventure."

Knowlton wondered if the family gossip had been so kind to note his desertion as *taking-leave*. "I shouldn't have left the *Patience*. But an adventure it was not. More like foolishness of a young man not wishing to take orders on a fisherman." He looked out over the harbor and the boats sitting at anchor.

"When we take the *Horton*, will you be up for whatever has to occur, Oliver?" Knowlton stared into his nephews' eyes. He saw Oliver swallow hard.

"Uncle, I've only been commanded to kill another man while in uniform. Luckily, while I was stationed in Virginia near the end of the war, I never had to fire—but once, and that was to shoot a wild boar for dinner. Our company was near death from starvation. And, I will say, that day, I was proud my shot hit the mark."

"Well, you might have to consider one of those red coats as being swine when the time comes." The captain searched his own fortitude to understand if he was willing to go to the gallows to reclaim his vessel. The prospect of hanging in Halifax for the crows to feed on him wasn't a pleasant thought.

"We don't even have guns, Uncle Harvey." Oliver's voice cracked.

"MacDonald is working on that aspect. He also has a six-pound cannon we will hide aboard before getting ready to sail."

"Hide a cannon? On the deck of the *Horton*? I don't see how that will go unnoticed."

"Nephew, I've gone unnoticed here as a miner for days now. The people here are not all too observant. Secondly, as a former captive pirate, one of my learned skills was that of hiding cannons in plain sight on a ship's deck."

Knowlton placed his hand on his nephew's shoulder. "All will be well. So long as you mind how you are approaching the feelings of that young lady." His eyes narrowed. "Go and sleep. We must be rested for what is to occur."

Stevens, still standing motionless at the rail of the *Sweepstakes*, watched a shadow approaching the wharf. He recognized the dory the man stepped into as belonging to the strange miner. He was about to discount any oddness in the miner being awake at such an hour, when off to his right, a light shone bright from the second floor of the boarding house. It was from the room rented by Oliver Knight. He knew the window. Under Captain Tory's orders, he had searched that very room while Oliver danced with the woman of his dreams earlier that very evening.

His search had been fruitless. He opined to himself that Tory was paranoid and all that was accomplished was he was missing out on dancing with Alice. He went about the search haphazardly. His only observance was that the foolish businessman's only possessions were several books, of which Stevens, not being a reader, hadn't even lifted to see the titles. Had he opened a book, from mere curiosity, he would have noticed a Gloucester owner's name inside the front cover. More so, he might have found a folded map of the harbor, one stamped with the seal of a crown's surveyor folded between the pages.

His inspection was completed in a hurry. He had returned to the party to cut in on Oliver who was dancing with Miss Tory.

Friday – October 6, 1871 – Morning

Blue skies and a fair breeze accompanied Oliver to the wharf following his breakfast. He intended to see Alice off. The two were standing close to the cutter, recalling dances of the night before, when they were interrupted by her mother.

"Good morning, Mr. Knight, but you must excuse Alice now." Mrs. Tory nodded.

Oliver was pleased at being acknowledged by Mrs. Tory. He returned the greeting. The prior evening, he had been entertained by the mother's conversation, and found her as charming as the daughter, and nothing like the coarse captain. He hoped her cheerfulness was maybe a sign of acceptance of his courting her daughter.

Mrs. Tory had come halfway down the gangplank to the wharf with her escort Officer Stevens at her side. She inclined her head towards her daughter. "Alice, your father wants you to come aboard. We're to be underway shortly."

"Yes, Mother, right away."

On reaching the deck, Mrs. Tory strode toward the cabin. The officer lingered, not taking his eyes from Oliver. Alice turned her back to Officer Stevens.

"I do wish you could sail to Halifax with us, Oliver. Certainly I can convince father to allow you to accompany me." Alice handed her sun umbrella to a crew member.

"No, Alice. As much as I'd like to spend the time with you, and dance with you at the ball, I must remain here for my business."

Behind Alice, at the rail of the *Sweepstakes*, Officer Stevens cleared his throat. "Miss Tory, we must sail on the tide."

Alice turned and gave a half wave to the officer.

"Goodbye then, Mr. Knight. I shall see you on my return. Father says we are to sail home on Monday, at the latest Tuesday." She patted his hand. "I'd wish to give you a kiss, but, well…" She motioned at the seamen of the cutter lining the deck, all pretending to be busy with the halyards and rigging, but likely ready to help Stevens wallop the man holding his girl's hands.

"Fair winds and following seas." Oliver bowed and took his leave. Alice safely boarded the ship and a deck hand pulled up the plank. From the end of the wharf, Oliver turned to wave, but Alice was being escorted aft by Officer Stevens to the captain's quarters.

On the height of McCaul Point, Harvey Knowlton watched the *Sweepstakes* sail out to the bay. With his expert eye, he watched as the orders were called to set sail and the cutter tacked to make first the right and then the left turn to deeper water.

Using his spyglass, he surveyed the now empty wharf and the warehouse. He counted only three Canadian seamen, all of whom he'd been watching for the past week. He knew where they lived, their typical work routines, where they took their dinners, and their tendency to stay below on a ship, or in the warehouse office when Officer Stevens wasn't barking orders at them. With both the captain and the officer on their way to the celebration, Knowlton didn't figure the men would be doing more than the minimum of checking the bilge on the smaller boats every so often.

On a sun-warmed rock, near the dying coals of his fire, he sat to think things through. The *Sweepstakes* shrunk away on the horizon. There wouldn't be a better opportunity to take his schooner. He packed his camp outfit and covered it in the bow of the dory with his mining tools. The day being warm, he rolled his coat and placed it on the seat beside him.

His first order of business was to ensure the town knew he'd found gold and made a claim. He pushed off.

The sparkle of the sun on the water brightened his mood. His plan was looking more feasible, and with the departure of Tory from Guysborough on his mind, he sang a shanty as he pulled the oars to and fro.

> "Oh, ho, blow the man down,
> please blow that Tory
> clear to Liverpool town.
> Oh, ho, give us some time
> to blow the man down."

Defiance Realized

Friday – October 6, 1871
McKenzie-Knowlton-Horton Wharf
Gloucester, Massachusetts

The office window slammed upwards. Three squawking gulls took off from the sill.

"Connie! Duncan!" The men, who were painting dories, looked up to the warehouse. Edward Horton beckoned them closer.

"Can you two good men assist Mr. Sweeney in lowering down the sails for *Defiance Too*?"

"Sure thing, Skipper," answered Cornelius.

Edward signaled a thanks with a wave. He looked off into the fog rolling in around Rocky Neck. An inbound schooner was trimming her sails. He thought he even heard the master give the command to, "Heave to!"

The scene beyond the window held him there looking out over the inner harbor. He admired the barnacle covered posts of the wharves and the skeletons of the ships on their ways being constructed. The rhythmic sounds of the hammers at work were a song. He took in a deep breath of the sharp, disinfecting stink from the rotting seaweed exposed at low tide. He read to himself the signs on the businesses he could see from his office window—he knew the owners, all of them, and many in their employ as well.

Pattillo's Chandlery.

Thomas Renton's Sheet Iron and Ship Stoves.

The loft of Allen Daniel's sail makers—(he'd worked there himself as a boy).

The yard of stonecutter Chris Amazeen.

Burnham Brothers Lumber, Railways, and Milling.

Coffey's Boarding House.

Tarr and Wonson's Copper Paint Company—(where, having sworn off the sea a decade earlier, Harvey Knowlton Sr. was employed as a foreman).

Cole and Cogswell's Blacksmiths.

Susan Barnetson – Dressmaker—(he remembered he had an order to pick up for Betty Tarr).

Samuel Fears – Grocery and Provisions—(he had to send the catchee up with the check to pay the invoice due).

G. Tarr – Quarry Equipment.

William Wonson & Son – Dry, Smoked & Pickled Fish.

A bit farther distant, he gazed at the signs of the shipwrights and boatbuilders—there were so many in view—including, Burnham's, Poland & Woodbury, the Davis Brothers, with still more beyond around the neck, and numerous others in Essex and Rockport.

He watched Connie, Duncan, and Frank finish up what they were doing as his thoughts ran to all the businesses beyond his line of sight. What of the netting and twine factories, manila rope dealers, coopers, box makers, tackle and bait shops, icehouses, painters, machinists, stables, smokehouses; there were the sparmakers, flake yards, oilskin suppliers, glue factories; and the fish dealers galore; then, of course, there were the salt dealers, teamsters, taverns, tailors, restaurants, saloons, hotels and boarding houses.

Not to mention those who worked as shoemakers, seamstresses, carpenters, bookkeepers, riggers, calkers, printers, masons, coachmen, plumbers, teachers, grocers, bakers, provisioners, barbers, pharmacists, the farmers of the outer acres, the wood cutters, and the scores of others that make life run when the schooners come home with their fish. There were even a couple of men with shingles on their sheds noting their trade as 'Oyster Opener.'

All these businesses were built by the men of Gloucester, and they employed the men of the town, who in turn provided for their families—it was a view he grew up with, one he helped build, and one he expected to see prosper into the future. *"Harvey, Godspeed, my friend. Godspeed,"* he thought.

He stepped back against the mist that was blowing in from the ocean. Down below, he heard Connie's bellowing voice as he came along the wharf with Duncan.

"Do you think Captain Horton plans to fish up the nor'then banks out of *Defiance Too*?" asked Connie.

Edward could tell Cornelius was huffing as he tried to keep behind the sprightly Duncan. He leaned over the sill, wondering what Duncan's response might be.

"Can't say. I doubt he'd do anything of the sort without hearing from Captain Knowlton on the fate of the *Horton*." Duncan slung a thick coil of rope over his shoulder. "Grab that other coil, we'll be needing it to wrap the sails. Besides, I don't know if they would be wanting to test the Canadians with a fourth new ship to seize—after they'd already detained the *Lily Rose Snow*, the *Alice Wonson*, and now the *Edward A. Horton*."

"When do you suppose we might hear word of what's going on up in Guysborough?" Connie pulled at the side door to the stairs.

The door swung open to reveal Frank Sweeney reaching for the handle on the opposite side at the same time. "For two weeks you two have been talking about the doings up in the Province worse than the women down doing laundry. Stop your worrying. Someone will get an idea that Harvey is up to something." Sweeney moved to the side of the stairwell. "I was coming to remind you to get that rope. Good to see you two haven't lost all your minds for details."

"Now, Frank, you know we was excited and busy when we got in that dory!" snapped Duncan. The side remarks on the missing oars hadn't stopped in the near month they'd been back to port.

"And besides, it was Oliver that was charged with getting the dory prepared that morning," added Cornelius.

"Yeah. Yeah. When I was a doryman I never let anyone be responsible for what was or wasn't in the boat other than meself."

Edward heard the outer door being pulled hard against the jam. He closed the window. When he turned, he caught the stare from Joseph Knowlton who was sitting at the table in the office. The two could hear the loud banter of the three men as they passed to the second landing.

"I must say, I'm as curious as Duncan and Connie for news." Edward dropped into his chair. He shuffled his papers to find the check to pay the provisions invoice.

"Aye. But don't let Sweeney fool you, he's as curious as all of us combined." Joseph walked to the map on the wall and adjusted the flags of the company vessels, mostly guessing on the location of each fisherman. He badly wanted to move the *Horton* from Guysborough out to the open sea, but busied himself with the fishing report in the paper. Ten minutes later he heard Sweeney back outside.

"*Slow! Easy now, you men.*" Sweeney's voice carried from outside on the wharf. Joseph turned to see the first bundle of sails being lowered on the pulley rope. He walked to the window to stand next to Edward.

"*Slow down!*" yelled Sweeney, his face turned upward to the men in the loft. "*You're bound to crush me.*"

"It appears the men will have *Defiance Too* ready to sail in four to five days, Edward." Joseph gazed down on the deck of the new schooner. Men were putting finishing brushes of paint on the trim of the cabin doors.

"She ought to get a trip in to *Georges* before the winter season." Edward turned slightly to Joseph. "To try her out."

"You and Harvey don't plan to send her for the winter season then?" asked Joseph.

"Ah, we've not had a chance to discuss it. With all this *Horton* business going on."

"Have you heard any news this week from Washington?" Joseph suspected that if there'd been news, Edward would have said something. Then again, he wasn't his jovial self and had been quieter over the past weeks.

"Nay. Seems they don't want to get involved with adjusting the agreements of the treaty. This business of letting duty-free fish be sold here in America from Canadian vessels, in return for the simple right for American fishermen to fish unmolested in open waters far from the Canadian coastline is lopsided in how things are in actuality."

"Isn't there something more the commissioners could be held to do for us, Edward?" Joseph indicated the stack of letters from Washington piled on Edward's desk.

"The last letter basically told me they wished to not bother President Grant with such matters. What I read in their words is he has bigger fish in the pan to deal with than Glo'ster mackerel."

"Does he even know the extent of the business here? The size of our fleet? The dependence on the fish coming to port?" Joseph, not as familiar as his brother, or Edward Horton with the fleet numbers, stole a look at Harvey's tabulation chart on the wall. "My gosh, Edward. For last year alone, there were over five-hundred and seventy vessels and more than six thousand men employed from this area around Glo'ster at fishing!"

"Yes. Yes, I know. But, we're herring in a sea of whales for what Grant considers important you see."

"*That's the last sail, Frank.*" Duncan's voice streamed from the loft above.

"*Very good. Come down. All of ye. Let's get them furled on the jibs,*" replied Sweeney.

"Guess I'll go up and take my dinner with Betty Tarr." Edward pulled on his coat. "Care to join me, Joseph?"

"No, thank you though. I think I'll stay here and help the crew bend the sails. It'll give me something to take my mind off this business of politics."

"Lucky you." Edward tipped his hat.

Within three hours, the sails on *Defiance Too* had been hoisted in the slack wind one by one and then furled. Joseph sat on the wharf watching the canvas rise and fall. He wished he was an owner in the company with the ability to order the vessel to sail that afternoon. She was a beauty.

"She'll beat any yacht in the harbor, Captain Knowlton."

Joseph turned to see a young man in the dark blue uniform shirt of the telegraph office.

"You likely are a good judge of hulls and sail, son. You'll want to save your money to put behind her come the races."

"That I will. This telegram came for Mr. Sweeney of your company. It's marked **URGENT**." The boy handed over the paper. "Post Master Humphries wanted it delivered straight away. Would you please pass it along to him? I see he's occupied." The boy pointed to Frank yelling commands on the deck of the schooner.

"Certainly." Joseph gave the boy a silver piece and thanked him. He began to read the slip of paper and then called the boy back. "Ho there, boy." Joseph handed him another silver. "Would you mind, please go up to the Tarr Tavern and ask Mr. Horton to come down to the office? Express to him—*promptly*."

The boy beamed. "Why, yes. Yes, sir!" He saluted and ran off.

"Frank! **Frank!**"

Sweeney who was still working the rigging with the men, gave some orders and came over the rail to Joseph. "What is it, Skipper?"

"From Harvey." Joseph waved the telegram. "I've sent for Edward to meet us in the office. Take a look at this."

Frank read it as the two went up the stairs.

"What's this all about?" Edward pushed the door closed behind him. "The telegram boy had no idea why you'd summoned me back down here? Betty Tarr had just set down to dinner with me."

Joseph placed a lantern on the office table close to where Edward, who was still breathing heavy from his walk down the hill, was holding the telegram close to his face.

"What the heck does this mean?" Edward pushed his glasses up on his head.

"Frank, I suspect it was meant for you to interpret," stated Joseph.

"Let me see it again, Captain." Sweeney walked from the window to the table. Edward pushed the paper closer to Sweeney who took it up in his hands.

URGENT WIRE:
TO: Mr. Frank Sweeney
Rocky Neck, Gloucester, Massachusetts

Cousin Sweeney:

I've made it to the Provinces. My nephew is looking well. We'll be departing with Gusto for our journey with the family, within a few days. Keep a watch out for us on hearing the next news — and Grant all may be well.

M. Burnham.

Joseph and Edward watched Sweeney twist his lips and crinkle his nose.

"Well, man?" asked Edward.

"Aye, I needed a moment." The chair Frank pulled out from the table screeched across the boards. He sat. "It all means,

Harvey is well. Oliver is with him, so that answers that disappearance of the boy." Frank looked at the partners. "And that means Harvey is aware of what Oliver wrote in the letter telling us of the Canadian plans to sail the *Horton* to England."

He studied the telegram again. "They've got up a crew they know. They'll be under full sail on the *Horton* within a few days. Seems they've reason to worry about being chased by the Canadian cutters. Captain Harvey is asking you, Captain Horton, to do what you can to have support off the coast through official channels of the President himself, but not until news breaks of the *Horton* escaping from Guysborough."

"You get that from that wire?" asked Edward. "How do you even know it's from Harvey?"

"I'm certain. You see, I figure he couldn't address the wire to yourself, the vessel having your family name, the operators in Nova Scotia would surely be alerted to it. Nor could he send it to his brother—for the same reason. Harvey's use of the name Gusto is for the 'A' of the *Edward A. Horton*." His misinterpreting the look on Edward's face, he added, "Gusto, being a less common nickname for Augustus."

"I know that! My own mother used to call me by such."

Sweeney pushed the paper back to Edward who was reaching for it again. "Of course, the capital 'G' in *Grant*, is indicating the President's name. He's signed it M. Burnham for the firm's vessel, the *Mary Burnham*. So, as sure as salt'll sting a cut, that there telegram is from Harvey." Sweeney tapped the paper.

"I'd say Frank has it as about accurate as Harvey meant it." Joseph examined the wall map again. "Do you suppose, Edward, you can get support to protect the men and vessel as they sail?"

Captain Horton blew out a gale of air from between his closed lips. "I don't see how. The commissioners have wanted nothing to do with our fishing war—as they put it." He paced to the window and looked at the harbor. Masts of hundreds of vessels bobbed on the tide. "I suppose if we don't take a stand now, with a shot to be heard across the ocean, we'll never get out from under the tyranny. I'm tired of taking insurance losses on our vessels, and paying fines, and worse, seeing owners having to buy back their own schooners at auction." He was roaring loud in his excitement. "I'll start at once with a telegram to the Boston yard. The local commanders may be more sympathetic to our cause."

"No!" Sweeney slapped the table. "You must wait. Once the *Horton* is found missing, or there is some chase through the Straits of Canso, we'll surely hear of it. Only then, per Harvey's instructions, are you to call on any support from the American naval forces."

"Frank is right, Edward. We must hold on any action until we hear, else the Canadian government will be alerted to the scheme."

"Humph. May as well return to my dinner then."

Frank and Joseph watched Edward trudge up the hill to the tavern.

"Do you think he'll be able to keep quiet?" asked Sweeney.

"You know Edward as well as anyone. But I have to hope he knows what it means in this case. Not only for the *Horton*, but for the safety of Harvey, Oliver, and the crew. Those past reports of the cutters firing on American vessels is serious business." Joseph Knowlton placed the telegram within the desk draw of company correspondence. He leaned back in his chair. His thoughts ran to wondering who might be dining at the Tarr Tavern that evening, and if they'd be within listening distance of Edward eating at his usual table near the kitchen door.

Gold in the Cove

Gold! Gold! What a sight to behold.
you'll find it here in Guysborough Town.
So, Handron, the miner, had told.

Friday – October 6, 1871
Guysborough Harbor

Captain Knowlton consulted his tide chart. The tides were not favorable the next few nights, unless they could outfit the *Horton* with sails and haul anchor during the light of day. That of course would not be feasible, even with Tory and most of his men away in Halifax. He knew his only chance was to sail the *Horton* under the cover of darkness. A confounding factor was the hinderance that the lowest tide would occur after midnight the next few nights. In his discussions with MacDonald, it was declared the water would be too low for this evening. MacDonald also warned that Fridays tended to have more night owls out and about, even in sleepy Guysborough. If wind conditions were favorable, they would make the attempt on Saturday or Sunday. It would be wonderful justice, thought Knowlton, if he could sail the *Horton* from Guysborough as Captain Tory was getting into bed following his party—the memory of the notes from *Sir Roger de Coverley* lulling Tory to sleep.

For his part, Harvey, on account of his current disadvantage of the low tide, figured himself for the one-legged boatman who was hired by Addison's fictional Squire Sir Roger de Coverley—

the one who rowed the squire across the River Thames at Vauxhall. A single leg was no disability for the boatman. So why should the matter of no water in the channel interfere with Knowlton sailing the *Horton* from beneath the Canadian's noses? Under his breath he whispered a verse from his days of pirate captivity:

> "Our captain stood on his quarter-deck,
> and a right mean pirate was he!
> If a hand spoke out of turn, he'd swat him
> with his peg leg; taken off below the knee."

In the late afternoon, he rowed across the harbor and made a sweep under the bow of the *Horton*. He noticed she was riding lower than he'd like, an indication that the Canadians were also derelict in their duties at the bilge pumps, or more likely another order from Captain Tory to fuddle any escape of the ship. He looped his dory rope around a wharf piling and went to place nuggets of information around the town.

As anticipated, he found the always-present men sitting around the stove at the center of the mercantile. They stopped their conversation when he stepped through the door. Each of them followed Harvey with their eyes as he walked across the creaking floorboards.

"Any luck with the yellow stones, Mr. Zadok Handron?" asked a fisherman who was seated at the bench. The others snickered.

Harvey didn't turn around. He spoke to the owner who was behind the counter. "I'll take a pouch of tobacco, twelve ounces of coffee, and a small bag of sugar."

"Must be lean picking out there on the rocks with an order that small." The bored fisherman had walked up behind Harvey to chide him some more.

Harvey's hand reached into his inner coat pocket. A little black pouch was cinched with a scrap of hemp. The store owner and fisherman watched him untie it. From the bag, Harvey removed a piece of black cloth. Gently the bag was tilted and three sparkling gold nuggets slid out onto the soft fabric bed.

The mercantile owner stepped forward. "I've never seen gold pieces raw from the ground before. You dug those here? Around Guysborough?"

Behind him, Harvey heard the men rise; their boots scuffing the wooden floor as they shuffled to the counter. He placed his hand over the two largest nuggets before they were able to see, and slipped them back into his pouch. The men stood close. He could smell their rum-coffee breath over his shoulder.

"This small piece here is worth near one-hundred dollars." He picked it up and waited for the shop owner to open his palm to accept it. "I'm low on cash with no time to get to Canso to trade this. I've found what I think will turn out to be a profitable claim."

"Where would that be?" asked one of the store loafers, not knowing miners weren't in the habit of advertising where they found gold.

Today, however, was his lucky day. Zadok Handron was a talker to begin with and it wasn't his plan to keep the location a secret from the small-town fishermen.

"So, you see," Harvey held open his hand for the gold piece back, "I'd like to trade this."

"Oh, I don't know," stated the owner. "I don't have any idea what such a piece is worth. And a hundred dollars, why, I don't even have that much here in the store."

Harvey nodded. "I'm a simple man. I don't like to bicker about money too much. As I said, it's worth that much, but I'd be willing to take fifty dollars for it. I'll be needing to buy some additional equipment here in town right quick."

The shop owner shook his head. He wasn't sure about buying a rock from a stranger.

"See here, Mr. Handron, my name is Captain Charles Davis."

Harvey turned to see Davis extending his hand. He was a sharp-dressed fellow wearing a jacket and tie, as opposed to the others in their wool pants and sou'westers that rarely left their heads. Knowlton shook the hand.

Davis smiled at the miner. "For fifty dollars I'll take a gamble and buy that gold from you. I'll give you a hundred, if you tell me whereabouts you found it. You don't have to tell me exact. I know a bit about how staking a claim goes."

The other men were straining to get a look at the gold and to hear where they might find themselves a nugget.

"I think we might work something out, Mr. Davis." Miner Handron let Davis hold the gold.

"Fine. Fine. Let's say you and me go over to the tavern and have a mug of wine."

By the time dusk had settled over the town, Harvey had let on he had staked out his claim up the shallow river that ran into the Saint Francis Harbor—a fifteen-mile water route from Guysborough, or ten through the thick woods, through which he knew no road ran.

"No, No," he told Davis. He couldn't rightly recall, not being from the area, how far up the river he'd gone, but he'd marked a tree with his axe, on the right side of the bank. "Oh sure, yes. There likely was plenty of gold up that way," he answered to further questions.

Davis, not knowing about mining, listened to what Zadok knew about gold, and terrain, and his self-study of geology. In him he saw an expert miner. The miner, for an extra twenty dollars even agreed to draw him a map. Davis made Handron an offer.

"Mr. Handron, I'm sure you could use more men up the river to mine before others descend on your claim. As a selectman in this town, I could arrange such an expedition. For a share, of course."

It was an outcome better than Knowlton had thought of. An agreement was reached and a slip of paper drawn with signatures. When he rowed away in his dory, a group of men were watching him from the tavern steps.

Around ten o'clock that evening, he'd beached his dory in a cove close to the path that led to MacDonald's home. But, to the barn he did not go. He walked back to town, keeping out of view of all the houses.

From the roof of the fish house he watched a contingent of men, directed by Davis, load up two boats with axes, picks, tents, food, and all sorts of supplies purchased from the mercantile. Theirs would be the *Expedition of Seventy-one*. There would be thirty fewer men loitering about the town for the next three or four days; it'd take them that long to not find any claim Harvey made along the river (he never having been there); and probably twice that many more days for them to dig and pick away at the ground trying to find gold that they figured must be there; it had to be, since Zadok Handron had discovered so many nuggets— not far from their very own Guysborough.

Before the last bell of twelve rang, the night watchman departed the *Horton*. Harvey noticed there was a difference in the man. Under his arm, he carried a book. A light was seen within the watchman's home until the hour of one. Thirty minutes after that, Harvey, along with Oliver, Gillis, McCloud and Webber, climbed over the rail of the *Horton*. Below they worked the pumps to empty the bilge in order to ready the ship.

It was near half past two when MacDonald arrived with his wagon. Using a warp and planking, the cannon was rolled onto the deck and secured to the planks in the fish pen. Under netting, rigging, ropes, and trawls it was hidden, but at the ready.

Exhausted, but confident, they rested at the forecastle table. MacDonald wiped his forehead with a rag. "News from Canso is the other cutters also sailed for Halifax to take part in the celebration. All the captains are to be honored for their service, not just Tory."

"We ought to have easy sailing then down the coast," said Gillis.

Knowlton nodded. "With strong winds we should hope to be beyond Halifax before they realize. With full sails under a decent breeze, even their steamboat could not catch the *Horton*."

The men, confident of not being detected below deck, lighted their pipes.

"Captain Knowlton, will you not drive the *Horton* out to sea before heading directly south by south-west?" asked MacDonald.

"All depends on the seas." Knowlton puffed on his pipe while considering his planned sailing route and MacDonald's question. He was certain that Canadian and British ships would be patrolling along the coast and banks. For weeks he'd been considering how to avoid all vessels on the seas. His best thought was to sail out far to the east of the Canso Bank. From there, he'd take a heading south between the Middle Ground and Sable Island Bank. All this, he kept to himself.

They left the *Horton* one by one. Through the darkness they walked past the homes of all the sleeping residents of the town. Once past the last house, MacDonald held the wagon and waited on the crew.

"It's a good thing my Bonnie sleeps on the opposite side of the house," said MacDonald, leading the group into his workshop barn. Neither Richards, Penney, or Dyer stirred from their bedrolls. "The snoring in here is louder than the two cows in the side stable. Those three might raise the roof with their exhales."

Knowlton turned up the lantern and examined the sacks the three sleeping men had earlier prepared for the departure.

"Looks like that'll make up three days rations per man for food and water," said McCloud.

MacDonald re-tied the sack he'd been examining. "Should you be discovered before you can sail, or Moby Dick forbid, you run aground in the channel, you ought to be able to hoist over your seine boat, land it, and make your way through the woods to Canso. Don't forget to take these supplies over the rail with you." He breathed out heavily. "Whatever you do, do not return to my barn!"

"You've done very good, Captain MacDonald. I'm grateful to you." Knowlton extended a hand to the smuggler, in which he held out a stack of crisp bills; the ones recently acquired from Davis for the map to the gold mine. Even though MacDonald's services were expensive, Knowlton admitted to himself, he'd made the plan all the more feasible—so far.

The bills counted and tucked in his pocket, MacDonald stated, "I'll be grateful when I get the remainder of the payment from ye, Captain Knowlton." He tipped the brim of his cap and headed out the door to his own bed.

A Fox in the Hen House

> Her dreams were of adventure
> far from the dory fishing town.
> And in the stranger there was mystery
> of what, she couldn't pin down.

Saturday – October 7, 1871
MacDonald's Barn

From his bunk, Richards watched his mate through one open eye. Before the rooster crowed the first time, he noticed Penney was awake and standing close to the inside barn wall; his right eye was set against a space in the boards that faced the hen house. Richards was determined to discover where his mate had been disappearing to the last two mornings—he had his suspicions— so, he kept still and waited.

Bonnie's cheerful morning song began as soon as she stepped from the back door. Soft notes, of what could only be a Sunday hymn, reached the barn and began to grow closer. Penney stepped abruptly back from the wall. Then he slowly approached his viewing port once again to peer out.

"Bonnie! Where are you going, my girl?" MacDonald's yell was purposeful enough to jolt the rest of the crew fully awake.

The men jumped off their bunks and made for the root cellar. Penney held up his hand for them to hold before raising the heavy door and the creaking possibly giving their position away.

"I was only going to look in your workshop for another egg basket, Father. I had so many yesterday morning to sell."

"Never mind there. Take this."

Through the space between the boards, Penney saw MacDonald hold up a wooden-handled tool crate. He started towards to where Bonnie stood along the worn dirt path halfway to the barn. She looked towards the back barn, shrugged, and went to take the box from her father. A minute later, an eruption of clucks alerted all the crew Bonnie had spread the flocks feed and their hideout was safe.

Once MacDonald was sure his daughter was on her way to town with her delivery, he took two dozen fried eggs and a slab of roasted pork out to the men. They were halfway through their breakfast before MacDonald asked, "We're missing two. Where be Richards and Penney?"

"Penney is surely taking care of his morning ablutions down by the water." Dyer pushed his hunk of bread around in the pan of pork fat. "Seems he's taken to this landlubber life with the bathing he's been doing every morning."

MacDonald peered through the back door of the barn. The woods were too thick and grown over to see down to the stream that ran behind the property. "And Richards?"

"Might you make the eggs a bit less done, Doctor?" Dyer poked his knife at the three eggs seated atop his greasy bread. "There's barely any yolk to run."

"You can cook 'em yourself then." MacDonald raised a fist.

"Aye, then, they're just the way I like 'em." A click came from his mouth. "Ah, Richards'll be down there with him, likely. Not bathing that skunk, just smoking a pipe."

"They ought to take care of that business after dark. You'd think they'd know better." He picked up the empty frying pan. "As for the eggs, I ain't been no sea-cook in over twenty years. You'll get them the way I cook 'em. And I do 'em one way."

"Don't mind Dyer, Skipper. He's like that with all the cooks," stated McCloud.

MacDonald grunted. "One of you sneak down there and tell those two to get back in here where no one can see 'em." He slid open the front door. "And if Captain Knowlton should show up after I've gone, let him know my brother-in-law sent the wire."

"What wire was that?" asked Gillis.

"He'll know." MacDonald pulled the barn door closed behind him. Not one of the men moved from their breakfast to take up his order to go down to the stream.

Richards crouched behind a blowdown to watch Penney. His mate emerged from the stream and dried off. But instead of dressing back in his sea clothes, he pulled on black pants, a white colored long-sleeved shirt, and an overcoat. Richards found the attire out of place; he wondered where Penney even acquired such clothes, and furthermore, why he was wearing them to sit in the barn. He couldn't quite make it out, but it appeared to him that Penney was tying his shoe with all things, a red ribbon!

A bigger surprise hit Richards when Penney struck off towards the road. His first instinct was to club his mate over the head with a stick and drag him back to the barn. Curiosity, largely from nearly a week cooped up like fowl, won out. He crept along, following through the woods. When Penney took to the road to sit on a boulder, he stayed back behind the trees. It wasn't long before he saw what, or rather who, Penney had dressed up for.

He listened to their conversation.

"Good morning, sir." Bonnie nodded, and then added, "I should think we'll have to name that granite boundary stone, Billy-boy Rock if you're so attached to the location."

"Maybe so. It could be the only monument ever named for me." He stood up and indicated with his hand. "But I see the king already has his arrow etched in it." Then, looking at the girl, said, "That is a lovely dress you're wearing today, Miss Bonnie."

"Thank you."

Her blush told him she was pleased he had noticed she wasn't wearing her worn housedress to make the deliveries.

"The shoelace is working out?" she asked.

He glanced down. "Ah, yes, it is. I haven't had time to shop for a new one."

She nodded.

He noticed her brow furrowed and her head was slightly tilted as she kept her eyes on the lace. Before she could ask a question he might not be able to answer, he went on, "I was out stretching my legs with a walk on this lovely road, observing the colorful autumn leaves and breathing the sea air, when I wondered to myself if I should wait here."

"Wait for?"

"To wait and see if I might run into you again, my fair lady."

"Oh, you wondered, did you, Mr. Billy-boy of the lane?"

"Um, yes. Well, to give you this." From his pocket he pulled a long coil of red ribbon. "It's not the exact match of the color." He pointed to his shoe. "But I wanted to replace the one you gave me."

"You didn't have to do that. I wasn't expecting you to pay it back." She waved off the ribbon.

"I felt I should repay your kindness." He held his hand out with the dark red, velvety-fabric which was rimmed in white lace, until she took it.

She ran the end of the ribbon between her fingers. "It is a quality weave. Thank you. And such a long piece. I'll find a better use for it than on my basket. That I promise."

"Won't you have a seat?" He sat down on the edge of the boulder, leaving room for her. "I thought maybe you might help me recall a few more verses of *Billy-boy*." He smiled.

Her head turned up the road toward her house. If her father was to come along, she'd see the wagon at the bend well before he spotted her. So, she sat.

As they talked, she thought of how the well-dressed, polite gentleman was different from the men in town and the crew from her father's boat. She couldn't quite place him, but she concluded he was not a local seaman or one of Captain Tory's men.

Using his concealed position behind the tree, Richards watched the two singing and laughing. He was of the mind to break up the two of them, and was getting up his courage, when the girl jumped up. He couldn't hear what she said, but she pushed Penney towards town and she went in the opposite direction, towards home.

Making his way closer to the road, Richards saw MacDonald driving their way on his wagon. He'd stopped in the road. His arms swung about as he spoke to his daughter. She handed him the egg box and climbed to the seat.

The wagon never slowed on its way down the dusty road. MacDonald veered his team up close behind Penney, so close, the fisherman had to jump into the tall grass. White seeds of the prickly weeds stuck to his wool pants, along with a coating of yellow pollen that puffed into a cloud from the dried goldenrod stalks. Richards snickered to himself.

"Father!" The girl looked over her shoulder and waved. Her father pulled her hand down.

Brushing himself off, Penney noticed MacDonald's left hand drop secretively over the side of the wagon; his index finger pointing back to the barn. How he was to explain his breaking of the rules to MacDonald, and worse to Captain Knowlton, he hadn't figured out. First, he had to change back to his clothes.

At the stream, he walked in circles trying to find his old sailing attire. There was no way he could appear at the barn in the dandy outfit he was wearing.

"Looking for these?"

He turned to see Richards holding his clothes on the end of a long birch branch. When Penney reached for them, his mate flicked them into the stream.

One Last Sleep

What shall we do with
the lovestruck sailor?
Best we keep him away from
the captain's daughter!

Saturday – October 7, 1871 – Evening

It was near dark when MacDonald returned to the back barn. He'd had to wait until Bonnie had left for a church meeting. By then, he'd had time to cool down, but not by much.

"Penney! What the heck were you thinkin,' lad?" He rushed at the younger sailor.

Penney dropped his hand of cards and fell back off the crate he was sitting on. Only MacDonald, he, and Richards knew what the scuffle was about.

Penney scrambled to his feet. "Well, Skipper, I don't see there's been no harm done."

MacDonald stood, feet apart, his arm outstretched grasping Penney's shoulder.

"What's this about?" Knowlton asked, getting up from where he and Oliver were studying the map of the cove they'd spread out on a barrel. He pushed his way between MacDonald and Penney.

"Your boy here, he's been playing dress up with my daughter!" MacDonald side-stepped Harvey and went toe-to-toe with Penney. "I ought to lay him flat right where he stands."

"Ah, Captain, we was only just talking." Penney gave a warm smile, his hands open in a friendly gesture.

"And don't forget the singing." All turned to see Richards swinging his head and pretending to play the violin.

"You knew about his sneaking around?" MacDonald spun towards the other.

Ready to fight, Richards jumped up. "Ah, only about ten minutes before you did!"

"Hold it. Quiet down." Captain Knowlton motioned to the crates. "Have a seat and explain it to me. MacDonald, you start."

The others shook their heads listening to the story. Webber complained about how Penney could have had them all thrown in a Province lockup if their plan was to be discovered. Captain Knowlton, madder than all the others combined, kept his cool. He needed the full crew and he couldn't discipline Penney who was near to a volunteer anyhow.

All were silent as the captain circled around the table. "Penney, your actions were likely to put this entire venture at risk." He looked at MacDonald. "What do you think Bonnie knows of his identity?"

"Ah. Nothing. I talked to her on the ride to and from town. I told her I knew him to be a traveling salesman."

"A salesman! That's the best you could come up with for me!"

"In those dandy clothes you were wearing, I could have made it worse."

There was a round of laughter.

"You ought to be glad MacDonald came along. It's a good thing." Richards elbowed Penney. "You'd have been libel to get us all caught. It's a fool thing you've been doing with the daughter."

"You met with her more than once?" Knowlton pounded his fists on the table across from Penney.

"Three times."

The captain's right fist slammed down again. He paced. When he stopped, he came to his point. "Tomorrow will be the night we sail the *Horton* for Glo'ster."

Each man had something to say along the lines of being glad the time had come.

"And based on the actions of Penney towards my only daughter, I'll thank the tide, the sky, and the wind if she may cooperate while most of the cutter men are still away in Halifax. I'd not be comfortable with him sneaking around behind my back any longer."

"Captain MacDonald, that's not how it was." Penney threw open his arms.

"Enough, Penney!" yelled Knowlton. "We've plans to go over. Men, we're here one more night and day. That means you are all to stay away from Bonnie MacDonald and any other girl that happens around." He gave a glance at Oliver. "You're all to keep here in the barn until we leave for the harbor." He motioned at MacDonald.

The smuggler rose. He pulled bales of hay aside to reveal the trap door in the floor which had already been discovered by the men. A lantern in one hand, he unlocked the hasp, and descended the ladder into the wood-lined, dirt hole.

"Here, here!" sang the men in seeing what he brought up with him.

"Compliments of his majesty in honor of your brave Captain Harvey Knowlton." MacDonald poured out a round of rum, filling each man's cup to the rim.

"Ah, I thank you, Captain." McCloud smacked his lips.

Knowlton took his mug in his hand, all the while knowing MacDonald would be expected to be paid for the drinks. "You men, I want to thank you. You have been more than patient and accommodating in taking part in this endeavor."

"Sailor Penney excluded, you might say." Richards held his mug, ready to toast.

"We'll let the error of Penney's ways go. United we will be from here out." Captain Knowlton raised his mug high over his head. "To Glo'ster! We are to teach Johnny a lesson he will soon not forget. It is not just for me we are taking a stand. All American fishermen deserve the right to fish in open waters."

"Here! Here!" There was a moment of silence as the rum was drained. In unison, the empty mugs banged down on the table.

MacDonald poured another round.

"This will be your last sleep, men. Tomorrow night and the day after you may see little time to close your eyes." Knowlton motioned to his nephew. "Oliver has something to share."

"Gather round, boys." Oliver stood over the map displayed on the barrel top. "Here's the chart of the harbor. You must all commit to memory the land markers we've indicated and the depths of the channel at those positions. A rogue wind, a slacked sail, a missed degree of the wheel, and the *Horton* will run aground. We will need eyes to watch all sides of the vessel." He ran his finger over the depth numbers calling out the fathoms. "You see how the river drops off. Here. And here."

In silence the crew listened to the details explained to them. MacDonald added his own expertise on the challenges to navigate the shallow harbor—particularly so on the lowest of tides. They heard of all the preparations that had gone on for the past week.

On the back of the map, MacDonald drew them a diagram of the inside of the warehouse; including the stairwells, the sleeping quarters, and where he figured their sails to be. "I've been through this warehouse myself many a times. The sleeping quarters for the men are on the far side of the building through many rooms. So long as you don't drop a pulley block, and you keep your wits about you, I'll do my part to keep them occupied."

"And how would you be doing that?"

"You have another drink there, Richards, and you'll see what His Majesty's rum can do!" MacDonald poured another round. "I happen to know those men enjoy a long drink."

"I trust once we are at sea again, our rum rations shall be restored to normal?" Webber shook his empty cup.

Captain Knowlton shook his head when MacDonald went to fill the mug. "That's the last for tonight. Once we're at sail, things will be more settled. You sailors will be back in the routine."

"The rum included?" Extending his empty mug, Richards tested to see if he might get another taste.

"Yes. But not tonight."

"Captain, should we be noticed, and an alarm rung in the town, what will we do?"

The question from Webber was on everyone's mind. They all waited on the answer.

"I for one will fight." Oliver raised a fist.

"Won't we be out gunned? Even if there are only a few cutter men left here at the harbor?" asked Gillis.

Once again, MacDonald went down through the trap door. He returned with a locked strong-box. Inside were five six-shot revolvers.

"I won't ask any of you men to shoot. In fact, these guns are to be a last resort. For self-defense." Slowly, Harvey looked at each man. "If there is any one of you who has had a change of mind for what we need to do, speak now."

There wasn't one among them who spoke out. Out in the barnyard an owl hooted.

"I'm with you until the end, Captain Knowlton." Richards stood up. All stood and repeated the same.

Questions were asked and details were clarified. Since only Oliver and Harvey had sailed on the *Horton* before, the crew wanted to know how she handled in the wind. Knowlton asked his nephew to brief the men and he took MacDonald aside.

"This nugget is for the cannon and guns. We won't be able to return them to you." He watched as MacDonald rolled the nugget around his palm. "I assure you, the sale of that single piece of stone will more than cover the artillery. The remainder of the payment for your help will be sent as agreed, once I can transfer it to you."

"Aye. But how am I to sell it without raising suspicions?"

The Gloucester captain was surprised. "You? A smuggler of the first degree, not able to sell that off?" The compliment hit the mark.

MacDonald pointed his finger at Knowlton's chest. "Of course, I can! Never let it be known that Tom MacDonald doesn't have connections." He pocketed the gold.

Rum and Cake

Sailors, they've worked at sea through the ages,
  those who obey commands are first raters.
A good captain knows, rum is as good as wages,
  but too much, and the men are useless freighters.

Sunday – October 8, 1871 – 4 p.m.
Guysborough Harbor

Allister MacDonald knocked on the side door that led to the cutter warehouse barracks. "Wire and delivery from Captain Tory." He waited. He pounded again—harder. The door opened to a revenue cutter seaman who looked as if he'd been asleep.

"What is it, Allister?"

"This wire came across from Halifax." He handed the man the paper. "And this box, I was given instructions to deliver it." He pointed to the crate he'd set aside.

"What is it?" asked the seaman who was unfolding the paper.

"I wouldn't know. I only type what comes over the clicks." He held out his hand, not that he should get a tip for this particular delivery, but he was playing his part.

"Oh, buggers. With me having the luck of answering the knock, while the others are on holiday in Halifax! Now's you want to pick my pocket." He handed Allister a coin.

"Good evening then." Allister turned. He felt like skipping down the street, but he held his calm.

The seaman pulled the box in, closed the door, and his lips moved as he silently read the telegram.

'All went splendid at the ceremony in Halifax. Each of you will also be getting prize money, but to thank you for keeping watch, please enjoy this bit of drink and cakes. I shall set sail from Halifax on Monday with a stop in Canso. Expect us to arrive on the tide Wednesday.
-- Captain J. Tory.'

He pried open the box. "Hey, mates, get a load of what the good captain sent us! We can make our own celebration."

By eight that evening, the men who were in charge of guarding the harbor had eaten all of the rum cake and had washed it down with an entire jug of rum. If anyone had walked by along the street beyond their window, they would have thought a deep-sounding fog horn had been left on inside the building.

Sunday October 8, 1871 – 9:00 p.m.
Tom MacDonald's Barn

"Your brother-in-law delivered the telegram alright then?" Knowlton bolted the barn door behind MacDonald as he entered.

"Aye. Sure did. Along with that rum cake I've had fermenting for six months. And the rum, I took it from Johnny's own warehouse stores after he took it from me." MacDonald winked and let out a satisfied laugh. He then gloated to them about how he'd put another one over on Tory and his men.

"I wished you had brought us another bottle of that rum, MacDonald." Richards slung his pack over his shoulder.

The others, readying for their march, added their wishes for the same.

"Hold on, men. We're just about out of this thing, but the hardest is yet to come. Once we've put Canso behind us, I promise, your rum rations will be restored."

"Three cheers!" exclaimed Penney.

"Shh!" MacDonald raised his hands. "I'll remind ye, my daughter is still up to the house. We don't want any noise alerting her."

Richards noticed Penney stealing a glance out the barn door towards the back porch of the house. Sensing someone watching, Penney turned to see the knowing grin on Richards' face. To be leaving the girl, without even saying goodbye, or her knowing his real name, was paining Penney. He hoped she'd understand.

It was half-past the hour of ten, when out the back door they slipped—one at a time—to the path that ran through the woods. At the feel of the northern, crisp October air, the men turned up their coat collars. Their breath turned white on the exhale, floating up as a fog shrouding the stars above their heads.

With the men spread out, MacDonald led the way. Harvey Knowlton was directly behind him; the pistols in his pack. The others kept a distance of ten yards between them, in order to reduce any chance of a group of men being seen walking together. Oliver was at the rear. Each carried a sack of spare clothes and emergency rations of food and water. They also had a supply of tobacco, which MacDonald had sold each of them for a good profit.

Before the march began, Captain Knowlton made it clear there was to be no confrontation with the locals. They'd only resort to defense if they were accosted while sailing his ship out to sea.

When they reached the crest of the hill outside of town, MacDonald had them gather around. He indicated the flags on the masts of the moored schooners. "She's blowing northwest. That'll be a favorable wind."

"Ah, and what a sweet sea breeze it is," said Gillis.

His mates nodded. Almost as one they took a deep breath of the salt air and looked out over the sea they longed to be on once again.

The men each took a position sitting at the base of a different tree, their shadows blending into the landscape. Oliver recalled the afternoons he'd spent with Alice on the hill. He fondly remembered her soft voice as she read to him under the same maple tree they'd taken to sitting under.

It was near midnight when finally they observed the remaining lights in the village houses get extinguished. The nightwatchman from the *Horton*, ascended from below deck and made his way home at the final bell from the tower.

The men went at once, staying close to the walls of the buildings, to retrieve the sails from the warehouse. Through the backdoor, opened with a key MacDonald produced, they slipped through the building. MacDonald stood guard, an oar by his side, at the door which led to the barracks where the seamen were still deep asleep, evidenced by the snores from their bunkroom.

On the second floor the sails were found furled and neatly bound. With one trip completed to the *Horton*, Gillis, Richards, and Penney returned for the remaining canvas.

"Stop!" came a hushed command. The captain met his crew as they were exiting the warehouse. He explained the bad news. "We've the wrong sails. They are not of the *Horton*!" remarked Captain Knowlton. "We must search again."

With valuable time slipping away, they searched the floors of the warehouse. A door was discovered behind crates. It was locked.

"Only a truly paranoid cutter captain would go through such lengths," stated Knowlton.

By this time the men were getting weary and anxious. A long metal bar was found and the door was pried open. A narrow staircase led to the attic.

"Captain, these *must* be our sails! They're the only ones here," stated Gillis.

For the second time that night, they went to lugging the sails—main, fore, topsail, staysail, fore topsail, jib topsail, jib, and jumbo—down three flights of creaking stairs. There was no time for rest. Songs usually sung while rigging a vessel were thought of in mind only.

Even with nine men fitting sails and walking the deck of the *Horton*, the sounds in Guysborough Harbor were the normal ones of the night. Buoy bells clanked. Rigging chinked in time to the rise and fall of the waves over the water. Only Tom MacDonald, who'd spent many nights as the only one awake in the harbor, could hear the out-of-place thumps, clangs, and groans of men fitting out a vessel.

Under the direction of Oliver, Captain Knowlton left the work to the men. He then went to pulling the Canadian flag and, in its place, raised the rightful American colors once again. The Dominion emblem he saved for a special purpose. Then he inspected his ship. The stores of food and water were still on board. He requested Oliver to take an inventory. In the captain's quarters, he found no instruments or charts had been left—not even a barometer. He only had his compass, and the harbor map Oliver had stolen, now marked with their additional depth measurements and shore markings.

"It's missing!"

Knowlton turned to see his nephew at the bottom of the companionway. "What is?"

"The *Horton* rum." Oliver pointed towards the forward galley. "We had two dozen jugs stored in the locker when we were boarded."

The captain frowned. At first, he was of the mind to say, *'what did it matter.'* They were nearly away from Guysborough. "Anything else from the stores missing?"

"No, sir. Tory even kept the ice replenished." Oliver read from a paper he'd taken of the inventory. "My check confirms there are six quarts of molasses, forty pounds of salted pork, plenty of flour, three crates of hard crackers, rice, and oatmeal. For vegetables and fruit there are carrots, potatoes, onions, and beets, along with dried oranges, beans, apples and peas. All the sugar, spices, tea, coffee and condensed milk seems to be untouched from before we were taken. In addition there are the ten barrels of fresh water. Added to that we have the eggs and brisket purchased from MacDonald."

"That ought to get eight men to Glo'ster." Captain Knowlton stared at his chart, focusing on every depth measurement in order. He added, "So long as we don't have to sail to the mid-Atlantic to avoid a chase."

His nephew did not move. "The men, sir. They've been more than patient and helpful. Especially for not being a Knowlton crew."

Harvey lifted his finger from the chart. He knew what Oliver was getting at. While he had a lot on his mind at the moment, he quickly realized that a week or more at sea, with nothing to drink for the men but strong tea water, could become troublesome on many fronts. "Go to MacDonald. See what he can do." He handed Oliver the last of his bills, figuring he'd have no need for the money at sea.

The mate found MacDonald preparing his dory. He was placing the oars between the thole pins. At his feet were a dozen lanterns. The old smuggler only had to hear a few words from Oliver and he placed the oars back to the bottom of the boat. "Follow me, lad. It 'twill only take ten minutes, and then I can go float these lanterns."

The two walked to the rear of the fish house. MacDonald lifted the loose plank of fencing along the alley. "Come on." He beckoned Oliver through. Once on the other side, he held Oliver's shoulder. "Seeing as you're leaving town, I don't mind letting you see this. But should anyone ever find out, you're the only other person that knows of it."

Taking a large skeleton key from his coat, MacDonald pushed aside a small board and inserted the key. A door, fashioned from the paneling of the building, swung outward. He indicated for Oliver to not say a word. Inside there were crates the size of soap boxes. He handed two to Oliver and picked up two himself. They hustled back to the ship.

"It isn't stealing if that's what you're thinking," huffed MacDonald when he handed his crate to Oliver over the bulwarks. "All that there—in that room, 'tis mine. Or mostly mine. The room is the back room of the cutter warehouse office. What Tory takes, I take back."

"The crew will be much obliged." Oliver tilted his head to the men who were finishing with the sails.

"Aye. It ain't free. I'll be expecting the captain to send me the money for it."

Oliver felt his left eye twinge. He knew the gold nugget his uncle had given MacDonald was more than enough to cover his expenses, the added jugs of rum included. Yet, he handed MacDonald the extra cash.

The smuggler took the time to count it. "Will do for now. Tell Captain Knowlton I'll settle up with him by letter." MacDonald turned down to the dory. "Good luck to, ye. I'll not light the first lantern until I see you're away from the wharf," he said as he checked the matches stored under the brim of his hat. Oliver watched him pull away, his oars not making a sound.

"Mate Oliver, this will never do." Gillis had a pole over the stern of the Horton. "There's less than three feet of tide here."

"You heard the captain back in the barn. He especially chose tonight *on account of* the low tide. These cantankerous cousins of John Bull would never figure American sailors could steal a boat out of this mudhole tonight."

"I don't know, I suspect they might be right. It's already nearing two o'clock. It'll be another three hours before the tide is in enough to float her. How are we to be free of this before daybreak?" asked Gillis.

Webber, McCloud, and Dyer had joined them at the rail. Oliver looked over the side into the black water.

Dreams of Memories

Her dreams—they held the answer
to the mystery of the man.
Was he really her romancer,
or someone harboring a secret plan?

Monday – October 9, 1871 – 2 a.m.
The MacDonald Home

A streak of moonlight found its way between the curtains of Bonnie's window. It may have been that light, or the owl hoot, that woke her from her dream. She'd been in a pleasant memory of when as young girls, she and Alice had dressed in men's clothes and played at being townsfolk and storekeepers. They'd found the outfits while her father was at sea, in a part of his back barn she was told not to play in.

Now awake, she sat up in her bed and parted the curtain. The light from the crescent moon was spreading long shadows over the side yard. She hesitated getting out from under her covers. She knew it was one of those cold Nova Scotian autumn nights, before the first coastal frost, but already making one wish for a warm fire in the stove. The air was so clear it permitted the stars to shine as pin-lights, focused on each tree top. Pulling on her robe, she slipped into the hall. The door to her parents' room was closed. Down the stairs she went, her bare feet on the cold pine treads not making a sound. The rooms were awash in a gray-blue from the light passing through the bare windows.

In the back hall, she lifted a lantern from the hook. She lit it and kept the valve open only enough to allow a dim beam to escape. Above her father's coat hook, she reached for his tinderbox on the shelf. She slid open the false bottom and removed a key.

Avoiding the crunch of the pebbly dirt path to the barn, she kept to the grass on the edge. The blades were stiff. Her feet left impressions in the dew behind her. She passed the main barn and went beyond to her father's workshop. The windows were covered in sail cloth, as her father always had them. She heard no sounds within. The lock clicked when she turned the key. Slowly she opened the door, remembering the exact angle the hinge would squeak, she pulled it fast, as one would pull a bandage. The door had no time to whine.

In the back storeroom of her father's workshop she came upon a plank table. Cups and dishes were set along the length. In some of the cups, there was still tea or coffee. The water pot on the oil burner was warm. Alarmed, she searched the barn. Blankets were folded, rolled, or simply thrown over trunks. She stood at the back door—listening. There wasn't a sound in the woods.

With her dream clear in her mind, she remembered the outfit the man was wearing. Her memory was of Alice once wearing nearly the same; the pant legs and arms twice as long as her friend could fill. The trunk of clothes was where they'd found it years ago when the two girls had rummaged through the items. Lying just under the lid, unevenly folded, were the clothes Billy-of-the-lane had been wearing. The black pants were covered in smudges of yellow pollen, and to them where stuck hundreds of tiny seed pods. Sitting atop a faded newspaper were the shoes; one laced with the ribbon that had a few days prior been on her basket. Another long coil of red ribbon, with white lace fringe, had been cut, the end showing a fraying. She reached around the back of her head to release the ribbon holding her pony-tail. In her hands she held an end of each ribbon—bringing them close together. A gasp escaped from her lips.

She gently closed the lid and hurried back to the house. In her room, she sat in a chair by the window, her feet curled under her. Her heavy nightdress and the comforter she had wrapped herself in wasn't enough to stop her shivering; she shook not from the cold, but more from the surprise of her discovery.

Bonnie stood and walked across the hallway; she turned the knob to her father's room. She found his bed empty. Back to the ell she ran, no longer concerned about her feet clapping on the floorboards. She found his coat and cap were gone. Up the stairs she ran to her room to dress. On her way to the front door, as she was passing the sitting room rocker, she threw her mother's quilt over her shoulders.

"We'll Warp Her Out"

"Said brave Knowlton to his crew:
'If you will follow me,
We'll take our vessel back again,
whate'er the cost may be.

We'll stand by one another,
like brothers brave and true,
We'll show those thievish Britishers
what Yankee blood can do.'"

Monday – October 9, 1871 – 2:30 a.m.
Guysborough Harbor

Captain Harvey Knowlton stood on the quarterdeck. It was now certain that the good Captain Osler of the *Sea Witch* had given him a competent crew of Gloucester sailors. The men worked without question, without delay, without making a noise. Each knew that to be discovered by any Guysborough fisherman, revenue cutter seaman, or some sleepless resident walking the wharf would place their entire escape in jeopardy. For seeing the shadows of seven men on the deck of the *Horton*, in the middle of the night, would surely raise alarm.

Captain Knowlton called Gillis, McCloud, Dyer, and Oliver to the captain's cabin. Gillis reported the sails were bent on the booms. Oliver noted the tide was yet too low for the ship to be moved. The captain opened the bag provided from MacDonald.

He handed each of them a pistol. "Here in the harbor, these are only to be used as warning shots, should the need arise, in order to buy our time. Should we be found out, and all hope lost, I want the ship burned. Johnny is not to have the satisfaction of this vessel."

"Aye aye, sir," said they all as one.

"Men, I had chosen this night for the low tide, knowing the Canadian officers would think it infeasible for the ship to navigate the channel, and few fishermen would be going out at this hour. Our time has come to sail."

The crew took his words without explanation. The ropes from the pilings were thrown to the deck of the *Horton*. The windlass was greased in order there be no telltale grating of the gear-teeth. When the anchor ran against the bow, a thump sounded across the harbor. Richards and Penney made ready with the warps. In a borrowed seine boat, the hemp was run to the available mooring of the Canadian cutter *Sweepstakes*.

On the row, with the oars wrapped in old shirts and rags, Richards whispered a chant. Penney, McCloud, Dyer, and Webber joined in, taking up the harmony.

> "Hoo-oo-rah! And up she rises!
> Hoo-oo-rah! And up she rises!
> *(Hoo-oo-rah! And up she rises!)*
> Early in the mornin'!
> What shall we do with a homesick sailor?
> Put him in the seine-boat and make him haul'er,
> *(Put him in the seine-boat and make him haul'er,)*
> So early in the mornin'!

"Quiet!" warned Oliver, in a hushed command.

With the mud on the bottom of the channel slick as grease, and just enough water for movement, they warped the schooner.

Their turns of the windlass were timed without a "Ho," or an "All hands, turn." The buoy bell in the channel was used to both time their rounds and conceal their grunts. Slack in the line was winched in until the massive seventy-ton ship inched across the mud below. The water ran brown along the hull.

Out in the center channel, with the rise of the incoming tide nearly indistinguishable, Knowlton could see the outline of MacDonald in his dory as he went about his task. The paraffin and candlewax lanterns he was setting were outfitted in floating bowls the men had whittled during their week in the barn. The beacons were anchored with a rock weight at the edge of the deep water. Each lamp was placed in accordance of the soundings that had been made of the channel.

On the captain's signal, the crew raised the mainsail. There was no call from the helm to "Make ready at the main," or the yelled response, **"Ready at the main."** Halyards were pulled at the raise of a hand. The hoops crept up the mast. Every clank and creak were acknowledged with a look towards the town for any movement. Windows were watched for signs of a lamp.

A path of light guided Captain Knowlton at the helm. Oliver, at his side, read off each reading from their chart.

"Looks as if we've a clean pair of heels, Captain," remarked McCloud.

The captain kept his gaze ahead on the beacons. "Let's make past Canso before we make any claims."

"Aye, Captain." McCloud used a spyglass to scan the shore.

"Ready to make foresail," stated the captain, to Oliver. The mate walked forward. A wave was given for the *Ready*. The sail went up.

At the cove across from McCaul Point, MacDonald pointed his bow to shore. He stood in the dory and saluted to Captain Knowlton and the crew of the *Horton* as they passed. A bit of moisture welled up in his eyes; his throat was tight. It wasn't on account that he'd helped the Yankees; rather he felt proud to have foiled Captain Tory once again. This was his biggest revenge in all his years, and one in which he'd have to keep to himself. For there'd been no alarm rung in the town, and, as far as he knew, no other person had witnessed the American schooner sail away.

Upon reaching the clearing on the hill, Bonnie stopped running to catch her breath. The snap of sails carried on the breeze caught her attention. She turned toward the bay. The ghostly image of a vessel against the night sky drifted across the water. A main topsail lifted. And then a fore topsail rose. The ship took on speed. A tear dropped to her cheek. The vessel's stern ran between Stony Patch and Peart Point.

She leaned against a tree; her body wrapped snugly in the quilt. A streak of moonlight glowed across the bay. "May you have following winds," she whispered, and then to the tune, she sang, "Billy Boy, Billy Boy."

Silently, Tom MacDonald rowed the dory through the harbor and collected the lanterns. At the now empty wharf, he smoked his pipe. All was calm in the harbor. He again was the sole nightwatchman of Guysborough.

When he arrived home, he looked in to see Bonnie sleeping in her bed. He went to put his workshop in order. Wanting to be in town when the *Horton* was discovered missing, he quickly fried eggs and warmed what tea was left in the pot.

He sat at the bench along the table, a half dozen tin mugs were positioned around him. It was a tea party for one. Flies buzzed over the dirty plates of dried chowder and crumbs of bread. The door creaking startled him, and he reached for the knife on his belt.

"Good morning, Father." Bonnie stood with the quilt wrapped around her shoulders.

He relaxed and spoke in a rhyme.

> "Oh, what brings you out so early?
> Bonnie, my Bonnie.
> Oh, what brings you from bed this fine morn',
> Daughter, my Daughter?"

He sipped his tea.

She played along, taking in the disarray of his workshop as she sang.

> "Oh, I've been to the bay,
> where the waters run green,
> and the purple sky looms
> o'er the rising tide."

The tin mug stopped midway on its way back to the table. His eyebrows raised, he asked, still in song,
> "What did you see, my daughter dear?
> What did you see on this morn',
> Bonnie, my Bonnie?"

> "Oh, I saw a Yankee ship go sailing by.
> Ov'er the water she schooned
> under the stars so high.
> The water she parted by and by,
> while the shrill wind caused her sail to strain."

Her voice, cracked, and her song ending in a hoarse whisper.

He nodded, knowingly, without addressing the glazed-wetness in her eyes. "I've got be goin' along to town. Don't you worry about this." He spread his arms to the mess in the workshop. "I'll straighten' it later, my Bonnie."

She followed him outside to the bright sunlight.

He latched the door with the hasp. "Keep this door locked today. We'll talk over supper. I've got to first ride to Queensport to fetch your mother home." He kissed his daughter on the forehead, but his thoughts were on what needed to be done. His first business was to visit his brother-in-law to ensure the planned wire had been sent at first light.

From the barnyard, Bonnie watched her father hitch his team and drive off. Slowly she walked to collect the eggs for her basket. Even the birds, if they were apt to notice these things, would have been saddened to hear her song.

"Twice on my lips, Billy boy, he pressed a kiss,
and now my heart shrinks in an awful bliss."

She looked to the bay.
A shrill wind ran up from the cove. The salty breeze ran over her lips.

"And o'er the wind, he sent me—a goodbye kiss."

A Bold and Yankee Trick

Come all you Province men,
　　and hear of Glo'ster's hero son.
I'll tell you of the Yankee trick
　　played in eighteen hundred seventy one.

Monday – October 9, 1871 – Morning
Gloucester, Massachusetts

The day began as a typical one for coastal New England in the fall. Change was in the air. Leaves were showing hints of orange and yellow, some fluttered to the ground mixing with the still lush green of the grass. Over the inner harbor, layered between the warmer water and the cool air, floated a blanket of mist. Yellow sunbursts reflected the morning dew dripping from the evergreen branches as the beams of light illuminated Cape Ann.

Frank Sweeney wasn't aware of the contrasts on his walk from the boathouse. He focused his attention on which vessels were out, which had returned to port in the night, and which crews hadn't yet rolled out to get to work. His nose was tuned to the smells of progress, not the wet leaves along the roadside indicating the all too soon change of the weather—the coming months when the schooners would be encased in ice from deck to mast, the days one could walk from Smith Cove, across Rocky Neck, and over to Harbor Cove on the frozen water. For Frank, he had other things on his mind than the season. Besides, things were far from typical in the offices of the *McKenzie-Knowlton-Horton* firm and along their wharves.

He shuffled through the stack of mail and newspapers that he picked up at the post and telegram office on his way to the warehouse. He paused at the top of the hill. From between the letters he found a slip of paper with the outside addressed to him. He unfolded it.

Mr. Frank Sweeney
Rocky Neck, Gloucester, Massachusetts

Cousin Sweeney:

We have sailed with Gusto.

M. Burnham

All along the street to the wharf there was an interest in Frank's stepping. Merchants and fishermen who remarked their usual *'Mornin'* to Frank waited for him to stop and talk. He hurried by without a wave.

The door to the office flew back against the wall.

Joseph's head snapped to the bang. "Good mornin,' Frank." Any interesting headlines?" He walked from his brother's desk to the table where Frank always placed the dailies. "What is it?" asked Joseph, when Frank hadn't moved, but stood breathing heavily.

Frank held out the telegram in his hand. His smile and excitement too much to state what it was about.

Joseph read the wire. His gaze rose slowly to Frank. "How do you figure? I mean, how did Harvey send this?" He paced the room. "Ah, never mind." He slapped Frank on the shoulder. "I'll run up and inform Edward."

Monday – October 9, 1871 – 7:00 a.m.
Guysborough Harbor, Nova Scotia

"Appears Captain Tory has sailed the Yankee ship out under the cover of night." The owner of the mercantile thumbed over his shoulder, indicating the empty berth to the two men waiting on his porch. The two were of the regulars not excited over the mining rush that led the others to follow Davis up the river.

"We was just discussing it," said the older salt of the two. "With the captain and most of his crew in Halifax, I don't see how he done it. Set a good surprise he did."

A noticeably smaller contingent of the Guysborough Mercantile unofficial town council filed in and huddled on the seats in front of the pot-bellied stove. It was silent while they waited for the heat. No gossip ever began until the coffee was poured. They lit their pipes in the meantime and were transfixed on the flames crawling up the pipe.

The door slammed open.

The owner halted his grinding of the coffee beans.

"You men!" Two Canadian revenue cutter sailors stood in the doorway. They were each fumbling to button their blue wool coats. The red stripe where the buttons were to connect from one side to the other was out of alignment with cross-buttoned holes. One sailor's cap was on sideways.

"Did you see what happened in the harbor?" demanded the taller of the two.

"What do you mean?" asked the store owner, turning on his knees from where he was adding wood to the stove.

"The Yankee schooner, the *Horton*. She's been stolen."

"I knew something couldn't have been right," declared the old salt. He rose to go have a look, as if he'd imagined the vessel being gone earlier. The others followed him out. The two seamen pushed their way through to the street again.

The wharf, beginning to get busy with the shore fishermen, fish buyers, and townsfolk, was crowded with excited talk and hand-waving. They all knew a ship the size of the *Horton* would require a deep tide to escape, and it was only now past flood.

"Must only have recently just sailed," yelled a man looking beyond the wharf at the river.

"Can't be far, likely right in the bay," said another, pointing to get the cutter men's attention.

The seamen ran to the home of the telegraph operator. They banged on the door to his attached office. "McGregor! Allister McGregor, wake up. Open this office at once!" The door opened and Allister welcomed them in. They demanded he send a message to which Allister stuttered excuses.

"What do you mean you can't send a wire!" declared the seaman. He examined the telegraph equipment. It was all disconnected with parts strewn over the counter.

Allister McGregor explained to the cutter seamen who desired to wire Halifax, that he was in the process of cleaning the equipment. "Gentlemen, the lever spring has worn out and the connections must be dusted and oiled. Shouldn't take longer than seventy minutes to be operational again."

They commanded he repair the equipment immediately and inform them at once. The ranking officer slammed the door. "We must get word to Captain Tory!" The two were in conversation when they noticed across the street, at the end of the road, the door at their mate's home opening. They leaped from the steps in unison and hustled up the street.

Driven out by the commotion down near the wharf, the nightwatchman of the *Horton*, stepped from his door. He stumbled over a stack of books left on the uppermost step of his threshold. He stared at the books now strewn across the dirt. A sound of surprise passed from his lips. It came initially from the shock of books being left out-of-doors; treasures he'd just kicked with his boot in his carelessness. But, more so, for he recognized the books. The collection of blue and green cloth covers were the same titles he'd placed on the table in the captain's quarters aboard the *Horton*. They were Melville's titles—*Typee*, *Omoo*, *Mardi*, *Redburn* and *White-Jacket*, books to be next in his reading order. He crouched down to pick them up. From between the cover and the first page of *Typee* a paper was showing. The beat of his heart increased as he read the note.

Dear sir of the *Horton* night watch:

For more than a week I've seen you reading the books from the captain's library on my vessel. You drank my rum, ate my bread, and made use of the *Horton's* library as your own. Due to your fondness of reading, please accept these titles as my gift to you. Because of your punctual bedtime hour, you unknowingly aided in the recovery of my ship. For that, I am much obliged.
Sincerely,
Harvey Knowlton, Jr. —
The McKenzie-Knowlton-Horton Company
Gloucester, Massachusetts
UNITED STATES OF AMERICA

He bent down and picked up the volumes.
"Hibbert! What is the meaning of this?" The tall seaman extended a finger at the books the watchman was holding. "Are

you to tell us, your negligence of duty was caused by more of your reading!"

Watchman Hibbert looked from the accusing finger, to the books in his hands, and back to the faces of his fellow seamen. He still wasn't sure of the full implications of the note and the commotion. "I, I…." he stammered.

"Come with us!"

It was true. The *Horton* had cleared Guysborough Harbor. Fishermen had rowed out in their skiffs around McCaul Point and reported no ship in sight out in the bay. The seamen stood on the wharf trying to figure how it was accomplished.

"But, but . . . it was lowest tide last night. I was on watch until midnight, as usual." Hibbert pleaded his case.

"Your head was probably so far in a book they could have sailed with you reading by lantern light in the captain's quarters!" The senior seaman poked at Hibbert's chest.

"And what of you two?" Hibbert wasn't going to take the blame. His orders from Tory were for a watch on the *Horton* until midnight. Captain Tory had been confident that no Yankee skipper could clear the shallow harbor, and certainly not in the dark. "Where were the two of you last night such that they were able to sneak the sails from under your noses in the warehouse?"

A hushed murmur went through the crowd.

Hibbert's point was not lost on the two men who had been instructed to alternate their watch. Each could not recall if they'd disposed of the remnants of the cakes and the empty rum jugs.

"Where's that rapscallion Handron?"

A booming voice came from along the wharf.

All looked over to see Davis and another man securing a dory. Their faces were smeared with dirt and ash; their clothes covered in river-mud.

It was admitted that the miner Zadok Handron hadn't been on people's minds that morning. Once reminded of the miner, it was odd to them that he hadn't been seen, as he'd been, every morning by this hour around the town.

A quick search found his dory tied up on the mudflat in front of the fish house. His mining gear and outfit were haphazardly stored in the boat.

Davis went immediately to searching through the ditty bag. He fell back on the dory seat with his discovery of a note.

> Davis, you old captain brave and bold,
> 　　do not cry, do not cry,
> All you old captains brave and bold,
> 　　oh, how I hear you cry,
> You old captains brave and bold,
> 　　though now it seems uncontrol'd,
> Don't for the sake of gold,
> 　　lose your souls, lose your souls,
> Don't for the sake of gold,
> 　　lose your souls.
> 　　　　Zadok Handron of Gloucestertown

" 'Tis was a bold and Yankee trick he played on us." Davis threw Handron's pick-axe into the muck.

"There's only one Guysborough skipper unaccounted for who could have sailed that vessel last evening!" remarked the old salt. "Would show he's as good as smuggling out, as he's in."

"And there he is now," shouted Davis. He jumped from the dory on seeing Tom MacDonald driving his team along the harbor road toward the wharf.

The cutter seamen ran to hold the bridle of the team. "MacDonald, where might you have been this last evening?"

With no doubt, MacDonald acted surprised to hear the ship was sailed out. He paced the wharf calling out the already discussed facts of low tide, the darkness, and the narrow channel.

"It couldn't be done. Not by Yankees!" His indignation roused the locals in their disbelief. He turned his attention to the three cutter seamen. He made a side remark about the two with the smell of rum on their breaths when they talked; and, from the other holding the stack of books, he coerced a confession that they were from the *Horton's* own library shelf.

Then MacDonald called attention to the *Horton's* hidden sails. He asked the guards, "And how did those Yankees manage to break in to the warehouse under your noses to steal the sails?" They looked at one another, knowing that they hadn't yet made any such inspection.

In a loud voice, for all the gatherers to hear, MacDonald continued, "It seems it would be near impossible for a crew of men to walk throughout that old, wooden, creaky warehouse— carrying hundreds of pounds of sail, and go unheard by two guards. Are we not sure this isn't some government rouse? And the ship, like the one before, the *Lily Rose Snow*, hasn't been smuggled to England? And Handron, a redder herring I've never seen." He straightened his tam o' shanter. "Maybe he was even a British captain."

Rumblings circled through the crowd.

The smuggler of Guysborough had cast enough doubt on the situation that all the men on the wharf were in a more confused state than before he'd arrived. The three guards huddled together at the door to the warehouse. MacDonald watched at an angle as they held a joint conference. It appeared they were in no hurry to get back to the telegraph office and wire Captain Tory, for even they were unclear if the ship had been stolen, or sailed by their own men. If it had in fact been stolen, they were surely responsible. And if not, wouldn't Captain Tory have informed them of his plan to abscond the ship? They were paralyzed to inaction.

The watchman, living in a world of tales and fanciful characters, remarked, "MacDonald could be right. He always seems to know more than he lets on. It could be Captain Tory has played his hand once again to foil the Yankees from regaining their schooner."

Still in disbelief the sails had been taken, the three entered the warehouse to inspect the storage room. Behind the once blocked and locked door, the loft was empty but for a flag—it was the Canadian flag that had flown on the *Horton*. Wrapped within was the head of a halibut.

Two streets over, Allister waited by his telegraph. The first town busybody arrived shortly to send a note to their relatives in Canso. It read, *"Be on the lookout for the Horton. The Gloucester men have stolen her back!"*

From the wire office at Canso, the news spread to Halifax even before the *Horton* guards, regaining their sense of duty, returned to Allister in order to place their official wire. When the Halifax telegraph operator sent word to the coastal cutter station, the message missed the recipient. Captain Tory and his men had already sailed for home on the *Sweepstakes*. The Halifax officer, not wanting to shame Tory, especially following his recent commendation, delayed informing his own superiors. When they finally were made aware, on account of their own embarrassment to the Dominion, their continued delay served Knowlton and the crew of the *Horton*—at least for the immediate hours following departure.

Call Out the Guard

Monday – October 9, 1871
Gloucester, Massachusetts

By late afternoon the news of the escaped *Horton* had spread along the northeast coast from St. John to Bangor and Portland to New York. The front pages of the afternoon editions declared:

Boston Courier:
Gloucester's *Horton* Retaken from the Dominion.

New York Herald:
Seized Gloucester Fishing Schooner Sailing Home.

Cape Ann Advertiser:
Horton's Gallant Crew Teaches Johnny a Lesson.

In Gloucester, the attitude wasn't one of complacency or immediate celebration. The seasoned sailors, skippers, and owners knew the trip could take more than a week under fair seas and a following wind. They were well aware that Captain Knowlton and the crew of the *Horton* had not only the seas to contend with, storms to avoid, and fog to navigate, but quite possibly they were being chased down by Canadian and British cutters and naval steamers. The men of the *Horton* were not yet safe from the lion's paw.

The patriotic people of Gloucester did not loaf around on the fish wharves to wait on news. From the docks, to the taverns, and into the offices of the vessel owners, plans of action were being made to assist Captain Knowlton as best they knew how.

Edward, not wanting to leave Gloucester during the crisis to lobby the commissioners in Washington, grew tired of the delays between the sending of wires with pleas for assistance and waiting on responses. Rather, he spent his recent days pacing the corridors of city hall and his evenings at Widow Tarr's tavern, where he kept council with the other vessel owners. There, he'd told them that since Gloucester had defeated the measure to be incorporated as a town, they were being given no official standing to argue a case.

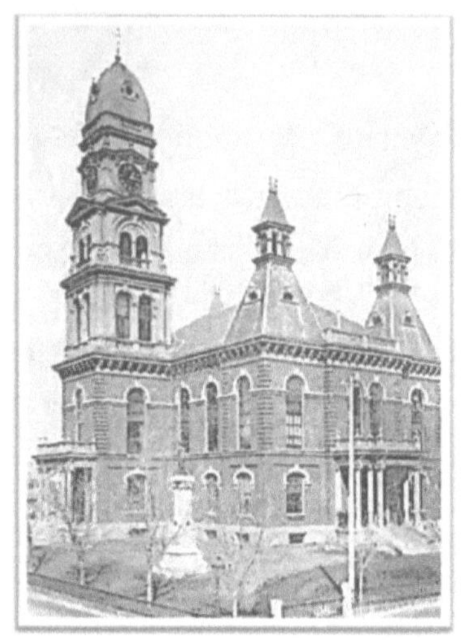

It was only through being united as fishermen, who President Grant and the Washington commissioners had little use of on account that political donations came from more affluent interests, that the town had any clout from which to muster support, however. In acknowledging this, partner McKenzie made the crisis a local one.

Robert McKenzie, the partner of Harvey and Edward, having arrived home from Ireland the week prior, began contacting his acquaintances in the state government. His angle was to assure a New England based vessel would be protected with all the resources that could be afforded. He received a positive reception, as the sting of captured schooners was seen as hostile aggression toward the not yet one-hundred-year-old Union.

McKenzie contacted his friend, Collector Fitz J. Babson, who took immediate interest in the situation. Acting with urgency, Babson devised measures to escort the *Horton* into port. He vowed to have forces ready, should the schooner be harassed off America's coast. At once, he held a council of his department, of which were comprised officers of the Civil War; these were men who had long family lines of American officers back through the wars of 1812 and the Revolution. Their sense of duty, patriotism, and a fire to fight off any Dominion injustice, no matter what the officials in Washington intended, ran swifter than a gale through the Southeast Shoal shallows of Georges Banks.

Unexpectedly, Collector David Russell of the Boston Custom House came to their aid. He barged into the warehouse office early Tuesday morning.

"Skipper Horton! How are you, old friend."

"Why, David, it's a surprise to see you in Glo'ster!" Edward pushed back his chair to shake the collector's hand. Introductions were made to Joseph and Frank. "And of course, you know Mr. McKenzie."

"Yes, yes, I do." He pulled five cigars from his inner vest pocket. "Ah, I've just enough," he said, handing them around to the men. "Have a smoke, my friends. To celebrate the nerve of Harvey Knowlton. Making all of New England proud is he!" His head inclined to allow Joseph to light his cigar. "And, you'll be the younger brother, I suppose?"

"That's right, Collector Russell."

"You were captain when the Canadians took the *Horton*. Isn't that right?"

Joseph bowed his head. "Aye, sir."

"Ah, son, you're a fisherman. Nothing you could have done against arms and bayonets." Russell placed his hand on Joseph's shoulder. "But after my business here, over a pint at the tavern, I want to hear all about it—how they came about under your bow, and what sneaky trick they played in order to board you!"

"Yes, sir!" Joseph nodded and smiled. He'd relish in telling the officer all about it.

"Good, good." Russell blew a gray cloud of smoke towards the ceiling. He turned and took a seat. "Tell me, Edward, what help might I give you and the crew of the *Horton*? For you know, I can't allow a ship, it being the namesake of a friend, to go without aid of guns and cannon."

"Have the commissioners in Washington sent you here?" asked Edward.

The end of his cigar burned a bright red as the collector took a deep, long inhale. Russell tapped the ashes into a tin can on the table. "If you prefer to think of it that way, we'll leave it at that."

Within the hour, Russell committed to dispatch an American government steamer to the waters off Cape Ann. This was immediately done by way of a wire. In addition, he personally contacted the coast guard station at Portland, Maine for assistance from the north. The Portland based cutter, *McCulloch* was sent to search the waters along the southern Maine coast in order to give assistance to the *Horton* and escort her home.

The commander of the Charlestown Navy Yard, also not one to wait for official orders from Washington, wired his offer of the steamer *Fortune*, to be armed with a navy crew. His telegram to Collector Russell read, *'Aboard this vessel are two howitzers of tremendous gunning power.'* The collector shared it with Captain Horton.

Edward pounded the table on reading the news. "This will burn Johnny's chances for sure. We've got the upper hand now!"

By Dead Reckoning

"There's a curl o' caps to loo'ard seems to beckon us away;
There's a rurrin' in the riggin' seems to whisper not to stay.
All the night the waves come pattin', like the hands o'
drownded men
Coaxed us down the sea to'ards Glo'ster
with the warnin', 'Home again!'"

Monday – October 9, 1871
On the Atlantic Ocean – East of Nova Scotia

It was inevitable, and Captain Knowlton knew it. At daybreak, when the *Horton* was discovered missing, a telegraph alerting the Dominion fleet commanders would be sent on the wire. MacDonald's brother-in-law would only be able to stall for so long.

The captain wrote in his ship's log:

"By daybreak we were passing far outside of Gunning Rocks. All I had to assist with navigation was my pocket compass, a spy glass, my memory and the brave Glo'ster crew. Gillis was an immense help with the local land observations, he having spent the most years of all the crew fishing off Canso. By first light we were past Hog Island. I had little comfort yet. Should we have the best of circumstances of wind we had likely six days of sailing to make the six hundred nauticals. My direction to McCloud

was to make the food last fourteen days, in order to account for weather and potential evasive maneuvers.

This first afternoon under the light of day was of most concern to myself and the crew. From my conversations with MacDonald on the plan to avoid vessels in the area, I held east sixty miles to sea, before turning south. We held watch forward, aft, and a man was kept aloft all the first day blessed by calm seas. I fought exhaustion and steered north of Canso Island with a course planned outside the Cranberry Islands.

I kept the Horton on a south-southwest course. We held a breeze from the north-northwest. When I turned in here for a short rest, Oliver was at the wheel. We had made the first day without seeing a single vessel. Not even another fisherman. If only that could hold for the remainder of our journey home."

The captain closed his notebook and his eyes shut.

Tuesday – October 10, 1871

A faint purple-orange line marked the sky to the east as the captain walked across the deck.

"Captain, you must have barely slept five hours." Webber accepted the mug of tea the captain had brought to him at the wheel.

"The ship is hardly moving, Webber. Makes for tough sleeping." Harvey drank from his mug as he surveyed the horizon.

Webber nodded. He knew a tired fisherman always slept better when the ship was tilted in the wind; the swishing of the water alongside the vessel singing a soothing song.

"Any lights spotted in the night?" asked Captain Knowlton.

"None, sir. The watches reported no sightings through the night."

"Very well." Harvey checked the log. Using a match, he read his compass that he'd fastened inside the companionway for the helmsman. "Can you keep the helm for a bit longer? I want to see what McCloud has in the pot."

"Aye aye, Captain." Webber checked the compass in the dying flame. "You'll find the beef stew and soft biscuits the best you may have had on the seas, skipper."

To Harvey's left, Richards had appeared, a biscuit in his hand. "My turn forward." He waved the biscuit toward the bow. "I think you've pulled it off, skipper. Ol' Johnny is sure gonna have a black eye from this one."

"We might be homeward bound, but let's keep the celebration for when we round Webber Rock and Eastern Point Light beckons us in." The captain pulled his collar up against the cold air.

"Aye aye, sir." Richards walked forward to his watch at the bow.

With the rising sun, they anticipated the wind. On throwing the common log, Dyer reported they were making four knots. It wasn't a racing speed to be sure.

The southwesterly course was continued all that day. When the men weren't on watch or trying to sleep, they played cards and harassed McCloud to make another pie. It wasn't common for fishermen to be so idle. They had no reason to bait up, set trawls, or sharpen knives; the last they did anyway, until the captain admonished them for wearing down the steel for no good reason without fish to gut.

It was coming on sundown of this second day, the sky to the west a deep orange, to the east it was blacker than a wet-molded log, when the mast watchman called out, "All is calm. No sails on the horizon."

"Captain, I suppose we'll be west'ard of Halifax by first light." Oliver stood across from his uncle in the captain's cabin.

Harvey had his pencil over a map. As they hadn't any charts on board, he'd found an old illustration of the coastline. He'd torn it from one of the books on the ship's library shelf, and he'd been making markings based on their speed and heading.

"Fairly close now." He marked the page with another X.

"I'd say this is our most dangerous heading we'll have, Captain." Oliver waited for his uncle to acknowledge the thought.

Harvey was thinking the same as his nephew. If Canada wanted to pursue the *Horton*, they'd have no better chance than to send their fleet in a flying set east from Halifax harbor. He worried that at this moment there could be a line of Canadian vessels positioned from the port all the way across to Sable Island on the lookout for them.

"Oliver, inform the watch of our position for these next hours. Might as well remind them to keep on high alert."

"No need, sir. They are well aware. They've taken it upon themselves to add a man. Gillis is forward. Richards is aft. Penney is aloft. Webber has the wheel. McCloud is the spare man; says he can peel potatoes with one eye and with the other watch the horizon. He's sitting atop the stacked dories with a sack of spuds and a knife."

"Ah. Very well. I recommend then we take our meals so we can turn in. Daylight may find us having to put all the wind we can find in the sails."

For a fishing trip, the calm seas and low winds would have been wished for in prayers of all dorymen. But for a captain driving for home, the conditions were a curse. Before turning into his bunk, the captain ordered sails to maintain headway. Lastly, he advised the night watches were to be reduced to helm, aft, and forward so men could get their rest.

Hours passed quietly. Tuesday turned into Wednesday.

Wednesday – October 11, 1871

In the still dark hours of the morning, not seeing anything but blackness, Richards left his watch on the bow and made a visit to the forecastle for a mug up. The seas were running so calm, he took two mugs topside with him and didn't spill a drop.

"This must be what a pleasure cruise is like." He handed Penney, who had the wheel, a mug of strong tea—on account it'd been steeping for four hours.

"Aye. Not sure as I like such weather in our situation, seeing we are not here to catch the fish. I'd rather a stiff breeze in the sails." He lashed the wheel to hold their course and took a seat to drink his tea.

"Might think of us as the fish being chased." Richards grimaced at the taste of the tea. "Doc must have left the leaves in the pot."

"I like it." Penney's grimace on his next sip said otherwise. "Certainly, not soothing. It'll keep me more awake anyhow."

"Best you not go to sleep or you'll be dreamin' of the girl you left behind." Richards avoided looking his mate in his eyes.

"You ought to leave that alone."

"Seems I saw you writing her a letter earlier."

"What of it?" Penney kept his eyes leveled on Richards.

"What good could come of it?"

Penney didn't see any good coming of furthering the talk about Bonnie. "Mate Richards, you take a watch aloft and give Gillis his watch forward."

"Aye." Richards obeyed the man in command without any more comment of the girl, at least for the moment.

Left to one another's own thoughts, it was peaceful on deck. The only sounds were a low swish of the sea running along the vessel and the occasional clank from the rigging. All around them the fog had closed in with a wall of white. Penney was checking the compass heading when the alarm was heard from above on the mast.

"Steamer!" Richards warned through his cupped hands.

The alert was relayed immediately as an "All Hands!"

As Harvey went to sleep with his red jacks on, and everything else but his sou'wester, he jumped up to the deck at the first call down the companionway. Oliver and Dyer followed.

"Don't know how Richards could spot anything in this muck." Captain Knowlton stood by the rail. "When'd this soup rise up?"

"About an hour ago, came on thick." Webber handed the captain a spy glass. "On the port quarter, off two points, sir."

Harvey lifted the scope to his eye. The fog horn of the steamer was a muffled, deep groan.

"Could be an Inman Line steamer bound for New York." Oliver stood on the stern grasping a halyard.

"Make mark of your current heading and turn her about, so'theast as far as we can," ordered the captain.

"Aye. Turning about so'east." Penney turned the wheel away from the steamer's position, and they headed farther from home.

The captain went amidships to give the orders for the sails. "Richards, to the deck!" Captain Knowlton beckoned.

Knowlton was taking no chances on it being a passenger line. It could be. But it might just as well be a British naval vessel. He focused his glass back on the steamer. "Let's drive her, boys. Drive her! Make all sails ready."

The crew sprang into action. The *Horton* was taken to full sail; a risky maneuver with the fog thicker and whiter than the choking air of a fish smoking-house—steamers weren't likely to veer off course for a yacht, no less for a fisherman. Not that they'd heard the *Horton* as she wasn't ringing her bells.

When they were hidden in the fog, there wasn't any way to know exactly how far they'd gone off their prior line and farther out into the Atlantic. There'd been no time to measure their speed. It was seven in the morning when the captain called to lower the foresails, topsails and jibs. The fog hadn't thinned and he needed time to calculate his next move.

Before the vessel even slowed, Dyer was climbing aloft. "No signs of her, Captain," he shouted. "I hear no horn or bells, either."

"Oliver, take the wheel from Penney and hold course. We'll put some space between us and that possible vessel lane for the day."

"Aye, Captain, relieving helm to hold course."

"Do you think the steamer had a sight on us, Oliver?" asked Penney once he'd relinquished the helm.

"In that dark and fog, doubtful. If it were a man-of-war, and he'd seen us, he'd have chased us down to see who we were. As it was, it was surely a passenger steamer." Oliver tried to sound confident.

They heard the captain yell aloft. "Come on down, Dyer. Get yourself some grub and sleep. We're clear now."

Below the men were holding court in the forecastle.

"I'd almost rather have seen a British navy steamer than any Inman liner," stated Webber.

"In our predicament! You've been drinking too much of Doc's rebrewed tea. Why's that you say?" asked Richards. He ran a biscuit around his empty chowder bowl.

"You surely recall that liner that cut a schooner in half, don't ye? Wasn't an Inman liner. I can't recall what company it was just now. But to me, they're all the same." Webber filled their mugs with coffee.

"Nay. Can't say I've heard that one." Richards handed his bowl over to McCloud at the stove. "Fill me up, Doctor."

"It was a night like we've just been having. All fogged in as it was. The schooner, *Wind Chime* was on the bank. They were a month on the grounds, with near a full hold, planning to head home the following day." Webber reached for the grub locker handle and took out the last of the apple pie. "We'll be starving to death in a day, McCloud."

"No you won't! We've plenty of salt pork and beans."

"I prefer pie," stated Webber.

"Go on!" said Richards. "And I want half of that."

"Well, on the *Wind Chime*, the catchee was at the bell. A young boy, he wasn't more than fourteen. The lad was ringing his arm off. That steamer kept right on course, blowing its horn for the schooner to move. Now, that steamer could have gone a notch or two off course. Easy done given her engines. As opposed to the *Wind Chime,* she hadn't enough wind or time to clear. That steamer sliced the *Wind Chime* dead in half."

"And the boy?" asked Richards. He'd been a catchee when he first started on a fisherman and held some concern for the lad he'd never known.

"Didn't make it. Six of the men were lucky enough to get the dories off and cut loose before she sank. Both ends, they said, rose high to the heavens and plunged under the rolling waves."

"Did they arrest that steamer captain?" A frown rose up on Richard's face.

"Bah!" injected McCloud. "You ever heard of a steamer line being blamed for anything?"

"Steamer never even slowed down." Webber shook his head. "Those men drifted for four days and four nights before the sea took them into a fishing lane. They ate raw fish and squeezed the mist from their clothes for water."

McCloud rationed out a drink of rum for all.

Richards hoisted his heavy legs into his bunk, boots and all. "I don't know, but I'd sure wish we were on a steamer now. How long on this course until we make Glo'ster?"

"You know as well as the wind," replied Webber.

Richards blew into his harmonica and sang an ode to the cook.

> "Our doctor's name it being McCloud,
>   the truth to you I'll tell.
> He was a jolly Irishman,
>   a good cook, I 'spose as well.
> He had a jug of rum on board,
>   that mustered the whole of our crew.
> And we drank the health of the Glo'ster girls,
>   wishing to meet once again a few."

All that day long, the fog didn't lift. To stare at the horizon, the sun burning beyond the blanket, would make your eyes tear. Captain Knowlton commanded the sails set to keep the *Horton* under three knots. The men were given rest between three-hour shifts on watch.

McCloud made a mincemeat pie with the last of the apples. He had no cherries, apricots, or cranberries, so he made due with raisins, figs, molasses, and extra rum. The smell of the baking cinnamon, cloves, and other spices made it difficult for the men to sleep. They took to playing cards and reading until their eyelids could no longer support themselves.

Thursday – October 12, 1871

On the fourth day, with daylight, the fog teased them with sporadic thinning. With long views of the water, the crew went about their duties with renewed energy. The captain called to raise all sails once again. The *Horton* schooned over the swells.

Knowlton figured, thirty miles starboard of their current position, Cadillac Mountain would be getting its first morning rays of sun. A Great Skua flew over the deck, nearly walloping Richards on the head. As it was, he flung off his hat at the bird, losing it overboard.

In the days since leaving the barn, Captain Knowlton had not had more than four hours sleep per day—if one could count interrupted twenty-four-hour periods in a bunk as a day. He told Oliver he was going below. Exhausted, he rolled his head into his wool jacket to cover his eyes.

Men of the sea weren't ones to count sheep. To set himself asleep, the captain closed his eyes and mumbled a ballad.

> "Mount Desert Rock it was well known,
> A brilliant light thereon it shone;
> And when this light it appeared in view,
> Our captain very well it knew.
>
> We brought our vessel to the wind,
> And cast both anchors from the bow.
> Thinking in safety there to ride,
> Although the seas run mountains high."

Captain Harvey Knowlton thought of the vessel *Sarah* for which the ballad was written, she wrecked near to that rock rising over the ocean, not far from their probable current position. He fell to sleep. In the darkness of his dream, he sensed the change in the air—those are the instincts that make men captains. In other times of less exhaustion, he might have woken with a premonition to command his crew to furl the sails before they were damaged, but that day he slept on.

By midday, the sun had given up and couldn't break the low cloud cover. The sky was a blinding, milky white. While the visibility was again poor, the seas remained calm. With the pleasant sailing, the concealment of the fog, and so far, having not seen a pursuing cutter, there was no man stationed aloft.

There was no warning from Richards at the bow. He'd closed his eyes against the bright white of the heavens in his need for sleep.

"Yo, ho!" he yelled. A rush of cold water drenched him through as the bowsprit dipped under the water from the first of the mountain-high waves.

Ahead of the ship the sky had turned to a dark purple in the time it took the bow to come up to the crest of the next wave.

"All above!" cried Oliver.

Richards called the men from below. Frantically, they secured items on the deck. Disadvantaged by the small crew, there was a delay in furling the sails.

By the time Captain Knowlton was topside, the sky was black all around them, the swells were crashing over the bow, and the foresail was split from the rigging.

While McCloud was securing the dory beckets, he heard the men near to him calling out a Psalm every seaman knew. They timed their lines to each rise and fall of the bow on the waves.

"For HE commanded a tempest
that lifted high the waves.

**The ship mounted up to the heavens
    and went down to the depths again;"**

"Furl the mainsail!" commanded the captain, interrupting the verse.
"Aye. Furling the main."

**"Our peril will melt our souls.
    We will reel and stagger like drunkards;
    All crew are at their wits' end."**

McCloud held tight to a halyard. The leeward side rose and the *Horton* was spun.

**"Then, we fishermen will cry unto to the Lord,
    and HE will bringeth us from our distress.
HE will still the storm to a whisper;
    the waves of the sea he will hush."**

"Hold course, Oliver." Captain Knowlton left Oliver tied at the wheel and he went forward, staggering along using a rope, to assist furling the sails on the jib. "Take care, men. Hold strong."

Before the crew could take in the sails, the wind ripped one free.

"Captain, the foretopsail!"

"Forget it. You can't save it yet."

The sheet ripped across the length of it; pieces flew aft to the sea.

"Watch your heads, boys!" yelled McCloud.

Gillis took a step forward and looked up at the exact wrong time. The foreyard smacked him across his back. He fell down, his face smacking the wet deck. McCloud and Webber grabbed at his legs as he slid through the pool of water. The foreyard spar bounced end-over-end and jammed in the rail; that was their luck, for otherwise, they'd have lost the spar overboard.

The men carried Gillis to the forecastle and lashed him in his bunk. There was no time to attend to him with all hands needed on deck.

Barrels which were tied strong to the rings on the house broke free, flipped on to the round, and rolled back and forth across the deck.

"Behind ye!"

At hearing McCloud yell, Dyer swung himself up on the boom as barrels went crashing by him. Ten feet of the bulwark by the quarterdeck was smashed into splinters and washed away clean.

"Heave to!" called the captain.

No one questioned Knowlton. The crew knew their jobs and went at it. Adjustment to the foresail caused it to turn and she filled with the wind. The *Horton* slowed to a near stop. And that's how they rode it out.

The gale—for not even a single Gloucesterman on the *Horton* that day would have called it a breeze, which they were apt to do unless it deserved the accolade—was relentless for six hours. In those hours, the *Horton* was pushed farther out to sea than they'd been since putting out east of Canso.

When finally the storm subsided, they sat in the forecastle. It was quiet for a time, the crew realizing their being short-handed by a man or two, made it all the more dangerous the longer they were to be on the sea.

"I thank ye, mate, for the earlier warning! Never did I see those barrels coming. I'd have been buried in the foam." The warm mug of rum coffee shook in Dyer's still trembling hands.

When Oliver was relieved at the wheel by the captain, he went below. He sat alone, ashamed he hadn't been able to predict the gale coming on. The *Horton* had survived the storm, but she was creaking, they had two damaged sails, and one sail was missing completely. Miserable, as he was, his thoughts turned to Alice. A verse he'd heard but once before, rambled in his mind. Taking up a pencil, he put it to his log with his own words to capture the injuries the *Horton* sustained that day.

"It was Thursday afternoon, no land did we espy;
The so'thard winds began to blow,
 the seas ran mountain high.
The so'thard winds began to blow
 and heavy squalls came on,
Which made our captain nervous
 and our sailors they did mourn.

Every sail was battered; to halyard, we could not get a hand,
Expecting every moment that our vessel she would strand.
Our foretopsail was split, my boys,
 our fisherman's sail blew straight away,
The bulwark by the quarterdeck was washed,
 leaving a gap in the deck that day."

Left alone by the crew, he kept writing verses. For his dinner, McCloud saved him the final portion of the mince pie. Although it was his favorite, most of it was left in the pan. He turned into his bunk, taking his notebook and a bottle of rum.

A Jonah Day

> "I pray you give attention,
>   and listen unto me,
> Relating to those noble men
>   who were drowned in the sea."

Friday – October 13, 1871

Morning started dark as the night. The gray clouds were so thick, they seemed to nearly touch the top of the mast. Never before had any of the crew experienced such gloomy feelings. Their lack of talking around the stove, mugs of warm rum ever-present in their hands, proved there wasn't anything more lonely than the dark sea after a week of no fishing, all worry, and the unknown of where their ship sailed on the rolling waters.

Sails were inspected for damage. The deck was put in order. Damage was reported to the captain.

"Once we hove to, she came out of it pretty good," stated Penney, aside the captain, who was checking the dories.

"I'll admit, it isn't too bad to be down the two sails and Gillis only with a bruised shoulder." Captain Knowlton looked to the gap in the rail. "You men see what you might find for wood to close that up some. Ought to be some boards above the ballast that can be pulled."

"Aye aye, sir," answered Penney. He motioned for Dyer and Webber to join him below.

Over lunch, the captain updated his map, although he wasn't certain by any account of where they were exactly. He wondered if Joseph or Edward were keeping up his pin-map of the fleet back at the office, with each of them guessing the *Horton's* position on every rise of the sun.

Confidently, Harvey rallied his crew with his optimism. With his small map on the forecastle table, he explained their likely location. He'd answered questions on when they'd arrive in Gloucester with, *"four to five days."* Their course was now set due west, hopefully to run into Cape Ann, the twin lights on Thacher's Island calling them home.

Still keeping to himself, Oliver sat that morning at the table in the captain's cabin. He was hunched over a loose sheet of paper he'd slipped from between the pages of his logbook. He'd only written two sentences, and was at a loss for how to go on.

My Dearest Alice,

I don't blame you if you never speak to me again. I hope that will not be the case and you will, someday, permit me to explain myself.

How could he explain. She must think he only took an interest to learn the plans of Captain Tory. His heart ached at how he may have hurt her. His mind drifted deep in thought.

Harvey had returned to the quarters and was reading a book. He noticed Oliver's pencil hadn't moved from the same spot for five minutes. Given the nephew's inwardness for the past twenty-four hours, Harvey thought he knew what was bothering him. He closed the book and took up his crude map in his hand.

"I don't blame you, Oliver. You've seen now how fast the sea can turn. It won't happen again to you." His tone was meant to show he forgave his nephew for not sensing the gale.

"Aye, sir. It was quicker than a mackerel flung from a line." He tried to put his mind off the damage and into the letter.

Harvey stole a glance across the table and caught the address line. "You know, Nephew, from what I understand of Miss Tory, she isn't at all like her father."

Oliver looked up and caught his uncle's smile. While he heard the meaning in the statement, he was more surprised at being addressed not as a crew member, but as a nephew. "What makes you say so, sir?"

"MacDonald. That smuggler, for all he was and wasn't, he had a saying. He said to me *'children should not be blamed for the sins of their fathers.'* He wasn't any fond of Tory, as you know, but Bonnie and Alice were lifelong friends and he didn't see any problem with that."

"Hmm." The young man sketched a bird along the edge of the sheet of paper. He added the horns of a lark.

"You see, Alice is likely to understand the predicament you were in, as well as your feelings for her."

"I can never go back to Guysborough. Tory would hang me."

"Well, true. That probably would not be a prudent move." Harvey moved his pencil over his map, contemplating where to make his next mark of their position. "But I don't think the captain would have grounds to hang you." He saw the corners of his nephew's mouth arc upward. "Although, he might tar and feather you, or put you on a British prison ship. So, you might want to stay clear of the Provinces for a time." The captain drew an **X** with his blunt pencil in the Atlantic. He labeled it *Friday Oct. 13th*. He added, without looking up, "And his daughter."

Forward in the forecastle, McCloud served up flat cakes.

"How's about a little more rum for the coffee?" asked Richards. The others raised their mugs in agreement. McCloud poured their mugs half full of coffee and half of rum. He then sprinkled into the mugs sugar and cinnamon. He'd been once told by a cook the spices were a remedy to calm nerves after surviving a storm. How much of it was true he didn't know, but he believed there was more about it to the rum than the cinnamon.

"This here, it reminds me of drink I had down while fishing near San Domingo," said Penney, smacking his lips.

"Lucky you came back from there," said Dyer.

"Why's that?" Richards swallowed, eyeing the jug McCloud was storing back in the cook's locker. He smiled when McCloud reached for the jug again. His grin flattened when he noticed Captain Knowlton and Oliver had entered for a mug up and the doctor was pouring only for them.

The captain indicated with a nod to the cook. McCloud poured another round for all.

"You were saying I was lucky, Dyer. How so?" asked Penney.

Dyer saw all eyes on him. He swallowed a long drink and started his story. "I had a mate, ten years ago this very day, Friday the thirteenth of eighteen-sixty-one. He sailed on the *Rosemary Louise*." He folded a flat cake in two and bit off a piece.

"They sunk?" interrupted Richards.

"No. Worse than that." Dyer scowled. "They found a ship, just floating along. Sails were up. Not a soul aboard."

The men sat still. Richards's arm froze with his mug near touching his lips.

"Was there a gale?" asked Gillis.

"No." Dyer chewed his cake.

"Ripped sails? Missing rigging?" questioned Webber.

"Nope. All was right as could be." Dyer held out his mug, sure his story deserved another. McCloud poured.

"From our quarterdeck, our skipper called and called. There was no answer." Dyer paused as he held his plate for another cake. "Add some of that molasses syrup over the top, Doctor."

McCloud obliged, knowing rationing sweets at this point in their journey wasn't going to matter much.

"You're saying, a perfectly fine ship, sails raised, was sailing the sea with no crew?" asked Richards, disbelief in his tone.

"Saying it as it was told."

"And it was Friday the thirteenth they found them?" Penney's eyes narrowed.

Dyer ran the cake around his plate to coat it in the syrup. "As it were, that was the date." He looked at the men. "As it is today."

"What'd the men of the *Rosemary* do?"

"Four men of the *Rosemary Louise* were able to get aboard the derelict in the calm seas. They furled the sails, and made an inspection. They found nothing. No lockers, no ditty bags, no ship's log."

"The dories?" asked three at once.

"Hooks and lift ropes lowered. Dories stacked where they'd been."

"Did they tow her?" the same three asked.

"No."

"Why not?"

"The captain considered her a Jonah. He ordered her burned as a derelict. A danger to the shipping channel. They watched her sink and then sailed away." Dyer sipped his drink slowly. He watched their reactions over the brim of his mug.

"And no one ever claimed her?"

"Or reported a crew missing?"

"Neither." Dyer hung his mug on the peg, kicked off his boots, and rolled into his bunk.

"What was her name?" asked Webber.

Dyer propped himself up on his elbow. "Joan H.—something. The last of the name had been washed off. Maybe."

Webber wrote the name in his journal. He closed the book, but opened it again.

Gillis stretched his neck to see what his mate was scribbling. He scowled. In arranging the letters of the ship's name over and over, he saw Webber had written in block letters—**JONAH**.

The remainder of that Friday was as dreary as Dyer's story. It was worse than foggy. The air was heavier than a wet quilt. You couldn't see from stern to bow. The watches, afraid of calling out and being heard by a lurking vessel, rigged a rope stern to bow to tug a signal if a sound was heard.

Captain Knowlton went up and took the wheel. Sails were set to hold the course at a creeping speed.

"Do you think they're chasing us?" asked Oliver.

"I can't imagine they wouldn't. Johnny's pride is as wide as our own." He checked the compass reading and made a notation in the log. "To our luck, Canada only has the one steamer in the revenue service. She'd be the only one of their vessels we'd have to worry about, her having the speed, guns, and men enough to take us. But with that storm, and our zig-zag course being what it's been, their finding us out here would be luck for them." The captain thought a moment. "They might be hauled up closer to Glo'ster, knowing that's where we're headed."

"Do you think Edward was able to gather support for us?" Oliver knew Edward would try, but what the response would be, he wasn't sure.

"He doesn't give up easy. If the commissioners in Washington weren't willing to help, or took offense to my tactics to regain the *Horton*, then I have to have faith in Joseph, Edward, Sweeney and the men. They might be outside the harbor now with gaffs, muskets, and rocks to fend off any Johnny vessel near the cape."

This was the most humor Captain Knowlton had shown in days. Oliver was glad to see him in positive spirits.

"I've been thinking this through." Knowlton lowered his voice, so even the watch aft could not hear. "I haven't come this far to lose the *Horton* again to the Canadians."

Oliver looked into his uncle's bloodshot, puffy eyes.

"Remember what I told you before. If we are to be boarded by any Canadian or British seamen, we must burn the ship." Knowlton looked squarely into his nephew's eyes. "I want you to prepare supplies for the seine and a dory, we could be rowing for several days should we have to abandon the *Horton*. Have kerosene positioned for easy access to light below on our exit."

A lump ran down Oliver's throat. The captain could see his nephew's concern. He placed a hand on Oliver's shoulder and swept the horizon with his other. "Ah, we've had Providence on our side this far. Things couldn't have worked out any better. It could be this fog has been sent as a final blessing. A Glo'ster blanket to hide us all the way home."

"I'll only feel blessed after we've anchored at Rocky Neck." Oliver retired to his bunk in order to be ready to take the next watch.

Saturday – October 14, 1871

McCloud started his day by throwing rotting vegetables and kitchen scraps overboard. Sea birds circled the deck and had a feeding frenzy off the stern.

"I can't see nothing from aloft." Richards swung down to the deck. "And McCloud, you've got the birds taking up residence on the halyards!"

"Be grateful. That's a good sign. Those gulls prove we're gaining on the mainland." McCloud picked up his bucket and disappeared down the hatch.

"With no wind we're floating here for the taking." Penney intently stared out to the open ocean; Richards stood beside him.

The fog hadn't lifted. Worse, there was not a breeze to blow a butterfly. The schooner seemed to be losing more distance than gaining for home.

"I've a mind to drop the seine boat and start towing this beast." Richards rested his hand on the seine gunwale.

"You and ten other boats of eight men at the oars each maybe could tug for a mile at that." Penney eyed his mate. "And not get more than where you started."

Richards peered over the side of the seine. "This boat is outfitted. It seems ready for a fishing trip!"

Penney stood beside him. "Aye. Oliver was making up emergency supplies. Just in case we have to abandon ship."

Richards lifted a tarpaulin. "So, the captain thinks they're following us then." He sat back on the top of the companionway. "If we get caught, you might be in luck, Penney."

"How's that?"

"Captain Tory will surely have us back to Nova Scotia to be tried for our crimes." Richards was bored of no fishing, the same old grub, and nothing to do. He was looking for some sport and Penney was his game.

"And that'll be lucky how?"

"The way I see it, MacDonald's daughter might be at your trial to make eyes at you."

"You leave any thoughts of Bonnie alone, Richards. You hear me?"

Richards was quiet for only a moment. "I don't know. It seems you taking a liking to the smuggler's daughter, a smuggler that assisted in the taking of the *Horton*, will not sit well with the jury of naval men handpicked by Tory."

Penney walked to the rail. His right fist was balled tight.

"I can still see you, in that silly outfit and the shoe tied with her ribbon. The two of you singing together on the lane." He sang a verse of *Billy Boy* in a mocking tone. The leap from Penney was so sudden, Richards had no time to brace his legs. He was on the deck staring up at the boom. Penney had his knees pinning him down at the shoulders. His yells were unintelligible.

"What's this!" Captain Knowlton pushed Penney off of Richards with such force the fisherman almost went over the lee bulwark.

"I'll have no bickering aboard my vessel. The two of you will report to my cabin at once. Webber, take the wheel." The captain called down to the forecastle for two men to take the watch.

"What was that all about?" asked Captain Knowlton once the two men were standing before him.

Neither Richards or Penney would offer an explanation.

"Now look, men, you aren't a typical crew on this ship. We're not fishing. I can't hold any pay from you or say I won't hire you again." Knowlton paused as Oliver stepped down into the cabin.

"What I can say is I've appreciated your help so far and I'd hate for any bad blood to be made on the *Horton*. I don't intend to say I'll keep any prize from you for your service, that wouldn't be fair either." He looked from face to face. The men both stared over his head at the far wall. "If you can't apologize to one another, I'll order you two to stay apart. You won't have any watches together. And Richards, you'll have to bunk aft here. Penney, you keep your bunk up in the fo'c'sle."

"Is that all, Captain Knowlton?" asked Penney.

"Yes. That is all."

Harvey watched the legs of the two men disappear up the stairs to the deck.

"What's the trouble?" asked Oliver, stepping further into the quarters.

"Something like it was bound to happen. Men on a ship with nothing to do." The captain took out his map. "If you've ever been a religious man, Oliver, start praying for some wind."

With their predicament of drifting along, McCloud suggested to drop some lines in order to have a fish dinner. The jigging for bait had no success, so pork fat was used. This seemed to do the trick in more ways than one. Soon they were pulling cod overboard and a competition was set up for the most fish caught.

"We'll be getting into Glo'ster with the saddest catch in years!" Gillis laughed as he threw a fish in the tank—the wooden crib on the deck that hadn't seen a fish in over a month.

"We might as well crown you the low-liner, Gillis, because I'm six ahead of you." Webber unhooked another cod.

"Someone keep an eye on him. I don't trust his counting." Gillis dropped his line again.

"Ho! I've got a tuna!"

They all turned to see a Bluefin thrust through the surface of the water on the end of McCloud's line.

"Play him."

"Don't let him break!"

"I can taste the steak already. Slow, McCloud! Slow."

The fishing went on until the fog darkened behind the setting sun.

"It may not look like much, but that was a good day," Penney said, as he admired their day's catch.

"Won't take long at all to gut 'em and put on ice. Come on, Penney, you and I'll take care of it as the doctor cooks that tuna."

Richards slapped Penney on the back. He then called out, "McCloud, I like my tuna seared lightly!"

"You got it, mate." McCloud threw the head over the side to the birds. On the rough-planks used as a deck table, he sliced steaks out of the hundred-pound fish.

Aft by the wheel, Oliver stood next to the captain.

Harvey removed his pipe from between his lips. "Remember this when you're a skipper, Oliver. Keep your men fishing and they'll be happy, they'll be making money, and, for you as the captain, bickering will be one less thing for you to deal with."

"Aye aye, Captain. Heard."

Sugar and Spice

> "Cheer up, crew, bright smiles await you,
>   From the fairest of the fair.
> Let the thought of it elate you,
>   You'll be happy when you're there.
> Sailing home, sailing home, sailing home across the sea!
>   Sailing home to good ol' Glo'ster—
> Coming home, dear Cape Ann, to thee."

Sunday – October 15, 1871

Other than the fog thinning, Sunday was more of the same for the crew of the *Horton*. They ate fish chowder at breakfast, and again for their noon meal, thanks to their prosperous catch from the day before.

One positive was a slight wind that kicked up. The sails were raised to catch all the breeze they could find. Spread over the deck, the split foretopsail was attended to by Dyer.

On the roof of the companionway, Gillis sat smoking his pipe; his right arm was done up in a sling. "Can you repair it, mate?"

"Aye. It wasn't on account of my looks the sails were my duty on the *Sea Witch*."

"It was good you had the clear mind to keep aboard the sails we mistakenly took on the first trip to the warehouse."

Through the fabric, Dyer threaded the long needle pulling hemp twine. "Always a smart idea to have extra sail in the hold. It has many uses." He pointed to the fabric holding Gillis's arm.

Due to the clearing skies, the watches kept alert scanning for vessels on the horizon. Others of the crew were gladly busy following their fishing yesterday. Lines had to be coiled. Hooks and knives had to be sharpened. Cutting boards were washed again. With four men working at those jobs they were soon back to the forecastle for a late afternoon snack.

For men stuck to the deck and cramped quarters below, they sure didn't lack for appetite. Doing his best at variety, McCloud cooked up a Dundee Pudding. Stale, hard bread was pounded into crumbs. To this he poured in a helping of rum-molasses to sweeten it, along with some flour to bind it. The dish baked in a cast iron skillet for forty minutes in the wood oven. When he sat it on the table, the crew didn't even wait for it to cool. Spoons were quickly dug into the warm treat.

"Doc, you've done it again," exclaimed Dyer.

"I'd like you to teach this recipe of yours to my wife." Webber wiped at his mouth with the back of his sleeve.

Later in the day McCloud used his saved crock of pork fat to fry strips of hard bread. The sizzling chunks he spread about the table and he coated them in salt that glued itself to the strips. The crackling from the men chewing the snacks was heard for two hours over a game of cards.

The cook's concoctions may have gone over with the crew as tasty, but McCloud was simply being prudent with the rations that were not going to hold out much longer. There'd be no more fresh bread. The surprise storm had soaked the flour. The pork remaining at the bottom of the barrels would only be good for fish bait, and that was questionable. Of the fish they caught yesterday, that might last two more meals, if he stretched it into hearty chowders of more dried corn than cod. What had calculated to be a fair amount of food proved to go faster while the men were aboard, than if they'd been fishing. With not much to do, they were all eating twice their normal amount. It was going to be pig's feet and potatoes soon for their meals.

Dessert that night was an old-fashioned apple pandowdy, apples baked in Doc's selections of sugar and spices of nutmeg, ginger, cinnamon, ground clove, and orange peel. For his crust, he'd had to improvise and used oatmeal. When he placed the deep cast-iron skillet on the forecastle table, Richards went immediately to dig his fork right into it.

"Hold!"

Richards froze at the yell from the cook.

"Ain't you ever ate a pandowdy? What are ye? An animal!" McCloud came at him with a five-inch round wooden spoon. Richards slid back away from the table.

The cook shook his head at him. "I ought to wallop you one. But, watch!" With the back of the spoon McCloud cracked into the crust. Down went the oats into the molasses and the syrupy-coated apples. "Now, let her sit for a minute in order to soak up the juice."

A minute never passed so fast. By the time McCloud had hung up the spoon over the stove, the men were already dishing out the pandowdy.

"Aye, Doctor, this would cure homesickness." A piece of coated apple dropped from Webber's fork to the table. Dyer scooped it up.

"If we ever get back to fishing with Captain Osler, I'm recommending you for the cook," stated Gillis, his spoon scooping out another helping to his plate.

"Save a bit for the captain!" Penney watched the pan being emptied faster than sharks swallow chum.

"No worries. I've got a second pan cooking now for the skipper." McCloud opened the stove door to add a stick. The crackling of the burning birch wood was the only sound heard along with the chewing of the apples coated in the sweet, dark-brown molasses.

A one-handed Gillis rummaged his ditty bag for his harmonica. "Here's a song that was written by that ol'salt of Glo'ster town, George Proctor. I heard him sing it at Tarr's Tavern."

The tune was of low, drawn, melancholy notes. Smoke from the pipes and the cookstove drifted past the single lantern to hover under the dark ceiling beams. On account of Gillis's chosen melody, and McCloud's satisfying dessert, most of the men closed their eyes and listened. It was only Oliver and Penney who both sat staring upwards at the yellow glow of the lantern, as verse after verse was recalled.

"That day so fragrant with its joy,
Her whom I loved—that pleasant stroll;
Pure happiness without alloy —
Heart answered heart and soul met soul.

She gave the promise — untold bliss!
Through all our lives our love should flow;
We sealed the promise with a kiss.
That summer day at Loblolly Cove."

"Guess, I'll take my watch." Penney tapped out his pipe.

"I'll join you to relieve the captain." Up the steps, Oliver followed.

Once the two had disappeared out the door, McCloud remarked, "You sure can clear a room, Gillis."

"Ain't my fault those two couldn't keep from letting a girl get under their oilskins." He began playing the chorus notes again, but stopped at hearing the heavy stomp of the captain's red jacks on the stairs.

"I hear you've made something to satisfy my sweet tooth, Doctor."

Before Harvey even took a seat, McCloud handed him a mug of coffee topped with rum. "Aye. It might at that." He placed a dish of the pandowdy on the table.

Soon after, Dyer, having been relieved by Penney, was beside the captain scooping his meal. "This 'ere is mighty tasty, Doc! The boys that came up weren't telling no fish story." He swigged down his mug and hoisted it to the cook. "A touch more rum, mate?" While McCloud poured, he looked to Gillis who was still blowing his doleful notes. "How's about a more lively song?"

With his only usable hand, Gillis placed the harmonica in his shirt pocket, and raised his mug to wet his whistle. "I might know a good drinking song. If the captain would permit the excitement."

"Never say Harvey Knowlton Junior doesn't run a tight ship, but yeah, you may sing a song to lift our spirits." The Captain lifted his mug. "We're near home, boys. Near home."

"I might have a tune you all know then." Gillis took out his harmonica once again. This time the notes changed to a sloop tune of long ago.

The captain let them sing it once through with the words they knew. Then, the crew was surprised as he stood next to Gillis. Harvey held his hand for them to hold. Accompanied by the low notes, he sang for them lyrics of his own making:

"We sailed on the *Horton* home.
My Glo'ster crew and me,
Towards our own Cape Ann, we did schoon.

Drinking rum all through the night,
They promised not to fight.
We're all so tired now,
        We want to sail home."

They all joined to repeat the last line,

"We want to sail home,
        we want to sail home."

The chorus melody seemed to float up the companionway. They all looked up the hatch, listening to the voices on deck singing along.

Before filing up the stairs, the mugs were refilled. The crew went above so that Oliver and Penney could join the harmony. Under the stars, the crew was in high spirits and they sang, verse after verse. Sails snapped in the wind, men drummed on the barrels, sheaves chuckled, the blocks ruckled. Had there been another ship within four miles, they would have surely come along to see what the celebration was about.

A Hero No More

Monday – October 16, 1871

Maybe it was the low of the morning following the night of drink and song; or possibly it was the fog that once again blocked out the sun making for dreary moods; or it could have been it was now the seventh day on the sea since escaping Guysborough. Whatever it was, McCloud's breakfast fare didn't seem all that grand to the men.

It ought to be well known on a ship not to insult the cook. Whether it was on account Richards had yet to quell his aching head with a drink, or McCloud was not feeling well himself, but the vow for no bickering was soon forgotten.

A slap of a spoon splattered the pork and black bean stew onto the table.

"What'd you do that for?" Gillis eyed Richards from across the table.

"This 'ere reminds me of a song we didn't sing last night." Richards lifted a hunk of pork on his spoon and let it drop to his bowl. "Doc, you probably have heard it. Goes like this."

Not one to be easily offended, unless it was on account of his food, McCloud paused his chopping of turnips. He held the ten-inch knife with the end pointed into the chopping block. The others stopped eating, what they themself thought was fine food for their predicament, as Richards more recited than sang the song he was remembering.

"Old hoss, old hoss, what brought you here?—
You carted stone this many a year;
From Scarboro' to Portland Pier.

But now worn out by sore abuse,
You're salted down for sailors' use.
We'll turn you over and pick your bones
And cast the rest to Davy Jones."

There was not a snicker in the galley. The knife rose in McCloud's grip and he slammed it into the already gouged block. Around the counter he came. One-armed Gillis jumped between the men.

Without pushing at Gillis too hard, McCloud yelled over his shoulder, "Richards, you complain about my grub, you ungrateful *Sea Witch* castoff, **you'll** be the one joining Davy Jones with the horse."

"Ah, it 'tis only a poem, McCloud. Don't ruffle your apron, man." Richards showed his toothy grin.

"It ain't a poem for this galley. Get out!" McCloud yelled, yanking a spoon from his apron pocket.

"You'd better go up top, Richards. Check the weather, maybe." Dyer nudged him up the companionway. "Don't let him get to you, Doctor. The rest of us appreciate all you're doin' to keep us fed."

Up above, Richards found the weather as sour as his mood. What breeze there was, was barely enough to maintain a heading. Remorse set in for how he'd treated the cook. He lifted the top of a locker and took out a knife and went below to the hold. There he pulled a piece of halibut that was caked in salt. On deck, he rinsed it in a barrel and baited a line to troll over the stern.

Captain Knowlton, who was sitting by the wheel, simply passing the morning in the salt air, heard Richards whistling the tunes of the night before. The whistling ended with the fisherman lowly singing the lines, "I want to sail home—I want to sail home." Harvey whispered the same to himself.

Tuesday – October 17, 1871

The slow sail of Monday continued into Tuesday. As did the fog. Oliver continued to state the shroud of mist was a blessing to keep them hidden. Captain Knowlton wondered why they'd yet to run into the coast.

The weather, if not sunny, cleared to an overcast with a breeze. Dyer threw the log and measured out three knots. Fresh air beckoned all the crew as the Horton sailed slowly westward searching for land.

Bowls of pickled pig's feet were eaten topside forward using the fried pork bread as scoops. Gillis played his harmonica.

At the wheel, Oliver kept his uncle company. "Captain, do you sense the crew is getting anxious?"

Harvey rubbed his eyes with his thumb and index finger of his right hand. In his left, a book was held open. He looked forward to the six men of the *Sea Witch* keeping to themselves; the figures against the white horizon triggered a memory of his days being held a pirate's hostage. He coughed; it seemed in order to clear his throat. But a ball of phlegm shot from his mouth over the rail.

"It isn't normal for fishermen to be so idle at sea, Oliver." From his jacket pocket he took a thin, flat piece of wood, about eight inches long and two inches wide. He used it to mark his place between the pages. "They'll hold up alright." He closed the book.

"How many more days do you calculate until we hit Glo'ster?" The younger Knowlton tilted his head to catch the book's title, *The Seaman's Medical Friend*. He doubted his uncle hadn't memorized every page in the worn book already.

Harvey gave his estimate with all the confidence he was certain. "One or two days. We can't be that far off, even with our setbacks."

"Permission to pass to the men, sir?" The answer came with a look and a nod of approval. Oliver walked forward.

Not wanting to interrupt the conversation, the mate took a seat on the deck, bracing his feet against the rail. Webber was telling another of his woeful tales.

"I tell you, such a thing happened not far south of Halifax at Port Medway, back in the mid-fifties, so the story goes."

"What was the fellah's name?" asked Dyer.

"He was Captain John Blackburn. Was said he knew that coast better than anyone, he being of a sailing family for generations."

"What happened?"

"As was typical for him, he was in the business of shuttling supplies and things along the coast between his port and Halifax." Webber's left eye twinged and slightly closed at the blinding sun-fog. "Some of the barrels on his two-mast pinky might have contained liquid considered a required necessity for the public health."

Hearing this, McCloud wondered how long their rum would hold out. It may not be needed for their health, but surely, it'd be required to maintain goodwill.

"I figure Port Clyde to Halifax is no more than ninety miles." A skeptical Richards stated.

"Less. Maybe seventy," corrected Webber.

"I don't see how, on such a short voyage, along the coast in a pinky, such a thing could occur." The grinding stone slid across the blade Richards was sharpening.

"It happened as I'll tell you." Webber sat forward. "The captain and two crew set sail from the port and headed north'ard. As it was a daytrip, they had some food and water packed along. Nothing out of the normal was anticipated for a sail they'd made nearly twice a month in all seasons." He paused and returned the gaze of each man. "Well, as you can imagine, else there'd be nothing to tell, a gale blew in from the no'theast. She didn't cease for four days. Turned out, they'd been blown clear across the gulf stream and out into the no-man's land of the Atlantic."

No additional swipes of the stone went over Richards's blade. All were silent. Oliver thought about breaking in with his news, but thought better of it; the captain's imprecise estimate didn't seem news to share any longer.

"It being February, Captain John told later it seemed warmer than it ought to have been. An expert seaman that he was, on a routine cruise, he hadn't even the thought to take a compass with him. It was more than a month before they spotted another ship."

"A month! So they were rescued? Where?" asked Dyer.

"No. The captain, being a proud man of the Provinces, asked of the ship where they were. On hearing they had a mere hundred miles to land and they'd stored some rain water, they decided to continue on with no help."

"What a stubborn old salt he must have been!"

"McCloud, what do you figure they cooked up all that time?" asked Richards, his smile wide to show his jest.

The cook, who knew of the story, signaled a crude hand gesture at Richards.

"Where were they headed then?" asked Penney.

"The captain and his mates found themselves in St. Martin's."

"From Nova Scotia to the West Indies?" Penney's head shook back and forth.

"That's right. On a straight run it would have been over two-thousand miles. With the course they blew on, Captain John said later he figured it was twice that."

"Did they sail the pinky home?" asked Dyer.

"Nay. They sold her and took the more direct route on a steamer to Boston."

Some chuckles came from the crew. This prompted Webber to tell of the moral he intended for them to digest. As he made the final statement, his head turned aft towards the captain who had his head down reading. "So you see, dead reckoning is often not a match for the whims of sea and wind. No matter the skill of the captain."

Oliver felt his face run flush. He stood and went to the cabin to have a rest; not trusting his temper at the moment with Webber.

Tuesday – October 17, 1871 – Evening

On their eighth evening out of Guysborough, the crew ran into an even denser fog. The mood aboard the *Horton* took a turn when the captain didn't come above to take his shift at the helm. Captain Harvey Knowlton, as the crew had come to realize, never needed to be called on. He arrived at the wheel ahead of his turn. They all knew he used no clock other than the one that ticked in his head. His lateness was talked of in the forecastle and on the deck.

"Gillis."

"Aye, Oliver?"

"Take the wheel please. I'll go below and check on the captain."

Oliver found Harvey, his face to the wall, covered in blankets and his two coats. Next to his pillow, made up of his canvas ditty bag wrapped in a wool shirt, was the book, *The Seaman's Medical Friend*. Lifting the book to place on the table, Oliver opened it and read the marked page.

"CONSUMPTION Comes on usually gradually and insidiously. The patient has for some time a slight cough, of which perhaps little notice is taken, until the…"

Harvey coughed in a set of four muffled-threes into his blanket. Oliver leaned in under the bottom of the upper bunk. His uncle's face was covered in sweat.

The steps creaked. McCloud stepped down carrying a pot of tea. Oliver indicated to place it on the table.

"Is he ill?" whispered the cook.

Oliver put a finger to his lip and took McCloud aside. He showed him the page. "He was reading this."

"Hmm. Then we must not give him this tea until it cools to temperature. You go adjust the watch. I'll remove his sweat-drenched clothes and start the stove in here. He must be kept warm and dry."

Harvey rolled over, groaning. "What's the heading, Oliver?" He coughed again, three times.

"Holding south south-west, sir. As you directed."

"Have we met with the north side of Georges Bank?" Harvey hadn't opened his eyes.

"I can't be sure of that, Captain. I might see the change in the sea with daylight. I'll report back once known. Stay and rest. Doc is here."

Harvey moaned and pulled the wool hat over his eyes.

Fortunate Defiance

Early in the morning, the *Fortune* steamed into Gloucester Harbor in order to again pick up Robert McKenzie, Joseph Knowlton, and Captain Robert Tarr, brother to Widow Tarr. The local Gloucester contingent had been leaving on the steamer each day. Their presence aboard the armed vessel was to serve two purposes. First, to provide positive identification of Captain Harvey Knowlton once encountered, and, second, to ensure the crew of the *Horton* recognized their pursuers on a large Navy steamer were of friendly disposition.

By all means, Gloucester, Boston, and Charlestown were prepared for war with any Canadian or British ships should they try and seize the *Horton* once again. Additional vessels had been cruising the waters from Cape Cod to Mount Desert Island. The steamer *Leyden*, the cutter *Mahoning*, and the tug *Hamlin* were given instructions that no foreign vessel was to be allowed to interfere with the *Horton's* sailing.

The American officers and officials issued a decree, "The *Edward A. Horton* was to be brought into port, at any hazard." When a copy of the memo reached Washington, the commissioners there decided to let Gloucester and the New England commanders fight their own battle. They did not voice support for, or interfere with, the objective.

News of the *Horton* had sailed on schooners heading to fish the Georges Bank and Long Island Sound. Gloucester vessels on hearing the developments, and only three-quarters full in their fish-hold, raised sail for home—the return of the *Horton* was not to be missed, the fishing would wait.

With his elbows propped on the office table, Edward was reading the Halifax paper. The journalists from Canada were having a fabulous time in relishing that the *Horton* had not been located. They speculated the ship had run aground, went over in a gale, or was met by a British gunboat and sailed to England. It seemed they'd write anything to add to the anticipation on the American side.

There was one article that Edward felt depicted the truth on the character of a Canadian cutter captain; the newsman wrote, "The *Horton,* when first brought into Guysborough, was stripped of all navigational aids, charts, and instruments."

Another article stated, "Captain Tory himself ripped even the compass off the wheelhouse." This disheartened Edward most of all.

He rubbed his temples. He wondered if Harvey and Oliver had managed to secure what they needed to find their way home. No longer could he sit idle and wait. With a grunt he lifted himself from the armchair and made for the stairs.

"Frank! Duncan! Connie!" Edward Horton beckoned his workers to where he stood on the rocks next to the wharf.

Throughout the harbor there were crews readying their ships for fishing trips. Others, having made port that morning, were unloading their catch. Although, even while they worked, the *Horton* was on everyone's mind. It seemed all kept one eye to the channel past Rocky Neck for their missing schooner.

"Yes, Captain Horton?" asked Frank.

"I want you men to get up a crew, six more men. Frank outfit *Defiance Too* to set on the evening tide for a two-week sail, plus contingency." Edward knew he didn't have to go into details with Sweeney on what was required; the seaman knew more about fitting a schooner than Edward could remember.

The two dory partners gave Frank a look; it was obvious they expected the master rigger to be spokesman. Frank stepped closer to Edward. "You want me, I mean the three of us on a crew? And to say, you'll be wanting *Defiance Too* fitted out? To fish? Who'll skipper?"

"Yes. I want the three of you on the crew. And, no, she's not going out to fish. Not tomorrow anyway." The glossy paint of the newest vessel gave him an idea. "But make it look that way."

He poked his cane hard on a rock to push himself back up to the roadway. "We'll be going out to keep an eye for Harvey and the boys. This sitting around is only good for old maids." He hobbled up the rip-rap. "As we'll be a crew, you might address me as captain until we reach port again. Sweeney, you're in charge to get the schooner ready."

Without a further question, the three watched him head into the warehouse. "Guess the old skipper is worried." Connie pulled down his hat against the cool mist that hung over Gloucester. "He must feel left out."

"I'd say, with Captain McKenzie out there on the steamer *Fortune*, with Widow Tarr's brother no less, and he left here in port." Duncan shook his head.

"Tarr was an officer in the war, so no doubt that's why he was invited along," said Connie.

"With that fog rolling in, I don't see how we'll see the *Horton*, or any vessel for that matter, unless she rides under our bowsprit." Duncan pointed a finger out towards the harbor entrance.

"Enough naysaying. We'll do what the skipper wants done." Sweeney started for *Defiance Too*. "Let's get busy." He stopped midway over the plank to the deck. "You two check the handlines, hooks, and knives. May as well put some bait on board to make a show of it. Besides, hand-lining will give the men a little to do while we're on patrol. I'll go to hunt up a fine crew and order down a supply of vittles."

"You'll be cook then, Frank?" asked Connie.

At the question, Sweeney thought back to his last voyage when he was a cook. The fog horn on the point blasted once again, pulling him from his nightmare memory of drifting in a dory for days. "Sure as heck ain't gonna leave that to you. There'd be a mutiny before we cleared the harbor."

"I take offense to that. I can cook a decent chowder." Connie stood with his feet apart, squared at Frank.

"Aye," said Duncan, "but that's about all. Men can't live on haddock chowder alone. Besides, your biscuits are so tight they can't sop up the bowl. Only thing, we might use them to shell Johnny with though."

Connie scowled at his mate and was about to offer a word, but Frank commanded attention.

"Hey! Seeing as I'm goin' out for this cause, I don't mind packing my old flapjack pan and serving up again. That is, should I be able to get us a crew. 'Tis short notice for sure. I'll be scraping the bottom of the bait barrel or paying twice the rate." Sweeney adjusted his black knit cap tighter down over his ears.

He shuffled up to the road. To himself he thought, *"At least with this fog, there ought to be men lounging here in port waiting it out."*

He started his search for men he knew, those who'd crewed on a *McKenzie-Knowlton-Horton* vessel at one time or another. As might have been expected, given the feelings around town, he had an easier time than anticipated in signing agreeable men. There were good sailors wanting to do the service free of charge so long as they had rum along and a chance to blacken Johnny's eye. His initial list of names contained more men than would fit aboard. Each selected man ran to their home, or rowed out to their vessel to gather their ditty bags, harmonicas, and extra pipes. More than one slipped in his bag an old musket, balls, and powder.

We Saw Three Ships

"There's naught upon the stern, there's naught upon the lee,
Blow high, blow low—and so sailed we.
But there's a lofty ship to windward,
    and he's sailing fast and free,
Sailing down along the coast, towards Cape Ann are we."

Wednesday – October 18, 1871
Massachusetts Bay

There was concern aboard the Horton. It had been nine days since they'd cut from Guysborough. The winds had been unfavorable, storms had battered their sails, the food was leaving a bad taste in their mouths, and now their captain was ill. What else could happen?—they didn't want to know.

"How's the captain?" asked Gillis.

"He's up and eating. His fever is down today," assured Oliver.

"Huh. Must have been something McCloud fed him." The remark from Gillis was more in jest than seriousness.

"Don't let the doctor hear you with that talk," said Oliver, pointing forward to where McCloud was smoking his pipe. "He'd done really good to figure it was only some passing ailment that rest would cure."

The rising sun straight off the stern shone forward over the calm Atlantic. It was looking to be the clearest day they'd have for weather in a week. Oliver wasn't so sure that was a good sign. The visibility was for miles over the ocean. Based on his measurements this morning, they had gone over the north side of Georges Bank. From this knowledge, and in consultation with the captain, he'd set their course to follow along the southeast edge with a turn north. Their course was to ride in on the outside of Cape Cod and approach Gloucester from the south. Captain Knowlton was gambling that any Canadian or British ships would assume a direct path from Cape Sable to Cape Ann and they'd be guarding that lane.

By noon, the captain was walking about and took his turn at the wheel. The wind was blowing a breeze to run five knots. In the lee of cool air, the sun warmed the deck and the shirtless men were relaxed, sensing the current taking them home.

"Hey, what is this?" Penney jumped up. On his shirt, which was crumpled lying next to him, a tiny yellow and black bird had landed.

"Looks like he needs a ride," stated McCloud.

"Some type of warbler," added Dyer.

"Must be off course." Richards stroked the bird's wing.

"He's exhausted." McCloud went below and returned with a dish of fresh water and cracker crumbs. He wrapped a shirt snugly around the bowl to keep it steady.

"Ah! That'd be my only good shirt," exclaimed Penney.

"It's for a good cause," shot McCloud.

After a time, the men (and bird) dozed off.

While on his turn at watch, Gillis tried out his bruised arm by playing a song on his harmonica using two hands. The melancholy notes woke the bird, who then discovered the crumbs.

"Hey, look, he's eating." Gillis broke up another cracker. The bird pecked at the bread.

"At least someone can eat that hardtack!" stated Richards.

Once he'd had his fill, the bird proceeded to take a bath in the dish of water. Round and round the bird flopped, washing off the salt of the sea mist that coated his feathers. It was more entertainment than the men had enjoyed in a week.

In midafternoon Oliver yelled from the mast. **"Three ships ahead, Captain! Two points forward of the port beam."**

All the crew turned out on the rail. Captain Knowlton relieved the helm to Gillis and he went forward with his spyglass. "Who are they, Oliver?" He yelled up as he passed the mast.

"Can't tell yet, Captain. The flags are flying straight aft."

"We'll run around them in this wind." The captain called for assistance. "Webber, give me a hand with the cannon cover." With a pry bar they pulled off the crating. "Gillis, keep the shot port side."

"Aye aye, sir."

"Red, White, and Blue on their mast, Captain!" yelled Oliver, holding his spyglass to his eye.

"Keep a close watch. We know their tricks."

"One's a steamer! Two schooners."

"Drive her. Drive her homeward. We won't stop now. Let them chase us!" Captain Knowlton hustled back aft and took the wheel from Gillis. "Oliver, to the deck! Guns at the ready, men."

At five knots the *Horton* was bearing east, the rail close to the water.

The steamer aimed head on to the bow of the *Horton* and blasted a horn every thirty seconds.

"What signal is that?" asked Oliver.

"Never heard it. I don't think it's a typical blast. But neither is their line of approach." The captain adjusted the wheel to keep his port side to the oncoming steamer. "Prepared at the cannon?"

"Aye aye, sir!"

"What is that steamer doing? Why are they coming on at us?" Oliver was now standing on the house, his spyglass to his eye.

"Steamer has cut engines, Captain," reported Gillis. "She's coasting for us."

Two blasts from the whistle sounded. The captain timed them. "Two seconds between each blast," he called out.

Two minutes later, a blast, two seconds, and another blast. This continued for six minutes until the Horton was close enough to see people on the deck of the steamer. The schooners by this time had circled wide and were now approaching aft of the *Horton*.

"Be alert, men!" yelled Captain Knowlton. He turned and spoke to Oliver in a whisper. "You go to the bottom of the companionway. Await my signal. If this is a trap and we need to burn her, you be ready."

Oliver grimaced, but obeyed. "Aye aye, Captain." He reluctantly disappeared below, preferring to see who was in the approaching vessels, and certainly not wanting to have to act on such an order.

"Captain Knowlton of the *Horton*, this is Commander Warren of the USS Fortune." Something else was said over the trumpet, but it was too faint over the wind and waves to understand.

"Can we trust them?" asked Gillis.

"We are not letting anyone on board or even close to this vessel. Hold your posts." Harvey Knowlton looked behind his ship. One of the schooners was closing in.

"That there is a swift schooner." Gillis peered out over the wheel.

"Take the wheel, Gillis. And give no ground." Knowlton walked aft and looked through his glass. A smile, wider than any he'd worn in two months, crossed his face. "Oliver, to the deck. Stand down men. All clear." He waved to the approaching schooner.

The schooner came up along the starboard side.

"Hello, Edward!" yelled Captain Knowlton through his speaking trumpet.

"Welcome home, Harvey, and the crew of the *Horton*!" answered Edward.

"Seems *Defiance Too* is all we thought she'd be," said Knowlton proud to see their latest vessel decked out in sail.

"By the looks of your damaged sails, seems you caught a breeze on the way home," called out Sweeney.

"Yes, a bit of one." replied Harvey.

By this time, the steamer had pulled up along the port side. From the deck, Joseph Knowlton and Robert McKenzie took turns at the speaking trumpet.

"How's the fishing been, boys?" asked Joseph.

"Good to finally see you. We're here to escort you into harbor." Robert pointed to the armed crew of the *Fortune*.

"Why so many guns? Do you think they expect trouble?" Oliver asked his uncle.

Harvey Knowlton was wondering the same himself. **"Are there John Bull patrols off the cape?"**

"None seen. Rumored to be. So, let's get this sea behind us," returned the Fortune's commander.

The sun by this time was dipping beyond the horizon towards home. The four ships set a course direct for Gloucester. The two schooners led the way, followed by the *Horton*, with the *Fortune* guarding the rear. They made their way to Gloucester protected by the cover of darkness.

"Hold this course." The captain turned toward Oliver, but quickly turned back. "And drive her, boy, drive her. Don't let Edward pull away." He smiled as his head shook, and his right arm pointed forward.

The first mate nodded and through his upturned lips managed a strong, "Aye-aye, Captain." He watched Knowlton descend through the companionway. His hands gripped the wheel spokes. Under his feet, Oliver felt the *Horton* cutting the water under full sails in the stiff breeze. He was full of pride riding along vessels flying the American colors.

The crew were all on deck now, rejoicing in knowing they were headed to port. McCloud opened the last jug of rum, one he'd hidden away for their home-coming occasion.

When Captain Knowlton appeared on deck again, he was dressed in his dark blue overcoat and clean pants. He'd even disposed of his miner's beard in exchange for a clean-shaven face.

Serene and Fair

"Ye sons of Uncle Samuel, come listen for awhile,
I'll tell you of a captain that was made in Yankee style;
Of the schooner *E. A. Horton* and the bold undaunted band,
Commanded by brave Knowlton, a true son of Yankee land."

Wednesday – October 18, 1871 – 7:30 p.m.
Gloucester Harbor

As soon as the *Defiance Too* reached the outer harbor, the men on the deck fired their guns—twice for a ten-shot signal. From the point of Rocky Neck came the **BOOM!** of the cannon firing a return.

The crew of the *Horton* gathered at the bow.

"Looks like the fleet has been expecting us," said Oliver. Lanterns began to shine on the rails of all the moored vessels.

Captain Knowlton took the wheel to enter the harbor. He needed no map or instruments for his home port. The thirteen feet of depth near Round Rock Shoal, and that in line with Mussel Point, was of no concern—he knew all the dangers well.

"Make ready to lower jib sails!" he yelled.

"Ready to lower jib," came the reply.

"Lower the jibs."

He schooned around Ten Pound Ledge. The bowsprit glided between Babson Ledge and Black Rock.

BOOM! The cannon roared as the Horton passed by the neck to the inner harbor.

The crew waved as the *Horton* schooned through the water.

"Ready at the sails, men," called the captain.

Aboard the *Fortune*, the naval band played the *Star-Spangled Banner*.

"Make ready to furl foresails."

"Ready to furl foresails."

"Furl foresails."

A line of vessels, all aglow with lanterns, were moored around the north side of Rocky Neck. The ships provided a lane of light for the *Horton*.

Commands to ready hawsers were yelled over the shouts of the crowds of people on the neck.

The captain brought his vessel close to the wharf that had been cleared for his arrival. Had the inner harbor not been so crowded with dories and skiffs of the welcoming town, Knowlton would have glided her right up along the side. As it was, the *Hamlin* tug was there to assist the ship alongside the piers.

Torches were flaming on the waterfront. A rush of men, women, and children were streaming from their homes to the wharves and streets along the harbor.

"It looks like the Fourth of July." Richards put his arm over the shoulder of Penney. "I bet we're in for some celebration at the tavern tonight, my friend."

In the inner harbor, the schooners at anchor were not only flying their top mast with the American flag, but their halyards were decorated in dozens of flags. Red, White, and Blue hung everywhere.

All across the town, the bells of each church were ringing. Guns were firing. Drums and bugles were being played to various tunes.

"Captain, did you ever expect such a welcoming?" asked Gillis.

Harvey Knowlton could hardly get the words past the restriction in his throat. "A most wonderful town Glo'ster is."

A plank was dropped to the ship and Captain Knowlton was then shaking hands with men of the *McKenzie-Knowlton-Horton* crews that had boarded the *Horton*. Men patted his shoulders and gave him their welcome and congratulations.

On the deck of the *Fortune* the navy band played *Yankee Doodle*, followed by *For He's a Jolly Good Fellow*. The townspeople erupted in song.

Captain Knowlton was swarmed by the jubilant crowd. Yells came for him to make a speech, but the noise was too great for anyone to hear. Still, through his speaking-trumpet, he thanked them for their appreciation, their welcome, and said the deed of honor was for all of Gloucester that night.

Edward, Robert, and Joseph whisked him, and all the crew of the *Horton,* up the hill to Tarr Tavern. A celebration was to be held there with the fleet captains, ship owners, and town dignitaries. The men were given rooms where hot baths and new clothes awaited them. Harvey's wife, Ellen, had the mind to bring him his best suit. She also brought with her a stack of newspaper articles about the *Horton's* escape. While he sat soaking in a tub, he read an article from the morning edition of the *Portland Daily Press.*

---

* * * *

PORTLAND DAILY PRESS

* * * *

WEDNESDAY OCTOBER 18, 1871

* * * *

A Speck of War

WHILE the President of the United States and the Governor-General of Canada are associating on the most friendly terms for the purpose of giving éclat to an event that is to strengthen the friendly relations of the two countries, it is most inopportune and unfortunate that a British man-of-war should be cruising along the coast, lying in wait for a Yankee schooner, while a navy force is dispatched by our own authorities "to uphold the dignity of the American flag." It is distressing to reflect that even a little matter of this kind may, by bringing on a collision through the agency of hot-headed naval officers, embroil the two countries in serious difficulties, and indeed war. The "E.A. Horton" is a little fishing schooner which was seized by the Canadian government for the violation of the fishing laws, and carried into the port of Guysboro, Nova Scotia. On Sunday of last week she was "cut out" by her audacious Yankee master with the assistance of his friends, and is now eluding the pursuit of outraged John Bull. So here is a genuine, serious international complication, requiring the action of the chief executive of both countries.

This is the state of things that the Canadians talk of perpetuating for the sake of keeping their neighbors from participating in their fisheries. If they conclude to reject the treaty of Washington, so far as it is applicable to the fishery question, they must not expect that a good providence will always in the future, as in the past, prevent dangerous complications from growing out of British and American rivalry on the fishing grounds. The situation will be one of constant danger. "Rumors of war," at least will be constantly exciting the apprehension of the public. Just now, were it not for this wretched little affair, the feeling between England and the United States would be excellent.

The piece, even though he knew it was written when the *Horton* was still *at-large*, infuriated Harvey. To his wife he complained, "They write the *Horton* is '*a little fishing schooner,*' and I, '*her audacious Yankee master.* And the whole month-long ordeal the *'wretched little Horton affair.'* I'd like to get a moment with the writer."

His wife handed him a towel. "You can't expect a typewriter man to understand the workings of a fishing town."

"Maybe not, but he ought to be more patriotic, if not sympathetic to the theft of American property."

Harvey flipped through several other articles, all of which, while somewhat understanding (mostly in order to not alienate their American readers), felt he was making more out of his ship being captured than was necessary. The editorials considered the relations between the United States, Canada, and England of higher importance than vessels, fishing occupations, and liberty. The general consensus was fishing captains should leave the international business to Washington, lest a Gloucester fisherman might start a war.

"You would think they'd be a bit more understanding of my actions and why it had to be done."

While Ellen trimmed his hair, she was understanding, but tried to calm him now that he was home safe. "Don't let it bother you, Harvey. There is nothing more you need to see for support than what is happening here in Glo'ster."

Outside guns were still firing. Drums were beating a march through the town. From the window on the second floor, he could see the lanterns shining bright on the vessels bobbing in the harbor.

"Yes, you're right, Ellen." He tightened his tie. "And maybe the newspapers are right too. Maybe it was a foolish stunt."

"You've done a brave and great service, husband."

"I don't think we've heard the last of it. News on the embarrassment to Canada may cause England to take action."

She handed him his suit coat. "Or maybe you have forced Grant's hand and the Washington fisheries commission will now enforce the treaty in order to protect the interests of the American fishermen."

"I pray you are correct, my dear wife." He took her hand. "It is good to be home."

Before he even descended the stairs from the upper room of the tavern, the press hounded Knowlton for all the details of his escape, much of which he held to himself, particularly his disguise as a miner and the help from MacDonald.

In the tavern dining room, Widow Tarr had prepared a feast for the men. Beyond her delicious roasts and the chickens, the men were appreciative of the ever-flowing cask of rum.

Once the dinner was concluded, Harvey saw his volunteer crew about to make their own escape from the tables of the vessel owners. He called them to the pantry room of the tavern. Out of earshot he spoke with some difficulty to acknowledge what he thought of their help.

"You men, each of you, I am thankful for your service to myself and the *McKenzie-Knowlton-Horton* firm. More than that, you should know that Glo'ster thanks you, the fleet thanks you, and your country thanks you." He handed each of them a stack of bills. "We will see about your right reward after this excitement blows down. For now, McCloud, Webber, Gillis, Dyer, buy your wives and children something. Richards and Penney, go easy on the town tonight, we want it still standing come the sunrise."

"Three cheers for the captain, then!" called Richards. The crew shouted their appreciation.

He shook each man's hand as they exited by the rear door. "Please keep our business in Guysborough, particularly concerning MacDonald's name, our own," he said to them as they left.

The crew of fishermen, even the married men, continued their celebration of free drink in the taverns along Main Street, and all-around Duncan, Wharf, and Middle streets, until the sun came up. It was the best homecoming of the most unsuccessful fishing trip they'd ever had.

The Horton's In!

> "**Boom!** and a cannon's voice rang out;
> **Boom!** and a mingled cheer and shout,
> With drum and trumpet, swelled the din —
> "**The Horton's in! The Horton's in!**""

> **Thursday – October 19, 1871 – 8 a.m.**
> **Rocky Neck, Gloucester, Massachusetts**
> **The Knowlton Boat House**

Harvey sat across from Frank Sweeney on a bench in the boat house. He had missed the morning view overlooking Gloucester's inner harbor. This morning was particularly spectacular. The sky reflected a dark blue. There wasn't a puff of white cloud in view. The birds in the canopy of trees overhanging the porch were singing—a more welcoming song than the gulls of the shore.

In the harbor, it seemed all of Gloucester were on holiday. From the absence of rigging being raised, sails being set, chants being sung, it appeared none of the still-moored schooners of the fleet were making ready to depart after the night of celebration.

The two talked business while drinking tea Frank had made over the oil burner in his apartment. Both were decidedly, yet uncharacteristically, late going to the office this morning. Frank had taken out the checkerboard and coerced Harvey into a game by saying he'd missed their matches.

Between moves they talked over catches the vessels had brought home while Harvey was gone, the pride of getting

Defiance Too ready to sail, and the gossip about why Knowlton was absent at the same time as Robert McKenzie. Frank told Harvey what he already knew, that all the owners and merchants in the town knew Edward Horton was the political arm of the business and it was McKenzie and Knowlton who made the day-to-day decisions. There was concern from the investors, as well as the fishermen, as to who was in charge. Frank assured him that through it all, Edward had kept everything running smoothly. Harvey knew Frank had a lot to do with it. Sweeney lapsed into a monologue about Edward.

"You see, as you can imagine, Edward was up to the Tarr Tavern for breakfast and dinner and supper. The men up there, they were constantly prodding him for information on the catches of our vessels. What they were really after was to determine who was directing our schooners and to what fishing grounds. Then came the day when Robert arrived home. He came at once down to the office looking for yourself. I informed him he'd find Edward up having his dinner. I felt it was Skipper Horton who should advise on your whereabouts."

Sweeney was about to go on, but Harvey interrupted.

"Frank, how did McKenzie take the *Horton* business?" His interest was in his partners disposition upon returning from Ireland to find Knowlton on his mission north.

"Well, you can imagine," Frank drew out his first words slowly, "he stormed around the office for several days. I kept to my work in the sail loft, but I could hear him. Edward had to listen to it all."

"As I suspected. He'd have likely wanted to simply make an insurance claim and build another schooner."

"His position was the schooner was simply wood and metal. He could commission a new vessel and be on with business rather than having trouble started. I gathered that much from the arguments I heard."

"Then it was all for the best he was away when I left then."

"Although, Captain, he had a change of heart."

"How might that have occurred?"

"Edward gave a rousing speech one morning and reminded McKenzie about King George the Third and his tyrannical rule over Ireland."

Knowlton laughed. "Ah. Good for Edward."

Through the window behind Knowlton, Frank saw the first schooner come around the point. She was outfitted in flags. "We might step outside on the porch for some air, Skipper." Frank rose and motioned to the door.

Harvey's lips closed tight as he took in the scene. Vessels were lined up in a row making a slow sail through the harbor. A band was playing on the quarterdeck of a schooner draped in banners.

"That'll be the Glo'ster Cornet Band on the *Freedom*," said Frank. "I see Eliot Friend conducting with Captain Jonas Buck at the wheel." Sweeney waved.

Behind the first boat was a second, then another. They kept on sailing around.

"It isn't without good reason for the vessels to begin gathering for a parade of the fleet, Captain."

"Aye."

Mrs. Knowlton arrived on the boat house balcony.

"A boy just dropped this letter for you, Harvey." She handed him the typed sheet. "It's from the mayor."

"Thank you, Ellen," said Harvey. He held the sheet out of the glare of the sun to read it.

He blew out a deep breath and shook his head.

Captain Knowlton:

My staff and I have declared that today, in your honor, will be a day of celebration in Gloucester. The arrival of the fleet will begin at 9 a.m.

Harvey paused in his reading and looked out over the water. The parade of boats—schooners, seines, dories, old pinkies, clippers, packets, and trawlers—was circling Five-Pound Island and the lead boats were heading past the Knowlton docks.

Captain Knowlton acknowledged the tribute with a salute. He recognized skippers from Gloucester, Essex and Rockport at their helms. "That explains why the inner harbor was so quiet this morning."

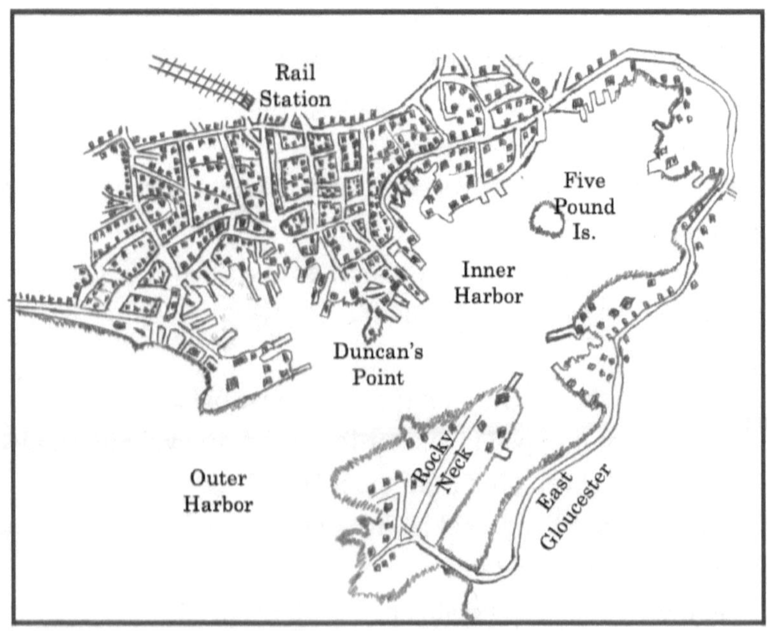

Frank smiled knowingly, his assignment of keeping Harvey occupied accomplished as the fleet was readied in the outer harbor.

Then came the Knowlton vessels. The *Defiance Too*, was again captained by Edward at the wheel. The *Phantom* was steered by Joseph on the quarterdeck. The *Mary Burnham* was under the command of McKenzie. These ships, and the others, had been outfitted with multiple American flags. Red, white, and blue banners, hung from the halyards. The *Samuel Adams* was packed forward with the high school choir. On the roof of the companionway stood the mayor. He saluted, turned to the choir and gave a double clap.

> "When the *Horton* comes sailing home again
> Oh yeah! Oh yeah!
> We'll give her a swinging welcome then
> Oh yeah! Oh yeah!
> The girls will scream and the boys will shout
> The old folks too will all turn out
> And they'll all go mad
> When the *Horton* comes sailing home again
> Well a ball be had
> When the *Horton* comes sailing home again."

The song faded away as the ship went around Rocky Neck to tack again. Harvey glanced down to continue reading the mayor's note.

> A band will play from Duncan Street Wharf all the day. School is on holiday. The events will be as follows in your honor:

11 a.m. — Recognition ceremony at City Hall. Guests
will include the captains and crews of the revenue
cutters and Navy vessels from Boston, Charlestown,
and Portland that assisted off the cape.

12:30 p.m. — Luncheon at the Gloucester Harbor
Hotel Ballroom.

3 p.m. — Special session in the mayor's chambers.
Discussion on the business of honorarium to the
Horton crew.

5 p.m. — Gala Dinner at the home of George Proctor.
Carriages will be sent for you and your family.

7 p.m. — Evening Parade – Assembling at Fort Square,
to Washington St., to Proctor St. (where at Mr.
Proctor's we will join the processions in the
carriages) down to Main and on to Duncan St. to the
wharf where fire-rockets will be launched over the
harbor.

"Seems our day has been planned for us, my dear Ellen." He handed Frank the schedule to look over.

Harvey waved at the ships passing. "I wasn't intending for the town to make such a distraction."

"Oh, dear, enjoy it." Ellen held his hand. "You can get back to business tomorrow."

Master George Proctor, commanding the schooner *General Grant* out of Essex, lifted his speaking trumpet. **"Thank you, Captain Knowlton— from at least this General!"**

Harvey could not hold back his smile, knowing the intended meaning.

"You ought to be aware, Captain Knowlton," Sweeney spoke in a low voice next to Harvey, "Master George Proctor supported you from the first story he printed to the last. And I bet we haven't read the last of it yet."

Knowlton nodded. "Captain Proctor is well aware of what is at stake in the Canadian Maritimes. He's always been a good friend. His asking for *that* helm today is by no coincidence."

BOOM!

The cannon on Rocky Neck caused Ellen to shudder.

"Good morning, Captain Knowlton."

Turning, Harvey was greeted by Oliver who handed him the morning's papers.

"Thank you, nephew. Did you sleep at all?"

"Ah, yes, sir. Two good hours. I was back to home at four and straight to sleep." Oliver smiled. "*The New York Times, The Boston Times, The Portland Transcript*—they all claim you are a hero for the fishermen."

The captain glanced at the headlines of the morning papers. As opposed to what he'd read the day before, these later stories, now that the *Horton* was safe in port without a shot fired between countries, were all supportive of Knowlton and what they were calling his *'brave act of patriotism.'* However, at odds with what he told reporters the prior evening, a few added their journalistic embellishments of how the captain *had evaded Canadian and British cutters* on the high seas. The editorials, at least, rallied the public's support for action from Washington.

"Sure, after they claimed it *Harvey's Folly* not more than a day ago." He ran his eyes over the front page of the *Times*. "And of course, they still claim I might have started another war with England, or this time Canada."

"Captain, listen here to this from *Old Locality*. An original poem of sorts. For the *Horton*." Sweeney read from the *Gloucester Advertiser*.

Knowlton closed his eyes and listened as Frank read. "Ah. That ain't half bad." He opened his eyes. "Frank, you know this poet Old Locality, I'm sure?"

"Aye. He lives across the harbor on Western Avenue."

"Send him word then. He's invited to this luncheon today and he'll be sitting at the captain's table with the rest of us. I'd prefer to hear from him than all the other speeches that'll be going on. That I'm certain."

Thursday – October 19, 1871
Lunch Reception – Gloucester Harbor Hotel

Harvey hadn't realized how much he was in need of sleep until the speeches began. The mayors of Gloucester, Essex, and Boston thanked Captain Knowlton for his brave act for all of the east coast fishermen. They offered their thanks and regards to the commanders from the Navy Yards for their patrols of the coast. He was presented a plaque with a brass relief of a schooner over a gold-plated key to the city.

When dessert was finished, Old Locality took to the podium and read his ballad. At the fourth verse, the chorus from the hotel could be heard through the open doors all the way to Eastern Point. The entire town had already memorized the poem and joined in as Old Locality recited his verses.

"The day retired serene and fair,
And lights came glancing here and there,
While gently swung the twilight down
On Rocky Neck and Gloucester Town.
The pulse of business life was still,
From Gardner's Brook to Beacon Hill,
On wharf and fish-yard, beach and bay,
The calmness of the evening lay.

Boom! and a cannon's voice rang out;
Boom! and a mingled cheer and shout,
With drum and trumpet, swelled the din —
"The Horton's in! The Horton's in!"

Safe from the lion's angry paw.
Safe from the lapdog's snapping jaw,
Hurrah! Cape Ann is sure to win —
"The *Horton's* in! The *Horton's* in!"

Hurrah! hurrah! rose loud and shrill,
From Duncan's Point to Banner Hill;
And Front and Park and Middle streets
Passed on the tidings to the fleet.

> **Hurrah! hurrah! for Yankee wit.**
> **Hurrah! hurrah! for Cape Ann grit,**
> **It's pluck and dash that's sure to win —**
> **"The *Horton's* in! The *Horton's* in!"**

> Here's three times three for the Captain, then,
> And three times three for his gallant men;
> For the strong and daring, free and brave,
> The olive-branch and the laurel wave.

> **Hurrah! hurrah! for Yankee wit.**
> **Hurrah! hurrah! for Cape Ann grit,**
> **It's pluck and dash that's sure to win —**
> **"The *Horton's* in! The *Horton's* in!"**

Old Locality had to perform his reading three times, after which he was escorted to the wharf to perform for the crowd who'd gathered on the streets.

At the afternoon sessions attended by the area councilmen, owners of vessels, and high standing businessmen the speeches continued for another hour. Harvey sat at a table with his brother Joseph, Edward Horton, Robert McKenzie, and the mayor. As much as Harvey protested that the act was one for the *McKenzie-Knowlton-Horton* firm, having three vessels seized, the town representatives were as adamant he'd done it for all the fishermen, owners, and even the wives and children who depended on the crews to make a living.

A vote was taken and the counselors agreed that each man of the *Horton* crew was to receive a monetary reward for their service. The people of the town had started the collection and it was rounded from the town treasury to the sum of one thousand dollars. Harvey and Oliver would not accept any of the gift money. Thus, Gillis, Richards, Penney, Webber, Dyer, and

McCloud received $200 each after the business owners added additional dollars to the funds. To this sum, the *McKenzie-Knowlton-Horton* firm quietly added $200 per man. With the bills Captain Knowlton included a note, "Each of you are *high-liners* for your service." This, of course, was in recognition to the fisherman aboard a vessel who landed the most fish on a trip for their high share of the profit.[1]

Each man later received a bronze plaque with an outline relief of the *Horton*. The inscription read, 'With gratitude from the citizens of Gloucester, Massachusetts, as a testimonial of the great service you have rendered the fishing interests, our town, and the United States of America in avenging the *Edward A. Horton*.'

---

[1] Such a sum would be equivalent to roughly $9,000 of buying power in 2024 dollars. This would be close to what a highliner fisherman would have received for a two or three month fishing trip.

Thursday – October 19, 1871 – 5 p.m.
Home of Captain George Proctor

"Captain Horton, may we have a word with you?" George Proctor ushered Harvey to his private study.

In the smoke-filled room waited Collector Babson, Commander Crowell of the Charlestown Navy Yard, his partners Edward Horton and Robert McKenzie, and Benjamin Corliss, Esquire, the lawyer for the firm's insurance company.

"What is it, gentlemen?" Harvey stood by the door, hesitant to enter.

"Come in, sir. Have a seat." Collector Babson indicated a chair at the head of the table. They all stood until Harvey was seated and then they sat down.

"We have news, from Washington, that Great Britain is taking up the *Horton* matter on insistence from Halifax." Babson passed a telegram towards Harvey.

"Meaning?" asked Harvey, not in the mood to read the long letter.

"What do you know of a Canadian smuggler captain by the name of Tom MacDonald?" asked Commander Crowell.

They all noticed Harvey's eyebrows twitch and his eyes narrow.

"It seems, Captain Knowlton, that Tom MacDonald has been detained by the Canadian officials as an accomplice in the escape of the *Horton*," said Babson.

"They have demanded the return of the *Horton*, on grounds she was stolen and violence was committed." Robert's right fist slammed the table. "It's an outrage."

"What is the result? Do they have any standing?" asked Harvey.

"It seems, two of Captain Tory's guards are claiming they were detained by drink, given to them by this MacDonald," added the commander.

Edward's right arm flew up from his side. "I don't see how that is relevant to any of this business. Someone can't be forced by violence to drink rum and neglect their duty."

"Gentlemen, may I?" The squire rose from his chair. "Captain Knowlton, as the Canadian cutter captain seized the *Horton*, he also took the ship's papers, isn't that so?"

Harvey nodded in agreement. "That's correct. The Canadians left nothing aboard for instruments or papers. Joseph and Oliver have given statements to that as I understand from the day the *Horton* was seized."

"True. Yes, they have." Squire Corliss smiled, as if he was making some argument to win over a jury. "And as such, you sailed the *Horton* into an American port without any papers. Do you agree with that charge?"

"Charge!" Robert McKenzie rose. "What is this, Captain Proctor?" The senior partner glared at his long-time friend.

"Just a moment, Robert. Let the squire continue," replied Proctor. A cigar hung in the corner of his mouth.

"Thank you, Captain Proctor." Corliss turned to Harvey. "Captain Knowlton, is that so?" asked the lawyer.

"Yes. How could I have the papers if Captain Tory had taken them?"

"Rightly so." The lawyer's smile grew wider. "Collector Babson, can you tell us the law on such matters?" Squire Corliss, as well as every captain in that room knew very well what the law was. Robert McKenzie appeared to relax.

Collector Babson rose. "You see, Captain Knowlton, as you arrived here with no papers, I have applied to the Secretary of the Treasury for a new set of documents for the *Horton*. They are being prepared today and will arrive by train tomorrow. At this point, as the ship is in Gloucester Harbor, without papers, we, I as the government revenue service official, and the navy," he indicated the commander, "can make no claim on the vessel in the name of the charges from the Canadian Government. Not at least until such time as legal proceedings of their claim of ownership can proceed."

Squire Corliss, unable to yield the plan's explanation, spoke again. "Under due process, a ship with no papers, must be secured by the government. The *McKenzie-Knowlton-Horton* firm is thus notified that, as the insurance agent, I have requested two navy guards be sent aboard, as keepers of the vessel. This action will remain until the papers arrive from Washington and we can then proceed with the British and Canadian request to hold the vessel."

"Now wait a minute!" McKenzie jumped up. He was again alarmed at the developments.

"Robert, I think I understand." Harvey motioned his partner to take a seat again.

"Let me explain further," stated George Proctor. He nodded at the commander, the collector, and the squire. All three left the room. Proctor stood. He placed his hands on the back of Harvey's and Robert's chairs. "Captain Knowlton, you took possession of the *Horton* while she was unguarded. Is that so?"

"Yes, George. You know it. We've been over this a half dozen times."

"Very good. And it is your position that the Canadian government left the vessel unguarded because?"

"My goodness, Proctor. You know it as well as I do. The Guysborough Harbor is difficult enough in flood tide and daylight to navigate. We took her during the night and low water. Captain Tory, in his hubris, believed such a natural defense was impossible for any American captain to conquer." Where Proctor stood, Harvey was forced to look over his right shoulder at Proctor's face.

Proctor took the cigar from his mouth and walked around the table to face McKenzie, Horton and Knowlton. He held his open hand to Edward.

Edward, who was a master of the law and politics, and architect of the arguments at hand, completed the explanation. "As such, Harvey, the departure of the Canadian guard from the *Horton*, as a result of their reliance on low tide, gave you the right, as the owner, to board the vessel and assume command."

"Is that so?" asked McKenzie.

"Rightly so!" stated Proctor. "As long as no violence was made in the retaking and the Canadian officers left the ship on their own will."

"There wasn't. And they did!" confirmed Harvey.

Proctor readmitted the lawyer to his office. The commander and collector remained in the hall.

Squire Corliss picked up the conversation as if it had been a practiced theatrical production. "Commander Crowell has ordered two men on the *Horton* as guard. This is due process while waiting for the papers to arrive."

The lawyer looked out the window. The band was playing on the corner. "The guards, due to low tide this evening, will not remain aboard the *Horton* on the outgoing tide, as the commander sees it impossible for anyone, Canadian or American, to sail Gloucester Harbor under such conditions in the *Horton*."

Everyone in the room knew this to be a fact of the tides, although not totally an infeasible feat. While there would be barely enough water to float the craft, a Gloucester skipper would have no fear of sailing on either end of the lowest tides.

Edward pulled his large frame up from the chair. "Harvey, Duncan and Connie have agreed to live on the *Horton*, as agents of our firm. Once the guards leave, the *Horton* then again becomes our possession, under due process, papers or no papers, so long as we have agents aboard. And the navy men leave on their own accord."

Both Harvey and Robert looked to the squire for confirmation.

"Yes. This is perfectly legal. As the American guards would have abandoned the ship and their posts, under the pretense of a low water barrier, the *McKenzie-Knowlton-Horton* owners have thus a legal right to claim the schooner."

"The same as Harvey did in Guysborough?" asked Robert.

"The same." The squire sat down, resting his case.

In this way, the commander had followed his orders from Washington and acted with reasonable protection of the schooner. In thus doing so, the commissioners in Washington would be able to inform their Canadian counterparts that the *Horton* had been guarded by men, and then subsequently by low tide with reasonable expectations of security. Under these circumstances, as permitted by law, the owners had legally taken possession of their vessel—with proof of ownership from the newly issued ship's papers.

Once the evening's festivities had concluded, and Harvey was seated in his chair near his own hearth, he finally relaxed. To Ellen's delight, he stated he had enjoyed the dinner, the parade, and the fireworks. The highlight, he told her, was seeing in the light of the rockets glare the American flag fluttering high on the mast of his ship. And, he felt vindicated in his actions to reclaim the *Horton*. With pride he recounted to her how Edward had once again proven his prowess in politics and relationships, to enact a plan to hold the vessel that displayed his own name.

In the days and weeks that followed, the local Gloucester guard assisted Duncan and Connie in guarding the ship; not against American forces, for it was sure there would be no acts of aggression from the navy, no matter what Canada or Britain petitioned. However, rumors persisted that Canadian cutters were seen cruising off Cape Ann. Strange characters in town, who came for a glimpse of the famous *Horton* were watched closely. They were pointed out as possible Canadian sailors hired to steal the vessel. Young boys, on constant high alert, would report anyone who wasn't a resident or local fishermen to the guards. Volunteers manned the lookout on Eastern Point, Rocky Neck, and Fort Square. The cannon was kept at the ready.

Through the remainder of 1871, the port of Gloucester, Massachusetts was likely the most watched and protected port on the American northern coast. With the oncoming of the winter months, the situation cooled and tensions were relieved. Harvey was pleased to read, in at least one periodical, praise for his actions.

No. 842—Vol. XXXIII.J   New York, November 18, 1871   Price 10 CENTS

CAPTAIN KNOWLTON proved himself an efficient person for such an undertaking, and he and his crew are entitled to the thanks of every fishing owner and fisherman in New England, as well as all others interested in the business, for their persistency in getting possession of this vessel, which it is hoped will awaken the Government to the necessity of taking prompt action in settling the vexed question of the fisheries. This branch of industry is an important one, and needs at this time the active sympathy and protection of the officials at Washington.

Bitter Port

November 1871
Guysborough, Nova Scotia

Six hundred miles over the Atlantic Ocean back in Guysborough, the subsequent days following the *Horton's* escape were long and embarrassing for Captain Tory. His rumored promotion never materialized. From Halifax, the official correspondence to Britain continued over the *Horton* matter. The waiting on news caused Tory mental anguish, which was further worsened by a new commander taking residence in the brick mansion on the waterfront. His wife, and daughter Alice, did their best to make a rented cottage on the outskirts of Guysborough feel like a home.

On a bitterly-cold, foggy November morning, word reached Guysborough that the Dominion Council's petition to Earl Kimberly had been successful. A copy of Kimberly's declaration was sent by express to Captain Tory. He sat by the crackling fire of the hearth, a glass of port in his hand, and read the statement, which encompassed three pages. The worst of it, his eyes settled on again:

> 'Due to the indignity to the flag of the nation, the prize money for the seizure of the American vessel the *Edward A. Horton* is hereby withdrawn. No payment shall be made to the captain of the *Sweepstakes* and crew. Furthermore, the council is ending any calls for reclamation of the said American vessel. This we proclaim is to serve as conduct to promote friendly

relations with our southern neighbor. It is our desire, and that of Britain, to maintain positive diplomatic relationships here forward.'

All in town knew Tory had hoped the government would take up the cause to regain the *Horton* on grounds the vessel was stolen with no fines paid. But news circulated that even the prize money for the taking of the *Horton* was being withheld. This was the worst of it. For Captain Tory had made little savings, having expected to continue in his revenue cutter command for years to come.

In a simple rocking chair near his fire, Tory drained his glass of port and closed his eyes. It was no secret in Guysborough that the captain blamed the smuggler, Tom MacDonald, for aiding the Yankees. In his dwindling state of finances, he planned his revenge.

December 1871
Guysborough, Nova Scotia
Home of Tom MacDonald

"Bonnie, it's not for myself I worry. The cottage we're now living in is small and there are no servants. Because of this my mother, who puts on airs she is fine, is worked to the bone, no matter how much I help her. How can I think of going now?"

"Oh, Alice. You must. You've already been accepted at full scholarship. You must not waste this opportunity for your own future. With such an education, you can help both of your parents. They know how much you desire to continue your studies." Bonnie truly wanted her friend to be happy. "Imagine the volumes in the college library. Not to mention the city public libraries—I hear there are several buildings!"

Miss Tory patted her friend's hand and rose from the smooth pine bench in front of the piano.

Bonnie played a few notes of *Silent Night*. "Have you heard anymore from Oliver?"

"Not since that first letter."

"Did you write him back?"

"Of course not! He ruined my family." Alice turned toward the darkness outside the window.

"Are you certain it was all his doing?"

"He took advantage of me and my position to spy on my father."

"Maybe. However, do you not believe his uncle would have taken the *Horton* regardless? Father says Captain Knowlton was not aware his nephew had remained in Guysborough. It came as a surprise when he heard him singing here that one night."

"His letter claimed the same. But, no matter." Alice flopped down on the sofa. "The way he went about the lie. And his secrecy. It wasn't right." Tears welled up in Alice's eyes. "Couldn't it be that such behavior runs in the Knowlton family?"

"What do you mean?"

"Rumor is your father is still waiting on his payment for services rendered to the thieving Yankee crew." Alice hadn't meant to sound mean, but if her father should suffer from this business, it served Tom MacDonald that he must suffer as well.

"I don't believe such rumors." Bonnie closed the sitting room door to keep their conversation private.

"Believe he hasn't been paid? Or believe he wasn't involved in the treasonous affair." Alice's two months of living with her father in the small cottage and listening to his rants had embedded feelings in her she wasn't aware of until the words left her lips.

Bonnie slapped a hand against her side. "Alice Tory! Such talk against my father shall not be permitted in this house."

"Then I may as well go."

"I guess you should." She handed her friend her coat.

At the slam of the door, Tom MacDonald and his wife appeared from the kitchen. "Wasn't Alice to spend the night?" asked her mother.

It was difficult for Bonnie to hide her watering eyes. "No. Yes. Well, she wasn't feeling well. Good night, Father. Good night, Mother."

It wasn't as if the two friends hadn't ever fought before. They'd had silly misunderstandings about likes and dislikes—as all girls do—but this was different. Alice was surely going to accept the college offer and leave Guysborough at the start of the New Year. What might be their final conversation weighed on Bonnie. She couldn't let Alice go without setting their friendship right again. Her distress was so, she couldn't sleep. She dressed and went quietly to the stairs. At the end of the hall, she could hear her parents talking in their bedroom. The gap under the door passed the sound to her ears.

"Didn't Captain Knowlton promise to send you the balance of money for your assistance?" she heard her mother ask.

"Yes, he did."

"And how long should we wait. You housed them in the barn. Nourished them with our food. Not to mention your assistance in the harbor."

A short gasp escaped Bonnie's lips. Her hand flew over her mouth. She surely had known of this, but to hear it directly, and to know her mother knew! That came as a surprise.

"He was to transfer the money to a Halifax bank. A letter was going to be sent care of Allister, so as not to go to our box. The

plan was, that letter would include the signature for me to withdraw the money."

"How long will you wait before you realize that this Yankee has made a fool of you, as he has of Tory."

"I shall make a trip to Gloucester after the winter."

"After the winter! You promised me new furniture from that money. In addition, we will need to replenish our winter food stores with the way those men ate."

Bonnie's stocking toes were lighted by a beam that shone under the door from a lantern that was just then lit.

"Must I also remind you of the need to send Bonnie to the school in Halifax. The money was to be used for that. She can't be expected to make anything of herself if she stays here in Guysborough."

"I know it."

The light under the door became brighter.

"Where are you going?"

"To the kitchen for a drink of water."

"The barn more likely and for a rum." This last, her mother said with disdain.

Quickly, Bonnie snuck back to her room and closed her door. The stairs creaked as her father went down. Her reconciliation with Alice would have to wait. Besides, now she wasn't so sure about the two Knowlton fishermen, their true intentions, or their character. Their other accomplice, she had her own thoughts about. Running the red ribbon through her fingers, she thought about just what she'd tell Billy Boy if ever she were to see *him* again.

One Turn Deserves Another

"O come list awhile and you soon shall hear.
By the rolling sea lived a maiden fair.
Her father followed the smuggling trade
Akin to a warlike hero that never was afraid!"

January 1872
Gloucester, Massachusetts

Tom MacDonald arrived at Gloucester on a gray winter day. Snowflakes blew left, right, and back up to the sky on the wind blowing off the Atlantic. The cobblestone streets were covered white on the edges and a rutted brown down the center where the horses and the grating iron carriage wheels rumbled over the stones.

He walked directly from the train station, only stopping for a time to admire the vessels in the Gloucester port. He'd always thought the numbers of boats in the fleet were inflated. Holding his hat down against the gale, the sleet stinging his eyes, he stood on a wooden wharf extending into the harbor. The booming industry for sails, barrels, bait, rigging, and all items necessary to design, fabricate, and outfit a ship were impressive, even for a smuggler who'd seen many northern fishing ports from the Provinces to Newfoundland.

"Where might I find Captain Harvey Knowlton?" he asked a fisherman who was coiling rope at the *Horton* berth.

The man pointed. "Office is on the second floor."

MacDonald found Knowlton arranging pins on the map of the Gulf of Maine.

"MacDonald?" Harvey was surprised to see the man. Below his tam o' shanter covered in white flakes, his face was in a scowl.

The smuggler wasted no time. "I've come for what ye promised me!"

"Meaning?"

"The money you owe."

"Captain MacDonald, I'm not sure what you're getting at, but please have a seat." Harvey's mind was working fast on how to quell MacDonald's pugnaciousness. He was wondering, since he'd sent the balance of the money as agreed, if MacDonald wasn't playing another of his schemes.

"Don't need to sit down. You need to explain your cheating me and my family from what was due!"

"I assure you. That money was sent." He opened a drawer of the desk. "I've got the receipt here in my papers." Knowlton indicated for MacDonald to sit at the table in the center of the room. The receipt from the Halifax bank was placed on the table, along with the notification of the funds being drawn. "As you instructed, I wired the note with the transfer approvals."

"When?"

Harvey looked through the papers. "It was November the second."

"Blimey!"

"What is it?"

"Officer Stevens! Stevens was relieved of his post in Guysborough. He took a position in the Halifax wire office after that."

"You don't think he…"

"Surely! Who else." MacDonald cut Harvey off to declare his conclusion.

"How could I have known!" declared Knowlton.

"Ye couldn't have." MacDonald then explained to Knowlton how it was a continued topic of discussion in the Guysborough mercantile as to Stevens moving to Halifax. Once there he'd established a tavern and tobacco shop on the waterfront.

The hat in MacDonald's hand was crushed into a ball. "Where he came upon the money for the business loan guarantee nobody in Guysborough knew. Most were glad to be rid of him. Now I think you and I both know how his position changed."

Having acknowledged that Knowlton hadn't cheated him, MacDonald relished telling Knowlton of Tory's demise. He told how he was moved from the grand, brick home with its white shutters; he told how the newspapers wrote of his failure to guard the *Horton*; he told how he couldn't hold his powdered, wig-covered head high around town any longer.

"I felt bad for his daughter. Little Alice, I've known her since she was five. The sins of the parent shouldn't fall to the children. In this case it was unavoidable I suppose." As if remembering some secret he'd forgotten to tell, MacDonald lowered his voice. "Ye might be interested to know, the House of Commons is still taking up Tory's appeal on the prize money from your earlier captured ship."

"My *Lily Rose Snow*."

"That'd be the one. The vessel which was sailed to England."

"He never collected on it?"

"Aye, he did." MacDonald laughed. "The crown did him one better. They confiscated it back on account of his dereliction of recent duty, what was left that they could get their paws on. Somehow, he thinks he deserves to get the money still. He's appealed to Commons."

Harvey didn't mind hearing the news that the prize money was confiscated, considering all the expense he'd gone through to right Tory's wrong. He was thinking, while MacDonald went on about how Captain Tory blamed him for getting his guards drunk the night the *Horton* was sailed out. "Even as it was proved them guards had taken rum from Tory's own storeroom of confiscated articles." MacDonald, his eyes squinting nearly closed, smiled at Knowlton.

The smuggler watched as Harvey went to the large safe in the corner of the office. He returned to the table and placed a large gold nugget in the center.

"Ye did find gold in Clam Harbor!"

Knowlton laughed. "No, MacDonald. That there is the last nugget from my '49 gold rush in California. It's worth more than what I offered to pay you for the *Horton* business by eight-fold, including what Stevens managed to steal." Now Knowlton found himself whispering. "For another bit of help, I'll pay you four times the original, plus all expenses."

"What do you have in mind?"

"Let me show you something." Together they walked the wharf. Knowlton indicated a schooner anchored in the harbor.

"She's a beauty."

"The *Defiance Too*."

"Defiant to what?"

"Tyranny."

Before the afternoon was out, MacDonald agreed to a mission with Knowlton aboard the *Defiance Too,* with a trusted crew they all knew.

Captain Knowlton had never told of the help MacDonald had given him in Guysborough. He hadn't wanted to implicate MacDonald in the affair. In keeping with this intent, he had to keep the smuggler hidden away from the busybodies of

Gloucester while he remained in town. Edward arranged a backroom at the Tarr Tavern where MacDonald boarded under a different name.

That evening, a private dinner was held in a room off the kitchen. The outer window shutters were kept closed. Aside from MacDonald, Harvey, and Edward, only Joseph Knowlton and Oliver were included. After the many toasts of rum on Tory's misfortunes, the talk was of fishing, the rivalry between Nova Scotia and Gloucester being the most of it. The bowls of steaming chowder were followed by rum drinking and pipe smoking.

After the drink had run out and the captains had departed, Oliver lingered in the hall and waited on MacDonald by the rear stairs.

"What is it, son? Seems you've been wanting to ask me something all night."

"Yes, Captain. About Alice Tory. I know you aren't any fan of that family."

With a grasp of Oliver's shoulder, the captain said, "I've nothing against the family. It's the once captain I've no use for." He held his arm firm and looked over the young gentleman. The boy was larger than himself and dressed in a suit of most expensive linen. *'Here's a lad that is going to be important in business,'* was his thought.

"Yes, Captain. Understood. So, then you don't mind me inquiring about Alice."

"You know, the people of town right quick figured out the miner was Harvey Knowlton and Oliver Knight was a mate on the *Horton* when the vessel was seized, the younger Knowlton of that crew. Ah, I'd say it only took them a few days anyway."

"Did you happen to hear how Alice took the news?"

"I heard it from Bonnie. She delivered the note you'd placed in that bottle. You should have told me you told her the truth and not the agreed story we discussed. I never thought to read it ahead, or I wouldn't have sent Bonnie along with it."

"But, I..."

"Never mind now. Nothing can be changed. You can be sure Alice was mighty hurt over it. As any woman would be if she'd thought she'd been played over."

"But that wasn't it! I didn't even know my uncle was coming back. My interest was in her. How can I convince her?"

"Aye, but that'd be a bottom-of-the-barrel halibut to try and sell."

Oliver hung his head.

"If you feel as you do, explain it to her, why don't ye?"

"I wrote a letter."

"Another letter!" MacDonald shook his head. "I may be an old salt when it comes to women and love, but I surely know, these things must be done face to face, my lad."

"I can't get up to Guysborough, not anytime soon. And to go, I might be thrown in jail."

"Who says you've got to go there." MacDonald bent closer to Oliver, his teeth showing in his open smile. "My boy, Alice is enrolled at the teacher's college in Boston. She has a scholarship there."

At seeing Oliver's expression, MacDonald began to laugh. It might have been brought on by the rum, but it was contagious to Oliver and he too laughed.

The next morning, a hand grabbed at MacDonald as he was turning the corner towards the train station. "Penney?"

"Aye, Captain."

"Well, son, you're looking well. Still fishing after all your fame?"

"Yes, sir. Ain't nothing else I'd want to be doing." Penney gazed around.

"What is it?" MacDonald looked around also.

"I was wondering, sir, if…"

"Out with it. I've got a train to catch."

"You see, Captain, I was wanting to ask you if I might ship on one of your fishing vessels."

"You want to leave Gloucester?" MacDonald waved his hand at the hundreds of masts in the harbor. "For Guysborough?"

"There's another reason, Captain."

MacDonald, rubbed his beard. "I'm sure I can guess it."

Penney's head fell.

"You might have had us all arrested, *Billy Boy*!" MacDonald watched as Penney raised his eyes to his. "Yeah, I know it, from that day I caught the two of you on the road."

"But, Captain, it was her voice, her singing. I had to meet her."

"Well, no harm done seeing we got away." He put out a finger towards Penney. "But my daughter deserves more than a common fisherman!"

"I've money saved and more from the gratitude the town has given us. I'd like to buy a vessel of my own. But I can't operate out of Guysborough as an American. For reasons you understand."

"Aye."

"With your sponsorship," Penney raised his chin, "and partnership in my vessel, I could fish the local waters."

"I see you've thought this out." MacDonald looked toward the station and the waiting train. "You come and see me in the spring."

"I've my bags packed and ready to join you now." Penney pointed to two ditty bags near the building.

The Province captain blew out a deep breath. "I suppose you'll be going whether I agree or not."

"Yes, Captain, that's true."

"And if my Bonnie won't have anything to do with ye after ye up and lied to her about who you were?"

"I'll pull that line when I come to it—if you don't mind, sir?"

"Alright then. I can always use a good man on the deck." For a good minute he eyed Penney, then he dug into his inner coat pocket. In his hand he held a red ribbon edged in white lace. "Bonnie asked, should I run into you, to give this to you."

Penney had plenty of questions, but the father couldn't say one way or another what the ribbon meant. Over the long train ride north, Penney had plenty of time to think on what to do if Bonnie wouldn't have him.

January 1872
Boston, Massachusetts

Two days after Tom MacDonald left for home, Oliver was seated in a coffee shop on Tremont Street in Boston wondering about what he'd say. He later paced along West Newton Street outside the new building of the Normal School. He was dressed in a fine, blue suit. His face was clean shaven and his hair cut close above the ears. On his head he wore a tall black hat.

Not knowing how to find Alice Tory, or where she might have classes, he asked the first student he saw come through the doors. The girl didn't know an Alice, but told him where to find the office. He was making his way through the halls, each full of young ladies staring at him as he passed. Twice he was mistaken for a lost professor.

At an intersection of four hallways he turned in a circle. While he observed the students rushing to their classrooms, he decided his idea was foolish. He turned toward the main corridor to leave. From a room came a woman holding a stack of books. He approached her.

"Excuse me, would you happen to have a copy of Miss Alcott's *The Mysterious Key?*" he asked.

Alice looked towards him. "Oliver!" She stumbled back. He reached to catch her.

"Unhand me. You lied to me! You took advantage of me!" She faced him and waited for an explanation.

"Alice, that was not my intent. I assure you. If you'll let me, I would like to explain the ordeal."

"Your family has broken my father. Why should I speak with you?"

"I work for my uncle—Captain Harvey Knowlton. It was partially, well, maybe wholly my fault those dorymen went adrift. Their error in fishing within three miles of shore, whether to fill a ship's hold or for two fish shan't be excused."

"True enough," she beamed at being shown right.

"Yet, is it right that an entire ship should be held captive for two fish? The entire catch auctioned to the highest bidder, for which the men who did the work received nothing? Should a government seize property and not levy a reasonable fine for the crime committed?"

"You'd make a fine lawyer, Mr. Knowlton."

"I'm only trying to explain. I first remained in Guysborough because of you, not the *Horton*. It was only a passing glance that first day I saw you—although it was enough to keep me there. I had no idea of my uncle's plans or that he'd travel to Guysborough."

Oliver remained in Boston for the week. Arguments were made. Positions were clarified. Statements were doubted. Throughout the spring, he returned at least once a week to see Alice. Far from home and the bitterness of her father, Alice was overcome with the fond memories of the times she'd had with Oliver on the hill outside of Guysborough.

Together they made new memories. They walked the paths of the Boston Common. They spent many hours in the public library, where Alice worked on her studies, and Oliver read books not contained on any of the Knowlton schooners. On the warm days of March, they sat under a tree overlooking the harbor. He took her on a visit to Gloucester. At a dinner hosted by his uncle, he made an introduction of her to the superintendent of schools.

Epilogue

> "Give me a laughing, parting kiss,
> That I afar may be
> Blest in the thought you gave me this
> To cheer me, lass, at sea."

September 8, 1872
A Year Since the *Horton* Affair Began
Gloucester Harbor

From the quarterdeck of the newest schooner commissioned by the *McKenzie, Knowlton, & Horton Company*, I watched as my nephew, now Captain Oliver Knowlton, said his goodbyes to his wife Alice at the wharf. The two embraced. His first and second mates stood by holding painters, ready to row him to take his command of *Nemo's Revelations*.

Hurriedly, I made my way below to the captain's quarters before my nephew boarded. I sat and wrote a note to the new captain to wish him a safe voyage. Within, I included the importance of adhering to a ship's hierarchy of command. In business terms, as the ship's owner, I reminded him that he was responsible for the vessel. As his uncle, I reminded him he was even more responsible for the men aboard and their loved ones back home.

From my pocket I pulled a folded news article. I felt my lips move upward in an arc at the rereading of the *London Times* page from a July issue:

"The *Lily Rose Snow*, a ship legally seized two years prior by the Dominion Government for illegal fishing in Canadian waters, suddenly sunk at its mooring near the mouth of River Avon, Bristol. The British Captain in charge said the sinking overnight was a mystery as the ship was recently overhauled with no noticeable issues. He was not ruling out foul play. The insurance agent for the ship remarked to the Times, *"Beyond the loss of the vessel was a collection of several rare navigational instruments. Our Agency had requested the new owners to relocate the items to a more secure location than a ship on the seas. We elected not to insure those items while on the vessel. Now they are likely lost forever."*

I placed the article at the top of the captain's correspondence drawer. From the crate Frank Sweeney had placed aboard earlier per my instructions, I unpacked my grandfather's instruments. The wall of the quarters had been designed in the same fashion for mounting the instruments when they sailed on the *Patience to-Knight*.

With care I secured the sextant with its gold arm, the ring dial, the astrolabe, and the ebony and brass quadrant with carved ivory scales. I held the two-hundred-year-old cross-staff and thought of my regrets from that last argument with my Uncle Nehemiah. I wondered if he had had the same regret when he tossed it to Frank Sweeney over the open ocean and into the dory.

Stepping up through the companionway, I went aft to the stern. I raised the long spy glass towards Rocky Neck. The Knowlton home on the hill overlooked the harbor, as it did in my grandfather's days, with a position to watch our ships swaying in their moorings. I swung the glass down to the boat house.

Sweeney was there, looking through his glass at me. He raised his right hand to his forehead in a salute.

Sweeney, the old cook, had cooked a good plan. And while sinking the *Lily Rose* was a tough choice, he was right, I didn't need to sail the *Lily Rose Snow* back home across the ocean. A new vessel could be built. It was only fitting to sail grandfather's instruments home.

On the deck, at noon with the sun blazing down, Oliver J. Knowlton was given command of the *Nemo's Revelations*, a Gloucester schooner of the finest kind.

At high tide, with myself at the wheel of the *Edward A. Horton*, I escorted our newest vessel out of the harbor. Our two ships raised sails and raced north by nor'east in search of the mackerel. We'd be in the Northumberland Strait in ten to fifteen days—the wind and seas willing.

My crew of the *Horton* sang as we rounded Rocky Neck:

> *The spirit true of 'seventy-six*
> *Lives in the land to-day;*
> *Thank God! — and no Dominion cliques*
> *Shall bar the Yankee's way.*

This is my story of the *Edward A. Horton.*
Harvey Knowlton, Jr.
September 8, 1872

The End

Postscript:

This would be Captain Harvey Knowlton Jr.'s final trip to sea.

Appendices

Ballads of the Edward A. Horton

The Horton was seized in the early days of September 1871. The news arrived in Gloucester about the eighth of that month. Fifty-six years later Fannie Hardy Eckstorm and Mary Winslow Smyth penned the preface to their book, *Minstrelsy of Maine*. In that preface, dated September 8, 1927, they wrote, "The old songs were fast vanishing. With them would be lost all they represented of the mental horizon of the pioneer, the cultus of the logger and river-driver, the hunter and trapper, the sailor and hand-line fisherman."

The *Minstrelsy of Maine* book is a gem of a collection from the woods and sea. Eckstorm and Smyth set out to perform a service of research into the ballads that were sung in lumber camps, in logging clearings, within dim forecastles, on wet decks of the schooners, and fish piers of old. In her typical fashion, Eckstorm was not satisfied in simply writing down the lyrics of the songs. She went deeper into the origins of the ballads, and where multiple versions existed, she documented those as well. Such was the case with the ballads about the *Horton*. Several verses of the *Horton* ballads were included within the book chapters. The full lyrics are reproduced here.

The first, *The Horton's In!* was published in Proctor's *Fisherman's Memorial* (1873) and was attributed to the local Gloucester poet, *Old Locality*. A rendition of the ballad, and several more from the Eckstorm and Smyth book, were recorded by Maine's Mallett Brothers Band on their album, *Falling of the Pine*.

The Horton's In!

The day retired serene and fair,
And lights came glancing here and there,
While gently swung the twilight down
On Rocky Neck and Gloucester Town.

The pulse of business life was still,
From Gardner's Brook to Beacon Hill,
On wharf and fish-yard, beach and bay,
The calmness of the evening lay.

Boom! and a cannon's voice rang out;
Boom! and a mingled cheer and shout,
With drum and trumpet, swelled the din —
"The *Horton's* in! The *Horton's* in!"

Safe from the lion's angry paw.
Safe from the lapdog's snapping jaw,
Hurrah! Cape Ann is sure to win —
"The *Horton's* in! The *Horton's* in!"

Hurrah! hurrah! rose loud and shrill,
From Duncan's Point to Banner Hill;
And Front and Park and Middle streets
Passed on the tidings to the fleet.

Hurrah! hurrah! for Yankee wit.
Hurrah! hurrah! for Cape Ann grit,
It's pluck and dash that's sure to win —
"The *Horton's* in! The *Horton's* in!"

Here's three times three for the Captain, then,
And three times three for his gallant men;
For the strong and daring, free and brave,
The olive-branch and the laurel wave.

The second was titled, *The Escape of the Horton*, attributed to *Yankee Ned*, and also published in Proctor's *Fisherman's Memorial* (1873).

Under the canopy of blue,
Under the starlit sky.
They crept—the daring, manly crew—
To cut her out, or die!

Into the store they climb,
With darkness all around;
Their nimble fingers quickly find
That every sail is sound.

With hank and halyard stout,
Her wings were bent anew—
Those gallant lads they ran her out
Across the waters blue.

Away from Scotia's shadowy shore,
With cruisers on her lee.
She travels o'er the deep once more,
To Cape Ann's port—she's free!

Old Eastern Point is dead ahead,
And the skipper's home in sight,
With flying colors she is sped
Safe into port at night.

The spirit true of 'seventy-six
Lives in the land to-day;
Thank God!—and no Dominion cliques
Shall bar the Yankee's way.

A third ballad for the *Horton*, was noted by Eckstorm as not being found in Proctor's *Fisherman's Memorial* (1873). She learned of it from a Mrs. Oliver K. Joyce, of Gott Island, Maine, some fifty-three years after it was supposedly penned at the return of the *Horton*.

Ye sons of Uncle Samuel, come listen for awhile,
I'll tell you of a captain that was made in Yankee style;
Of the schooner *E. A. Horton* and the bold undaunted band,
Commanded by brave Knowlton, a true son of Yankee land.

Now the schooner *E. A. Horton* in the British harbor lay;
She was taken by the *Sweepstakes* while cruising in disguise;
Our treaty they rejected, our government defied,
They captured our fishermen, now, Johnny, mind your eye!

On the eighth day of October, in the year of seventy-one,
Our bold, undaunted heroes the daring work begun.
Said brave Knowlton to his comrades: 'If you will follow me,
We'll take our vessel back again, whate'er the cost may be.

'We'll stand by one another, like brothers brave and true,
We'll show those thievish Britishers what Yankee blood can do.'
While Johnny's sons were sleeping, with red ruin in their brain,
The sons of Uncle Samuel took their vessel back again.

On the next Monday morning, when Johnny looked about,
He found his gold prospector and the *Horton* had stepped out;
And now the news began to penetrate the Britishers
    called so thick,
They finally acknowledged 'twas a bold and Yankee trick.

Now the schooner *E. A. Horton* and the gallant band are free
From the New Dominion government and many miles at sea;
While the news of her recapture are circulating round,
Our gallant sons of freedom to their native land are bound.

Now, Johnny, there's a jolly time in Gloucester tonight;
The heavy guns are firing, the torches burning bright,
And the band plays 'Yankee Doodle' and it makes
    the welkin ring;
Young Americans are shouting, 'The *Horton* has got in!'

Of the New Dominion government I warn you to beware;
Why don't you join the treaty and settle this affair?
And learn to do by others as you'd have them do by you,
And not abuse your neighbors, as Old Johnny used to do?

Of this ballad, Eckstorm wrote:
> "This song no doubt was adapted from 'Johnny Bull,' a prize-
> fighting song upon the fight between Sayres and the Benicia
> Boy (John C. Heenan) which took place April 17, 1860. That
> song was a great favorite, both with woodsmen and with
> fishermen. It contains expressions, like 'Johnny, mind your
> eye,' which, with the similarity of meter, indicate that this
> song of the Horton went to the familiar tune of 'Johnny Bull.'

Author note: This ballad was published by George Proctor in
Fishermen's Ballads and Songs of the Sea (1874), with slight word
differences and attributed to William E. Lakeman, under the title,
Recapture of the Schooner E. A. Horton.

A fourth ballad, written in Nova Scotia, was discovered during
research for this book. See reference, *"The Story of the E. A.
Horton: a letter to the Editor."*

Ballad, Verse, and Quote References

First lines of the quoted material used in the chapters are repeated here with the source. It is noted, where lines were modified to fit the story of the *Horton*. If a ballad is not listed here, it is original to the novel.

Opening Ballad

"This is the song of the seaman." Modified from, Minstrelsy of Maine (page 199), attributed to Bertrand L. Shurtleff. Collected by Fannie Hardy Eckstorm and Mary Winslow Smyth, 1927.

Chapter: A Patriot Wronged

"I purchased a glass of stiff Glo'ster grog." Modified from, *Tale of the Sea-Faring Man*, by Holman F. Day, in *Up in Maine: Stories of Yankee Life Told in Verse*. 1900.

Chapter: The Chase

1. *"Our captain's name, all know, was Knowlton."* Modified from a ballad documented by Eckstorm, with a late version from 1873. She wrote, "this very popular old song is commonly changed to suit any ship and voyage that is preferred."

The news stories of the *Horton* state Harvey Knowlton left Gloucester on September 20th, 1871. So for this ballad, the captain is noted as being Joseph Knowlton when the *Horton* was seized. The first mate, was fictionalized to be another Knowlton family member, a nephew given the name of Oliver.

Also, fishing schooners from Gloucester rarely had a second command in rank known as a *mate*, a position more commonly given on military vessels. On a fishing vessel there was the captain, or better termed the master, and the crew of fishermen. In this novel the terms *captain* and *mate* are used for more common reader nomenclature, even if not Gloucester history specific.

2. *"A Yankee sloop came down the strait."* Adopted from an old shanty. Eckstorm characterized this as a *chantey*, the word

derivation she gives in her book, as opposed to the more common spelling of *shanty*.

3. "Singing, Row, Row, Row, bullies, Row." Modified from an old chanty. Eckstorm had similar words contributed by a Captain J. A. Creighton, of Thomaston, Maine. In 1925, the captain wrote: 'This is a chanty the writer has never seen in print but helped to sing over forty years ago. There must have been fifty verses to this chanty, and it told of a sailor's life from beginning to end and was one of the best chanties the writer ever heard.'

Chapter: Harbor Blues

"What looms upon our starboard bow." Modified from *The Yankee Man-of-war* and *The Stately Southerner*, two ballads about the American sloop-of-war Ranger, built on Badger's Island, Maine and commanded by Captain John Paul Jones.

Chapter: Advice of Friends

"Farewell to friends, farewell to foes," modified from a verse in, *Blow the Man Down*, Holman F. Day. 1916.

Chapter: Miner Days

1. "Don't fret your life," from a verse titled, *Moral*, Holman F. Day, in *Up in Maine: Stories of Yankee Life Told in Verse*.

2. "O little, Fannie, here is a song, so listen to me." Original to the tune of the ancient shanty, *Blow the man down*.

Chapter: Billy Boy

1. "Won't you tell me Alice darling," modified from *Mollie Darling*, written and composed by Will S. (William Shakespeare) Hays (1871).

2. "Where have you been all the day, Billy Boy, Billy Boy?" modified from an old English folk song (or sea shanty) that was based on *Lord Randall*, an Anglo-Scottish border ballad.

Chapter: Choosing Sides

1. "Dory here, an' the Horton there." Modified verse from *The Doryman's Song*, Holman F. Day. Pine Tree Ballads. 1902.

2. "Dixey Bull was a pirate bold," From the lyrics of *Dixey Bull* in, *Minstrelsy of Maine.* Collected by Fannie Hardy Eckstorm and Mary Winslow Smyth, *1927.*

Chapter: The Mysterious Key

"Love comes to all soon or late," from The Mysterious Key (1867), by L. M. Alcott. Chapter IV.

Chapter: Auld Offenses Be Not Forgot

In, *The Court and Character of King James* (1650), Sir Anthony Weldon wrote, "The Italians having a Proverb, He that deceives me once, it's his fault; but if twice, it's my fault."

Chapter: Victory Declared

"When in safety or in doubt," from a verse in *Blow the Man Down*, Holman F. Day. 1916.

Chapter: Mutiny and Murder

"Oh—I am not a man-'o-war, or privateer," modified from *Shanty of the Prince Luther*, in *Clothes Make the Pirate*, Holman F. Day. 1925.

Chapter: Gold in the Cove

"Our captain stood on his quarter-deck," modified from *The Whaler*, in *Clothes Make the Pirate*, Holman F. Day. 1925. Referenced in Harvey's remembrance of the one-legged boatman, who was met by Sir Roger at Vauxhall. In, the Sir Roger de Coverley Papers, 1712. [Tuesday, May 20, 1712. Addison.] The passage is written as: "We were no sooner come to the Temple Stairs but we were surrounded with a crowd of watermen, offering us their respective services. Sir Roger, after having looked about him very attentively, spied one with a wooden leg, and immediately gave him orders to get his boat ready. As we were walking towards it, 'You must know,' says Sir Roger, 'I never make use of anybody to row me that has not either lost a leg or an arm.'"

Chapter: One Last Sleep

"What shall we do with the lovestruck sailor?" An old sea chant, now known to the tune of *Drunken Sailor*. Modified from, *Clothes Make the Pirate*, Holman F. Day. 1925.

Chapter: We'll Warp Her Out

1. *"Said brave Knowlton to his crew,"* see *Horton* ballad attributed to William E. Lakeman in appendix, *Ballads of the Edward A. Horton.*

2. *"Hoo-oo-rah! And up she rises!"* same as, *"What shall we do with the lovestruck sailor?"*

Chapter: A Bold and Yankee Trick

"Davis, you old captain brave and bold," in the note left for Davis, modified from a *Captain Kidd* ballad of the 1800s.

Chapter: By Dead Reckoning

1. *"There's a curl o' caps to lee'ard"* from, *Christmas Time in Glo'Ster.* Holman F. Day. Pine Tree Ballads, 1904.

2. *"Our doctor's name it being McCloud."* A verse modified from, *The Eastern Light*, a ballad of an 1866 Gloucester schooner of near the same tonnage as was the *Horton.*

3. *"Mount Desert Rock it was well known,"* In *Minstrelsy of Maine*, Eckstorm wrote, "In 1835 the *Sarah*, a packet sailing between Boston and Eastport, was wrecked off the Maine coast, and half of those on board were lost."

4. *"For HE commanded a tempest."* From Psalm 107.

5. *"It was Thursday afternoon, no land did we espy."* Modified from, *The Loss of the Albion*, in, *Minstrelsy of Maine.* Eckstorm wrote of this ballad, "The ship Albion, Williams master, from New York to Liverpool, was wrecked on the Irish Coast, probably not far from Kinsale, at 4 A.M. of the morning of April 22, 1822."

Chapter: A Jonah Day

"I pray you give attention." From, *On the loss of the George Vessels, in 1862*, in Fishermen's Ballads and Songs of the Sea.

Chapter: Sugar and Spice

1. *"Cheer up, crew, bright smiles await you."* A modified Boston shanty, from, *Clothes Make the Pirate*, Holman F. Day. 1925.

2. *"That day so fragrant with its joy."* Modified from the ballad, *That Summer Day At Norman's Woe*, by George Proctor in, *The*

Fishermen's Memorial and Record Book. The line ending in Norman's Woe, replaced with Loblolly Cove, a cove on Cape Ann between Gloucester and Rockport.

3. *"We sailed on the Horton home."* Original, to the melody of the traditional Caribbean shanty, *The John B. Sails,* as documented by Richard Le Gallienne in his article *Coral Islands and Mangrove-Trees,* (December 1916, pp. 81–90). Harper's Monthly Magazine.

Chapter: A Hero No More

1. *"Singing Hi derry, Ho derry, Hi derry down."* Old shanty chorus.

2. *"Old hoss, old hoss, what brought you here?"* From lyrics known as, *Old Horse* in, *Minstrelsy of Maine.* In 1927 Eckstorm wrote, "Fifty years ago every Maine child knew the sailor lines on, *The Old Horse…*if a particularly bad piece of beef is found, one of them takes it up and addresses it thus."

Chapter: We Saw Three Ships

"There's naught upon the stern." An ancient shanty, from, *Clothes Make the Pirate,* Holman F. Day. 1925.

Chapter: Serene and Fair

"Ye sons of Uncle Samuel, come listen for awhile," see *Horton* ballad attributed to William E. Lakeman in appendix, *Ballads of the Edward A. Horton.*

Chapter: The Horton's In!

1. *"When the Horton comes sailing home again, Oh yeah! Oh yeah!"* Modified from *When Johnny Comes Marching Home Again,* a Civil War song.

2. *"Boom! and a cannon's voice rang out."* From, *The Horton's In!* in, *Minstrelsy of Maine.* Collected by Fannie Hardy Eckstorm and Mary Winslow Smyth, *1927.*

Chapter: One Turn Deserves Another

"O come list awhile and you soon shall hear." From, *The Female Smuggler,* a traditional English ballad.

Epilogue

"Give me a laughing, parting kiss." From, A Kiss to take to Sea, in, *Fishermen's Ballads and Songs of the Sea.*

The *Edward A. Horton* in the News

1871: The *Daily Press* article in the chapter *Serene and Fair* which Harvey reads upon his return is an actual account.

1874: Reported in The Fishermen's Own Book (1882): **1874 Lost in Dories:** David Henderson from schooner *Edward A. Horton*, Feb 26.

1879: February 20, 1879, seven years after the *Edward A. Horton* was seized, the Boston Post reported:

> The schooner *Edward A. Horton* of Gloucester, arrived from an off-shore fishing trip on Wednesday, reports that one of the crew, Michael O. Malley, was lost overboard and drowned. He was a young man, unmarried, and belonged in Gloucester.

1880: Reported in, *The Saga of Cape Ann*: Two dory men of the crew of the *Edward Horton*, were caught in a fog. They rowed for 5 days until they reach Newfoundland.

Further details were reported in, *The Fishermen's Own Book*, including the names of the dorymen (page 152):

> At the Mercy of the Seas.—*Five Days without Food or Drink.*—John Whitlaw and Samuel Orgrove, two of the crew of fishing sch. *Edward A. Horton* of this port, left that vessel on Grand Bank, Thursday, July 1, 1880, for the purpose of hauling their trawls. After loading their dory they found themselves unable to return to their vessel, on account of a heavy fog having shut in, and rowed aimlessly away in the hope of finding succor. After undergoing great exposure and hardships, on the following Tuesday they effected a landing upon the coast of Newfoundland, greatly reduced and almost in a dying condition from their enforced abstinence from food and drink. They were kindly

treated, and were forwarded to St Johns, N. F., where they arrived on the evening of July 9.

> Note: In this novel, this event was used in the year 1868 when the fictional character Frank Sweeney and a mate went adrift in a dory from the fictional vessel *Patience to-Knight*.
>
> The most famous stories of a Gloucester doryman surviving being lost at sea, is that of Howard Blackburn. See the book, *Lone Voyager*.

1898: On November 9, 1898, the *Edward A. Horton* was fishing off of Digby, Nova Scotia, Canada. The schooner ran aground off North Point, Brier Island, Bay of Fundy. The ship was lost. The crew was saved.

Knowlton Family Tree

The following was compiled from various records for illustration only to show some of the fictional characters. The accuracy of names and dates for the real people cannot be certain.

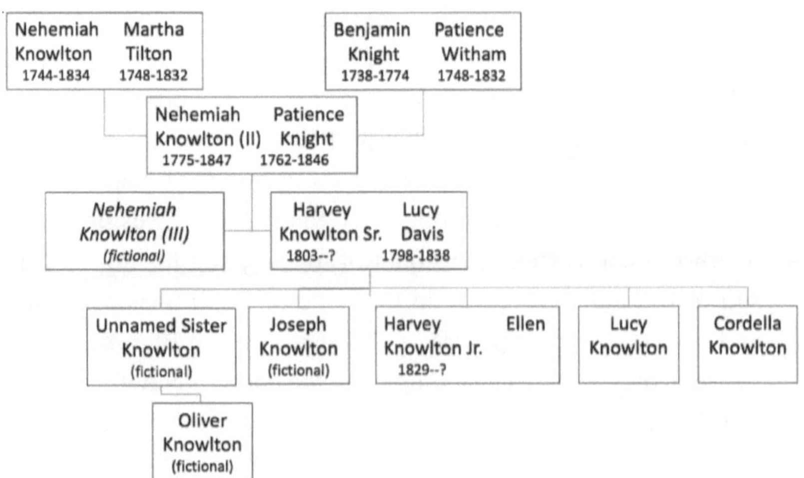

The Saga Continued

Canada was seizing fishing vessels and levying fines long before 1871, the year the *Horton* was seized. The practices even continued into the following decades. Several examples are noted here, some sixteen years after the *Edward A. Horton.*

Fishery Seizures, from, *History of the Town and City of Gloucester, Cape Ann, Massachusetts,* by James R. Pringle, 1892.

1887, page 265

"Notwithstanding the attitude of our government in adopting the retaliatory law, the Canadian cruisers pursued their operations as before.

July 25, the schooner *Annie W. Hodgdon* engaged in cod fishing was seized at Shelburne, N. S., on suspicion of violating the fishery law, and was released on payment of a fine of $400.

Later in the summer a large fleet of vessels were engaged in fishing off East Point, P. E. I., and two seine boats and seines belonging to the schooner *Col. J. H. French* and *Argonaut,* together with 14 of the crew of these schooners, were seized for alleged fishing within the three-mile limit. They were taken to Souris, the men delivered to the U. S. consul, the paraphernalia to the collector."

1889, page 271

"Early in the spring the schooner *Mattie Winship* was seized off Cape North charged with fishing inside the three-mile limit. She was released on payment of a fine of $3,000.

The schooner *David J. Adams,* the first Gloucester vessel seized since the expiration of the Washington Treaty, was ordered to be sold by the Canadian authorities.

1890, page 274

April 24, the schooner *Abbie M. Deering*, was seized by the collector of customs at Canso, N. S., on a charge of smuggling fresh fish ashore during the night. The *Deering* put in to land a sick man. The captain and crew belonged in Nova Scotia, and stated that they considered themselves perfectly secure in landing and selling fish where they were so well acquainted. The fish were ordered sold, and the vessel was fined $800, which was paid under protest.

May 2, the schooner *Howard Holbrook*, in the cod fishery, was seized at Harbor Breton, Newfoundland, for an alleged infraction of the bait law. She was released upon the filing of a bond of $2,500.

The schooner *Davy Crockett*, in the mackerel fishery, was seized September 28, at Souris, P. E. I., charged with fishing inside the three-mile limit, preferred by Capt. Gordon of the Canadian service. She was taken to Charlottetown and secured to Peak's wharf. A warrant and summons was nailed to her mast, the Crown claiming the condemnation of the vessel and appurtenances in violation of the treaty of 1818.

1870 Directory of Gloucester Vessels

There were over 506 schooners in the District of Gloucester in 1870.

The McKenzie, Knowlton & Co. vessel that was captured in 1870 was the *Alice. H. Wonson*. There are minor typographical errors in the records for the vessel's middle initial and the tonnage. The ship was new in 1870.

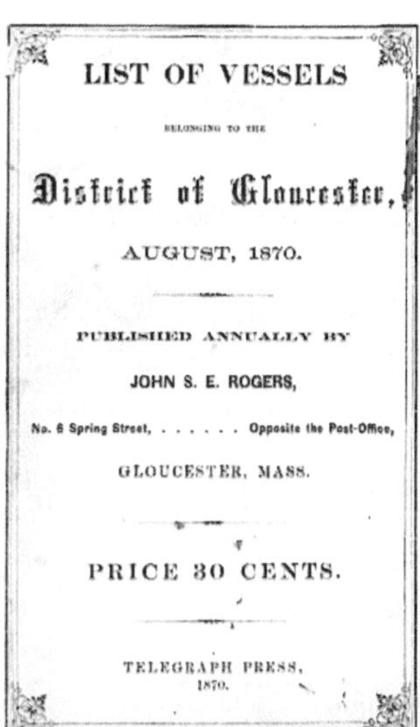

LIST OF VESSELS

BELONGING TO THE

District of Gloucester,

AUGUST, 1870.

PUBLISHED ANNUALLY BY

JOHN S. E. ROGERS,

No. 6 Spring Street, ... Opposite the Post-Office,

GLOUCESTER, MASS.

PRICE 30 CENTS.

TELEGRAPH PRESS,
1870.

GLOUCESTER HARBOR. 1870 1

Name of Vessel.	New Tonnage.	Master's Name.	Number and Letters.	Where Built.	When Built.	Owners' or Fitters' Names.
Aaron Burnham, 2d,	69.09	Lemuel Hobbs,	1913	Essex,	1870	D. C. & H. Babson, Jr.
Abby Dodge,	59.61	John Daniel,	1772	Essex,	1868	Smith & Gott.
Abby M. Heath,	58.98	Edwin Flagg,	483	Essex,	1860	Solomon Pool.
Abigail,	35.08	Bowen King,	490	Essex,	1837	George Dennis & Co.
Abigail Brown,	47.50	Ezekiel S. Call,	495	Essex,	1850	George W. Plumer.
Ada Herbert,	89.28	Josiah A. Gould,	464	East Haven, Conn.,	1858	Elisha Crowell.
Ada L. Harris,	42.69	James Blatchford,	476	Boothbay, Me.,	1863	McKenzie, Hardy & Co.
Addie M. Story,	61.36	John J. Rowe,	497	Essex,	1867	Solomon Pool.
Addison Gilbert,	48.54	John Chisholm,	489	Chelsea,	1866	David Low & Co.
Adelia Hartwell,	60.29	Edward Morris,	1777	Essex,	1869	D. C. & H. Babson, Jr.
Aerial,	25.98	Mark Lane, Jr.,	253	Gloucester,	1830	Aaron D. Wells.
		George C. Johnson	1501	Essex,	1867	Daniel Sayward.
A. H. Wonson,	63.68	Benjamin Webber,	1779	Essex,	1868	McKenzie, Knowlton & Co.
		John M.	470	Essex,	1854	Rowe & Jordan

Alatamaha,
Alfalfa,
Alfaretta,
Alhambra,
Alice G. Wonson,
Alice M. Lewis,
A. Lincoln,
American Eagle,
Amos Cutter,

ADDITIONS TO THE LIST.

The following are the new vessels, thirty-seven in number, 2557.20 tons, that have been added to the List, which was made up to August 1st, 1870.

Aaron Burnham, 2d,	69.09	J. J. Clark,	69.68
Alice G. Wonson,	64.18	Job Johnson,	64.07
Annie Hooper,	69.21	Knight Templar,	73.26
Annie E. Lane,	50.85	Mary Louise,	68.15
Barracouta,	68.57	Messenger,	66.20
Carrie E. Sayward,	62.18	N. H. Phillips,	66.93
Clara B. Chapman,	68.19	Oliver Eldridge,	65.86
Cora E. Smith,	49.24	Restless,	66.47
Dauntless,	69.67	Sarah C. Pyle,	52.62
Edward A. Horton,	66.46	Southern Cross,	65.20
Edith Wonson,	69.41	Sultana,	69.84
Elisha Crowell,	67.78	Tragabigzanda,	68.03
Frederic Gerring, Jr.,	70.88	Varuna,	83.80
F. W. Homans,	66.21	White Eagle,	70.41
Gail Hamilton,	69.	White Fawn,	64.49
George J. Tarr,	59.85	Wm. Parsons, 2d,	64.41
Janet Middleton,	66.43		

Knowlton Vessels as of 1878

From the list of Vessels Belonging to the District of Gloucester, August 1878.

Vessel Name	Tonnage	Master	Ship Numbers	Built
Alice H. Wonson	64	Benjamin Webber	1773	Essex, 1868
Defiance (boat)	18.97	Elisha C. Wheeler	6904	Essex, 1876
Edward A. Horton	66.46	E. M. Hodsdon	8623	Essex, 1870
Emma S. Osier	23.91	Charles W. Osier	135,326	Essex, 1878
Equal. (boat)	10.89	Eben A. Brazier	7 1 3 6	—
Jennie and Julia (boat)	14.21	Daniel Rowe, 3rd.	75,947	Gloucester, 1877
Martha Jane (boat)	16.89	Jeremiah Gaskell	17,081	—
Phantom	30.05	Joseph F. Wheeler	150,017	Salisbury, 1875
Procter Brothers	77.05	Edward Trevoy	150,066	Essex, 1876

Knowlton also fitted ships for others as accounted in this note:

"Lizzie and Namari, 94.09 tons, one year old, lost near Matinicus, Aug. 31. Owned by George Laturen, master, and Almon Mason of Pigeon Core, and was **fitted at Harvey Knowlton, Jr.'s**. Valued at $7,000, and insured for $6,000 in the Union office of Provincetown. Wreck sold for $50."

— — — — — —

Edward A. Horton 1878 Listing

LIST OF VESSELS   **1878**

BELONGING TO THE

DISTRICT OF GLOUCESTER,

AUGUST, 1878.

The following List of Vessels gives the name, tonnage by new measurement, master's name, official number, where and when built, and the fitters' or principal owners' names. The Letters assigned to vessels of one hundred tons and upwards are also given with the numbers.

All are Schooners with the exception of those otherwise designated.

GLOUCESTER HARBOR.

Name of Vessel.	Tonnage.	Master's Name.	Number and Letters.	Where Built.	When Built.	Owners' or Fitters' Names.

GLOUCESTER HARBOR—*Continued.*   **1878** 3

Name of Vessel.	Tonnage.	Master's Name.	Number and Letters.	Where Built.	When Built.	Owners' or Fitters' Names.
Della Maria, **D**	55.75	Charles H. Jackman,	6176	Essex,	1864	Dennis & Ayer.
Dexter, (boat,)	6.24		6910			
Dictator,	63.18	Antone Joseph,	6721	Gloucester,	1872	John Pew & Son.
Eastern Light, **E**	70.29	I. M. Tilden,	7423	Kennebunk, Me.,	1866	Maddocks & Co.
Eastern Queen,	60.11	William Corliss,	7387	Essex,	1860	John Pew & Son.
Eben B. Phillips,	66.91	William N. Walls,	7431	Essex,	1866	Walen & Allen.
Eben Parsons,	91.48	Thomas F. Parsons,	135,106	Gloucester,	1875	William Parsons, 2d & Co.
Eclipse,	49.69	James Thurston, 2d,	7416	Gloucester,	1851	McKenzie, Hardy & Co.
Edith, (yacht,)	27.97	Henry S. Hovey,	7434	Bridgeport, Ct.,	1861	Master.
Edward A. Horton,	66.46	E. M. Hodsdon,	8623	Essex,	1870	Harvey Knowlton.
Edward E. Webster,	98.80	Charles H. Nute,	135,176	Gloucester,	1875	Dennis & Ayer.
Edward Grover,	77.26	Daniel Crew,	8991	Essex,	1874	Sidney Friend.
Edwin C. Dolliver,	87.07	William Morris,	135,041	Essex,	1874	Walen & Allen.
E. K. Kane,	52.29	Joseph Weeks,	7414	Essex,	1856	Master.
Electric Flash,	82.19	John McDonald,	7415	New London, Ct.,	1858	Dennis & Ayer.
Elisha Crowell,	67.78	Thomas Goodwin,	8605	Essex,	1869	Walen & Allen.
Eliza Abby,	40.29	Epes M. Parkhurst,	7391	Essex,	1854	Shute & Merchant.
Eliza K. Parker,	57.05	Daniel Douglass, Jr.,	7388	Essex,	1857	William C. Wonson.

Edward A. Horton – The Person

The novel has placed Edward Horton as a partner in the fictitious firm of *McKenzie, Knowlton and Horton* for poetic license in relation to the ship's story.

Research for this novel did not definitively discover the full middle name represented by 'A' in the name of the vessel. However, the middle name of *Augustus* was attached to an internet record of the Gloucester 1860 census for Edward A. Horton, and thus this is most likely the representation for the ship as well. The nickname *Gusto* in the telegram from Harvey was applied for the story.

An *Edward A. Horton* is buried in Oak Grove Cemetery, Gloucester, Massachusetts in plot 2 Oak 63 (according to the website *Find a Grave*).

Birth of September 14, 1835.

Death April 23, 1910 — at the age of 74.

His father was Barnabas Horton, who, per the census, was a fisherman.

Edward A. Horton was listed in the 1870-71 Gloucester & Rockport Directory. He __was__ in fact employed with *McKenzie, Knowlton, & Co.,* a discovery only found after the novel was completed.

Photo and Illustration Credits

The illustrations included are from various sources intended to add to the reader experience. The text includes explanatory notes and indicates if the image has been revised for use in this fictional work. Original illustrations and author photos are not noted.

Chapter: A Patriot Wronged
1. Sketch of two-mast schooner. The Fishermen's Memorial and Record Book, George H. Proctor, 1873

Chapter: The Chase is On
1. The cabin of mackerel schooner. Plate 55 in, *The Fishery and Fisheries Industries of the United States*, by George Brown Goode, 1887 (hereafter as, Goode's Fishery.)
2. Fishermen pulling in their net from their seine boat. The dorymen have tied up the dory alongside. A seine net could be 800 feet long and 100 feet deep. (Photo by Gordon Parks. The contents of the Library of Congress Farm Security Administration/Office of War Information Black-and-White Negatives are in the public domain and are free to use and reuse. Credit Line: Library of Congress, Prints & Photographs Division, Farm Security Administration/Office of War Information. Cited 2024, https://loc.gov/item/2017856605/

Chapter: Harbor Blues
1. Depiction of warehouses and wharfs in the harbor.
2. The old post office.

Both from: History of the Town And City Gloucester, Cape Ann, Massachusetts. By James R. Pringle. 1892.

Chapter: Advice of Friends
1. Masts in the harbor. Plate 185 in Goode's Fishery

Chapter: Tory Celebrations
1. A revised image with the name plate of the Edward Horton added on the schooner. From Plate 66 in Goode's Fishery.

Chapter: A Miner Again

1. Map of Guysborough. Fictional with labels. Based on 'Dominion of Canada, Nova Scotia, Guysborough Harbor (Chedabucto Bay),' from a British survey in 1850. Issuing body: United States. Hydrographic Office Engraver.

Chapter: The Mysterious Key

1. A barn. From Plate 125 in Goode's Fishery.

Chapter: Defiance Realized

1. A cropped image of a wharf building. From Plate 133, in Goode's Fishery.

Chapter: "We'll Warp Her Out."

1. Lighting lanterns. Edited for use. Plate 163 in Goode's Fishery.
2. A schooner photo. Edited for use. Captioned: "The day's begun for the men of the Grand Bank Shoals." From, *Pine Tree Ballads*. (Page 72 facing.) Holman F. Day. 1902.

Chapter: Call Out the Guard

1. Gloucester City Hall as rebuilt in 1969, page 224 in, *History of the Town And City Gloucester, Cape Ann, Massachusetts*. James R. Pringle. 1892.

Chapter: Serene and Fair

1. Men on shore. Plate 106, in Goode's Fishery.

Chapter: The Horton's In

1. Boat parade. Plate 88, in Goode's Fishery.
2. Wharf image. From Plate 239 in Goode's Fishery.

Select Further Reading and References

Connolly, James B. *Out of Gloucester*. New York. Charles Scriber's Sons, 1906.
Includes the short story, *Echo o' the Morn'*, a highly fictionalized account of the Horton including a chase by the Canadian cutters, which did not occur.

Connolly, James B. *The Port Of Gloucester*. New York. Doubleday, Doran & Company, Inc., 1940.
Includes a brief chapter on the *Edward A. Horton*, which mirrors Proctor's account in the *Fishermen's Memorial*.

Copeland Melvin T. & Elliott C. Rogers. *The Saga of Cape Ann*. Freeport, ME. Bond Wheelwright Co., 1960.

Eckstorm, Fannie Hardy, and Mary Winslow Smyth. *Minstrelsy of Maine — Folk-Songs and Ballads of the Woods and Coast*. Boston and New York. Houghton Mifflin Company, 1927. Eckstorm's commentary on the *Horton* account from Proctor's *Fishermen's Memorial* book. In addition, she has notes relevant to further ballads, some of which were included in this book.

Eckstorm, Fannie Hardy. *Fannie Hardy Eckstorm – Short Stories and Essays*. Burnt Jacket Publishing, 2023. Includes the account of James White finding the great keel timber on Mt. Kearsarge in New Hampshire.

Garland, Joseph E. *Lone Voyager. The Extraordinary Adventures of Howard Blackburn. Hero fisherman of Gloucester*. 1963. Captain John Blackburn, who was noted in this novel, was Howard's grandfather. The included account was taken from Howard's notes and other stories.

Garland, Joseph E. Down to the Sea – *The Fishing Schooners of Gloucester*. Boston. David R. Godine, Publisher, 1983.

Goode, George Browne, et al. *The Fisheries and Fishery Industries of the United States*. Washington: U.S. Commission of Fish and Fisheries, 1887.

Hawes, Charles Boardman. *Gloucester By Land And Sea – The Story of a New England Seacoast Town*. Boston. Little, Brown, and Company,1923.

Frank Leslie's Illustrated Newspaper. The Schooner "E. A. Horton." New York. 18 November 1871. No. 842-Vol. XXXIII.

Morris, John. *Alone at Sea: Gloucester in the Age of the Dorymen, 1623-1939*. Commonwealth Editions, 2010.

Pringle, James R. *History of the Town and City of Gloucester, Cape Ann, Massachusetts*. Gloucester, Mass., 1892.

Proctor Brothers Publishing. *The Fishermen's Own Book: comprising the list of men and vessels lost from the port of Gloucester, Mass., from 1874 to April 1, 1882*. Gloucester, Mass., Proctor Brothers, 1882.

Proctor Brothers Publishing. *Fishermen's Ballads and Songs of the Sea. 1874*.

Proctor, George H. *The Fishermen's Memorial and Record* Book. Gloucester, Mass., Proctor Brothers, 1873. (This book includes the most complete factual account of the *Edward A. Horton*.)

The Atlantic Advocate. An article about the Horton was published from the perspective of a Gloucester native. To this came a letter to the editor from Guysborough native.
Richardson, Evelyn M. "Bully of the North Defied." The Atlantic Advocate 48:11 (July 1958): 93-95.
Boyd, Cecil. "The Story of the E.A. Horton; a letter to the Editor," The Atlantic Advocate 49:5 (January 1959): 66-67.

Author's Note

In 1871 reports of the schooner *Edward A. Horton's* capture and return to Gloucester were written in the papers. The most complete summary of the ordeal was written by George H. Proctor in *The Fishermen's Memorial and Record Book (1873)*. Author James Connolly wrote of the *Horton* in his book, *Out of Gloucester (1906)*. Connolly's telling omits some of the facts as provided in Proctor's earlier writing. Connolly also wrote a short story based on the *Horton*, in which he christened the captured vessel, *Echo o' the Morn*. In Connolly's account, the ship was chased back to Gloucester by Canadian cutters, which, of course, did not occur with the *Horton*.

Certainly, the specific details of what occurred day-to-day during the time the ship was seized, or while sailing home, cannot be known, and thus, this book is a work of creative historical fiction. This brief note provides background for the reader on some of the story line. Beyond what is specifically noted here, and anything not documented in the references from the news accounts, this book is a work of historical fiction.

Most accounts place Captain Harvey Knowlton Jr. in Gloucester at the time his vessel was captured. The writings on his travels later in the month to arrive in Nova Scotia were fabricated for the novel.

Several of the ships noted as owned by Harvey Knowlton are accurate. However, the *Lily Rose Snow* and the *Patience to-Knight* are fictitious vessels. The latter was named for Patience Knight, Harvey's paternal grandmother. The Knowlton fleet included a 19-ton vessel named, *Defiance*. In the story, the fictitious, and much larger vessel, was named *Defiance Too*. The *Paul Revere* was a Gloucester schooner, but could not have carried the *Horton* crew home in 1871, as that ship was not built until 1875. In fact, I have found no documentation on how the stranded crew arrived home, whether by land or sea. The listing of the fishing vessels seized by the Canadian cutters in the years 1870 and 1871 were taken from various references. History on the actual *Edward A. Horton*, and the suspected namesake, was covered in early appendices.

Characters were added to tell the story of what occurred in Guysborough and Gloucester. Most importantly, Harvey Knowlton, Jr. did not have a brother named Joseph. Census data shows he had two sisters. Grandfather to Harvey, Nehemiah Knowlton Jr., had only one son, Harvey Sr. (who <u>was</u> employed at Wonson Paint.) Thus, Uncle Nemo, Nehemiah Knowlton III, is fictitious, as is the nephew Oliver. The names of the crew that assisted Knowlton are as given by Proctor, and were recorded as Daniel Richards, John Penney, Charles Webber, Malcom McCloud, Peter Gillis, and D. Isaac. A change was made for D. Isaac to be Isaac Dyer. This was purely for the story. Dyer was used as the last name to avoid two people with a similar surname, since the Goldboro hotel owner was written to be *Isaacs*. (In that area, there is an Isaacs Harbour location and the author desired to keep relevance to that actual place.) The involvement of Guysborough's Tom MacDonald is unsubstantiated in Gloucester history, but comes from Nova Scotia storytelling. Given this book is a fictional account, a MacDonald character has been included in the story.

Harvey Knowlton's Guysborough true mining ploy was carried out under the novel's fictitious name of Zadok Handron. Knowlton did mine in California around 1849, and there was a vessel named the *Boston* that did sail for San Francisco with men chasing the gold rush. Harvey's mining during the years of the Goldboro, Nova Scotia rush in the 1860s is fiction; as is his time at the Brewer shipyard and his meeting with David Stone Libbey.

The story of James White finding the great keel on Mt. Kearsage is true, and told in, "The Broad Axe Man," a chapter in *Fannie Hardy Eckstorm – Short Stories and Essays* (2024).

Acknowledgments

In prior books I've made mention on what seem to me to be coincidental occurrences in meeting people, or finding related facts from my life, being relevant to the story I was writing. As these things go, this book was improved with help through a coincidental meeting of my now good friend, Allen Humphries. A more widely read reader of books than Allen, I do not know. Someone with more diligence to details, I'd be hard pressed to name. Allen is very busy with day-to-day life, and yet, he still found time to not only offer story feedback, but with his curious nature, he researched valuable information for several characters. He dug like a clam digger into the genealogy of the Knowlton and Horton families by pouring over census data. His findings improved the manuscript significantly, as several changes were made to make the historical fiction more accurate. After his initial reading, Allen wrote to me, *'this is one of the most interesting books I've ever read.'* That is indeed a very high compliment to receive.

My initial acquaintance with Allen was previously noted in my introduction to the book *David Stone Libbey – He was Penobscot.* What I did not mention in that book was a remarkable occurrence that Allen and I knew a particular person. The explanation of why having this particular common acquaintance is remarkable, requires a little background. When I first met my wife-to-be's grandparents, her grandfather gave this young engineer a desired tour of his basement in Saugus, Massachusetts. Chet, a retired tool and die machinist for GE, was still making custom parts using lathes and metal working tools in his workshop. Behind the room of bandsaws and borers and milling machines, where boxes held metal filings and it smelled like oil, Chet had a small room with his ham (amateur) radio equipment. He 'called up' a friend to give me a demonstration.

What's remarkable is that Allen Humphries once stood in that same radio closet. Back in his high school days, some thirty years before I was there (before I was born even), Allen had visited that basement with Chet's son, Dick, as part of the school's ham radio club. It was only after having a side conversation, did Allen and I discover that I had married Chet's granddaughter, and future niece of his high school acquaintance. I'd say the odds are pretty low that I'd have a chance of meeting Allen, and he'd end up assisting me with Libbey family history for a book I was writing, and later, he'd contribute to this book about the *Horton*. Permutate those odds, with the odds that I, a Brooklyn-born boy, would write a book about Mainer David Libbey, who descended from the same lines of pioneers as Allen Humphries of Massachusetts, who happened to have a casual school association with the uncle of the woman I would marry—and that is *pretty remarkable*. One of my degrees is in mathematics, and I'd say the probability is very low of this association combination-permutation occurring. And this book is better because of my crossing paths with Allen.

One more thing. As a young man, Allen spent time as a crewman for two-man racing sailboats in Marblehead, Massachusetts, and he also has a boating connection directly to Gloucester. As a youngster, his family had a cottage at Wingaersheek Beach in Gloucester. During his toddler years, his father took him sailing along on the Annisquam River. When he was around six, he even remembers going out with his father in their dory. In my book, that counts as being a doryman. Allen, thank you for your assistance in helping this story schoon.

(And, by the way, the Gloucester postmaster in the story named *Allen Humphries* was fictional—for, of course, Allen is not that old. I did find a single Humphries in the Gloucester directory of 1875, Jacob Humphries, who lived in Annisquam and was a clerk at the Cape Ann Granite Company. I suspect Allen will check the genealogy on the name.)

Of course, I must thank Chet's granddaughter, my wife, Meredith, for her help again in editing. In her multiple readings of the manuscript, she caught many inconsistencies that arise in writing a novel which escape the author's eyes. The corrections she made improved the story, the flow of the words, and my 'fat-fingered' typos. Even more so, I appreciate all the evenings she was patient while I 'closed out' one more sentence before dinner.

One early reader enjoyed the book so much he read it in under forty-eight hours and offered his enthusiastic encouragement. He rightly caught I used way too many "*Arghs,*" in the initial draft. Thank you, Peter.

Help also came from the "Provinces." Don, an Executive Member-at-large, from the Guysborough Historical Society was kind enough to answer my question about *Hortons Cove*. I stumbled across a recent map with that cove name *after* I had placed the fictitious location of Tom MacDonald's barn, two coves north of the now *Hortons Cove*, which on early 19th century maps was considered part of the Salmon River. The name *Hortons Cove* was applied around the 1920s—decades after the *Horton* incident——by postal authority orders to distinguish the Salmon River locations. But isn't it a remarkable coincidence for a Guysborough cove to end up with such a name?

Thanks for reading. As always, please drop me a line to let me know how you liked the story.

Tommy C.

About Maine Author Tommy Carbone

Tommy Carbone lives in Maine and spends a wicked amount of his time exploring the waterways and trails of the north woods. He writes from a one room cabin, on the shores of a lake, that is frozen for almost six months out of the year, and moose outnumber people three to one.

His first novel, "*The Lobster Lake Bandits – Mystery at Moosehead*," has made those 'from away' want to visit Maine. It's a big state – come explore.

www.tommycarbone.com